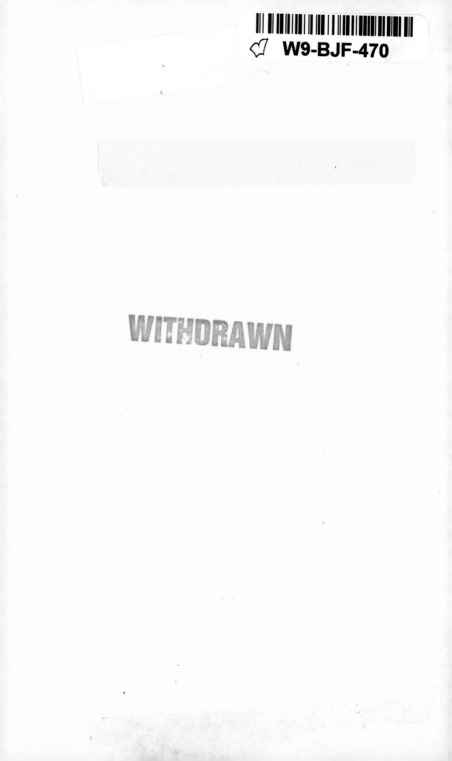

W9-BJF-470

MY WIFE AND MY DEAD WIFE

a novel by Michael Kun

MacAdam/Cage
155 Sansome Street, Suite 550
San Francisco, CA 94104
www.macadamcage.com

Portions of this novel have appeared, in different forms, in
USA Today, *The City Paper (Baltimore Edition)*, *Fiction* and
Story Quarterly.

Library of Congress Cataloging-in-Publication Data

Kun, Michael.
    My wife and my dead wife / by Michael Kun.
      p. cm.
    ISBN 1-931561-69-9 (hardcover : alk. paper)
     1. Tailors–Fiction. 2. Widowers–Fiction. 3. Atlanta,
(Ga.)–Fiction. 4. Country musicians–Fiction. 5. Women
singers–Fiction. 6. Memory–Fiction. I.Title.

    PS3561.U446M9 2004
    813'.54–dc22

                                   2004000961

Manufactured in the United States of America.
10 9 8 7 6 5 4 3 2 1

Book and jacket design by Dorothy Carico Smith.

MY WIFE AND MY DEAD WIFE

a novel by Michael Kun

MacAdam/Cage

For my parents

ACKNOWLEDGMENTS

At this stage, I believe it is my duty as your author to acknowledge all of the fine literary societies, humbling awards, and generous artistic grants without which I would not be standing before you today, presenting you *My Wife and My Dead Wife*. However, I have never received any grants of any kind, generous or otherwise, and the only relevant award I ever received was a giant Hershey bar for winning a spelling bee in Mrs. Cantello's sixth grade class at Sicomac Elementary School in Wyckoff, New Jersey. So, without further ado, I'd like to thank Mrs. Cantello and the fine people who make Hershey products. Thank you, thank you. Without you, this book would be chock-full of misspelled words. And my skin would have been much clearer during my teenage years.

Much more importantly, I'd like to acknowledge the fellowship, patience, and good cheer of the following people, all of whom continue to put up with my stuff and nonsense. They are, more or less alphabetically: Jeff Aghassi, Jamie Allen, Scott Allen (MacAdam/Cage CEO, who will send me larger and more frequent checks if you each buy more copies of this book), Luis Alvarez, the Andersons (look, Charlotte, that's Uncle Mike on the back cover), the Andresinos, Chris Antone, Mark Attwood, Cecily Banks (who once lent me her pants, which is all I'll say), Valerie Barnard, Lori Bauer, Andy Bienstock (Baltimore's best DJ), David Block, Howard Bloom, Sandra Bond (world's nicest agent), my friends at BookWorks in Albuquerque (especially Nancy Rutland, Lindsay Lancaster, and Carolyn Valtos), Terri Boyd, Bert Brandenburg, Jeff Brody, Pete Bulmer, the Callahans, the Campbell-Corrys (the closest thing to my family, if you don't count my family), the Cherofs, Jim Crane, Mike Curran, Harrison Darby, John Daugherty, Stephen Dixon, Peter Farley, Karen Fazekas, Robin Federman, Eric Feinstein, Doug Fellman, Evelyn Giammona, Melissa Goldsmith, Maricela Gonzalez, Clare Grossman, Rich Hafets, the Hennellys, David Hoiles, Brent Houk, my friends at Jackson Lewis (especially the Los Angeles office), Bert Johnson, the Johnsons (Scott and Ben, look who's on the back cover), the Kennedys, Tasha Kepler, Dallas Kingsbury, Susan Krell, the Kuns, the Larias, the Lebaus, Cecily Lesko (did you notice that I have two close friends named Cecily—imagine the odds), Holly Levin, Ann Lloyd, the Longos, the McGees, Nancy Miles, the Millspaughs, Melanie Mitchell, Agnes Muscianese, Kate Nitze, Mindy Novick, Maria Olsen, Rob Pattison, Tom Piekara, David Poindexter (MacAdam/ Cage publisher who may or may not have had his arm twisted quite severely before he signed me to a contract), Jeanne Vaeth Porter, Terry Prince, Bill Quinn, Richard Rabicoff, Kristy Raska, the Richardsons, Phil Rosen, Anne Rumsey, Avril Sande, Evan Shenkman, the Sienas, Teresa Siriani, Dorothy Carico Smith, Doug Smith, Stan Smith, pretty much anyone else named Smith, the Solitars, Jon Spitz, Larry Stone, Jackie Sumanis, Wanda Thomas, Amy Toboco, the Tobocos, Guy Tully, Todd VanDyke, the Visages, Pat Walsh (editor/nemesis/supporter/confidant—a more complex relationship would require a therapist), Doug Warren, the Weymers, Anna Williams, James Williams, Cara Wilson, Serena Wiltshire, Doug Wolfe, and Michael Yockel (the only person ever to risk his job in support of my writing—shame how that worked out, wasn't it).

Special mention, and special thanks, must be given to the Class of 1984 of the Johns Hopkins University and the Class of 1988 of the University of Virginia School of Law. Never mind all the support and encouragement they gave me; they frequently offered to take notes for me so I could skip classes to write. Those are special people.

To all of you, I offer my thanks.

And to those of you who will believe this book to be autobiographical, I say, "Oh, please." For one, the narrator and I have different names. For two, the narrator grew up in Georgia, while I grew up elsewhere. As for the fact that the narrator is single, dim-witted, and putting on weight...well, I suppose you've got me on that one.

CHAPTER 1: COWBOY OUTFIT

Renée is NOT my wife.

Sure, she says she is. She's a sweet girl, sweet as cake batter, but she is NOT my wife and we are NOT married, despite what she may be telling people.

After what happened in Decatur, she signs her name "Renée Ashe," and she runs all over town saying, "I'm Renée Ashe. I'm Hamilton Ashe's wife." Not, I'm Renée YATES, Hamilton Ashe's GIRLFRIEND. She even signs her name "Renée Ashe," with a big loop at the end. I don't know how she ever got it in her head to tell people she's my wife. We don't have a marriage license, we never had a wedding ceremony, we never did any of the things you have to do to become man and wife. NONE. She just started saying she was my wife, and she keeps saying it over and over.

"Hello, this is Renée Ashe," she'll say when she answers the phone.

Or she'll say, "Mr. and Mrs. Hamilton Ashe," when she introduces us. She'll walk up to complete strangers, people we've never seen before and will never see again, and she'll extend a hand and say, "Mr. and Mrs. Hamilton Ashe. We're pleased to meet you," like we're running for public office and we're looking for votes.

"My husband's first name is an old family name," she'll

say. "He goes by 'Ham,'" she'll say, then she'll spell it for them as if they've never heard the word "ham" before, as if they came from some remote country where they've never heard of such things as "ham and eggs" or a "ham sandwich."

I'll ask her calmly, "Renée, why do you keep telling people that you're my wife?"

And she'll say, "Because I am."

And I'll say, "My foot you're my wife," only I don't use the word "foot."

And she'll say, "I am so your wife. We're married."

And I'll say, "By what power can you declare us man and wife?"

And she'll say, "There's a little thing known as a common-law marriage."

And I'll say, "I've never heard of any such thing, and I know people who are lawyers," which is true. My older brother Carl is a lawyer. Not only that, he's a good lawyer with a top-notch Atlanta law firm.

But she'll say, "A) You don't know people PLURAL who are lawyers, and B) even if you did know lawyers, they'd have to be the stupidest lawyers in the world if they've never heard of something as obvious as a common-law marriage."

That's another way things changed. Before, we used to just talk like normal people do. I'd say something, then she'd say something connected to that, then I'd say something connected to *that*, and it'd go on and on and, before you knew it, we'd be in bed and naked. But now we don't have what you would call normal conversations. Every time we talk about something, it's like she's a scientist trying to prove some theory. And she's always using A's and B's to do it. Or 1's and 2's and 3's.

For instance, I'll get dressed in the morning and she'll say, "Go get changed. I don't like 1) your shirt, 2) your pants, and 3) your socks."

Or I'll ask what she's cooking for dinner and she'll say, "We're having A) hot dogs, B) cole slaw, C) potatoes, and D) lemonade."

I'd never heard something so funny as someone trying to sound intelligent because they say "D) lemonade." As if the king or queen of some country runs around saying, "D) lemonade." As if some professor at Harvard University comes home from work at the end of a busy and frustrating day and his wife will say, "We're having D) lemonade." As if anyone's wife talks that way.

That's a bad example, of course, because Renée is NOT my wife. She's not my wife because A) I never asked her to be my wife, B) we never got a marriage license, C) we never had a wedding ceremony, and D) lemonade.

Here's another way things have changed: Renée's always telling me I'm fat. If I'm fat, why does she keep baking all the things she bakes? Cakes and pies and cookies. She used to bake once in a while, but after what happened in Decatur, she does it every single day like normal people might brush their teeth or wash their hair or things of that nature. I'll come home from work and have dinner, and then she'll say, "How about a nice piece of yellow cake?"

I'll say, "No, thank you."

And she'll say, "I baked it just for you. It has chocolate icing."

And I'll say, "I'm full, Sweet Potato," which is what I call her sometimes.

And she'll say, "Come on. I baked it special for you. Why

don't you sit down in front of the television and I'll bring you A) a piece of cake and B) a glass of milk."

So, I'll do it. I'll sit down in front of the television with the remote control, and I'll find something to watch, and then she'll bring me some A) cake and B) milk, and then she'll watch me while I'm eating, watch me like a cat watching a bird, ready to pounce. When I'm finished, she'll say, "There, now, wasn't that good?"

I'll say, "Yes," which is usually true, because Renée is a very good cook.

And then, not ten minutes later—*not ten minutes*—she'll pat my stomach and say something like, "Do you have a baby in there?"

Or, "Looks like I've got a chubby hubby."

Now, why would she say something like that after she practically stuffed the cake in my mouth in the first place? Why would she say something like that when I am NOT her husband?

Why?

Why?

★

When you get right down to it, everything really started to change when Renée lost her job at the hospital. She was working in the gift store where they sell cards and candy and stuffed animals and things of that nature. One day she came home from work and said, "Ham, honeypie, I need to talk to you about something." She had a very serious look on her face. She wrung her hands the way people do when they have arthritis.

I said, "What?"

And she said, "I lost my job. They fired me. They said it

—4—

was a layoff, but it still means I don't have someplace to go to work tomorrow."

I said, "Oh, God, that's terrible."

And she said, "No, no, it's okay."

And I said, "Don't worry, sweetheart, you'll find another job."

And she said, "That's just it. I don't want to get another job."

And I said, "Why?"

And she said, "I've got dreams, Ham. I've got things I want to do with my life, and I want to try to do them."

And I said, "What sort of dreams?"

And she said, "I'm too embarrassed to tell you."

And I said, "If you can't tell me, who can you tell?"

And she said, "Well, I suppose I should be able to tell my boyfriend."

She said "boyfriend," not "husband." And at no time since—at NO time—did we ever get married. I may not be a genius, but I'd sure remember something like that. Anyone would.

That's when Renée said, "What I really want to do is to be a singer."

And I said, "Really?"

She looked down at her shoes and said, "Really. I want to sing and play the guitar. I want to be a country-and-western singer like Patsy Cline and Dolly Parton." She named some other people whose names I forgot right away.

Here I'd known Renée for more than three years, almost four, and I never knew she wanted to be a singer. The only times I ever heard her sing were when she sang "Happy Birthday" on someone's birthday or when she sang some

Christmas carols at Christmas parties. "Rudolph the Red-Nosed Reindeer." "Silent Night." "I'll Be Home for Christmas." She wasn't half-bad, but she wasn't so good that you'd say to yourself, "Lord, that girl can sing! She could charm the birds right out of the trees. Heck, she ought to be a professional singer." No, when she sang, she just blended in with everyone else, that's all.

And another thing: I never heard her listen to any country-and-western music the entire time I'd known her. Never. She always listened to the same music as me, which is rock and roll. Aerosmith. The Doors. The Rolling Stones. Music like that.

"You think it's silly of me to want to be a singer, don't you?" she said. She was still wringing her hands. She looked up from her shoes.

I said, "No, of course I don't think it's silly."

"I mean, me wanting to not look for another job and everything so I can be a singer? You don't think it's silly?"

"No, no," I said. "We can get by on my paycheck. Things will be tight, but we can do it," which I wasn't really sure about. I work in a tailor shop. I don't make a fortune like some people in Atlanta do. But I didn't want her to get more upset than she already was, so I said what I said about how we could get by on my paycheck.

Renée said, "It won't be for long, I promise you that. I figure I need to take some time to stay at home and write some songs, and then I'll go to some of the clubs in Decatur and see if they'll hire me to play. Then, if I can play a couple times a week, I bet I could make as much money as I was making at the hospital. Maybe more."

And I said, "What if they offered you a record contract."

which I don't know why I said, getting her hopes up and all.

And she said, "Why, I'd be the happiest woman in the world."

She threw her arms around my neck and kissed me.

I've never seen Renée so happy as she was at that moment. Never, except maybe a few days later when I bought her a guitar on the way home from work. I bought it used, so it wasn't too expensive, and the salesman threw in a black guitar case for free because we once worked together somewhere, although neither of us could remember where. You've never seen anyone so surprised as when I came in the front door and gave her that guitar.

"We can't afford this," Renée said. "You should take it back." But I knew she didn't want me to take it back. She was already stroking the wood.

"Don't worry," I said. "We can afford it."

And she said, "How?"

And I said, "I'm going to quit smoking. I've been meaning to quit smoking anyway. I figure I must spend fifteen dollars a week on cigarettes. That is fifteen dollars a week we'll be saving, which we can apply to the cost of the guitar. So, when you consider the savings, the guitar will be paid off in a couple of months, then we'll start *making* money. Hell, if I quit drinking, too, we'll be millionaires before you know it."

I was joking, but it all made perfect sense, how the money for the cigarettes would pay for the guitar. Only I didn't figure on the guitar lessons she needed, which were ten dollars an hour, two nights a week. That alone was MORE than the cost of the cigarettes. Two nights a week, a boy from the college would come by. He couldn't have been more than nineteen, and he had oily black hair that was long in the back and stained his shirt collar. They would sit on the sofa in the living room, him and Renée, each one playing a guitar.

"This is such-and-such chord," he'd say, and he'd strum his guitar. He was good with a guitar and if you gave him the name of a song, any song, he could play it for you, note for note. "Stairway to Heaven." "Get Off My Cloud." Et cetera. His name was Walter Something-or-other.

After he showed her a chord, Renée would try it, and she'd make a sound that sounded something like what the boy had played. Not quite, but close, like when you try to make a photocopy of a photograph. Then they'd move on to another chord, then another. I'd try to watch television or read my sports magazines while they were doing that, but I couldn't concentrate. Eventually, I'd end up sitting out on the front steps, waiting for it to get quiet so Renée and I could go to bed.

★

I suppose Renée was practicing her singing and her guitar playing while I was at work. Except for when that boy was giving her lessons, I never heard her practice, not once. And she must have had a lot of extra time on her hands, because that's when she started baking. At first, it was once or twice a week. Cakes or pies or cookies.

"Did you bake all day?" I'd say.

And she'd say, "No."

And I'd say, "Did you work on your songs at all?"

And she'd say, "Yes, I did. I just did some baking to take a break."

But with all the cakes and pies and cookies, I have to

admit that I was beginning to think she wasn't practicing at all. When I'd get up for work, she'd still be sleeping in bed. When I'd come home from work, there would be the cakes or the pies or the cookies, and she'd still be dressed in her pajamas. And I never heard a single note come out of her pretty pink little mouth. Never.

That's why I was so surprised one night when I came home from work and Renée was dressed in a red blouse and blue jeans, with a cowboy hat and cowboy boots and a bandanna tied around her neck. You could only see a little of her blonde hair hanging down at the back of the cowboy hat.

She said, "I want to play you a song I wrote, and I want you to tell me what you think of it. I want you to tell me the truth."

And I said, "Okay," and sat down on the sofa.

And she said, "The truth? No sugar-coating it?"

I said, "I'll tell you the truth," and crossed my fingers over my heart.

And then Renée sat down and played the WORST song I've ever heard in my life. It was called "Winona Forever," and it was about a girl who had a puppy named Winona who ran away, and the girl was so sad that she had the words "Winona Forever" tattooed on her arm, only the puppy came back a few months later and was missing an ear. It was a stupid, stupid song, and Renée kept messing up the chords the boy had taught her. Her singing wasn't bad, but it was hard to focus on it because of the words, which made you want to laugh out loud. Except for the part where she sang, "Winona forever, I'll love you, Winona, forever," which was very sad, especially because she had her eyes squeezed shut whenever she sang that part.

When Renée was finished, she said, "So, what did you think?"

I couldn't lie to Renée, but I didn't want to make her unhappy either, so I tried to sound positive. I smiled and said, "That's not bad for a first try."

And she said, "What do you mean?"

And I said, "Just what I said. For your first song, it's not bad. Just think how good you'll be when you improve."

The tip of her nose got red like it did when she was getting out of the shower. She said, "Ham, I spent a lot of time writing that song. I've been working on that one song since I lost my job."

It'd been three months. Three months writing about a dog without an ear.

And I said, "It sounds like you put a lot of time into it."

Now she was crying and crying, and I had to put my arm around her. When I did, I accidentally knocked off her cowboy hat. It landed on the floor, upside-down. There was a drawing of a girl with a lasso inside.

"You're going to leave me, aren't you?" she said.

And I said, "No. No, Renée, no."

And she said, "I can tell you will. I can tell you're going to leave me."

All I could do was say, "No, no, no," then I carried her to bed and she fell asleep, still dressed in her cowboy outfit like a child who'd stayed out too late on Halloween.

★

After Renée lost her job, money became a problem. We still had to pay the rent, and for food, and for heat and hot water, and for car insurance for the cars.

And we had to pay for the guitar and the guitar lessons.

And we had to pay for the cowboy outfit, even if Renée kept insisting that's not what it was. "It's not a *cowboy* outfit, silly," she'd say. "It's just a *rustic* look I'm going to use." Then she'd name someone famous whom I'd never heard of who supposedly dressed the same way. I don't care what she wanted to call it, it was a cowboy outfit. The red blouse and the jeans, the cowboy hat, the cowboy boots, the bandanna. They weren't cheap, either, especially the boots, which were leather and had stitching all over them. We couldn't afford them.

One month we were late with the rent. Another, with the telephone bill. I ended up having to borrow some money from my brother Carl, the lawyer.

"I promise this will never happen again," I said. "It's an emergency."

And he said, "No need to worry about it. You don't need to pay me back."

Thank God for Carl, or else we would have been sleeping naked out on the street, just me, Renée, and the guitar.

Every once in a while when I got home from work Renée would sing one of her songs for me in the living room. She would sit down on the edge of the coffee table and start strumming the guitar. Her guitar playing improved, and you could tell she'd been practicing. Some of the songs she wrote were pretty good, too. She wrote one called "A Whisper Tames the Wild Horse," which was slow and pretty and made you smile if you thought about it. The chorus went like this:

Like a hush that stops a baby's cry,
Like mothers wash and fathers dry,
Like a compass keeps a ship on course,
A whisper tames the wild horse.

The song was about a man who was wild—smoking, drinking beer, driving fast cars, gambling—and about how a woman was able to calm him down and get him to straighten out. I don't think she wrote the song about me because I don't drive fast. I usually stay at the speed limit, give or take a couple miles per hour. I don't gamble much, either. Sometimes I play cards, but that's where I draw the line. The smoking and the beer? I suppose that part could've been written about me, which is *very* flattering.

When Renée was done singing that song, I said, "That was wonderful," and I started clapping and whistling.

She said, "Do you really mean it?"

And I said, "Of course I do. It was wonderful. It was as good as anything I've heard on the radio." I was proud of her, really, truly proud.

She was smiling so big. She sat on my lap.

"Say that again," she said.

And I said, "Say what again?"

"Say that about the radio. I want to hear you say it again."

And I said, "That was as good as anything I've ever heard on the radio."

That night, we had a good night in bed.

★

There were some bad nights, too. Sometimes she would play a song that was so terrible that I had to tell her for her own good. Even though it broke her heart, I had to tell her. I remember she played one song called "Dance with Me, Bobby Bailey" that was almost as bad as that "Winona Forever" song. It was about a boy in a wheelchair who went to the school dance alone, but a girl approached him and asked him to dance.

How could he dance if he was in a wheelchair?

How?

HOW?

And there was another one called "Grandma's Kitchen." Nothing happened in that song. It was just a list of things that Renée's grandma used to cook:

Meatloaf, pork chops, apple pie,
Noodles, turkey, my oh my,
Cookies, bread, Yankee stew,
Chicken soup so good for you,
Beans, potatoes, cobs of corn,
The kitchen floor was always worn,
We'd start at five and end at seven,
Bet Grandma's cooking up in heaven.

I had to tell her that was a bad song, and Renée stayed up all night in the living room, writing a brand-new one to prove that the song about her grandma was just a mistake. And it was. After I'd told her how much I liked the song about the whisper and the wild horse, most of the songs she wrote were pretty good. The bad ones were exceptions to the rule, as they say. She started to get up when I got up to go to work in the morning, and she'd get dressed, and then she'd have a whole plan mapped out for what she was going to do that day, how much time she'd spend writing her songs, how much time she'd spend practicing her chords, how much time she'd spend doing this or that or the other thing. Every couple of nights, she'd play a new song for me in the living room while I ate some cake or pie or cookies, then we'd go sit on the porch. I'd smoke a cigarette, and we'd each have a beer or two, and I'd tell her how much I liked the new song.

The cigarettes. The cigarettes that were supposed to pay for the guitar.

That didn't work out at all.

I've been smoking since I was thirteen. The only other time I'd tried to quit was back in high school, when I had to go to the funeral of a boy from school who had died. My friends and I didn't want all the teachers and parents to smell smoke on our clothes, and we even scrubbed our hands, the notches between our index and middle fingers, to try to get rid of the yellow stains there.

That time, in high school, I'd quit for two full weeks.

This time, trying to save money to pay for Renée's guitar, I'd only quit smoking for six days.

Probably closer to five.

Which didn't even save us enough money to buy a picture of a guitar, let alone a real guitar.

★

One night when I came home, Renée was dressed up in her cowboy outfit again. The same blouse and jeans and cowboy boots and cowboy hat. The same red bandanna. She had her purse with her, and her guitar was in its case and propped up near the door.

I said, "Hey, Sweet Potato, what's going on?"

And she said, "I want you to come with me to Eddie's Attic tonight. I'm going to sing some of my songs. I'm going to make my singing debut."

And I said, "They're going to pay you to sing your songs?"

And she said, "No, not yet. It's Wednesday, and every Wednesday is Amateur Night. They let people get up and sing their songs, and if you're good enough, they might have you come back to sing for money. That's how the Judds got started."

And I said, "The Whos?"

She grinned and rolled her eyes a little and said, "The Judds, silly," like I should have known who they were. Like they were the Kennedys or the Rockefellers.

So I drove Renée into Decatur, to Eddie's Attic. I was almost as excited as she was. While we were driving, I asked her which song she was going to play, and she said, "I'm not sure. I'm thinking about playing "A Whisper Tames the Wild Horse."" It was her best song. That, or the one about the woman who got lost on her honeymoon. The woman went out to run an errand, then couldn't remember the way back to the hotel where she and her new husband were staying. When she finally found the hotel, he'd already checked out because he thought she'd run away from him. Only his tuxedo was left in the room. That one was called "Lost Honeymoon." The chorus to that one went:

> *It was a lost honeymoon,*
> *She returned too late,*
> *He had left too soon.*
> *On the pillow where he'd laid his head,*
> *There was just a bowtie instead.*

I really liked that one.

When we reached Eddie's Attic, I carried Renée's guitar from the car. The entrance was on the side of the building, and the club was on the second floor. There was a line of people standing in the stairwell leading upstairs, leaning their instruments against the banister. There must have been thirty people in line to sign up to sing, all different kinds of people. Fat men, skinny women, scrawny boys, girls with puffy hair on top, and Renée in her cowboy outfit.

Renée was nervous, and after she'd signed up we went and sat at a table in the back and drank beer as the other people got up on stage to sing. Most of them sang songs by famous singers. I recognized the songs by rock groups—the Rolling Stones, Bruce Springsteen, the Beatles—but I didn't recognize the country-and-western songs. Renée would lean over to tell me who wrote those songs.

"That's a George song," she'd whisper to me.

Or, "Johnny Cash wrote that."

Or, "That one's by Emmylou Harris."

Her skin was white from being so nervous, but I could tell she was eager, too. She kept squeezing my fingers the way she might do when we were on a carnival ride together, spinning round and round, screaming. When a girl finished playing a song by someone named Lucinda Williams, Renée grabbed my hand and said, "I'm next. I'm next. Wish me luck."

I said, "You're going to be great."

And she said, "I owe this all to you."

And I said, "No, you don't, Sweet Potato. You did this all yourself."

Then the owner announced, "Ladies and gentlemen, let's give a nice, warm, Eddie's Attic welcome to our next performer, Ms. Renée Yates."

Everyone applauded. Renée took her guitar and walked up to the stage, and I took a drink of my beer and lit a cigarette. It was like dreaming, Renée sitting up there on stage, on a stool, a circle of white light on her face. She fixed her blouse with her fingertips, and said, "Thank you," then started strumming her guitar. Strumming her guitar and smiling, her teeth white like piano keys. Only she wasn't playing the song about the whisper and the wild horse, like she said she would. And she wasn't playing "Lost Honeymoon," either. She was playing "Winona Forever."

Why would she play that song?

Why?

Why?

She started singing about the dog, and how the dog ran away, and you could see that she was practically crying just singing about how much she missed that stupid dog. People started laughing, quietly at first. I don't know if Renée could hear it. Her eyes were closed, and she kept singing, "I love you Winona, forever." I looked around the room, and the people were laughing and laughing out loud now like she meant the song as a joke, which she didn't. There were two men at the table next to mine, laughing with their mouths wide open. You could see their fat red tongues. You could see the beer running down their chins.

Even though there were two of them and they were both much larger than me, I leaned over, and I pointed at them, and I said, "Hey, will you both kindly shut the hell up so I can hear the young lady sing?"

They ignored me and kept laughing with their enormous mouths and their pointy teeth like beasts.

So, a little louder this time, I said, "Will you SHUT THE HELL UP so I can hear the young lady sing?"

And one of them said, "Shut the hell up yourself, jackass," and started to rise from his seat like he wanted to fight me.

And then the other one said, "Who is she to you anyway?"

And I said, "For your information, she's my wife," which shut them both up.

But she is not my wife.
She is NOT my wife.

CHAPTER 2:
ELECT HAMILTON ASHE FOR A BETTER TENTH GRADE

That was how it started. That was the night Renée started saying she was my wife. That was the night she stopped being "Renée Yates" and started being "Renée Ashe." Or, actually, "Mrs. Renée Ashe." Even though A) I never asked her to marry me, B) we never got a marriage license, C) we never had a wedding ceremony, and D) lemonade.

That's the night Renée started saying we were married, even though she doesn't even know how to say my name. Not my last name, Ashe, which rhymes with "cash." No, she says my FIRST name wrong. Ham, which rhymes with "lamb" and "wham" and "sham" and plenty of other words. THAT's the one she doesn't know how to say.

Whenever she says my name, it comes out "Hay-yum," like it's two words, instead of "Ham," which is only one.

"We need to pay the rent, Hay-yum," she'll say.

Or, "You need a haircut, Hay-yum."

Or, "Have some peas, Hay-yum."

Or, "Have some cookies, Hay-yum."

Or, "Have some A) cake, B) pie or C) muffins, Hay-yum."

Or, "Have some hay-yum, Hay-yum." She said that on Easter Sunday when she made ham and potatoes for dinner. They were very good.

When Renée says my name in the bedroom, it's very provocative, I'll admit. She's normally very quiet when we're in bed, quiet like there's someone in the next room listening with a glass pressed to the wall, but sometimes very softly she'll say, "Oh, Hay-yum. Oh, Hay-yum."

But you can't be married to someone who doesn't even know how to say your name, no matter how provocative it can be. You CAN'T. It just wouldn't make sense. It wouldn't make sense to be married to the one person in the world who can't even pronounce your name.

Sometimes, when she says it wrong, I'll try to help her say it right.

"It's Ham," I'll say. "Like lamb and wham and sham."

And she'll try it, only it'll still come out "Hay-yum."

And, a little louder and more slowly, I'll say, "Ham," the way you talk to a foreigner or a baby to get them to understand what you're saying. "Ham," very slowly.

But she'll still say, "Hay-yum."

And I'll say, "Ham."

Usually she'll get frustrated and say, "I feel like I'm the girl in *My Fair Lady*."

And I'll say, "What girl?"

And she'll say, "The fair lady. You know, the girl with the accent, and the professor tries to teach her to say things the way he does. I have a southern accent. I don't see why you want to change me."

And I'll say, "I don't want to change you, Sweet Potato. The only thing I want to change is the way you say my name. And besides, look what happened to the people in *My Fair Lady*. They ended up falling in love, right?"

Only instead of being glad when I say that, she'll say

—20—

something like, "Are you telling me you don't love me already?"

And I'll say, "No, that's not what I'm saying."

And she'll say, "Or are you saying that you'll only love me if I do things the way you want?"

I'll say, "That's not what I meant at all."

And she'll say, "Well, if you want my candid opinion, Hay-yum is a silly name to give a human being. I mean, what kind of people name their child after luncheon meat? Other than Oscar Mayer, I mean."

And I'll say, "A) Oscar Mayer is the BRAND name, and B) I wasn't named after luncheon meat."

Now she's even got me doing the A's and B's.

She'll say, "For your information, A) I was making a joke about Oscar Mayer, and B) if you weren't named after lunch-meat, then where on earth did your parents get that silly name?"

And I'll say, "You know very well that Ham is just a nick-name and my name is Hamilton. It's an old family name," which isn't true at all. The truth is that I got the name from my mother, but I don't feel like explaining that to Renée because it's none of her business.

And she'll say, "Well, just because it's an old family name doesn't mean it's not silly. What if you had a grandfather whose name was Birdbrain, so they named you Birdbrain?"

And I'll say, "That's a bad example."

And she'll say, "Why?"

And I'll say, "Because I *did* have a grandfather named Birdbrain."

She'll start to smile, and I'll start to make up some story about a grandfather named Birdbrain, about how he flew his plane backwards during the war, or something like that.

And she'll start laughing.

And we'll start kissing.

And I'll put my hands inside her shirt and pluck at her bra straps.

And before you know it, we're in bed and she's saying my name just the way I like it.

★

When I get up in the morning, Renée is already sitting at the kitchen table. It's been almost four months since she lost her job at the hospital. She's wearing only her underwear. A black lace bra, black lace underpants. She wears pretty underwear; some women don't, but Renée does. She's drinking a cup of coffee, and she has her guitar balanced on her lap. Every once in a while, she writes some words on a white notepad that she keeps next to her coffee cup. She'll write, then she'll close her eyes like she's trying to work out a math problem in her head, then she'll start writing again.

"Morning, Sweet Potato," I say.

And she looks up and smiles and says, "Morning. There's coffee on the stove." She gestures toward the stove with her head.

I say, "Thanks."

And she says, "There's orange juice in the refrigerator."

I say, "Fresh squeezed?"

And she says, "Not by me. By some nice men in Florida. And they were kind enough to put it in a carton, too."

"That was nice of them."

"It was, wasn't it? We should add them to our Christmas card list."

"We don't have a Christmas card list."

"Then they'll be the first ones to be on the list." She pretends to scribble on her notepad. "Christmas card list. Send card to the fine people at Minute Maid."

I pour a cup of coffee and sit down at the table across from her. Her eyes are shut tighter this time like she's working on another, more difficult math problem, like this one involves calculus or trigonometry. I try to read what she's already written on her pad, but just when I crane my neck, she opens her eyes and catches me looking.

"Don't look," she says, and she puts her hand over the pad quickly the way people cover themselves with a towel if you walk in on them when they're naked.

And I say, "What is it?" even though I know what it is. She's working on a new song. We've been back to Eddie's Attic three or four times, and each time she plays two songs: one new song, then that "Winona Forever" song about the dog. The new songs get better and better. That "Winona Forever" song stays the same.

"I'm writing some new lyrics."

I say, "What's this one about?" But I'm thinking, *Please, Lord, don't let it be about a dog.*

And she says, "It's about life."

And I say, "Couldn't you find a bigger topic?" because I'm trying to be funny.

Renée doesn't realize I'm joking, so she says, "No," then writes something on the big white pad. I could swear she's writing the word "banana." How can a song about life have the word "banana" in it, that's what I want to know. Then I think, *Please, Lord, don't let her be listing all the fruit in her grandma's kitchen.*

"Can I hear some of it?" I say.

And she says, "Not until I'm done. It's a work in progress."

So I say, "Okay, whenever you're ready," then finish my coffee and get ready to leave for work. I kiss her on the top of the head, and she looks up and smiles. She smells nice. Her shampoo smells like strawberries. Her grandma probably had strawberries in her kitchen, too. Right next to the bananas.

"Good luck with work," she says. "Say hi to Palmeyer for me."

Palmeyer's my boss. He owns the tailor shop where I work. Renée's only met him once or twice, but she always says, "Say hi to Palmeyer for me," which I never do. What would be the point? Palmeyer would just think I was trying to trick him into giving me a raise.

"I'll tell him that," I say, "and you have a good day with your songs."

I start to leave, but before I reach the door, she calls out my name. She pronounces it wrong.

"Yes?" I say.

And she says, "Can you think of a word that rhymes with umbrella?"

I stop and think for a second, then say, "Salmonella?"

And she says, "What, the bacteria?"

And I say, "Yes."

Renée shakes her head and says, "I don't think I can use that one."

I go to work safe in the knowledge that she is NOT writing a song about all the fruit in her grandma's kitchen. And she's not writing a song about spoiled food, either.

But what IS she writing about?

What song could be about bananas AND umbrellas?

I almost drive through a red light just thinking about THAT. I almost get into an accident.

★

On the way to work, I stop at the bank machine to get some money because I only have two dollars in my wallet and I need money for lunch. I used to eat lunch most days with a girl at work by the name of Bobby Jean Krueger, but she quit, so now I usually eat by myself. It's not bad eating by yourself. It gives you time to think. Only lately I've been thinking about Renée and her cowboy outfit, and about how we're running out of money, which can leave a bad taste in your mouth. A man should have more than two dollars in his wallet. What if something happened? What if there were an emergency? Two dollars won't get you out of a lot of emergencies.

I try not to talk to Renée about how we're running out of money because I don't want to get her upset. She's upset enough as it is, so why make it worse? I didn't even tell her about the money I borrowed from Carl, though I'll bet she figured it out. Where else did she think the extra five hundred dollars came from? From the Bank Fairy? No, she knows.

When I get to the bank machine, I push the little buttons on the keypad to withdraw twenty dollars. I wait for the sound the machine makes when it's sorting the bills, the sound like a card dealer shuffling a deck, only it doesn't make that sound at all. Instead, it makes a clicking noise—*click-click-click*—then a message flashes on the screen in fluorescent green letters saying we have insufficient funds. I try it again, and the same thing happens: INSUFFICIENT FUNDS. PLEASE SEE BANK MANAGER.

I push the buttons to find out what our account balance is. There's a clicking noise again, then the screen says: *$17.73.*

It's three days to pay day, and we don't even have twenty dollars between us.

What has Renée been spending all the money on? What? She doesn't go anywhere. She just stays at home and practices her songs. Practices her songs and bakes. I guess all the ingredients in the cakes and the pies and the cookies cost something, but not so much that we'd only have $17.73. Beggars on the street have more money than that.

When I get to work, I say hello to Palmeyer, who just nods, and then I call Renée. The phone rings eight or nine times before she picks it up.

"Hello, Ashe residence," she says. "This is Renée Ashe speaking."

And I say, "Renée?"

And she says, "Yes."

"Renée," I say, "Sweet Potato, we've got a problem."

She says, "What is it?"

And I say, "Have you been buying anything lately?"

And she says, "What?"

And I say, "Have you been going out buying things lately?"

And she says, "Why would you ask a question like that?"

And I say, "Because I just went to get some money from the bank machine, and it says we don't have any money left in the checking account."

And she says, "Why do you need money?"

And I say, "Because I need to buy lunch. I've only got two dollars. All I can buy with that is a soda pop."

And she says, "Well, maybe that's good. It'll be like you're on a diet. Maybe then I won't have such a chubby hubby."

There she goes again with that "chubby hubby" thing.

I never know what to say when she says it because Renée is NOT my wife and I am NOT her husband. If I say, "You're not my wife," though, I know she'll start crying and we'll get into an argument, which I don't want, especially when I'm at work with Palmeyer sitting five feet away from me, pretending he's not listening, but he is. I can tell. His machine's running, but there's no thread in the bobbin. Which is fine, because there's no fabric underneath anyway.

I say to Renée, "That's not the point, Sweet Potato. The point is that I'm running around town with two dollars. What if something happened?"

And she says, "For instance?"

And I say, "What if I ran out of gas?"

And she says, "Then I'd come pick you up, and I'd drive you home, and I'd sing you a song, then I'd make love to you."

So I say, "Okay, what if I got sick?"

And she says, "I'd bring you home and undress you and give you a bath, and I'd kiss you everywhere you hurt."

And I say, "Renée, stop it please. I'm at work."

And she says, "I'm just giving you something to think about while you're working."

I picture her sitting there in her black underwear, which is NOT something I should be thinking about at work. Especially when I'm not going home for another eight or nine hours.

On a piece of paper I write STOP LISTENING in big, black letters. I hold it up. Palmeyer reads it. He acts offended until I point to the empty bobbin. Then he pops a spool of green thread into his bobbin and whistles along to a song on the radio.

I say, "I've got enough to think about, Sweet Potato. What I really need to talk with you about is the money. I know I haven't been spending it. And if YOU haven't been spending it, then the bank's made a big mistake, and we need to call them to correct it." It all sounds very reasonable, I think, especially since it just popped into my head as I was talking.

Then Renée says, "Well, honey, I did buy a few things."

I say, "Can I ask what?"

She says, "Yes," but she doesn't tell me right away.

I wait a couple seconds, then finally I say, "What?"

And she says, "Well, I was talking with Walter."

And I say, "Who's Walter?"

And she says, "You know very well who Walter is."

And I say, "No, I don't," because I want to hear her say it.

And she says, "Guitar Walter, the one who's teaching me to play the guitar. He says if I want to sell my songs, I can't just go to Eddie's Attic every week expecting to get discovered. I need to make tapes of my songs and send them out to radio stations and record companies."

She pauses, and I say, "Okay, so what does that have to do with us not having any money?"

That's when she says, "Well, the other day we went out and bought a tape recorder and some cassette tapes, and we bought some envelopes to put them in."

And I say, "We?"

And she says, "Me and Walter. We went to Phipps Plaza."

Phipps Plaza. That's the EXPENSIVE shopping mall. That's where the rich people go. That's the mall my brother Carl and his wife go to. You can't buy a soda pop there without a credit card.

And I say, "How much did this little shopping spree cost?"

And she says, "Not much."

And I say, "How much is not much, Renée?"

And she says, "I don't know, two hundred dollars."

I try to keep from getting angry, but it's hard. I say, "Goshdarn it, Renée, I'm not goshdarn Ted Turner," only I don't say "goshdarn" either time. "I don't have money coming out of my ears." I don't say "ears."

And Renée gets mad and says, "Don't you *dare* talk to me like that. Don't you *dare* talk to me like I'm a dog or something."

And I say, "I'll talk any way I want. I don't have that kind of money that you can just be going out and buying things like that. You're buying tape recorders, and I can't even buy a goshdarn hamburger."

And she says, "When you're married, the money belongs to *both* people."

And I say, "I'm not having this conversation again, Renée."

This time when I look over, Palmeyer is giving me a dirty look. He's shaking his head and clucking his tongue. I look up at the racks. We have a lot of work to do: there are suits everywhere; suits and pants and jackets and dresses. I shouldn't be on the phone. I write another note: I'LL BE OFF IN A MINUTE. Palmeyer runs his tongue over his front teeth.

Renée's talking, only I can't concentrate on what she's saying. All I hear is, "Mumbo jumbo mumbo jumbo money mumbo jumbo mumbo jumbo wife mumbo jumbo money mumbo jumbo mumbo jumbo mumbo JUMBO."

And I say, "Renée."

And she says, "Mumbo jumbo."

And I say, "Sweet Potato, slow down."

And she says, "Mumbo jumbo money mumbo jumbo money mumbo jumbo mumbo jumbo."

"Listen," I say, "I have to go to work. I'll talk to you about this later."

And she says, "Fine," very forcefully like SHE's the one who's right.

And I say, "Don't go buying any diamond earrings or sports cars until I get home."

And she says, "It's *our* money, Hay-yum." It doesn't sound the least bit provocative.

"It's Ham," I say. "Ham."

And she says, "I know. It rhymes with slam," and then she slams the phone down, which I have to admit was pretty clever of her.

When I hang up the phone, Palmeyer says, "Problems with the missus?"

He knows Renée and I aren't married. He just says it to get my goat, which it does.

"Very funny, Palmeyer," I say, "very funny."

Then he points to the racks as if to say, *Get to work already*.

I get the point.

I get the point.

★

Carl is a very good lawyer. He's so good, that there have been articles written about him in *The Atlanta Journal Constitution*, articles with his photograph in them. They're framed and hanging up in his office behind his desk. One of them has a big picture of Carl standing next to a horse. It's funny because Carl doesn't own a horse, Carl has NEVER owned a horse, and Carl has never even been on a horse. Carl is AFRAID of horses.

When I asked him once why he was posing for a picture next to a horse, he said, "It was because I was working on a big case involving a horse breeder who was trying to defraud an insurance company."

I said, "Oh, well, I guess that makes sense."

And he said, "God only knows where they'd have wanted to take a picture of me if I was working on a case involving skydivers."

And I said, "Were you afraid standing next to the horse?"

And he said, "Sometimes, Ham, we have to confront our fears," and he tipped his head back the way he does when he thinks he's said something meaningful.

And I said, "Cut it out. You're still afraid of horses, aren't you?"

And he said, "Scared to DEATH."

I don't visit Carl at work very often, but since I'm going to have to ask him for another loan, I'd rather do it there than at his home where his wife and kids might hear, which could be an embarrassing thing for me. So I ask Palmeyer if I can take a long lunch, and he says it's fine as long as I work late that night to make up the time, which makes sense. I'm not trying to take advantage of Palmeyer, not at all.

When I show up at Carl's office, his secretary tells me to sit in one of the leather chairs outside his office because he's on a telephone call. Only she says it's a "teleconference," which must mean it's important. Which means my call with Renée about not having any money in the bank was a tele-conference.

Carl's secretary's name is Cecily. She's been his secretary for at least five years, maybe longer. She's pretty, with a thin waist and long, fluffy black hair like the girls in Renée's magazines. If I wasn't living with Renée, I would probably ask Cecily on a date. You can tell she wears pretty underwear. Today she's wearing a thin, beige blouse. You can see that she's wearing a white camisole underneath. You can hear your heart racing whenever you see her.

"Ham, can I get you some coffee while you're waiting?" Cecily says to me.

I say, "No, thank you."

She says, "We also have tea and soda."

"Are you sure you didn't used to be a stewardess in a previous life?"

"I don't think so."

"Well, you sure are attractive enough to be a stewardess."

She smiles a little, then says, "You're very sweet, Ham." That's when I notice that she has an engagement ring on. An engagement ring and a frilly white camisole. Whoever she's marrying is a lucky dog. I'll bet she doesn't go out buying tape recorders without talking with him first.

It's five minutes that I'm sitting in the chair across from Cecily. I try to make myself stop thinking about the camisole, but then I find myself thinking about the tape recorder. And when I try not to think about THAT, I find myself thinking about that stupid song of Renée's, the song about the dog. I'm thinking, *I love you, Winona, forever.* When Cecily looks up at me over her computer, I realize that I'm humming the song out loud.

"It's a song," I say.

And she says, "That would have been my guess."

"My girlfriend wrote it."

"That's nice. What's it about?"

I lie and say, "It's about a trip to Paris." I'm not about to tell her the truth.

The little red light on Cecily's phone flicks off, and she says, "He's off the phone now, Ham. You can go in," which I do.

Carl's office is huge. It's almost as big as my entire apartment. You could fall down in his office and not hit your head on anything, that's how big it is. In our apartment, you can't even bend over without giving yourself a concussion. It's still a nice apartment, though.

"It's good to see you, buddy," Carl says when I walk in. There's the picture of him from the newspaper in a frame right behind him, so it's almost like seeing double. The same slightly off-center smile, the same slicked-back hair. When I reach Carl, he shakes my hand. He's wearing a navy blue suit with a white shirt and a red tie. The tie has little curlicues on it, like fish hooks. He's a good dresser. He shops at the expensive mall.

I say, "It's good to see you, too. When did Cecily get engaged?"

"Last month. Some guy who works for a computer company."

"Well, good for her."

Carl says, "Not sure I trust the guy, but it's not my place to say anything. But, oh, never mind. To what do I owe the pleasure of this visit?"

And I say, "Remember the five hundred dollars you lent me a couple weeks ago?"

And he says, "Yes."

And I say, "Darn it, I was hoping you'd forgotten."

And he winks at me and says, "It's forgotten, buddy."

That's the way Carl is. He likes to wink, and he likes to shake hands, and he likes to call people "buddy." That's the way I imagine most lawyers are. Winking, shaking, calling you "buddy." Pretending they're not afraid of things.

I say, "I'm just joking, Carl. I promise to pay it back to you, but I was wondering if maybe you could lend me another hundred dollars. It's just that—"

He doesn't even wait for me to explain about the tape recorder. Instead, he holds up a hand beside his face and says, "Hey, it's no problem," and he opens his top desk drawer and removes his checkbook. Then, very quickly, he scribbles on one of the checks, pulls it out of the checkbook, folds it in half and hands it to me the way your grandfather slips you a couple dollars when your parents aren't looking. I open it up. It says "One hundred dollars and 00 cents" on it in perfect handwriting, just like they teach you in school.

"Thanks, Carl," I say. "I really promise I'll get it back to you."

And he says, "Whenever you get a chance. But it's okay if you don't." It's hard to tell if he is being nice or if he pities me. Either way, it's fine with me. I need the money. I'm getting hungry.

That's when I say, "Listen, Carl, there was actually something else I wanted to talk with you about while I was down here."

And he says, "You didn't quit your job, did you?"

And I say, "Worse."

And he says, "You killed your boss?"

And I laugh and say, "I can't say it's never crossed my mind, but, no, I didn't kill my boss. Actually, it's about a puppy."

Carl gets a funny look on his face, his eyebrows curling toward his nose, and he gestures for me to sit down in one of the big, overstuffed chairs across from his desk. Everything on his desk is perfect. The papers are all in neat piles. The pens are all arranged in a coffee cup. The coffee cup has golf clubs painted on it. They're crossed like swords.

I sit down across from Carl and I tell him everything. I tell him all about Renée, and about how she lost her job at the hospital, and how she's taking the guitar lessons. I tell him about the cakes and pies and cookies. I tell him about the cowboy outfit and the tape recorder, and then I tell him about "Winona Forever." I even sing part of it for him:

No matter the day,
No matter the weather,
I love you, Winona,
Winona, forever.

"It's a love song to a *dog*?" he says.

And I say, "Yes."

And he says, "A *dog* dog?"

And I say, "What?"

And he says, "Maybe she's using the word 'dog' to refer to a person, like rap singers do when they refer to their friends. Like when they say, 'You don't want to mess with my dawgs.'" His voice deepens and he makes quotation marks in the air with two fingers on each hand when he says "my dawgs."

And then, sarcastically, I say, "That's right, Carl, she's a rap singer. She sings songs about 'ho's' and about how she wants to 'bust a cap' in someone, and she refers to people as 'dogs.'"

And he says, "I was just brainstorming."

I say, "I appreciate it, but she's not referring to a person when she says 'dog.' Besides, there's part of the song where the dog is sitting on her lap licking food off her fingers. No, she's singing about a real dog. A *dog* dog."

"So maybe she just had a dog once that she really loved," Carl says.

"That's just it, Carl—she's never *had* a dog."

"Never?"

"Never. I asked her mother once when she called, and she said Renée's never had a dog. Heck, she's never even had a cat."

Carl scratches the tip of his nose like he's thinking, then he says, "What does that mean, 'She's never had a cat'?"

And I say, "What kind of person has never had a dog or a cat?"

And he says, "A lot of people have never had a pet."

And I say, "We did," which is true. We had a beagle named Clementine.

And he says, "But we never had a cat."

And I say, "Lots of people have never had a cat."

Then Carl says, "Maybe the dog in the song represents something. Maybe the dog is a metaphor for lost innocence. Maybe it's a metaphor for, well, I don't know what it could be a metaphor for, but maybe it's a metaphor."

And I say, "No, it's about a dog, Carl. I've resigned myself to that. It's about a stupid dog who runs away from home, then comes back."

"And it's missing an ear?"

"Yes."

And Carl says, "Which ear?"

And I say, "Does it matter?"

And he says, "Not really," and shrugs.

And I say, "That's where this whole thing leads to a legal issue."

And he says, "This dog that doesn't even exist leads to a

legal issue?"

And I say, "Sort of. Here's the legal question I was hoping you could answer. Let's say there's this guy and he's living with this girl. And let's say they're living together for a long, long time. A couple years, let's say. And let's say he NEVER asks her to marry him, and they NEVER get a marriage license, and they NEVER have a wedding ceremony or anything like that, okay? Now, at some point in time, just because they're living together, are they considered to be man and wife? You know, are they considered to be a married couple as far as the law goes?"

Carl starts smiling. "Renée thinks you're married?" he says.

And I say, "She doesn't just think we're married, she's telling everyone we're married. We get bills in the mail addressed to 'Mrs. Renée Ashe.' Carl, I swear, there's NO SUCH PERSON AS MRS. RENÉE ASHE."

And he says, "So where's this coming from?"

"She says it's something called a common-law marriage. She says that just because we've lived together for so long, it means we're considered to be married. That's crazy, isn't it? I mean, she's out of her mind, right? Right?"

"Well, she's right about common-law marriages," and I can't catch my breath. I feel like I do when some food goes down the wrong pipe. "She's right as long as you've been holding yourself out to the public as man and wife for ten years."

I start to breathe again. "Ten years. I haven't even known her for ten years," I say. "You know that. And that business about holding yourself out—what's that?"

"It means, do you tell people you're husband and wife?"

"*I* don't, that's for sure."

Carl says, "Congratulations. By the powers vested in me by the state of Georgia, I hereby proclaim you *not* man and wife." So there's a legal opinion, from a LAWYER, that Renée and I are NOT married.

I say, "Thank God."

And Carl says, "God had nothing to do with this one. Now, do you want my opinion as to whether or not you *should* marry Renée?"

I already know his opinion: he thinks we should get married. Every time we have dinner at his house, he and his wife, Judy, will pull me aside in the kitchen and say, "You really should marry her, Ham." But I don't want to hear his opinion now, so I say, "No, I only came here for some legal advice, not romantic advice. Besides, I already got married once, and look how that worked out."

It didn't work out too well, to say the least.

And Carl says, "Well, for what it's worth, I happen to think she's great."

And I say, "She wrote a love song to a dog, Carl. A dog with one ear."

"Oh, yeah, I'd already blocked that out of my mind."

"Well, don't."

Then I go back to work.

The rest of the day, every time I try not to think of Cecily's camisole, I think of the tape recorder Renée bought.

And every time I try not to think of the tape recorder, I end up thinking about that stupid song about the DOG.

And every time I try not to think about THAT, I end up thinking about Renée mispronouncing my name. Hay-yum. Hay-yum. Hay-yum.

★

I know I have an unusual first name. I'm not stupid.

Once, a long time ago when I was in high school, my mother told me how I got my name. I was sitting at the kitchen table while she was cooking dinner.

Out of the clear blue sky, my mother said, "You know, Ham, you will never forget your first love. Never."

And I said, "Is that right? Who was yours?"

I thought she'd say my father, but she didn't. Instead, she said, "Well, we never talk about it, but I was engaged to another boy before your father. His name was Hamilton Cray, and he was just the most handsome man you'd ever want to meet. Handsome and quite an athlete. We got engaged on the night of our senior prom, and then he joined the service. The military service, I mean. He wrote me the most beautiful letters, which I kept for years and years, even after your father and I married. They were very lyrical. You might even say poetic. Your father finally asked me to throw them out when we were moving here. That's a small sacrifice to make for your husband, I think."

So I said, "So you named me after him?"

And she said, "What?"

And I said, "So you named me after your first boyfriend, Hamilton Cray?"

And my mother turned her back to me. She may even have blushed, it was hard to say.

After a while, she said, "Why on earth would you think that?"

I said, "Because his name was Hamilton, and my name is Hamilton."

She turned around and waved a wooden spoon at me and said, "Whatever you do, don't tell your father."

And I said, "What do you mean, don't tell him?"

And she said, "He doesn't know."

And I said, "What do you mean, he doesn't know? You'd have to be an idiot not to figure it out." Her boyfriend's name was Hamilton. My name is Hamilton. It doesn't take a private detective to figure it out. It'd be like having a child name Michelangelo, then saying you didn't name him after THE Michelangelo."

She reached out and squeezed my elbow, and she said, "Whatever you do, just don't tell him."

I promised her. And I didn't tell my father. Although a few weeks later, when we were driving to Atlanta to see a baseball game, I asked him where my name came from, just to see what he would say.

"Heck if I know," he said. "Your mother picked it out. I'm sure it was the name of someone she knew, like an uncle or something. She probably explained it to me, but I have to admit my radar only picks up about forty percent of what your mother says." Then he put his hand on my wrist and said, "Whatever you do, don't tell her I said that."

That was when I was in the ninth grade. The next year, I ran for class president. I shook hands, and I painted posters and passed out buttons that said ELECT HAMILTON ASHE FOR A BETTER TENTH GRADE. It was very exciting, but in the end I lost the election to a pretty Irish girl named Shellie O'Connell. She had red hair and freckles on her nose, and she was a cheerleader. Her campaign posters, which she taped up right next to mine, read HAM IS A PIG!

I ended up marrying her five years later.

SHE knew how to say my name.

"Ham is a pig," she would say, not "Hay-yum is a pig."

CHAPTER 3: BLESSED ARE THE LITTLE FISHIES

My first marriage didn't work out too well, to say the least. My ONLY marriage.

I grew up in a town called Cadbury, Georgia. "Cadbury," like the chocolate bars. It's a fishing town not far from Savannah. Fish and shrimp. Shellie and I both went to Cadbury High School, as did Carl. The name of the sports teams was the Cadbury Poets, which seemed like a silly name for a sports team at the time.

What do sports and poetry have to do with each other?

Only now, the name seems very sweet to me: the Cadbury Poets.

Carl and I played for the basketball team, though I hardly ever got off the bench. Carl was the starting center. He was tall and fast. He'd salt away 20 points a game, and the girls loved him. Me, I played guard sometimes because I was a pretty good dribbler. Not good enough to start, though. There was always someone better. Sometimes there were two boys who were better.

While I sat on the bench, the cheerleaders would jump and dance and sing our school cheer right in front of me. They would be so close I could touch them if I wanted to. They'd sing:

Keats, Yeats, Browning, Frost,

The Cadbury Poets have never lost.

Shellie was one of the cheerleaders, though I didn't know her very well. She was too pretty for me, with those freckles and that red hair and those short, short skirts that showed her legs while she was jumping up and down in front of me, calling out the names of Keats, Yeats, Browning, and Frost.

Then she started with that "Ham Is a Pig" business.

★

"What happened in Cadbury isn't for the weak of heart." That's what my mother would say.

She was right: it wasn't for the weak of heart. Or the weak of stomach, for that matter. It was in the newspapers. The newspapers had pictures of it. The newspapers often have pictures, which isn't always good for those who are weak of heart. Or stomach.

Cadbury is where the body was found. Actually, the body parts. Hands. Legs. Feet. Ears. You name it. Body parts that only doctors could dream of. The coroner had to put the body together like a model airplane. They wrote about it in the newspapers, and it wasn't a story for the weak of heart. There were pictures. One article said that the boy was put back together with his right arm where his left arm should have been, and vice versa. The report, it turned out, was false. My father asked the coroner himself.

Cadbury isn't the sort of town where people murder each other. But it happened anyway, there's no denying it. It's not the only town where murders happen, though. Far from it. I don't know how many hundreds or thousands of murders occur each year, but I know one thing: They all happen somewhere. And most of the time I'd bet you'll find someone saying, "This is not the sort of town where people murder each other."

Except in New York. In New York if someone gets murdered, they probably say, "Big deal. Happens every day," which is why I don't like to go to New York. I went there once. Once was enough in my book.

★

After I graduated from high school, I interviewed for a job with a large soda company right here in Atlanta. I wore a suit and tie that belonged to my father. He had bought it at Small's Clothing in Cadbury. It was just a rinky-dink little place no bigger than a hamburger stand.

At the job interview I spoke with a man from the personnel department. The man who interviewed me for the job was about the same age that I am now. He had a crewcut and a round face, with crow's feet at his eyes. He seemed bored with me until I mentioned that I was from Cadbury. He asked me if I knew where Crow's Point was, and I said I did: Crow's Point is ten miles or so from Cadbury, southeast.

"I once knew a girl in Crow's Point," he said. "In fact, I was engaged to her. She was a beautiful, beautiful girl. She was murdered. It was very strange. You see, she was collecting money for charity, and when she knocked on the door, the guy answered and—boom!—he just shot her in the head with a pistol. Then he took her out back and buried her in the backyard like he was burying tulip bulbs. Her parents filed a missing person's report with the police when she didn't come home that night, and it only took them an hour or so to find her. They found her car parked right in front of the guy's house, and then they found her body in the backyard. It's a very sad story, not a story for the weak of heart."

The man told me this story matter-of-factly, like a

teenager reading Shakespeare aloud in class. You could tell he'd told that story, that EXACT story at least a thousand times. When I left the office I knew he wouldn't offer me a job. Everything worked out fine, though. Had I worked for that company, I wouldn't have ended up going back to Cadbury that summer to work in the appliance store where Shellie worked. We wouldn't have ended up getting engaged and married. So everything worked out fine. Except for the girl in Crow's Point. I have to remind myself of that sometimes.

Except for the girl in Crow's Point.

★

It was only two days after they found the body that the police arrested Victor Smalls. He was forty-eight years old, according to the articles in the newspaper, and he owned Smalls' Clothing, the same place where I had bought my suit. He was a widower and he dressed well, which made sense since he could get all the clothes he wanted. They arrested Victor Smalls, and the following morning my mother and Carl and I bumped into one of the police officers who'd arrested him. We ran into him at the post office, where we were in line to send off some packages, and my mother asked him if they were certain it was Victor Smalls who'd committed the murder.

And the policeman said, "There's some very damaging evidence."

And my mother said, "What's the evidence?"

And he said, "I'm not at liberty to discuss it."

Already there was a rumor in town that Victor Smalls had tortured the boy in the cellar of his store. My mother asked if that was true, and the policeman said, "I'm afraid I can't tell you anything, ma'am. But I will tell you this. When we arrested him, Smalls said, `There are some crazy people in this town.' Well, if that's the case, we ought to elect him Mayor."

The best I remember, though, Victor Smalls had never done anything crazy. He was not some shifty brute. He sold clothes. He was a normal, quiet man, like most men in Cadbury. But the fact that Victor Smalls was a normal, quiet man could only mean one thing: he was guilty. Anyone who's ever been to the movies knows that being normal and quiet is considered incriminating evidence.

Very incriminating.

But there was something unusual about the murder, too. The boy had a fresh cigarette burn on the palm of his hand.

And Victor Smalls didn't smoke.

★

The school had counselors come talk to all of us about our grief. They told us that after a tragedy, it's not unusual for sick, insensitive jokes to run wild, and that's what happened in Cadbury. It happened after the *Challenger* spaceship blew up. The counselors said that psychologists excuse these jokes as "defense mechanisms." They say jokes are natural. One of the jokes went like this: "Did you hear that Victor Smalls was voted class clown in high school? Yup, he was a real cut-up."

The first time I heard that joke, everyone laughed, but they did so in a strange way, as if they were pretending they hadn't heard the joke at all, but instead had thought of another, harmless joke of their own at precisely the same moment. Later, I'm sure, they each repeated the joke to someone else. Like I just did.

Here's something else: On one of the bridges in town, some boys painted "VISIT CADBURY, GEORGIA! BRING

THE KIDS!" At least I suspect that boys painted it. I can't imagine girls doing that. It was the only graffiti I ever saw in Cadbury.

Later, when our basketball team went to play a game against Magruder High School, the students at Magruder wore T-shirts that read "I SURVIVED CADBURY, GEORGIA." On the back was a drawing of an old, well-dressed man clutching an ax.

In the cartoon bubble coming out of the man's mouth, it said, *Here come the Cadbury Poets, I killed their kids, but they didn't know it.*

It was all very natural.

★

In high school, our phys ed teacher was named Mr. Mennori. He'd been in the Marines. The Marine insignia was tattooed on the inside of his arm. To get us to run faster, Mr. Mennori would shout to us, "Pretend a madman is chasing you with a knife." That was BEFORE what happened with Victor Smalls.

The sports teams there are now called the Cadbury Bulls, and the students all cheer:

Rattle, rattle, rattle
Here come the cattle
Moo moo MOO!

There aren't cattle within fifty miles of Cadbury, for godssakes. It's a fishing town.

Why would they do that, change the name of the sports teams?

Why?

★

Victor Smalls was listed in *Who's Who in Cadbury, Georgia*. My father was, too. It wasn't so much an honor as it was a fact of life: all of the men in town were listed in *Who's Who*. The Chamber of Commerce didn't want to get anyone angry, so they decided to include everyone. That would never happen in a large town like Atlanta. God knows what they do in New York.

Victor Smalls' entry read: "Proprietor of Smalls' Clothing." That was all, one sentence. He wrote it himself. Everyone wrote their own entries each year. My father once wrote, "Samuel J. Ashe, Jr. King of Spain," and no one edited it. They ran it just like that: "Samuel J. Ashe, Jr. King of Spain." So I guess that made me and Carl Princes of Spain.

It's strange what crosses your mind at times, how in the midst of a gruesome event like what happened to that boy, you could think, *Where is everyone supposed to buy clothes now?* I thought it, and I'd bet I wasn't the only one who did. But what was everyone supposed to do? Were we supposed to drive to another town?

★

My grandfather was a fisherman. My grandfather on my mother's side. He once met Ty Cobb, the great baseball player, in a parking lot outside a liquor store in Albany, Georgia, and got him to autograph a baseball. He gave it to me, but I don't have it anymore.

The largest tiger shark ever caught weighed 1,780 pounds. It was caught by a man off Shady Grove, South Carolina, in 1964. Not a week later, not a *week*, my grandfather caught one that weighed 1,777 pounds—three pounds less!

"I should've put my thumb on the scale," he told us.

Each morning, even today, dozens of fishermen steer

their crafts into the bay, then set off for deeper water and larger fish. At night, most of the boats are tied to the docks by the grocery store.

One night, when I was in high school, I took a walk through town, and I wound up by the grocery store. I looked at the boats as I walked down one of the docks, not looking too carefully. All of them had women's names. *Linda. Silly Sue. My Maria. Amy Sweet Amy*. When I reached the end of the dock, I sat down and just watched the water. Several hours passed before I got up and started to walk back toward home. It was then that I saw the boat nearest the grocery store. I hadn't seen it when I'd walked out. The boat was listing to one side so that it had filled with thick, brown water. It was painted light blue, but the paint was chipped, peeling, and the bow had turned green-red with rust. The lantern in front was broken. So were the windows. The cabin was filled with garbage. A wooden basket with its slats broken, with a single line of string running into the water. A red rubber hose. A broken navigation panel. A wire cage. A rusted motor, on its side. Twigs. A broom. A cardboard box with "Perishable Fresh Seafood" on the side. Some soda pop cans. Crumpled cigarette packs. Pieces of wood. I remember looking at it and thinking I could pull it out of the water and fix it up. Keep it in the garage and work on it on weekends. Put it up on cinder blocks like some of the boys in school did with old cars. Sand it down, slap on a fresh coat of paint.

I decided to pace off the boat to see how large it was. I walked on the dock, alongside the boat, counting off my footsteps. When I turned again to consider the boat, I saw its name painted on the bow: *Kathy*. Suddenly, I was light-headed. A few months earlier, two of my classmates found a boy's hand in that same boat. It was the hand with the cigarette burn on the palm. The other pieces of the body were found in the bay, in very shallow water, beside the boat. Pieces only a doctor could dream of.

My grandfather used to keep his boat—the boat in which he caught that tiger shark—no more than 50 yards away, back when he was still living, of course. The first time he took me fishing, we left at five o'clock in the morning. He showed me how to bait the hook, and how to cast, and how to reel in. I was the first to make a catch, a tiny bluefish that couldn't have been more than four inches from end to end. My grandfather twisted the hook from its mouth and explained to me that it was too small to keep.

"Blessed are the little fishies," he said, and he dropped it back into the water.

★

Our entire high school attended the funeral. The counselors said it would be a good idea, but they never explained why. It was the first funeral I'd ever been to, and I've hardly gone to any since, just my grandparents'. I can't stand to look in the caskets, or even to imagine what's inside. "People always seem to look smaller without their souls," as my mother used to say. I don't know if I agree with that. I just know that the body in the casket didn't look like anyone I'd ever seen before.

Several days later, there was a photograph of the boy's mother on the front page of the *Cadbury Weekly* newspaper. She looked dignified in her black dress and dark glasses, with a white handkerchief in one hand. She was holding an umbrella because it was drizzling. The caption said something like, "The mother of the slain child grieves at the grave of her son." In the article beneath the picture, she said, "He was a joy. He was a bright, ambitious boy. He wanted to be an astronaut. And a professional football player. And a private detective." It was enough to make you wonder whether you should ever even dream about being an astronaut or a professional football player or a private detective. It was enough to make you wonder whether you should ever dream about doing anything at all with your life.

In the article, they also quoted a poem that one of the girls in our class read at the funeral. She was the editor of the school yearbook, *Serendipity*. I don't remember her name, but I remember the poem word-for-word, even after all these years, as if I'd just heard her read it a moment ago:

Let's pull the stars down from the sky,
Let's help the moon turn its back,
Let's drain the oceans til they're dry,
Let's make the sun turn brown, then black.
Let's be strong and not meek,
Let's turn the clocks back a week.

Spin the dials counterclockwise,
Seven days in reverse,
Wipe our noses, wipe our eyes,
A friend returns, none the worse.
A friend returns, and always stays,
Only now it's been eight full days.

And now it's nine, and now it's ten,
And there's much to do before we're through,
Too many clocks to turn back, friends,
Too much rewinding for us to do.
So let's close our eyes and get some sleep,

Let's think of him and not weep.

Let's leave the stars up in the skies,
Let's keep the moon in its place,
Let's let the oceans fall and rise,
Let's look the sun right in the face.
Let's not be meek, let's be strong,
Let's let the clocks just tick along.

Maybe that's why I think the Cadbury Poets was a lovely name for a sports team. Maybe that's why I don't like the new nickname.

★

Several days after Victor Smalls was arrested, my mother and I were in the grocery store, and we overheard an old married couple talking. It was a couple by the name of Mr. and Mrs. Steen. They were talking about the murders, about Victor Smalls.

"I don't know," the woman was saying, "I always thought he was very nice."

And her husband said, "He's a murderer."

And then she said, "Maybe, maybe not. Besides, how do you explain the cigarette burns on the boy's hand if Victor Smalls didn't even smoke? Hmm?"

And her husband said, "Maybe he had an accomplice, like in the movies and TV shows."

I remember something else I heard the woman say. She said, "Even if he did do it—and he's innocent until he's proven guilty in this country—even if he did do it, we'll never know why. Only God knows why someone would do something so brutal."

Her husband said, "At the very least—I mean, at the very

least—we should vote to take him out of the *Who's Who*."

And she said, "What if he's innocent?"

Then he said, "Well, if he's innocent, we'll just put him back in next year," which is exactly what the Chamber of Commerce voted to do: remove Victor Smalls' entry from the *Who's Who* and put it back in the next year if he was found not guilty. Only they never had to put his name back in the book.

★

Shellie and I had hardly spoken after she'd beaten me in the school election. We ended up working at the appliance store together a couple summers later, though, the summer after we'd graduated. She was pretty, and she was charming in the way only southern women can be, and she was good at selling vacuum cleaners. She'd pretend vacuuming was fun. She smiled while she demonstrated whatever vacuum she was trying to sell.

"I pretend a parade is going past," she explained to me once. "That's how I do it. If you pretend a parade is going past, you can't help but smile."

Sometimes she'd even sing while she was vacuuming.

It was hard to stay mad at her about the election. The whole "Ham Is a Pig" thing was actually pretty funny, if you think about it. "You didn't miss out on much," she said. "Not being our class president, I mean."

And I said, "Is that so?"

And she said, "It's not like a lot of foreign dignitaries flew in to meet me."

And I said, "No?"

And she said, "No, but I was on a first-name basis with the president of the math team."

Sometimes, when business was slow, we would sit on top of the dishwashers and tell each other stories. For instance, I told her about how my grandfather met Ty Cobb and how Carl was going to go to law school. Once, sitting on the dishwashers, she told me about her brother. Her twin brother. He was the boy who was killed. He was the boy with the cigarette burn in the palm of his hand. She said he'd wanted to be an astronaut, and a professional football player, and a private detective, et cetera, et cetera, et cetera.

She said, "Let's not kid ourselves. I only beat you in the election because I got the sympathy votes."

And I said, "No, you beat me fair and square."

Later that year, when she said she loved me, I asked her to marry me. It's hard not to marry someone who's pretty and sad and who loves you. It's hard not to give her everything she wants.

★

I remember our wedding like it's a movie I've seen on television too many times. We were married in Cadbury at the Church of the Holy Angels. It was the same church where I'd been an altar boy when I was in school. It was the same church where Carl and I had been baptized. Shellie and her brother, too.

Shellie wore her mother's wedding dress, which was creamy white with a scoop neck and a long train; the seamstress had done a wonderful job. Carl was my best man. My mother sat in the front row and cried. My father patted her hand like he was the bearer of bad news. The bridesmaids wore blue dresses the color of the ocean where it's stopped being brown or green, a color you can only reach by boat.

Near the end of the ceremony, the priest said to me, "Do

you, Hamilton Ashe, take Shellie O'Connell to be your law-fully wedded wife?"

And I said, "I do."

He turned to Shellie and said, "And do you, Shellie O'Connell, take Hamilton Ashe to be your lawfully wedded husband?"

And she smiled at me with those pretty white cheer-leader's teeth of hers, then leaned forward slightly and in a tiny, tiny voice so quiet that only the priest and I could hear she whispered, "Ham is a pig."

That was how our marriage STARTED.

CHAPTER 4: TAILORS NEED SEAMSTRESS

Palmeyer and I work late, until about eight o'clock, and when I get home, Renée is already sitting on the couch with Guitar Walter, the college boy. The first thing I notice is the tape recorder.

The tape recorder Renée bought is as large as a microwave oven, maybe larger. I'd expected it would be one of those little tape recorders that you hold in the palm of your hand, the kind you see people carrying when they're running or riding their bicycles or doing some other kind of exercise. Only it's not. It's ENORMOUS, and it has dials and knobs and red lights on it like the control panel of a jet airplane.

Then I notice the microphone. Renée didn't say anything about a microphone, but there's a microphone, too. A big microphone with a foam ball on the top the size of your fist.

Then I notice Renée's clothes. She's not wearing a T-shirt like she normally does. No, she's wearing the chicken shirt. MY chicken shirt. It's a white collared shirt with drawings of chickens on it that I usually wear while I'm just sitting on the couch reading the newspaper or watching television or something else of that nature. Sometimes Renée wears it when she goes to sleep. It's not the kind of shirt I'd wear outside the apartment. It's not the kind of shirt I ever show anyone other than Renée.

Renée and Walter have their guitars on their laps. They're fiddling with the dials on the tape recorder like they're trying to tune in a faraway radio station. When I close the front door, I say hello, and they both look up from the tape recorder.

"How are things going?" I say.

And Renée says, "They're going good. Walter's teaching me some new chords."

She plays a chord, only instead of looking at me to say it was good, she looks at Walter.

I say, "That sounds good," anyway, but Renée doesn't say anything back like she's supposed to. She's still mad at me about what I said about her spending the money for the tape recorder, which I said THREE days ago. We've hardly talked since. You'd think I was the one who'd spent HER money on a tape recorder.

And I haven't even said anything about the microphone. Yet.

I just stand there for a while, and finally Guitar Walter says to me, "That's a pretty funny shirt you have." He's not talking about the shirt I'm wearing, which is just a plain, blue button-down shirt. He's talking about the chicken shirt.

So I say, "It's not supposed to be funny. It's supposed to be comfortable."

And Renée says, "It's the funniest looking shirt I've ever seen, and I've seen a lot of shirts in my day."

I almost say, "If it's so goshdarn funny, then why are you wearing it?" but I don't because I don't want to start a fight. If I start a fight, we'll end up fighting about the tape recorder, then we'll fight about the microphone, then we'll fight about whether we're married again, and I'll have to tell her that

Carl says we're NOT married. Legally speaking or otherwise.

Then Guitar Walter says, "I'm sorry, I didn't mean anything by it."

And I say, "It's okay, I know you didn't," which is a lie. I can tell he likes Renée. I can tell by the way he's always leaning toward her when he talks to her, like a man leaning out his window to check on the traffic outside. I can tell by the way he breathes, like he's always smelling her perfume. Even though she hardly ever wears perfume.

Which leads to another question: Why does Renée wear perfume when Guitar Walter comes over?

Why?

You don't need perfume to play the guitar.

Renée says, "You don't have to apologize, Walter. It *is* a funny shirt. I mean, A) who would even think of buying a shirt with chickens on it? And B) who would ever think of spending their family's money on something like that?"

That's when I say, "If it's so goshdarn funny, then why are you wearing it?" Only I don't say "goshdarn," and then I walk to the bedroom to get changed. I keep waiting for the door to open for Renée to come in to apologize, but she doesn't. They just keep playing their guitars in the living room like nothing happened, nothing at all. Playing this song, then that song like all is right in the world. Like they weren't just making fun of MY shirt in MY home. I change into some jeans and a T-shirt, then I walk out to the porch. When I pass through the living room, Renée and Walter don't even look at me. They just keep playing their guitars like I'm some kind of ghost. The kind of ghost who pays the rent and pays the bills and buys all of the food.

And a tape recorder.

And a MICROPHONE.

I sit on the porch and light a cigarette, and I watch the cars driving by. I can hear Renée and Guitar Walter playing their guitars, and Renée starts singing. It's the new song she was working on in the kitchen. I think it's called "Umbrella Steps," which is from a game called "Mother, May I?" In the game, you have to ask whether you can move, and someone will tell you what kind of steps you can take. "Take five banana steps," they'll say, which means you have to take steps that curl like a banana. Or if it's baby steps, you have to take tiny, little steps like a baby would. Or if they tell you to take umbrella steps, you have to take umbrella steps, only I don't remember what those steps are supposed to look like.

> *If you want to kiss me*
> — Renée is singing —
> *Take four umbrella steps*
> *If you want to hold me tight,*
> *Take two umbrella steps*
> *If you say you love me,*
> *Turn off the lights.*

It's one of her better songs. Near the end, she rhymes "umbrella" with "young fella," which isn't bad. It really is hard to find something to rhyme with "umbrella."

When she's done, I walk to the car and drive to a convenience store to buy some more cigarettes, even though my pack is still half-full. I buy a hot dog and soda pop, too, because I haven't had any dinner yet. On the drive home, I try to think of something else other than the fact that I'm angry at Renée, but my mind keeps going back to the same thing: If you think a shirt with chickens on it is funny, why would you wear it?

Then I start thinking of her on the couch with Guitar Walter, making fun of my shirt and looking at each other and singing love songs. I think of them going out on shopping sprees to buy tape recorders and microphones and God knows what else with MY money. I think of her in her underwear, putting on perfume before Guitar Walter comes over. I think of him leaning over to smell her, his eyelids closing slightly as he does.

If she WAS my wife, I'd be pretty angry. I'd probably even pick Guitar Walter up by his shirt collar and toss him out of the apartment, which wouldn't be too hard to do since he's all skin and bones with hair on top. But she is NOT my wife, so I don't throw Guitar Walter out when I get home. Instead, I just sit outside and listen to them sing like two lovebirds.

★

You know something's wrong at home when you'd rather be at work, but that's the way I feel, what with everything that's going on with Renée. And I don't even LIKE work. I'll sit on the porch, and I'll listen to Renée and Guitar Walter playing their guitars and singing and laughing—*ha, ha, ha*—and I'll think to myself, *I'd rather be at WORK right now*. Eight o'clock at night, and I'd rather be at work. Nine o'clock, and I'd rather be at WORK. Ten o'clock. Eleven o'clock. Weekends. That's not the way it's supposed to be, but that's the way it is now.

Almost two years ago, I saw an ad in the newspaper. The ad read: "SAILOR NEEDS HELP." Who knows what a sailor would need help with here: Atlanta's three hours from the ocean, even if you're driving fast. Working with a sailor sounded like it could be very interesting, so I applied. I called the number in the ad, and an old man answered. You could hear big band music playing in the background.

"I'm calling about the ad," I said.

And the man said, "You have any experience?"

And I said, "A little. I grew up in Cadbury. My grandfather was a fisherman."

And the man said, "Jesus Christ. I meant experience in this field."

And I said, "That's what I was saying. My grandfather was a fisherman, so I've been on boats. Only a few sailboats, though, but I'm a quick learner."

And he said, "What kind of sewing do you do on boats?"

And I said, "Sewing? What are you talking about?"

And he said, "What are YOU talking about?"

It was a couple minutes before we realized there was a typographical error in the ad: It should have said "TAILOR," not "SAILOR." But I took the job anyway because I needed the money, and money's the same color if you're working for a sailor or a tailor or the man on the moon.

Even though I've been working with Palmeyer for nearly two years now, I still tell people it's a temporary job. I don't like people to think I spend all my time sewing buttons and putting hems on pants. There's more than that. It's hard work, especially working on jackets, but people don't think it's a man's job. People think pouring tar is a man's job, but who wants to do that? Not me. I did that once before, pouring tar on roofs; you thought your back would break in half like a pretzel rod. I worked in a car wash once, too; it felt like it was raining all day. No, there are worse jobs in the world than working in a tailor shop.

There are only two of us at work these days: me and

Palmeyer. He's old, and mostly bald, and he has a puffy face. When I first started, I had to listen to his rantings and malarkey for hours on end:

"The best-looking women are redheads," he'd say, which I had to agree with. Shellie was a redhead. Palmeyer didn't know anything about Shellie, and he still doesn't. I haven't mentioned her name even once.

Or he'd say, "Here's my favorite sandwich: turkey, a little provolone, some lettuce, tomato, and a healthy dab of Russian dressing."

Or, "The Braves will win the pennant if they trade for a power hitter."

Or, "There are three things every man thinks he can do better than anyone else: Build a fire, run a restaurant, and manage a baseball team."

Or, "The best Sinatra songs are 'Summer Wind,' 'All or Nothing at All,' 'Luck Be a Lady,' and 'Nancy.' `My Way'? 'My Way' is nonsense."

Then I guess he ran out of things to tell me about. Now, we hardly ever talk except about work and sometimes about baseball or music. He likes big band music, and he keeps the radio tuned to the big band station. Harry James. Cab Calloway. Benny Goodman. Duke Ellington. Count Basie.

Sometimes he'll shout, "Get me some black thread, Salami," over the music. He likes to call me Salami, which he thinks is funny because my name is Ham, but it is NOT funny.

And I'll say, "You're a riot, Palmeyer."

And he'll say, "What do you mean?"

And I'll say, "You know exactly what I mean."

And he'll keep it up and keep it up until finally I'll say, "My name's not Salami. It's Ham."

And he'll say, "Salami, Ham, what's the difference? It's still something my doctor says I can't eat. Too salty."

There used to be three of us: me and Palmeyer and Bobbie Jean, who was the seamstress, only she quit. She had curly brown hair, and she used to wear tight clothing that looked like it had shrunk a size or two in the laundry. I don't think she wore nice underwear. Once, I saw part of her bra when she was bending over, and it was as old and worn out as my own underwear, which is really saying something. But she was still cute as could be. She had big brown eyes. Sometimes, she would sit on my knee and say, "Bet we could get things done twice as fast if we worked on them together." And I'd tell her I thought she was wrong about that. VERY wrong.

One day when we were at the lunch counter at Woolworth's, just before she quit, I told Bobbie Jean about that "Winona Forever" song. I told her about the dog running away, and about the girl getting the tattoo that says "Winona Forever," and about the dog coming back with part of its ear missing.

"That's not so bad," Bobbie Jean said. "I once dated a guy in a band, and he wrote a song about his arms."

I said, "His arms?"

And she said, "Mm hmm," and took a bite of her hamburger. "It was about how his left arm tasted saltier than his right."

"You're kidding, aren't you?"

"Nope. One day he came to bed, and he looked all upset. I thought maybe his mom died because she had cancer or leukemia or something like that. So I asked him if he was okay, and he said, 'Bobbie, I think something's wrong.' And he said, 'My left arm doesn't taste the same as my right.'"

"What was he doing tasting his arms?"

"You've got me on that one. Anyway, the funny thing was that it was true: His left arm *did* taste saltier than his right. He went to a doctor. There was no medical explanation for it, one just tasted saltier than the other. Not that that means you have to write a song about it. He wanted me to do the same test on his feet, but I said, 'Forget it, pal.' I don't care how much he washed them, a girl does have to draw the line somewhere."

And I said, "That's true."

She said, "So, in comparison, a song about a dog's not too bad."

I said, "Only in comparison."

Bobbie Jean quit working at the tailor shop because she got a better job as a seamstress at Saks Fifth Avenue, which is at Phipps Plaza. The expensive mall where they sell tape recorders and microphones to people who don't need them.

Things haven't been the same since Bobbie Jean left the tailor shop. Palmeyer and I still work on the big jobs, like always. The alterations, the fittings. Things like that. Since Bobbie Jean left, though, there's been no one to work on the smaller jobs. The zippers, the buttons, the buttonholes. And no one to work on women's clothing, either. So Palmeyer and I work on them, too. Until Palmeyer hires someone new, that is.

But that isn't all that's different, though it's hard to put a finger on exactly what it is. Maybe it's just that, since Bobbie Jean left, the shop has seemed lifeless, although that might not be the right word.

Things were never like this before. But they are now.

★

After Bobbie Jean left, Palmeyer took out an ad in the newspaper. It said:

TAILORS NEED SEAMSTRESS. *Must have 2 yrs. experience. Good listener. Must enjoy big band music. Call 293-9627.*

It could have been worse. It could have said "SAILORS."

When I called to place the ad, the man at the paper said, "So where do you want it, in the Help Wanteds or the Personals?" I told him to stop being such a wise guy. But it was a legitimate question.

The ad's been running in the paper for a few months. There haven't been many responses to it, though, except for the phone calls we keep getting from some boys from the high school, disguising their voices, claiming to be Tommy Dorsey's mother. Tommy Dorsey was a big band leader. God knows how high school boys know who Tommy Dorsey was. Maybe they looked it up in a book.

Few of the women who have applied for the position have been qualified. Almost everyone can sew, but only a few can be happy doing it all day long. That's why Palmeyer turned down the housewives who have called, figuring that they'd get bored and leave after a day or two, which I don't think is true. I'm bored, and look at me: I've stayed for two years. Imagine how long I'd stay if I LIKED it.

Palmeyer only asked one woman to come in for an interview, a woman in her forties named Christine Something-or-other. She'd worked for three years for one of the best tailors in Gainesville, and before that she'd worked as a seamstress in a men's shop in Decatur. She knew her stuff. You could tell from the calluses on her fingers.

When he was nearly finished questioning her, Palmeyer asked Christine who her favorite bandleader was.

"Glenn Miller," she said, and I could tell that Palmeyer had already made up his mind not to hire her. When they finished, he took her hand and told her he was sorry, that we wouldn't be able to use her services.

"Why did you do that?" I asked when she was gone.

And he said, "She didn't know a thing about big bands. Only someone who doesn't know anything about big bands would say Glenn Miller. He's the one everyone knows. If she were really a fan of big bands, she would have said someone else, someone more obscure. Don't you agree?"

And I said, "Yes, but what if Glenn Miller really *is* her favorite bandleader?"

Palmeyer just looked at my face for a while. He looked sad.

But it was true.

What if Glenn Miller really is her favorite?

CHAPTER 5: NINES

I've got a long list of things I'm trying NOT to think about at work.

How Renée and I aren't married.

The stupid one-eared dog song.

The tape recorder.

The microphone.

The chicken shirt.

Bobbie Jean.

I'm trying not to think about any of them while I'm working on a suit that a man by the name of Robert Minnifield needs for his niece's wedding on Saturday. I doubt Minnifield even has a niece. And she's not getting married. No, Minnifield lied about all that. People always lie to tailors, just like they always lie on their taxes. I'd bet Minnifield only said that there was a wedding on Saturday so he could get the suit back quickly. Otherwise, he would've had to wait a couple weeks because we are so backed up.

Palmeyer gets up from his table and puts his coat on.

"I'm going to the post office, Salami," he says. "Need anything?"

And I say, "Nothing."

Palmeyer shrugs and leaves, and the bell over the shop door tinkles. Not two minutes later, he's back.

"I don't know why I thought I had to go to the post office," Palmeyer says. "It was yesterday that I had a letter to mail, remember?"

"No."

"Remember, I had that envelope?"

"Oh, yeah," which isn't true, but what's the point? I don't feel like arguing over mail.

Palmeyer hangs his coat on the rack and looks over at me while I'm running the cuffs of Minnifield's suit pants through the machine.

"Look at this," he says. He points to the racks. "Look, Salami, look."

The work is piling up.

At last count, there are twenty-seven suits to be altered. The cuffs on this one, the jacket sleeves on that. Four of them, including Minnifield's, are being made by hand in the shop. The pants don't take long to make. Maybe three hours, including interruptions, with another half hour or so added on for the zipper and the button on the back pocket. The vest is another three hours, and the jacket could take up to seven hours. The lining is the hard part. People never think of that.

There are fifteen sport coats, some brand-new from Macy's or Hechts, all of them needing to be taken in or let out, or the sleeves lengthened or shortened. A few are old ones that customers brought in to have the lapels narrowed to stay in style.

There are some pants, too, thirty-four pairs in all, which isn't as bad as it sounds. They either need to be lengthened or shortened, or let out in the waist, all quick jobs.

Then there are the dresses. Seven dresses, all winter weight, none of the thin and flowery summer material, but still softer than the cloth for the men's suits. Most of the seven have to be hemmed, bringing the material up to cut across the knee, which is most nearly the same as putting cuffs on slacks, only it's a more delicate job with dresses. No one looks at a man's cuffs. Everyone looks at the cut of a woman's dress. The stitching has to be straight, perfectly straight, and as invisible as a sound.

The dresses. They haven't been touched in four days, and a lady by the name of Mrs. Broquette is due to pick hers up tomorrow morning. At least that was the date on the ticket. March 14. One of us will have to tell her she was mistaken, that the four is really a nine, that her dress won't be ready until next Tuesday. Monday afternoon at the earliest.

Lately, almost everything has become a nine, thanks to Palmeyer's sloppy handwriting. It's worse than any doctor's handwriting you've ever seen. Bobbie Jean had complained about that: ones were nines, and fours were nines, and sevens were nines, and nines were nines. And sometimes a three becomes an eight. There isn't much you can do with twos, fives, and sixes, though, except to get the job done on time.

★

At twelve-thirty, Palmeyer clears a spot on his table and opens his lunch sack. He unwraps a tuna salad sandwich and puts it on top of the wax wrapper, then pulls an orange out and places it on the table. It rolls until it hits the sandwich. He takes a small carton of milk out of the sack, then unfolds a paper napkin and lays it across his lap.

Palmeyer presses the carton open, brings it to his lips, and drinks some milk. Only he doesn't really drink it. He makes a face and spits the milk back into the container. A string of saliva hangs from his chin like tinsel from a

Christmas tree.

"Dammit!" he says.

And I say, "What?"

And he says, "The milk's spoiled."

So I say, "So go take it back and get another."

"It's not worth the time." He drops the carton into the waste basket beside the table, along with the napkin he'd used to wipe his lips. "I'm just going to go out for a walk." He begins to wrap the sandwich again, then holds it out toward me and says, "Do you want this?"

"What's it on?"

"White."

"Is it toasted?"

"No."

"I only like sandwiches on toast," I say, which is the way my mother used to make sandwiches for me. Shellie, too.

"Well, it's not on toast."

"Then I don't want it, thanks."

Palmeyer pushes the sandwich and the orange off his table and into the trash, then leaves. I wait a couple minutes, then I lock up the shop and go to get some lunch myself at the lunch counter at Woolworth's. There are two women and three men sitting at the counter, each separated by a seat. I take a seat at the end of the counter where I can look at the front door. A teenaged girl gives me a menu, and I pretend to browse through it, but what I'm really doing is looking at the front door. A lady comes in, then a boy. I see Palmeyer pass by the window. He sees me, too. He makes an obscene gesture with his middle finger, which makes me laugh.

When the girl comes back, I order coffee and a roast beef sandwich on toast. I fold the menu closed and hand it to the girl, then watch the door, pretending I'm not watching it at all.

★

Bobbie Jean never shows up like I'd hoped she would.

I don't know why I thought she might. She doesn't work anywhere near here anymore. She probably eats at the food court in the expensive mall. They have a place where they cook fresh pasta for you with whatever sauce you like. And the whole thing only takes a minute or two.

When I'm finished eating, I take some money out of my wallet and leave it on the counter. The girl who'd served me wipes off the countertop with the dish towel she has tucked in the waistband of her skirt.

I smooth the front of my shirt.

"Say," I say, "you wouldn't happen to be acquainted with Bobbie Jean Krueger, would you?"

She says, "No."

I hold my hand across the bridge of my nose and I say, "She's about this tall. Brown hair, very curly. She used to work over at the tailor shop. She'd come in here for lunch all the time."

The girl says, "Sorry."

And I say, "It's okay. It's not your fault."

I walk outside, and I walk over to a pay phone right outside the door. I find Bobbie Jean's telephone number on an old alteration ticket in my wallet, and I dial it. There's no answer, which is good because I don't know what I would say.

The answering machine answers after four rings. It's Bobbie Jean's voice: "Hi, we're not in right now. Leave your name and number, and if you're someone we like, we'll call you back." She lives alone, but she says "we" on the message so people will think there's a man living there and leave her alone. It's a pretty clever idea, unless you already know she lives alone.

At the beep, I wait a second before I say, "Bobbie Jean, it's Salami. It's been a while since you left, and I just wanted to see how things were going. I'll be at the lunch counter at Woolworth's tomorrow to grab a bite, if you can stop by." Then, before I can stop myself, I say, "I really miss you." I'd meant to say, "WE really miss you."

Then I return to the shop. When I get there, I give Palmeyer the same obscene gesture that he gave me. And he says, "Well, I *never*," then laughs.

★

Minnifield's suit is on the rack, covered in plastic, when he comes by to pick it up.

"You boys been outside today?" he says. "It's cold as a refrigerator out there today."

"Sure is," I say, hunched over the table, reading the sports page. It's forty degrees. People in Atlanta think that's cold. When it snows here, even a little, people act like it's the end of the world. There are long lines at the supermarket to buy bread and milk, and toilet paper. Because if the world is going to end, these are the things you'd want to take with you into the afterlife, I suppose. Bread, milk, and toilet paper.

Palmeyer walks to the rack and pulls the Minnifield suit down, then removes the plastic and hands the suit to him.

As Minnifield changes in the dressing room, Palmeyer calls out to him, "So, when's the big day?"

Minnifield says, "What's that?"

And Palmeyer says, "The big day. The wedding. When is it?" Palmeyer winks at me. He knows there's no wedding.

"Oh, sure," Minnifield says. "This Sunday."

Palmeyer says, "Nothing's nicer than a wedding. All the pretty dresses and the dancing and the food. There's not a thing in the world that I enjoy more, no matter what time of year it is."

I fold my newspaper into thirds and put it on the shelf, then start to mend a tear in a pair of gray wool slacks. Tears are tough to fix. You either have to put on a patch, which looks terrible, or you have to reweave the material around it, which takes FOREVER. As I work, I try to guess what Renée's cooking for dinner. It'll probably be macaroni and meatballs. She's good with macaroni and meatballs. That's what it'll be. Probably. I picture her in her red underwear, fixing macaroni and meatballs. Then I picture Guitar Walter coming into the room carrying a microphone, which ruins everything.

Minnifield steps out of the dressing room and stands in front of the mirror. He's smiling. It's hard to tell if he's admiring himself or the suit.

"A good-looking fellow?" Palmeyer asks.

Minnifield says, "Who?"

And Palmeyer says, "The groom."

Minnifield pauses for a moment, then says, "Oh, I wouldn't know. I've never met him."

Palmeyer gets down on one knee and tugs at Minnifield's pants leg, pulling it tight over his shoetop. "Good job?"

Minnifield says, "Hmm? The pants?"

"No, no. The boy. Does the boy have a good job?"

Minnifield pulls at the front of his suit jacket and turns to face the mirror sideways. "Sure," he says. "Works in a bank. Manages the place, to tell you the truth."

I turn in my chair and switch down the volume on the

radio. I hate it when people lie, like Minnifield's doing right now. I hate it how they don't think they'll get caught. So I say to him, "Whereabouts?"

And he says, "What?"

And I say, "Where's the bank that he manages?"

And he says, "Up by the river."

And I say, "Which bank? I happen to do my banking up there, maybe I know him."

Minnifield pretends he doesn't hear me. He pulls at the material at the seat of his slacks, and Palmeyer smiles into the mirror to let him know that there's more than enough room back there.

Up by the river.

Minnifield didn't have to say, "Up by the river." He could have said anything, anywhere, considering that there is no niece, and there is no wedding, and there is no bridegroom, and there is no bank. At least not one where the bridegroom works. He could have said the bank was near the highway or out by the airport. As a matter of fact, it didn't even have to be in the area. He could have said that the boy managed a bank in Peru. Or Rhode Island.

But "up by the river" is near where Bobbie Jean lives. Bobbie Jean, whom I just told I miss.

Minnifield raises his arms like a bird spreading its wings. The bottom of his jacket rises to his belt, and Palmeyer smiles in the mirror again.

"Interesting place, up by the river," I say before returning to work. I turn the volume up again and think of macaroni and meatballs with tomato sauce.

★

I'm considering starting on one of the dresses when the

phone rings. I haven't taken one of the dresses from the racks yet, but at least I'm thinking about it, and that's a start.

I answer the phone on the third ring. "Palmeyer's Tailor Shop," I say.

Someone with a thin, scratchy voice says, "Hello, is this the tailor shop?"

I say, "Yes. Yes, it is."

"I'm calling about the position in the paper."

Thank God, I think, *maybe we'll finally get some help.*

I reach for my pen, then grab an alteration ticket to write on. "Yes," I say. "Are you interested in applying?"

There's a pause.

"Hello, are you still there?" I say.

"Yes, I am, but I can't make out a word you're saying. Would it be possible for you to call me back?"

And I say, "Sure. What's your number?"

"Pennsylvania 6-5000."

There's laughter, and then the click of the phone.

It's lunch break at the high school. Worse, Palmeyer was right: everyone knows Glenn Miller. Even high school kids. "Pennsylvania 6-5000" is the name of one of Glenn Miller's songs. It's the one he's famous for.

I tell Palmeyer that it was just another prank call, but I don't tell him about Pennsylvania 6-5000. And I don't tell him that I'd written PENN6 before I'd figured out the joke.

It's not fifteen minutes before the phone rings again, and I answer it, turning my machine off and lowering the volume on the radio.

"Tailor shop," I say.

"Who is this?" It's a woman's voice.

And I say, "Ham. Ham Ashe."

And she says, "Is that you, handsome?"

And I say, "Yes."

And my heart is beating fast.

And she says, "I called to ask a favor. Could you pick up some ground beef at the grocery on the way home?"

It isn't Bobbie Jean after all. That's what I'd been thinking.

It's Renée.

And there's a good chance it'll be macaroni and meatballs.

So I say, "I'll make a note of it."

I turn the radio up again, catching an advertisement for Wonder Bread. On the back of one of the alteration tickets I write GROUND BEEF, then tack the ticket to the bulletin board and flick my machine on.

When another advertisement comes on, I glance up at the ticket. It looks like GRAND BLIP.

I pick up the phone and dial home. "You didn't say how much you needed," I say.

Renée says, "A pound."

I write 1 POUND on the ticket.

Only the one looks like a nine.

★

With the racks full, there's every reason to work late, but we clear off our tables and are ready to leave by six o'clock. I don't want to go home, but I don't want to stay either.

The suits we've been working on are folded over the backs of our chairs. There are strips of white tape holding down the ends of thread, in part so we'll remember where we left off, mostly to keep the stitches from popping loose.

There's a vacuum in the closet, but it's hardly been touched in weeks. Not since Bobbie Jean left. Even when she was here, we'd have to beg her to vacuum. Snippets of thread, mostly black and gray, are scattered about the floor, along with jagged strips of cloth and neat rings clipped from pants legs.

Palmeyer is out the door first, waving a hand to say good night. We used to say, "See you in the morning," or "Have a pleasant evening." Sometimes I would say, "Give my best to Louise," which is the name of his wife, or he would say, "Give my best to Renée," which is NOT the name of my wife.

But not anymore.

Now it's just a quick hand wave, and only by the first one out.

I pull my coat on, flick the lights off, then lock the door. I drive to the grocery store to get the ground beef for Renée. Once I get there, I walk directly to the meat cooler. I pull a package of ground beef out of the cooler and walk to the express checkout lane, then take a chocolate bar off the rack, setting it down beside the meat on the conveyor belt. On the rack beside the belt are a lot of magazines. *Newsweek. People. The Star. Redbook. Women's Day.* The women's magazines have the best headlines.

"I LOST 64 POUNDS OF UGLY FAT!"

"LOSE WEIGHT—AND EAT, EAT, EAT!"

"I WAS A TEENAGE FATTY!"

"18 SPECIAL WAYS TO SHOW HIM YOU LOVE HIM."

"THE LIGHT AT THE END OF THE TUNNEL WAS THE REFRIGERATOR!"

"MY SISTER'S A PANTY THIEF!"

What's THAT story about?

Does the woman's sister steal underwear from her? Does she steal it from other people? Does she steal it from department stores?

When I reach the front of the line, the girl at the cash register points to the ground beef and asks, "Just that?"

I say, "The candy, too."

She says, "I got it."

I hand the girl three dollars, take my change, and watch as the girl slips the package into a small plastic bag. It's funny how little the slab of meat resembles meatballs.

I pull the wrapper from one end of the candy bar and hold it out to offer the girl a piece. She pats her stomach and shakes her head no.

With the ground beef tucked under my arm, I walk out to the sidewalk. I walk past my car, passing the bakery, the pharmacy, and the appliance store before stopping in front of Thompson's Jewelers. The display case is empty. No rings, no bracelets, no necklaces, only black velvet cubes where they usually put the jewelry boxes. Whenever I walk past the store with Renée, she'll point to something and say, "Someday my husband's going to get that ring for me."

My nose is getting cold. I sniff, then walk into the florist shop next door. The shop is warm with perfume. I walk a circle around it, pausing to look at some of the larger arrangements.

The man behind the counter approaches me. He's wearing a white smock, and his hands are clasped together behind his back. "Could I be of any assistance?" he says.

I say, "Maybe. Maybe you could tell me how much a dozen long-stemmed red roses would cost."

He says, "I could check." He goes into a back room, and when he comes back a few minutes later he says, "Thirty-eight dollars."

And I say, "Is it extra for deliveries?"

And he says, "An extra five."

I open my wallet. I have a twenty, three tens, and six ones. It's all I have left from my last paycheck, but it's only two more days until payday.

"Let's take a dozen," I say.

And he says, "Yes, sir," then moves back to the counter. "And you're sending these to—?"

I think for a moment.

I think for a moment about sending them up by the river.

"No," I say, "I'll take them with me. I was just curious about the cost of sending flowers."

The man wraps a dozen roses in green-and-white paper, and I fill out a card to go with them. I use my best hand-writing, and it still looks like something Palmeyer wrote.

I tear the card up. "Would you mind writing out the card for me?" I ask. I hold up the callused hand.

And the man says, "I'd be happy to." He takes another card from the rack and holds a pen above it. "What would you like it to say?"

If it wouldn't be too embarrassing, I'd ask him to write something about macaroni and meatballs. Or something about how we should forget about the tape recorder and the microphone. Instead, I say, "To Renée. I liked the song about the umbrella. Ham."

And he says, "Ham, like the meat?"

And I say, "Yes."

And he says, "H-A-M?"

And I say, "Yes. YES. H-A-M, like the meat. Like the salty meat."

CHAPTER 6: THE SUITCASE WITH THE STICKERS ON IT

The apartment smells like tomato sauce. There's a large pot on the stove, and Renée is sitting at the kitchen table with her tape recorder and some cassette tapes and some big manila envelopes. She has them all laid out like a production line.

I carry the flowers behind my back so she can't see them while I put the plastic grocery bag on the counter.

"Did you get the ground beef?" she says.

And I say, "Sure did. I got something for you, too." When she turns around, I hand her the flowers.

"For me?" she says, and she smiles a little less than I'd hoped she would.

And I say, "Who else would they be for?"

And she says, "I thought we were fighting."

And I say, "We are."

And she says, "Okay, but this isn't fighting fair."

She opens the card and reads what I wrote about the umbrella song, then stands up and kisses me on the neck. She looks into my eyes for a long time. Her eyes are the color of good clear coffee.

"Thank you," she says, "I needed this." Then she says, "I did something to make up, too. I baked you a cake. It has two layers. One's white cake, the other's chocolate."

And I say, "Sounds good."

She walks to one of the cabinets and takes out a vase. It's a vase that Shellie and I were given as a wedding gift, but I've never told Renée that. She thinks it was mine. Renée fills the vase with water at the sink. While she's doing that, I sit down at the kitchen table. There's a stack of cassette tapes with white labels that read, "RENÉE ASHE, RECORDING ARTIST," and there's another stack of cover letters. I pick up one of the cover letters to read it. Renée doesn't try to stop me.

The letter says:

Dear Sir or Madam:

Please let me introduce myself. My name is Renée Ashe, and I am a country-and-western recording artist based in Altanta, Georgia. I sound a lot like Tammy Wynette, with a little Patsy Cline mixed in, and maybe a pinch of Trisha Yearwood, too. (It sounds like a recipe, doesn't it!)

At the present time, I do not have a recoding contract. Accordingly, I am enclosing for your enjoyment a cassette tape that will give you a sample of my musical skills. I hope that you will find it pleasing to your ears.

I must tell you that I am sending copies of the tape to other radio stations and record companies. While I cannot say that money isn't important, I will give my strongest consideration to whichever company offers me a contract first.

I look forward to hearing form you soon.

Musically,

Renée Ashe

Renée puts the vase in the center of the table, then sits across from me and starts stuffing envelopes again. I don't tell her that she misspelled "Atlanta" and "recording" and "from." She's already got half of the envelopes stuffed and sealed. She'd have to reopen all of them.

Without looking at me, Renée says, "A good hubby would lick the envelopes for me."

I stick my tongue out, and she says, "That looks like it could do a good job of licking, Ham." She says "Hay-yum" instead of "Ham," and this time it sounds provocative. We both smile. Then she starts laughing and says, "I'm a bad, bad girl, aren't I?"

I smile at her, then try to wink like Carl always does.

"Can I hear the tape?" I say.

And she says, "Maybe later, if you're good."

And I say, "Is it just you singing and playing?"

And she says, "No. Walter's on it, too. He's playing the guitar and singing the backup vocals."

And I say, "How many songs did you record?"

And she says, "One."

And I don't even ask her which one.

I know. I KNOW.

And it's not the umbrella song, that's for sure.

★

We finish stuffing the envelopes with the cassette tapes and the cover letters, then Renée makes some meatballs, mixing the ground beef with eggs and bread crumbs and spices from the spice rack. I change my clothes while she's cooking and setting the table. When we finish eating dinner, Renée brings out the cake she baked. On the top it says, HAM STINKS in white icing.

"Oops," Renée says, "that's a typo."

It's a good cake, though, and we each have two pieces. When we're done, we put the dishes in the sink, and our shoulders bump, and soon we're kissing right in the middle of the kitchen. Then, in the hall. Then, in the bedroom. I help her pull her sweater over her head. She's wearing a white, lacy bra. I kiss her shoulders and her arms. I help her out of her jeans, then we lie down on the bed.

She says, "I'm not going to be a famous singer, am I?"

And I say, "Of course you are." I almost say, "You just have to stop singing that dog song," but I don't.

And she says, "Do you really think so?"

And I say, "Yes."

Even though it's dark, I can tell she's smiling.

She licks my ear. She kisses my forehead.

"Are you still mad about the tape recorder?" she says.

And I say, "No."

And she says, "Good."

And I say, "But I'm furious about the microphone."

And she says, "I'll bet you won't be furious in an hour."

She kisses my lips.

She says, "Say something sweet to me."

And I say, "Cookies, cake, chocolate candy."

She laughs and says, "Really, say something sweet to me."

And I say, "I couldn't love you any more than I do at this moment," which is the first thing that pops in my head. I heard it in a movie once.

That night, we have a good night in bed.

A VERY good night.

★

We're so busy at the shop that we have to start turning down some work. And Palmeyer still won't hire a new seamstress. Either they don't have enough experience, or they haven't heard of "Minnie the Moocher."

"It's a Cab Calloway song," I've heard him say to some of

the women he's interviewed. "Jesus, it's CAB FREAKIN' CALLOWAY."

I'm eating lunch and Palmeyer's off somewhere. Maybe mailing a letter. I have a chicken sandwich on toast, cut into halves, a can of soda, and a sugar-glazed doughnut. I have them spread out across the newspaper, blocking out advertisements here and there, the sandwich wrapper covering an entire story.

I'm eating the sandwich and reading an article about a burglary at Thompson's Jewelers downtown when a woman enters the shop. She has a man's pinstriped suit slung over her shoulder like those sashes that the Miss America contestants wear.

"Excuse me," she says, "but I'd like to get my husband's suit altered. We marked it up at home this morning."

"Can't do it," I say, reading around my doughnut, then taking another bite of my sandwich. "He'll have to come in for a fitting."

The woman tips her head to the side and says, "I don't see why. The suit's already marked up." She held out the slacks, chalk marks at the ankles for me to look at. People do that sometimes, they bring in clothes they've already marked up with chalk or pins, and they ask us to alter them. Every time—EVERY time—they end up complaining about the job we did. They never will admit that they're the ones who marked the clothes wrong in the first place.

I say, "Nothing personal, ma'am, but how can we be sure that it's marked properly? We're very precise about our work, and we prefer to do the marking ourselves. We can't be responsible for any errors someone else might make."

And she says, "But I did a good job of it. If there's any

problem, I'll take responsibility for it."

And I say, "That's what you say now, but before you know it, we've got lawyers involved and the Supreme Court's deciding this, that, and the other thing."

The woman shakes her head side to side.

"Besides," I add, "it really would be easier to just bring your husband in next time you're in the area."

The woman says, "Fine," then she leaves.

I can't tell if she meant fine, she'll be back later, or fine, she'll take the suit elsewhere. I hope it's the latter. Things are already too busy.

Things were never like this before Bobbie Jean left.

But they are now.

Not only are we turning down work, but we have to work late most nights just to keep up with the work we already have.

★

Early one morning, not even six o'clock, I hear noises in the kitchen. Renée's not in bed. I climb out of bed and walk to the kitchen, and I see Renée folding laundry. Except she isn't folding it and putting it in the laundry basket like she normally does. Instead, she's folding it and putting it into her suitcase, the old brown one she used when we drove to Cadbury for a weekend to see my parents, and when we drove to Florida to see Disney World and Sea World. The suitcase has stickers on it from cities she's never been to. New York, Paris, London, et cetera, et cetera. The New York sticker has a drawing on it of the Statue of Liberty. Paris has the Eiffel Tower.

"You've never been to Paris," I say when I see the suitcase in the kitchen. I try to kiss her, but she pulls away. I don't know why she pulls away because we're not fighting about anything. At least, not as far as I know.

She says, "I know I haven't been to Paris."

And I say, "So why do you have a sticker on your suitcase that says Paris?"

And she says, "A) Because you don't have to go somewhere to buy the sticker, and B) because I plan to go to Paris someday."

I say, "When?"

And she says, "I don't have airline reservations yet, if that's what you're insinuating."

I still don't understand it. Why would you put stickers on your suitcase if you hadn't been someplace yet? It would be like putting up a doctor's license in your office because you were planning on being a doctor someday. It'd be like having your *Redbook* magazine sent to "Mrs. Renée Ashe" when you aren't even married, which Renée DOES. *Redbook* and *Cosmopolitan*.

Renée keeps putting her clothes in the suitcase, so I say, "So, where are you going this week? Rome?"

Only she doesn't laugh. I try to kiss her, but she turns her head away from me. She's acting like she's mad about something, only I don't know what. I haven't done anything wrong lately.

"No," she says, "I'm not going to Rome."

"New York then?"

And she says, "No," again.

So I say, "Los Angeles?" The sticker for Los Angeles doesn't have a drawing on it because there's nothing famous there.

And she says, "No."

And I say, "Then where?"

And that's when she says, "I'm thinking of going to Nashville."

And I say, "Nashville?"

And she says, "It's in Tennessee."

And I say, "I KNOW where Nashville is. Why are you going on a trip there?"

And that's when she says, "I'm not thinking of going on a trip there. I'm thinking of MOVING there. That's where all the singers go."

So I say, "You're thinking of moving to Nashville? When did you get this idea?" Just as I say that, I think of the answer: GUITAR WALTER. A picture of him pops in my head. He's sitting on the couch with Renée. His hair is oily. He's strumming his guitar. He's smelling her perfume.

"Did Guitar Walter tell you you should move to Nashville?" I say.

And she says, "Do you have to call him Guitar Walter?"

And I say, "Well, my only other choices are Oily-Haired Walter and Funny-Smelly Walter."

And she says, "He doesn't smell funny."

And I say, "My nose disagrees." He DOES smell funny. He smells like he's been working on the engine of a tractor-trailer all day. Gas and smoke and things of that nature.

She says, "Can't you call him just Walter?"

"Fine. Did Just Walter tell you that you should move to Nashville?"

Renée's mouth turns sour. Instead of answering my question, she says, "It pains me to say this, Ham, but do you think we should get a divorce?"

"What?"

"You heard me, Ham. Do you think we should get a divorce? I mean, it doesn't make much sense to stay married if you're here in Atlanta and I'm living in Nashville. So I was thinking that maybe we should get a divorce. What do you think?"

I don't know what to say because we are NOT married. It's like your boss asking you if you'll stop stealing money from the cash register. If you say "Yes," you're ADMITTING that you've been stealing from the cash register. If you say "No," it means you're going to KEEP stealing from the cash register. Either way you lose. So when Renée asks if I want a divorce, there's nothing I can say. You can't get a divorce from someone who's NOT your wife.

You CAN'T.

Right?

Right?

"Well?" she says.

And I say, "Well, what?"

And she says, "I asked you a question. I want to know if you want to get a divorce?"

And I say, "I already got a divorce," which is true. I got a divorce from Shellie, my first wife. My ONLY wife.

And she says, "I mean, do you want to get a divorce from *me*?"

"From you?"

"Yes."

And I say, "Renée, Sweet Potato, how can we get a divorce if we aren't even married?"

Renée looks at the ceiling and shakes her head side to side and says, "I am NOT having this conversation with you again." She folds some of her underwear and places it in the suitcase. The underwear is the color of a matador's cape.

I come up from behind Renée and put my hands on her hips. Although she tries to pull away, I kiss her neck, and I say, "Now, what conversation was that, Sweet Potato?"

And she says, "Don't try to change the subject. You know perfectly well what conversation I'm talking about. I'm talking about the conversation where you deny we're husband and wife. You keep denying it. You're like a killer who keeps denying he killed anyone even though there's a dead body, and there's blood on his hands, and there's the murder weapon with his, his—"

"—Fingerprints?"

And she says, "Exactly. There's the murder weapon with his fingerprints on it, but he still says, "Oh, no, I didn't kill anyone, Mr. Police Officer. There must be some mistake.'"

"Well," I say, "I *didn't* kill anyone."

And she says, "Look, I don't want to go over this for the billionth time."

And I say, "Neither do I. So, there, we're in perfect agreement."

And she says, "I guess so. I guess we're in perfect agreement that we should get a divorce."

I make a growling noise because she's driving me CRAZY. First she wants to get married, then she wants to get divorced. It doesn't make any sense. None at all.

Then Renée makes a noise in her throat and goes back to packing. I want to stop her, and I can tell she wants me to, the way her eyes keep darting toward me, but I can't think of what to do. She keeps packing the suitcase, her eyes darting over at me, and when she's through she closes it and snaps the latches shut. She picks up the suitcase. It's heavy, and you can see the muscles in her shoulders tightening. She carries the suitcase out of the kitchen, and I follow her, trying to think of what to say. Only she doesn't go to the front door.

She takes the suitcase into the bedroom and puts in on the floor of the closet.

"You're not moving?" I say.

And she says, "I never said I was moving right away. I only said I was *thinking* about moving."

Renée closes the closet door and walks into the living room. I hear her turn on the television set.

I start dressing for work while she's watching television. Renée doesn't say anything else about her suitcase, not while I'm shaving, not while I'm having my coffee. The suitcase just stays packed the whole time, sitting there on the floor of the closet where I'll see it whenever I go to get a clean shirt and pants. I don't have to open the closet to get clean underwear or socks, but I still know it's in there.

When I'm ready to leave for work, Renée's still on the couch. We don't look at each other, and we don't say anything. Just as I'm about to close the door, I hear her say, "For the billionth time, it's called a common-law marriage. C-O-M-M-O-N L-A-W. Do you hear me, Ham? Ham?"

"Yes," I say. "I was just trying to figure out what you were spelling. I thought you were spelling 'communist' at first."

And she says, "I was spelling 'common law.'"

And I say, "I figured that out."

Then I leave.

CHAPTER 7:
SHE WAS ONLY THE GROCER'S DAUGHTER

We're out of money.

Again.

At lunch, I drive to Carl's office to borrow another hundred dollars, only he's not there. He's at a meeting somewhere.

"When will he be back?" I ask Cecily.

She says, "Probably not until five." She's wearing a short black skirt with a blue sweater.

I say, "I can't wait that long."

"Is it something I can help you with?"

I say, "No, thanks." But before I know it, I'm telling her all about what's happened with Renée. Everything from how we met to her losing her job to Guitar Walter and the suitcase with the stickers on it.

"A song about a dog with one ear?" she says when I'm done.

And I say, "Yes."

"It sounds kind of sweet."

"Well, it's not. And that's the song she sent to all the record companies."

"Oh."

"What I don't understand, what doesn't make any sense

at all, is why would she be talking about picking up and moving to Nashville? Why?"

Cecily says, "You don't have a lot of female friends, do you?"

And I almost say, "I don't even have a lot of MALE friends," but I don't. Instead, I say, "Since Bobbie Jean quit, I don't have any female friends at all."

"Bobbie Jean?"

"She used to work at the tailor shop."

"Oh. Anyway, if you did have some female friends, they'd tell you that this is an easy one to figure out."

"Really?"

"Sure."

"So why is she talking about moving to Nashville?"

"Ham, she's leaving you before you leave her."

"But I'm not leaving her."

"Really?"

"Yes."

She says "Really?" again.

I say, "Yes" again.

"Well, that's just my opinion."

And I say, "But I'm NOT leaving," only I say it much louder than I'd intended.

Cecily brushes her fingertips over my lips and says, "Shh, sweetie. This is a law office."

I say, "Sorry."

And she says, "It's okay," then turns around to return to her work.

On the drive home, I imagine kissing her fingertips.

★

Renée keeps the suitcase in the closet. It's hard to forget

it's there. Sometimes she even leaves the closet door open when we go to sleep so I'll remember that she's THISCLOSE to moving to Nashville to become a singer. THISCLOSE, the distance between your thumb and your index finger when you're holding a pin.

At night, I sit on the steps and smoke and listen to her practice her songs.

She has a new one called "Biology" that I like:

Can a love like ours ever truly last,
When we are just biology,
Biology and years gone past.

There's another song called "Deep, Dark Secret," about a woman with a secret that she never tells her boyfriend. It's a good song, only you never find out what her secret is. Was she married before? Does she have a baby? What's the point of saying you have a dark secret if you're not going to tell what it is? If she doesn't want to reveal her secret, then she shouldn't say that she has a secret at all.

On Wednesdays, we drive to Eddie's Attic for Amateur Night. Sometimes Guitar Walter comes with us, sometimes he doesn't. When he comes, he always tries to clap louder than me, as if that's how you prove your love to someone, by clapping louder than everyone else. I want to say to him, "Walter, the way you prove your love is by taking a shower every once in a while," but I don't.

Every Saturday afternoon, I watch Renée as she waits for the mailman, then runs to the door to see if she got a letter from a radio station or a record company. I watch her as she flips through the mail, and then she'll say, "Oh, well, nothing today. They must still have my tape under consideration."

I know she does the same thing during the week when I'm at work, waiting for the mailman, flipping through the mail. I can picture her face as she sits at the window. I can picture her face as the mail slips through the mail slot and onto the floor, and when she sees there's nothing there from the radio stations or record companies. I can picture it, and it makes me feel sorry for her. Until I picture the suitcase.

After a while, some of the envelopes with Renée's tapes come back in the mail. The envelopes are unopened. They have RETURN TO SENDER stamped on them in fat red letters. Renée leaves them on the kitchen counter.

"It happens sometimes," she says. "The record company will move or something. If it comes back unopened, it doesn't mean they didn't like your music. It means they didn't even have a chance to listen to it," which makes sense. "It doesn't mean your dream's not going to come true," she says.

★

But I don't know if she really believes that or not. One day, I find a pad of lined notebook paper on the coffee table under Renée's magazines. On the front sheet, she'd written:

—PRESS RELEASE—
NEW COUNTRY MUSIC SUPERSTAR!
The world of country music has a new superstar, and her name is Renée Ashe!

Renée's debut album, "Winona Forever," has skyrocketed to the top of the Billboard country music charts and has already sold 10 million copies in the United States alone!

Her rise to fame is truly an American success story. She grew up in a small town, where she was only the grocer's daughter. Now, she's an international superstar, but one who hasn't forgotten her roots.

"I write songs for people like me," Renée says, "people who may not have been born with a silver spoon in their mouth and who yearn for more."

Only Renée had drawn a large "X" over the entire page and written "Stupid! Stupid! STUPID!" in the margin in letters you could tell she'd traced over a hundred times until the pen practically poked through the weakened paper.

★

My pants are getting too tight in the seat. At first, it's one or two pairs, and I think maybe they're shrinking in the laundry, which happens sometimes. That's why we always leave a little room when we're fixing someone's pants. A little room in the waist, a little room in the seat. Only now it's not just one or two pairs of my pants that are too tight. It's six or seven or eight.

They're not shrinking.

I'm growing.

Specifically, I'm growing in the seat region.

I know what it is.

IT'S THE CAKES AND PIES AND COOKIES. IT'S THE BROWNIES AND THE MUFFINS.

Renée is making me fatter, as if I were a balloon she was inflating.

Luckily, I happen to work at a tailor shop, so I bring my pants with me in the morning and let the seats out an inch or so.

It's the cookies and cakes and pies.

I'd stop eating them if Renée would stop baking them. But it's rude not to eat something that someone baked for you. It's rude not to have a taste. It'd make her feel like she wasted her time.

One day when I get to work early to fix my pants, I see Palmeyer there with a woman. He introduces me to her. Her name is Debbie Something-or-other.

"It's a pleasure to meet you," I say.

She says, "You, too. I'm looking forward to working with you."

Finally.

Finally, Palmeyer has hired a new seamstress, which makes me happy for a few days. But only a few days. After a while, I start to feel worse. There's not much I can say about the woman he hired except that she's a WITCH with a capital B.

Debbie is a large, sleepy-eyed woman who looks as if she used to work building houses. She's about Palmeyer's age, which means she's old, except she's not old and sweet like most old people. She's old and mean. She says nasty things for no reason whatsoever, and she curses under her breath, which I can hear but Palmeyer can't since I have better hearing. "Goshdarn this" and "goshdarn that," she'll say in a voice that's gritty like coffee grounds, only she doesn't say "goshdarn." She jerks her head while she talks, like a hen pecking. She moves around the shop slowly like she never gets enough sleep. She's always taking my thread or my pins without asking, and she never returns them when she's done. Instead, she makes ME ask for them back, so I end up having to be the one to say, "Thank you." What's worse, she's not even good at her job. Half the time the buttons are too loose or there are threads hanging off like cat whiskers going in every direction. I end up having to redo them.

"Palmeyer," I finally say, "you've got to get rid of Broom Hilda," which is what I call her. "Broom Hilda" was the name of a comic strip about a witch. A witch with a "W," not with a "B."

And he says, "Why?"

And I say, "Well, for starters, she can't SEW."

And he says, "Yes, she can."

And I say, "Look, look," and hold up something she sewed wrong, like a button on a pair of pants, for instance.

And he says, "Looks fine to me," which I know he doesn't mean. Palmeyer likes everything to be perfect.

Then I say, "Heck, Palmeyer, she doesn't know what she's doing."

And he says, "She's better than nothing, which is what we had."

And I say, "Not much better."

Then Broom Hilda returns from lunch or the bathroom or wherever she was, and Palmeyer says, "Debbie, our friend Ham here doesn't think you know how to sew. Do you or do you not know how to sew?"

And she says something like, "I've been sewing since before he was even in diapers," which I don't doubt for a minute. She was probably sewing when the baby Jesus was in diapers, which doesn't necessarily mean she's any good at it. Then she curses at me under her breath, and Palmeyer doesn't hear it. Then she turns on some big band music on the radio, which is the only reason she got the job in the FIRST place.

Whether or not you like big band music has nothing to do with whether you can sew.

They're completely unrelated.

★

The worst part about all of this is that for two years Palmeyer hardly spoke at all. He hardly said anything to me, and he never said ANYTHING to Bobbie Jean when she worked here. Now, he's a talking machine. Talk, talk, talk, talk, talk. All day, non-stop, like that pink rabbit on the television commercials, the one with the batteries in his back. All day, he and Broom Hilda talk and talk and talk. Usually, it starts with one of them saying, "Do you remember," and then they're off to the races, talking about old times as if they once knew each other and have recently been reunited.

"Do you remember when Truman beat Dewey?" Broom Hilda will say.

And Palmeyer will close his eyes and grin like someone's rubbing his neck and say, "Ah, yes, yes, I remember."

And Broom Hilda will say, "I volunteered for Truman. I went door to door passing out buttons."

And he'll say, "I voted for him."

And there's nothing I can say, so I just keep working. I remember how Truman beat Dewey, and how some of the newspapers got it backwards. Only I remember because they taught it to us at Cadbury High School. I don't remember because I was THERE, like Palmeyer and Broom Hilda.

Sometimes I try to join in, but it never works.

"Do you remember the *Hindenburg*?" Palmeyer says.

And Broom Hilda says, "Yes, I do. My cousin knew someone who was on it."

And he says, "Oh, I'm sorry," and frowns.

And then she says, "Do you remember penny candy," as if penny candy had anything to do with the *Hindenburg*. As if they sold penny candy on the *Hindenburg*. As if anyone of sound mind who was talking about the *Hindenburg* would start thinking about penny candy.

And he says, "Yes, I do. Do you know how much penny

candy is today?"

And she says, "No."

And he says, "Ten cents, that's how much."

And she puts her hand on her chest and says, "No!"

And he says, "Yes! Ten cents! A dime!"

And she says, "No!"

That's when I say, "But if it's ten cents, it's not really penny candy. It seems to me that you can't call it penny candy if it doesn't cost a penny," which makes sense if you think about it.

Both Palmeyer and Broom Hilda look at me like I'm crazed, like I've dared to sing to the birds.

"Do you remember when gasoline cost ten cents a gallon?" Broom Hilda says, and I go back to work.

Sometimes, when she's gone to lunch or the bathroom or wherever, I think about pulling Palmeyer aside and saying, "Do you remember how nice it was before she got here? Do you remember THAT?" Only I don't.

★

Renée doesn't tell me about the letters. She never says a word about them.

"Anything today?" I'll ask her.

And she'll say, "Nope. But in this business, no news is good news. Everyone knows that."

Then we'll have dinner and I'll tell her about work. I'll tell her about Truman and Dewey, and about the *Hindenburg* and penny candy, then we'll go to bed.

Only one night after we finish dinner, I clear the table while Renée is in the bathroom. As I'm scraping off the plates, pushing food off the plates and into the garbage can with a knife, I see a manila envelope sticking out from beneath some balls of paper towels. I pull it out and wipe off a piece of lettuce that's clinging to it. There's a stain where the lettuce was. The envelope's from one of the record companies, addressed to "Ms. Renée Ashe."

I open it and read the letter:

Dear Ms. Ashe:

Thank you for submitting your music and/or suggestions for our consideration. At this time, we are not accepting unsolicited submissions. For legal reasons, we have not listened to your music and/or read your suggestions. We thank you for your interest in our company and wish you the best of luck with your musical endeavors.

Sincerely,
Alan Solitar, President
New Sounds Music, Inc.

No, Renée's not going to Nashville. She's not going anywhere.

When I hear her coming back into the kitchen, I crumple up the letter and put it back in the trash. I kiss her on the cheek.

"What's that for?" she says.

"Just for being you," I say. "You cooked a great dinner. That was a great pot roast."

She knows I'm joking, but still says, "It was chicken."

She smiles, but it's the sad kind of smile you smile when everything's going wrong. It's the way you smile when someone comes to visit you when you're sick with the flu.

Then she says, "Come on, I'll get us some coconut cream pie," and she walks to the refrigerator with her shoulders drooping.

CHAPTER 8: MISS REDBOOK

Things with Renée go from bad to worse, and quick. So quick you couldn't see it coming.

One day I'm at work, and "One O'Clock Jump" is playing on the radio. It's a Benny Goodman song. I'm repairing the waistband on a pair of slacks for a man named Grimaldi. It's not as easy as it might seem. First, you have to pin the waistband, then turn it up and press it. Then you have to grade the seam to eliminate the bulk. After you've done that, you have to fold the waistband inside out and trim the corners. Then you turn it right side out again, clip it and tuck the seam allowance, then fold the clipped corner under at an angle. When you're done with that, you have to pin the edge in place and stitch in the ditch of the waistline seam. It's not easy work, and it's harder when Palmeyer and Broom Hilda are sitting three feet away having another one of their "Do you remember" conversations.

"Do you remember *The Maltese Falcon*?" Broom Hilda says.

And Palmeyer says, "Yes, yes. I saw it when the carnival was in town. Do you remember the first time you went on a Ferris wheel?"

And she says, "Oh, yes. What fun. Do you remember the first time you ate a hamburger?"

DO YOU REMEMBER THE FIRST TIME YOU ATE A HAMBURGER? Who remembers THAT? It's like asking, "Do you remember the first time you heard a whistle?" "Do you remember the first time you saw a circle?"

Who remembers things like that?

Who CARES about things like that?

The phone rings, and Palmeyer answers it.

"It's for you," he says.

And I say, "Who is it?"

And he says, "It's your wife."

Only before I can say, "She's NOT my wife," Palmeyer hands me the phone and goes back to talking with Broom Hilda about the Cuban missile crisis.

"Do you remember when there was that Cuban missile crisis with Cuba?" Palmeyer says, as if that's related in any way to hamburgers, which is what they were discussing before the phone rang. Maybe the Cubans were grilling hamburgers at that time. Maybe they were grilling hamburgers and the *Hindenburg* flew past and dropped some penny candy on them.

Broom Hilda says, "Yes, yes, I remember the Cuban missile crisis. With President Kennedy. He was very handsome for a president. Do you remember poodle skirts?"

I pick up the phone and say, "Hello, Sweet Potato. Want to hear what kind of skirt President Kennedy wore?"

I just hear sniffing on the other end.

"Renée, are you okay?" I say. "What's the matter?"

And she says, "Oh, Ham, it was terrible."

And I say, "*What* was terrible? *What*? Are you okay?" I'm thinking that maybe she was in an accident. Maybe someone died. Who knows?

"I'm fine. I just need to catch my breath."

"Tell me what happened, Sweet Potato. Tell me."

"Okay."

Then she tells me what happened. There she was, she says, standing in the bedroom, looking at the clothes she'd spread out on the bed, when she saw the gas man reading the meter outside the window. When she screamed he glanced up from the meter and saw her through the window, and, for a second, the time it takes to cough, their eyes met. The gas man put his clipboard in front of his face, but there was no mistake about it: he'd seen her all right, as naked as the day she was born, as they say. Only, to Renée, she was *more* naked than the day she was born because she was larger and there was more of her to see. It was logical, I suppose: she's been eating the cakes and the pies and the cookies, too.

"You're either naked or you're not, Sweet Potato," I tell her. "There aren't any degrees of being naked. It's an all-or-nothing sort of thing."

She doesn't say anything, so I say, "Everything will be okay. Everything will be fine."

And she says, "Regardless, I'm going to cry."

She sniffs.

I say, "Sweet Potato, don't cry. There's nothing to cry about."

And she says, "You're a fine one to talk, Ham. You weren't the one he saw. I was. Me."

She sniffs again, and I picture her wearing her white terrycloth bathrobe, sitting on the floor beside the bed, her back to the bedroom window. It's terrible to hear her like this, just terrible.

"Renée, it's really nothing to get upset about. It was an accident," I say.

And she says, "It doesn't matter that it was an accident. What's important is that that man knows what I look like now. He *knows*. You know what I look like. I'm fat, fat, fat. Now that man knows what I look like, too. He can tell people. He can go back to work and tell people, 'You should see the fat lady I saw today. A regular piggo.'"

All I can say is, "Sweet Potato."

Again, she sniffs into the receiver.

I whisper, "Renée, you're not fat."

She says, "Liar."

And I say, "Renée."

"If I'm not fat, then why did he cover his eyes? You tell me why he covered his eyes."

I say, "What?" even though I'd heard her.

"The gas man. The second he saw me, he put something in front of his eyes. He looked right at me, then he put some paper in front of his face so he wouldn't have to look at me because I'm fat. He went like this."

And I say, "Sweet Potato, I can't see what you're doing," but I know what she's doing. I even know what she's holding in front of her face. It's the *Good Housekeeping* magazine she has on the nightstand beside the bed. It has a picture of Heather Locklear on the cover. She's one of Renée's favorite actresses.

Renée says, "I wasn't doing it for you. I was doing it for me, to re-enact the crime, like they do on that TV show."

And I say, "There was no crime. Just an honest accident that could've happened to anyone. If he covered his eyes, it was to be polite. It was—"

And then Renée interrupts and says, "Right, it's not nice to stare at fat people. It makes them self-conscious."

And I say, "No, that's not what I mean. I mean, well, he was probably very embarrassed. That's an embarrassing situation for a man to be in, I'd bet. Take me, for instance. Let's say I'm at Macy's and I go to the dressing room to try on some clothes. I'm not paying attention, and I push open the door to one of the dressing rooms, and there's a woman standing there naked. Well, of course I'd be embarrassed. I'd probably turn beet red. It's natural."

"They have separate dressing rooms for men and women so you couldn't walk in on a woman. In fact, that's exactly *why* they have separate dressing rooms, so things like that won't happen."

And I say, "I know, Renée. I was just offering that as an example."

And she says, "It's a bad example."

There's a pause before Renée says, "You know, Ham, you're supposed to be on my side."

And I say, "I am, but there really are no sides."

For several moments, neither of us speaks. Renée huffs deep breaths into the phone as if she'd been running, and I start to sew a button.

"Stop working when I have a problem," Renée says.

And I say, "I'm not working. Renée, listen."

Then she says, "Don't tell me to listen. I'm twenty-nine years old, Ham. I don't have a job. I can't sing. I just sit around all day eating and eating. It's not my fault."

And I say, "Sweet Potato?"

And she says, "Yes?"

And I say, "Sweet Potato, you're not twenty-nine years old. You're thirty," which is true. She turned thirty in August. We went to dinner at her favorite restaurant, Camille's, where they serve Italian food. Then we went to the movies.

Renée starts to laugh, then stops.

"Oh, yeah," she says.

"Thanks for reminding me," then she sniffs.

And I say, "You're welcome."

Then she says, "Darn it, Ham, the gas company knows what I look like naked." Only she doesn't say "darn."

I say her name again.

"The gas company," she says. "The goshdarn gas company." Only she doesn't say "goshdarn," either.

The next few days are horrible.

Renée stays in bed all day crying. Her nose is red like she'd been ice skating. I bring her soup and sandwiches for dinner, but she doesn't eat them.

Two more envelopes come back in the mail marked RETURN TO SENDER. I throw them in the trash without telling her about them.

Palmeyer and Broom Hilda play their "Do you remember" game every day, all day.

The radio plays big band songs.

The worst part about that is that it plays the same songs over and over and over, which makes sense: there aren't any new big band songs.

I would quit the job except I need to support myself. I need to support myself and Renée.

★

Renée isn't the same after the gas man saw her naked. She finally gets out of bed, but she doesn't laugh at any of my stories, and she doesn't even play the guitar at all anymore. It sits in the bedroom closet, propped against the wall.

I'll say, "Renée, why don't you play me a song?"

And she'll say, "I don't think so."

And I'll say, "Come on, just one song."

And she'll say, "Ham, you don't understand. There's no such thing as a fat singer."

I don't know how to respond to that. If I say there is such a thing as a fat singer, if I say that OPERA singers are fat, she'll take that to mean I think she's fat. And if I agree with her, she'll only feel worse. So I don't say anything at all.

And the guitar stays in the closet.

With the tape recorder.

And the microphone.

And the suitcase with the stickers on it.

Although Renée sometimes jokes about her weight—puffing her cheeks out and saying, "Give Big Mama a kiss" is the one example that comes to mind—more often than not I'll come home to find her in the bedroom in front of the full-length mirror. I'll catch her looking over her shoulder and smoothing her slacks against her rear end, or plucking at her hips or her waist, or slapping at the undersides of her arms.

"Cassie," I heard her saying to a friend on the telephone, "Cassie, I have underarm dingle-dangle. I'm turning into my grandmother."

Or I'll find her in front of the television set in a pair of my sweatpants, following along with an exercise show, kicking up her legs, and twisting, and flapping her arms as if she were swatting flies. One night, I hear her say in her sleep, "No, I'll have a salad."

Though she's a good cook, she's stopped eating dinner. Instead, she'll set the meal on the table for me—a meatloaf, roast beef, spaghetti and meatballs—just setting a glass of ice water in front of her chair or chewing a stick of gum while I eat.

There are no more cakes or pies or cookies.

"Are you embarrassed to be seen with me?" she asks me one night as I climb into bed. She's holding a magazine to her chest.

And I say, "What?"

And she says, "I said, are you embarrassed to be seen with me because I'm so fat?"

And I say, "Sweet Potato."

And she says, "I mean, you always look so disappointed when I take my clothes off. You think I'm fat, I can tell. You know, I used to be an interesting person. Thin and interesting. Now, all I do is read stuff like this." She waves the magazine in the air so I can see the cover. There's a picture of some movie actress knitting a sweater beneath the word *Redbook*. "Now I'm even reading magazines for fat, old housewives. Articles about 1) cooking and 2) sewing and 3) needlepoint. I've practically turned into Miss Redbook. Just some fat lady who stays home all the time."

I say, "Sweet Potato, that magazine's not for fat women. It's just for women, period."

"Well, just the same, I'm fat."

"Sweet Potato," I say, "you're not fat."

She says, "Yes, I *am* fat. I have more chins than a Chinese phone book. My shadow weighs fifty pounds."

"Renée, please stop making jokes about yourself like that. You're not fat."

Then she says, "Then why don't we ever go out anywhere where people can see us? Why don't we ever *do* anything? People *go* places and *do* things, Ham. I know there are places to go—I've seen maps. And there are things to do, there must be?"

The answer is that we don't have any MONEY. We can't afford to go anywhere. But I don't want to say that, so I don't say anything.

After a while, Renée says, "Remember when we used to do things together? Remember? Maybe that's why I'm fat, Ham. That's what it says in the article I was reading. It says that a lot of women eat, not because they're hungry, but because they feel neglected. It's like we eat to fill ourselves up. Listen to this." Renée takes a magazine from the nightstand. There's a pencil marking her place. "It's an article called 'The Truth about Fatness.' It says—and I quote—'You are not alone in taking solace in the fork and knife. Many people do, men and women alike, and for many it's a sign that something is missing in their lives.'" She closes the magazine and returns it to its place, then repeats, "Something is missing in their lives," in a tone that you normally hear people use in church.

So I say, "Renée, people eat because they're hungry. It doesn't mean anything."

And she says, "This is in a MAGAZINE, Ham. It's proven. Remember when we used to go to the movies? I didn't eat as much then. Remember when we used to go up to the Tara to see a movie, or we'd go over to the Screening Room on Piedmont? Remember how we used to go play miniature golf, or watch the Braves play baseball, or watch the Falcons play football games?"

And I say, "The Falcons stink, Renée."

And she says, "I know that. I was just giving examples of things we used to do together. Football games. Movies. Baseball games. Shopping. We used to go on trips, remember?

Remember when we drove to Florida?"

And I say, "Renée, please. I don't want to talk about that. I've just had a rotten day, and all I want to do is to relax and have a little peace and quiet." Before she says anything, I add, "And be with the woman I love."

Only Renée says, "But I've got things I need to talk about."

And I say, "I'm listening. I just don't feel like talking about things that happened a long time ago. I'm just not interested in ancient history. I'm interested in the here and now."

"It wasn't that long ago," Renée says. "Florida, I mean."

I know what she's talking about. She's talking about the time we drove to Florida, about how we went to Sea World, how one of the dolphins snatched a fish out of her fingers, and how I'd laughed because I was nervous.

Renée says, "You always make it sound like we're a hundred years old or something. And besides, time is just a relative thing. What's long ago to you is nothing to someone else. To me, Florida seems like it was just yesterday."

So I say, "Well, it wasn't yesterday. It was a long, long time ago. I was working at the furniture store still. That wasn't just yesterday."

And she says, "I know, but it is to me. Remember the dolphin, honey?"

And I say, "It was just some ordinary fish, Renée. Some ordinary fish from a long time ago."

There's silence, and Renée looks at the ceiling.

Renée begins again. "I remember everything like it happened yesterday," she says. "I remember the day my family moved here like it was yesterday. I remember the day I graduated from high school like it was yesterday. I remember the day we moved into this apartment. See, honeypie, I remember everything like it was yesterday."

So I say, "Well, yesterday was yesterday, and nothing happened yesterday. I went to work. You went grocery shopping. That's it. Everything else happened a long time ago."

Renée looks at the ceiling again.

That's when she says, "I remember when we were driving to Florida, how it was raining so hard that we couldn't see and we had to sit in that truck stop for four hours until the rain let up. Remember that, how we ate hot dogs until it stopped raining? I even remember the name of the place. It was called Stuckey's—remember?—and they sold fireworks and little games for the car and pecan log rolls. Remember, we bought some pecan log rolls to eat in the car and I fell asleep and when I woke up one of them was stuck to my leg, and when I tried to pull it off it ripped some of my skin off with it?"

And I say, "I don't want to talk about Florida, Renée. I just want to go to sleep."

Only she doesn't hear me. She says, "Remember how you got sunburned on your eyelids, and we had to put that white stuff on them? Remember, zinc oxide from the drug store?"

And I say, "Please, Renée."

And she says, "Remember Sea World? How could you forget Sea World?"

"Renée!" I say her name in a burst, louder than I'd intended, and you can tell it startles her. For a moment, she seems to lose her breath.

"That's one of the biggest differences between us," she says, "how I've got a good memory and you don't."

How could I forget Sea World?

It was impossible. I couldn't forget about that. I just don't want to talk about it.

The way the girl in the Sea World shirt picked Renée from the crowd and led her to the edge of the pool.

The way everyone applauded.

The way she called up, "Ham, if I don't make it back from this alive, you can finish my orange juice."

The way everyone in the crowd laughed at what she said.

The way I held both of our orange juice containers on my thighs.

The way the Sea World girl held Renée's hand and guided it into the bucket.

The way she pulled out a fish and it danced in her hand, but she kept squeezing it. Not like the man at the two o'clock show. We stayed for that one, too, and that man let go, and the fish just plopped into the water, just like that.

The way Renée squeezed the fish. She wasn't going to let go.

The way everyone laughed.

The way Renée held it out over the water, her arm extended, her head tipped back slightly.

The way the black shadow of the dolphin approached.

The way everyone gasped. They *gasped*.

I remember the way I felt when the dolphin sprang out of the water, toward Renée's tanned arm, her little browned hand. The way I was more afraid than she was. It may as well have been my grandfather's shark, it seemed so big.

Renée is still looking at the ceiling. Finally, I say, "You're right, we should do things. Miss Renée, will you do me the honor of accompanying me to dinner tomorrow evening? It'll be your day. Whatever you want to do, we'll do. What do you say?"

Only she says, "No," then turns her face away.

And I say, "Renée?"

And she says, "No," very loudly.

So I say, "Why?"

And she says, "Ham, weren't you listening to a word I was saying? I'm fat. That would be the worst thing in the world for me, to go out and have a big dinner. That's the worst thing in the world for a fat person to do. To go out and eat all those calories."

"Renée," I say. "Sweet Potato."

And she says, "Ham, I'm fat. Let's stop kidding ourselves."

When I put my hand on her hip, she pushes it off. She opens her magazine and starts reading, or pretends to. If she's reading it, she's reading it very fast. She's reading it like one of those ladies on the speed-reading commercials that used to be on television, whipping the pages.

I close my eyes and try to go to sleep. I listen to Renée turning the pages of her magazine.

I have to admit to myself that it's true, though: Renée has put on some weight since she lost her job at the hospital. Not much, but enough. Enough that you'd notice. Enough that sometimes I feel as if I'm looking at her through someone else's reading glasses. Enough that some days I'll wake up and look at her asleep beside me and think, *Who are you? What have you done with my girlfriend?*

CHAPTER 9: MARIO LANZA WAS HERE

Palmeyer and Broom Hilda are at it AGAIN.

"Do you remember spats?" she says.

And he says, "Yes. My father owned several pairs."

Then she says, "Do you remember Mario Lanza, the singer?"

And he says, "Sure, I do."

And she says, "Do you remember how he died?"

And he says, "Yes, it was very sad." Then, without pausing to take a breath he says, "Do you remember when the Lindbergh baby was kidnapped?" as if that had anything to do with Mario Lanza. As if there were anything in the world connecting the two. To my knowledge, there wasn't.

And Broom Hilda says, "Oh, yes. Wasn't that terrible?"

And Palmeyer says, "Just terrible. Kidnapping is a horrible crime."

And she says, "How about when the Japanese invaded Pearl Harbor? Do you remember that?"

As if the Japanese had anything to do with the Lindbergh baby. As if anyone else in the world has conversations like this other than Palmeyer and Broom Hilda. As if anyone else in the world has to listen to it other than me.

It goes on and on and on like this all morning. They talk, and I work, sewing this, that, and the other thing. I put a stretch seam in a skirt for a woman named Callahan. I sew a new plastic molded zipper into a ski jacket for a man named Fellman. The only time Palmeyer and Broom Hilda stop talking is to answer the phone. The first few calls are people checking to see if they can pick up their clothes. When it ends up that one of the calls is for me, they both look at me as if I'M the one who hasn't done any work all day.

"Hello," I say.

And Renée says, "Is it still my day?"

I don't know what she's talking about, so I say, "What?"

And she says, "Last night, you said that today was my day, that we could do whatever I want. So what I want to know is, is it still my day?"

And I say, "Of course it is, Sweet Potato. I'll be home to pick you up at seven. Whatever you want to do, we'll do."

And she says, "Good. I'll see you at seven."

And I say, "Seven."

And I hang up the phone.

And Palmeyer and Broom Hilda look at me as if maybe I'M the one who kidnapped the Lindbergh baby, which I wasn't. I wasn't even alive then. And I wasn't alive when Mario Lanza attacked Pearl Harbor, either.

Maybe I should start looking for a new job.

That's what I think about the rest of the day.

Maybe I should find a new job, a better job.

★

I don't have enough money to take Renée out to dinner. I have eighteen dollars, which won't be enough if we go somewhere nice; it would barely be enough if we went somewhere rotten. I could ask Palmeyer for an advance on my paycheck, but then I'd have to interrupt him and Broom

Hilda while they're reliving the entire Twentieth Century. Instead, I decide to ask Carl for another loan, only there's no way I'll be able to get downtown to his office in time. No, if I get out of work at six, I'll have to go to his home, which is exactly what I DON'T want to do, because it'll be embarrassing, his wife and his kids standing right there while I'm asking to borrow money. Again. But I don't have a choice. When you have to take your girlfriend to dinner, you have to get enough money to take her somewhere nice, no matter how much you might embarrass yourself.

Carl's house is beautiful. It's located in a nice section of the city known as Morningside. The area is filled with trees. The trees are what you notice first about the neighborhood, big oaks with thick trunks. In the summer, they smell wonderful; in the winter, their brown limbs reach toward the sky like the arms of a gospel choir. Although there are several apartment complexes in the area, all with fancy names meant to suggest that they have some history to them—"The George Washington Estates," "The Gables," and other nonsense—most of the homes are one-story affairs with front porches and short asphalt driveways and, of course, the trees. Carl's house is different. It's enormous. Two stories, with five bedrooms, most of which are unused.

When I arrive at their house, Judy answers the door. She's wearing a green-and-blue dress and her hair is pulled back in a ponytail. She smiles when she sees me, but it's the kind of smile that lets you know you're interrupting dinner. I can smell the chicken from where I'm standing. I can smell cornbread.

"Ham," she says. "We haven't seen you in a long time. Is everything okay?"

"Everything's fine," I say. "I was just dropping by."

And she says, "Well, come on in." She leans forward, and we kiss each other on the cheek like we always do. Even though she's had two children, she's still very thin; you'd think the children were adopted. Every time I see her, she's so gentle and sweet and pleasant, and I have to tell Carl how lucky he is, as if he'd forget.

"Carl," she calls into the dining room, "your brother's here." Then she calls, "Kids, your Uncle Ham's here."

They have two boys, Jon and Emmett. They're nice boys who look more like Judy than Carl, which is good for them. Carl looks like he has a broken nose.

The boys come running out of the dining room, and I crouch down to hug them. Then Carl walks out. He's wiping his lips with a napkin and fingering his tie.

"Hey, buddy," he says, "we never see you around here."

He shakes my hand.

I say, "I just wanted to drop by. I'm interrupting dinner, aren't I?"

"Technically, yes, but don't worry about it. In fact, do you want to join us?"

Carl and Judy look at each other. I can tell what they're thinking: *Do we have enough chicken?*

"No, thanks," I say. "I have dinner plans."

And he says, "Is everything okay?"

And I say, "Fine, fine. There just was a matter I wanted to get your advice on. It's a complicated legal matter."

Judy takes the boys by the hands and says, "Boys, say good-bye to Uncle Ham. He and your dad need to talk in private."

The boys say good-bye, and Judy curls her fingers into

her palm to say good-bye, too. Carl and I step outside onto the front lawn. The grass is green and thick like carpeting in a nice hotel, the type you'd stay in on your vacation. Like the time Renée and I went to Sea World a hundred years ago.

"Do you mow your yard yourself?" I say for no reason.

"Are you kidding? I pay one of the neighborhood kids to do it."

"How much do they get these days?"

"Twenty-five dollars."

I almost say, "I'll take the job." Instead I say, "Listen, Carl, there's no use beating around the bush. I don't have a complicated legal issue to discuss."

And he says, "Good. Last time you had a complicated legal issue, it ended up being about a cat missing its tail."

And I say, "It was a dog."

And he says, "Oh."

And I say, "And it was missing its ear, not its tail. A song about a cat missing its tail, now THAT would probably be a good song."

And he says, "Sorry."

And I say, "Anyway, the reason I'm here is I have to take Renée to dinner tonight, only I don't have enough money."

And he says, "You *have* to take her to dinner?"

"Yes."

"You *have* to?"

"If I ever want her to talk to me again I have to."

Carl winks and reaches for his wallet and takes out all of the bills. He counts it to himself, then he says, "How's eighty dollars?"

I say, "Eighty dollars is great," and he hands it to me. "I'll get it back to you. Unless you want me to cut your yard for the next month instead."

He laughs and says, "Don't worry about it. Just make sure Renée has a nice time tonight."

I say, "I'll try. Thanks." I put the money in my pocket, then I say, "What are you going to tell Judy I stopped by for?"

"What do you mean?"

"She's going to ask you why I stopped by, right?"

"Yes."

"What are you going to tell her? I'd rather you didn't tell her I stopped by just to borrow money."

"I'll tell her whatever you want me to tell her, buddy."

I think for a second, except I can't come up with anything that sounds logical. Finally, I say, "Would you tell her I came by to talk with you because my job is killing me?"

Carl smiles and says, "I think she'll buy that one."

And I say, "Good," then before I leave I say, "By the way, do you have any idea who Mario Lanza is?"

And Carl says, "Never heard of him."

"He didn't kidnap the Lindbergh baby, did he?"

"Not to the best of my knowledge."

I turn to leave, then I say, "You're very lucky, what with Judy and the boys and everything."

And he says, "Tell me something I don't know."

And I say, "Okay. Did you know the Japanese kidnapped the Lindbergh baby?"

And he says, "I have to admit I didn't know that."

And I say, "There, I guess I told you something you didn't know."

★

When I get home, Renée's already sitting on the steps of the apartment building. She's wearing a blue dress with black pantyhose. She looks pretty, like a photograph you keep in your wallet and show your friends at work. If you have friends at work, which I don't. All I have are the Reminiscing Twins.

When Renée climbs into the car, she leans over, and she kisses me full on the lips. She runs her tongue over my teeth, which I like.

"So," I say, "where are we going?"

And she tells me she wants to go to an Italian restaurant called Alfredo's, so I take her there. It's only a short drive from our apartment, but it's on a strange little street called Cheshire Bridge Road. There are nice little restaurants, but there are also strip clubs with names like the Palomino Club and Bare Bottoms. Who would put an Italian restaurant near a strip club? Who?

When we get to Alfredo's, we don't even have to wait for a table. The maître d' seats us at a table along the wall and hands us each a menu. I look at the prices first. The entrées aren't too expensive. Eighty dollars will be more than enough.

"Renée," I say, "you order whatever you want. It's your day. Whatever you want, you order."

"Okay," she says, "but I'm on a diet, remember."

"That's okay. You order whatever you want, because it's your day. I even wrote it on my calendar: 'Today is Renée's day.'"

She smiles and says, "You don't have a calendar."

"No, that's true. That's very true. But what if I did? What if I ran out right now and bought a calendar. Do you know what the first thing is I'd write on it?"

"Your name?"

"No. The first thing I'd write on it would be, 'Today is Renée's day.'"

The waitress arrives at our table. She says her name is Tammy. She doesn't look Italian at all. She has blonde hair and blue eyes. She has bright red lipstick, only it's outlined with black pencil that makes it look like she just ate a candy bar.

Tammy tells us what the specials are, but I don't listen because I already know what I'm going to order. I always order chicken parmigiana when Renée and I eat at Italian restaurants. Tammy asks us if she can get us anything to drink, and we both order a beer.

"Listen," I say to Tammy, "would you mind putting a little umbrella in Renée's beer—it's her day."

Tammy says, "Oh, is it your birthday?"

Renée blushes, which makes her look even prettier, and she says, "No," and I say, "It's just her day. Anything she wants, she gets."

Tammy says, "Anything?"

"Anything," I say.

"You should ask him for a trip to Bermuda," Tammy says.

And I say, "If she wants a trip to Bermuda, it's hers. How about it, Sweet Potato. Do you want a trip to Bermuda?"

And Renée says, "No."

And I say, "How about a swimming pool?"

And she says, "Where would I put it?"

And I say, "We have a little room between the couch and the TV set."

And she says, "That wouldn't be a pool. That'd be a puddle."

So I say, "Okay, then. How about a mink coat?"

And she says, "In Atlanta. I'd wear it once a year."

"Well, anything you want today, it's yours."

Suddenly, Renée smiles and looks at the menu. "You know what I want," she says, which really isn't true at all. Either she wants to get married or she wants a divorce. They're two extremes with one thing in common: I don't want to talk about either one.

And I say, "Oh, no. Let's not talk about that, Renée. Please. I just want to have some fun tonight."

The waitress leaves, and Renée says, "I thought it was my day."

And I say, "It is your day, Sweet Potato."

And she says, "Can't I talk about what I want to talk about then? You'd think I'd be able to talk about what I want to talk about on my day. I can have 1) a swimming pool or 2) a mink coat, but I can't talk about what I really want to talk about? That doesn't seem right."

And I say, "I'll have to consult the rulebook on that." I open up an imaginary book and pretend to read from it. "The official rules for your day, section 19, paragraph A read as follows: 'On your day, you are entitled to eat at whatever restaurant you want. You are entitled to eat and drink whatever you want. You are entitled to pick whatever movie you want to see. You are entitled to talk about whatever you want to talk about —'"

"—A-ha!" Renée says, and she points a finger at me.

And I say, "I'm not finished. 'You are entitled to talk about whatever you want to talk about provided the subject doesn't give me a headache.'"

And Renée says, "I'm giving you a headache?"

"You're starting to," I say.

And she says, "Well, that's a nice thing to say to your wife."

"Renée," I say.

And she says, "What?"

And I say, "Nothing."

We don't talk for a couple minutes. There are about a dozen other couples in the restaurant. All of them appear to be speaking to each other. I get up from my seat and extend my hand toward Renée.

"May I have this dance?" I say.

A puzzled expression appears on her face, and she looks around the restaurant, turning her head left, then right. "Ham," she says, "there's no music."

And I say, "I know, Sweet Potato. But on your day, we don't need music. We have the music of our hearts. The music of our internal organs." I tug at Renée's fingers.

And she says, "*Hay*-yum."

And I say, "Can't you hear your heart singing, Renée? Your kidneys? Your liver? Your spleen?"

I pull her from the table, but she wriggles free and sits.

"Sit *down*," she whispers loudly. "People are looking at us."

It's true. People are looking at us. They're looking at us the same way you look at people who are standing on the side of the highway next to a broken-down car.

And I say, "Who cares who's looking, Sweet Potato? "

And she says, "I care. They probably think you're on drugs. They probably think I'm here with some kind of drug addict."

And I say, "It's your day. It's a day to celebrate."

Again, I take her hand, squeezing her fingers in mine, and I try to pull her from her seat. Renée clamps her free hand on the edge of the table. The table shakes. The water glasses rattle. Some water splashes onto the table. I'm trying to be funny and spontaneous, but it isn't working out very well. The harder I try, the worse it gets.

Renée says, "People are watching us, Ham. Stop it. Please stop it."

Finally, I stop and release her hand. Everyone's looking at us, and all I can do is smile weakly.

"God," Renée says, "I feel so embarrassed."

Renée's eyes are red, and tears begin to run down her cheeks. I hand her my napkin.

"Oh, Sweet Potato," I say, "I'm sorry. I'm honestly, truly sorry. I was just trying to do something special. Don't cry. Please don't cry."

And she says, "Don't tell me not to cry. That just makes me cry more." And she does. Her head bobs slightly, almost but not quite imperceptibly. She folds and unfolds her red napkin.

I say, "I'm sorry."

And she says, "Please don't say that." She keeps trying to catch her breath, but she can't.

That's when Tammy arrives with our drinks. There's an umbrella in Renée's beer. Renée had almost stopped crying, but when she sees the umbrella she starts again.

"Is everything okay?" Tammy says. Her mouth looks enormous, with those puffy red lips with the chocolate drawn around them. She looks at me like I'm some kind of animal, which I don't think I AM.

"We just need a moment," I say to Tammy. "We were talking about a sad movie we saw."

And she says, "Okay."

She leaves, and Renée wipes her nose on the napkin and says, "A sad movie?" She's smiling a little at my lie. She wipes her eyes with her fingertips. It smudges her makeup.

And I say, "That's the best I could come up with on short notice. I didn't feel like telling her your boyfriend's a jerk."

And Renée says, "I think she figured that out on her own."

And I say, "She probably did. But you have to admit that I came up with a pretty good explanation for why you were crying."

And Renée says, "But what if she asked you the name of the movie we were talking about?"

And I shrug and say, "Well, I guess that's why I'm no criminal mastermind."

And Renée says, "I would've said something then. If she asked you what movie we were talking about, I would've said *The Lion King*."

And I say, "*The Lion King*?"

And she says, "Mm-hmm. Remember when Simba's father gets killed?"

"Oh, yeah," I say. We saw that movie together in a movie theater that was filled with children. Renée was crying louder than anyone. She held my hand and pulled it to her chest when the lion cub's father was killed.

"Remember that his own brother planned it so he'd get killed?"

And I say, "Yes."

And she says, "That was sad." Then she says, "Or maybe I would've said *Sleepless in Seattle*."

And I say, "That would've been a good choice, too."

And she says, "Remember when Tom Hanks and Meg Ryan almost missed meeting each other at the top of the Empire State Building, and you think that maybe they won't fall in love after all?"

And I say, "Yes."

She says, "That was sad, too."

I reach out and grab Renée's hand. She braids my fingers in hers. We just look at each other for a while, half-smiling, half-frowning.

"You know," I say, "I think we made a mistake. I don't think today's your day after all. I think *tomorrow's* your day. I think I just got the days mixed up because I don't have a calendar."

And Renée says, "It's tomorrow?"

And I say, "Yes."

And she says, "Then what's today?"

And I say, "Today's just a dress rehearsal for your day."

And Renée smiles and says, "You know, in our drama club in high school, whenever we had a really bad dress rehearsal, that meant the show the next day would be great."

And I say, "Then tomorrow should be the best day of your life," and she laughs. Then I say, "You pick the restaurant, the movie, everything. I'm just sorry I got the days mixed up. Tomorrow's your day, not today. It's all my fault."

And she says, "You should get a calendar."

And I say, "Yes, yes." Then Renée orders pasta and I order chicken parmigiana.

"Renée," I say, "do you remember when they used to call pasta 'macaroni'?"

And she says, "*Yes*. Why did they change the name?"

And I say, "I have no idea."

And she says, "It's like drapes. When I was little, we used to have drapes in our living room. Now everyone has 'window treatments.'"

We smile at each other.

Then she says, "Do you remember the New Kids on the Block?

And I say, "The singers?"

And she says, "Yes. I used to have all their albums."

And I say, "Do you remember when Ronald Reagan was president? Ronald Reagan with that funny haircut?"

And she says, "Yes, *yes*," and pats my hand.

And I say, "Do you remember Mario Lanza?"

And she says, "No."

And I say, "Me neither. I was hoping you would."

★

The meal is very good, although I suppose it's pretty difficult to ruin pasta and chicken parmigiana. It's one of the easiest meals to cook. I can even cook it myself. When we're finished eating, Renée excuses herself and walks to the ladies' room. I can't help smiling. It started out terrible, what with Renée crying and all, but it ends up being the best time Renée and I have had in months.

I see the maître 'd standing in the corner. I wave for him to come over to our table. He's a large man with tan skin and black hair that curls on the top.

"Can I help you with something, sir?" he says.

"Maybe. Are you Italian?"

"Yes, sir."

"Have you ever heard of a person by the name of Mario Lanza?"

"The singer?"

"Yes, that one."

And he says, "Not only have I heard of him, but he ate here once."

"Really?"

"Really. It was a long, long time ago, but he ate here. We used to have a picture of him on the wall." He points to a painting of a gondola on the wall. "That's where the picture was, right there."

"Is he dead?"

"Oh, yes, he died a long time ago. A *long* time ago."

"You wouldn't happen to know how he died, would you?"

"I believe he had a heart attack. He put on a lot of weight, and his heart just couldn't handle it. He ate and ate and ate, then he died."

And I say, "Whatever you do, don't tell my girlfriend that."

And he says, "It'll be our little secret, sir." He twists his fingers in front of his mouth as if he's turning a key in a lock.

And I say, "Thanks," and he leaves just before Renée returns. She's smiling and smiling and smiling.

We put on our jackets, and Renée picks up the styrofoam containers that have our leftovers in them: half an order of pasta and a little sliver of chicken. As we're leaving, she says, "Ham, this has been perfect."

I turn and say, "It's just how I planned it."

Just as we reach the front door, someone entering swings it open too quickly. It bumps me on the forehead. It stings, and I rub it and say, "Darn it, darn it, darn it," only I don't say "darn."

"Are you okay?" Renée says, and she touches my scalp with her fingertips.

I don't want to ruin our night, so I try to make a joke. I say, "I think so. But suddenly I remembered that I'm married to Erica on *As the World Turns*."

Renée laughs loudly, then puts her hand over her mouth for a moment. Then she says, "It's worse than I thought. I watch that show, and Erica's married to Chad. She's not married to you."

And I say, "No?"

And she says, "No."

And I say, "So I shouldn't feel guilty about being out with you tonight?"

And she says, "No. Not at all."

★

The drive home is a quiet one, so quiet that I can hear the pieces of the car engine at work. One piece rubbing against another. Something ticking away, *tick-tick-tick, tick-tick-tick*. Some liquid flowing. Gas? Oil? Water?

I can feel a little bump rising on my forehead. I can feel the skin stretching there. Renée leans over and kisses it every time we stop at a traffic light. Renée and I just look at each other from time to time, and it's all I can do not to pull over to the side of the road and start kissing her. It's all I can do not to undress her right there in the car.

When we get home, she carries the styrofoam containers to the kitchen while I go to the bedroom and start getting changed. I look at my forehead. There's a bump there, the size of a walnut; it's turning purple. When Renée walks into the bedroom, her dress is already unzipped in the back, revealing her bra strap and delicate white skin.

"Are you still mad at me?" I ask, and she says, "Not at all."

She flips her hair to one side and tips her head.

"Are you going to help me take this off?" she says, and I help her pull her dress off. She's standing in front of me in her bra and slip. They're white and lacy like the kind you order from a magazine. Her hair smells like oranges. I kiss her neck, and I whisper in her ear a poem my father used to say to Carl and me at bedtime:

> *I love you in blue*
> *I love you in red*
> *But most of all*
> *I love you in blue.*

"That's your father's poem," Renée says. I'd forgotten I'd told her about that once before. She remembers EVERY-THING. She runs her fingers over my shoulder. She kisses the bump on my forehead.

And I say, "It's my poem now. I bought it from him."

And she says, "How much did you pay?"

And I say, "Ten dollars."

And she says, "Well, you got ripped off."

And I say, "Really?"

And she says, "Yes. My God, Ham, it doesn't even *rhyme*."

I start kissing her and plucking at her bra straps, and before you know it we're in bed and happy.

★

In the morning you can hear delivery trucks outside our apartment, but it hardly ever wakes up Renée. I shower and shave and watch her sleep, her chest rising and falling, a smile on her face like she's having a nice dream. You can't wake someone up from a nice dream, so I let her sleep and I'm out of the apartment before she's even gotten up.

In the middle of the morning, she calls me at work while I'm putting some darts in some slacks for a woman named Millhouse. If they're done right, they're straight and smooth. If they're done wrong, they pucker at the ends. And if they're not all the same length, they look terrible.

"That was great last night," Renée says when I pick up the phone.

Palmeyer and Broom Hilda look at me and clench their jaws at the same time. They're not even WORKING and they're upset with ME for answering the telephone.

"I agree," I say. "That was terrific."

And Renée says, "You know, I love you, Ham."

And I say, "Me, too."

And she says, "Say it."

And I say, "I can't, I'm at work."

And she says, "Embarrassed?"

And I say, "No."

And she says, "Then say it."

And I say, "Oh, listen, Palmeyer's calling me."

And she laughs and says, "Liar. Now say it."

And I pretend that I'm talking with Palmeyer, "Yes, Palmeyer, I'll be right there."

And Renée laughs and says, "You are *such* a liar."

And I say, "No, I'm serious. He sewed his tongue to a pair of pants. Can't you hear him screaming?" Then I say, "I'm coming to save you, Palmeyer. I'm coming to save you."

And Renée says, "You are such a liar."

And I say, "I have to go save Palmeyer. I'll see you tonight."

I go back to work on the darts.

That night, on the way home, I think of stopping at the florist, but if I do I won't have enough money left to take Renée out to dinner again. So, instead I stop at the grocery store. There's a cooler along the far wall, filled with flowers wrapped in cellophane. Three other men are crouched like catchers and peering in when I arrive.

"Birthday, anniversary or argument?" one of the men asks. He's speaking to me.

"Anniversary," I answer, "sort of."

"I'm a birthday," he says. "It's the same day every year, but the hell if I can remember."

And I say, "You should get a calendar."

And he says, "No kidding."

I pull open the door, a fragrant wave hitting me, and pull out a bouquet of tulips, then walk to the front of the store to pay for them.

When I get home, though, Renée isn't dressed for dinner. Instead, she's in bed with a giant textbook propped up on her thighs. The book is the first thing I notice when I enter the room. Behind it, Renée looks small and young, and not different from my memories. She looks like she did when I first met her. What a gumdrop she was then. Small and young and happy to be wherever she was.

With the flowers behind my back, I say, "Hello."

And she says, "You're awful late."

And I say, "I know. I had to stop on the way home."

And she says, "Well, there's some of that pot roast from the other night in the refrigerator if you're hungry. And there's still some pasta and chicken left over from Alfredo's."

And I say, "I thought we were going out for dinner again tonight. Remember, it's your day."

And she says, "There's been a change of plans."

I sit on the edge of the bed and pull the flowers from behind my back, doing it swiftly like a magician. Voilà'!

"Here," I say.

And Renée says, "What for?"

And I say, "No reason."

And she smiles and takes the flowers in one hand. She puts her nose in them and says, "Thank you."

"I love you, Sweet Potato," I say.

And she says, "I love you, too," like she really means it, not the way people sometimes do. Not like she felt obligated to say "I love you" back.

We look at each other the way lovers sometimes do. Finally, I gesture toward her book with a jerk of my head. "What are you reading?"

Renée holds the book up so I can see the cover, a picture of a gold-and-black sarcophagus, then says, "It's called *The Royal Treasure.*" She pauses and adds, "Ham, it's a textbook. I was talking to Walter today—"

And I say, "Guitar Walter?"

And she says, "Yes. I was talking to Walter today, and I was thinking about that magazine article, and it just hit me that maybe I should take a few night classes, you know, to broaden my horizons. So Walter came and picked me up, and he took me over to the school and helped me pick out some classes and find everything at the bookstore."

"Well, it sounds like a great idea," I say, which I don't mean at all. "You should definitely sign up."

And she says, "Well, I already enrolled. I signed up for two classes. They're two hundred fifty dollars a class, but before you say anything, I want you to know that I'll pay for them myself. I don't know how, but I will."

She sounds exactly like me promising to pay money back to Carl, and I know how well that's worked out. I haven't paid him back ANYTHING yet.

So I say, "Renée, you don't have to do that. If you want

to take some classes, then take some classes. Just take the money out of the account."

We don't have any money in the account.

And she says, "I already did. I wrote a check. It's just that I'm going to put the money back in."

And I say, "Renée, please, don't worry about it." I take the book from her and thumb through the pages mindlessly, occasionally focusing on a piece of jewelry or something else bright and shiny. "So, tell me, what classes did you sign up for?"

And she says, "I signed up for a film class, where they show old movies and we analyze them. And I signed up for an archeology class because, well, I'm not sure why."

And I say, "Because you're planning on going to Egypt to hunt around for old pots and stuff?"

I run the back of my hand along her cheek. When I reach her lips, she kisses my fingers.

"They're not old pots," she says. "They're relics of past civilizations. They're treasures. I don't know, I was just in the bookstore, and the books looked so interesting. Like that one." She gestures to the book I'm holding. "Isn't that interesting? And just the idea of digging and digging and digging and finally finding something valuable way down just sounds very interesting."

"Great," I say. "I think it's a great idea. Just promise me that if you dig up anything dead, you won't bring it in the house."

Renée puts a hand over her heart and says, "Promise."

And I say, "Now, I've got to get something to eat. I'm starving."

I hand Renée her book and start toward the kitchen. Renée stops me.

"Honey," she says, "would you take the flowers and put them in water?"

I take them from her and head toward the kitchen, then stop in the hallway and call out, "Renée?"

And she calls back, "Yes."

I'm about to ask her why she's taking night classes. Aren't night classes for people who work during the day? Shellie took night classes, but she was working in a dentist's office during the day. That was before she left me.

CHAPTER 10: MONKS IN THE KITCHEN

It's a good idea for Renée to take some classes. It'll be good for her. I keep telling myself that over and over.

Only now I never see her. During the day, I'm at work. "Do you remember this," "Do you remember that," and the big band songs all day. On weekends, Renée studies at the kitchen table. Sometimes I go to Carl's house to play football with him and his boys or to watch television with them. At night, Renée's at her classes and I end up eating dinner by myself, eating dinner and reading the newspaper or a sports magazine.

Sometimes I'll make myself a sandwich. Sometimes I'll go out to a restaurant, although I feel like people are looking at me when I eat by myself, looking at me and thinking, *Look at that poor man. No one likes him.* I wish I could say, "I have a girlfriend. It's just that she has class tonight." But it's none of their business.

There's a place where I like to eat called Fat Matt's Rib Shack. It's just around the corner from our apartment, and I've been eating there a lot while Renée's at her classes. It's across the street from the church Renée goes to, and it's right next door to June's, which is where we take our dry cleaning when we have dry cleaning, which isn't very often.

There's a big sign painted on the brick wall in front of

the building. It says FAT MATT'S RIB SHACK in yellow let-ters on a green background, and there are paintings on the windows of the food they serve: barbequed ribs, and barbe-qued chicken, and chopped pork sandwiches. At night they have blues singers who sing while you're eating your ribs or chicken or pork, and while you're drinking your beer.

This time, the place is fairly crowded with people eating like Teamsters, leaning over their plates and shoveling their food in. Only there's not a blues singer. Instead, there's a band playing. A sign says they're called Sidebar. They're all white men, and some of them look like they're older than me. The one playing the keyboards is bald. He keeps looking up from the keyboard and waving to a pretty, black-haired woman in the back. She smiles and waves back. She's prob-ably his wife, I bet.

I sit and listen to the band, and I eat some chicken, and I drink some beer, and when I start to get a little tired I walk home. Renée isn't home yet, so I watch a little television and smoke. I fall asleep on the couch with the television still on. I never hear her coming in.

Sometimes Renée goes out after her night classes with her classmates and doesn't come home until I'm already asleep. Sometimes a few of them will come by the apartment after class. I can hear them talking from the bedroom.

A couple weeks pass, and we hardly see each other.

Renée is changing.

Again.

★

One night after work, I'm in the bedroom when I hear a car pull into the parking lot, then I hear a car door slam. I hear the front door open and close. I get up from the bed so

I can tell Renée about how Broom Hilda sewed the legs of a pair of pants together, which was VERY funny to see, but from the bedroom I hear two voices: Renée's and another one that I don't recognize. I walk into the hall. The light in the kitchen is on.

"Oh, Hamilton," Renée says. "I thought you'd be asleep."

Renée NEVER calls me "Hamilton." It's always "Hay-yum." What's going on?

She introduces me to the woman sitting at the kitchen table, and I shake her hand and wish she'd leave.

Renée's friend is a round-faced woman, with a mess of red hair that hangs down in front, a narrow forehead, a small nose, and the large, owl-eyed glasses that smart children wear. She's very thin. Her figure doesn't seem to be much, and a ring of her slip shows beneath the hem of her skirt. All in all, very plain looking, as plain as tap water, and already I've forgotten her name. It could be Cheryl. It could be something else. She has a Jewish last name, I remember that much. Cheryl Steinberg. Cheryl Schwartz. I can't remember.

Whenever I meet a woman with red hair, the first thing I do is try to see if she reminds me of Shellie. If she does, it makes me sad. If she doesn't, that makes me sad, too. This one doesn't remind me of Shellie at all.

"How was your night?" Renée says.

And I say, "Fine."

There's a pause, and both women stare at me. I excuse myself, saying, "I've got some work to do," then return to the bedroom. They both nod. They hadn't wanted me in there in the first place, I know. None of Renée's new friends do. They come to the house and sit in the kitchen, quiet as monks whenever I enter the room. The conversation will die, and they'll look at me blankly, as if I couldn't possibly understand their thoughts. When I leave, they start up again with their talking.

"Hamilton moves around quite a bit, from room to room," I hear Renée say. "He's very *transient* that way." Then she and Cheryl start talking again.

I sit on the bed and try to read one of Renée's magazines, but I can't. I can hear them talking in the kitchen, but it's hard to make out their words. I just pick up the sensation of a conversation, the humming of two voices, then I hear Cheryl laughing. They all laugh in the kitchen, all of Renée's new friends, and she has plenty of them. At first I tried to keep them all straight, which one was Guitar Walter and which one was Robert, which one was in her archeology class and which one was in her film class, but now I don't even try. It was so much easier when we had the same friends. It was so much easier when we didn't have any friends at all. Now, Renée brings people over to the house two or three nights a week, and they sit at the kitchen table and drink coffee and keep me awake. They talk about "digs" and "zooms" and other things like that, things I don't know about and, until recently, Renée didn't either. It's strange to hear her saying these new words. It's as if she's still breaking them in, like they were new dress shoes.

Cheryl's a new one. Walter's a regular. Guitar Walter. He still comes by every Tuesday night, only now he doesn't bring his guitar. Samantha and some thin boy are Thursdays. They might be married, I don't know. There are more, and they come by so often that I can guess what class they're in just by the way they look. The ones from the archeology class are all thin, thin people who don't look like they enjoy their food. The ones from Renée's film class are pale and messy, and they never smile, as if blood doesn't flow to their faces. The one in the kitchen is a Film, I bet. I thought it the second I saw her in the kitchen: she had "Film" written all over her pale, round face.

They look distinct, the Archeologies and the Films. They look distinct, except for Renée. Renée doesn't look like any of them. She looks like my girlfriend.

"Hamilton," Renée says, standing in the hallway, dipping her head into the bedroom. "Hamilton, do you want a snack? Claire and I are fixing sandwiches."

It's Claire, not Cheryl.

"Sure," I say. I get up from the bed, smooth the bed-spread flat, then walk to the kitchen.

Renée is standing at the counter, and her friend is sitting at the table, her thin legs crossed at the knee, revealing even more of her slip than she had before.

"Roast beef?" Renée says. "We're having roast beef sand-wiches."

I'm surprised to see Renée eating.

And I say, "That's fine." I take a seat across from Claire.

"On white bread?" Renée says.

I'm confused. Renée knows I like sandwiches on toast. So I say, "No, on toast, like always."

Claire laughs, then puts her hand to her mouth. Renée is laughing, too. Her back is turned, but her shoulders are bouncing up and down.

"Did I miss something funny?" I ask.

Renée keeps laughing. After a while she says, "Did I tell you he'd say that, or didn't I?"

"Yes, you did," Claire says. "I owe you a quarter."

And Renée says, "Hamilton is just so *intractable* about

his toast. Everything has to be on toast. Who on earth ever heard of roast beef on toast?"

Claire puts her fingers to her lips again.

Renée isn't finished, though.

"And not just toast," she says, "but *warm* toast. It has to be warm. He won't eat it if it's cold. He's like a little boy. You know how little boys have to have the edges cut off their sandwiches. Well, Hamilton has to have warm toast. Isn't that right, Ham? If the toast is cold, I have to throw it out and put the sandwich on fresh toast. It's like it's *ceased* to be toast once it's gone cold. It's moved from one state of existence," she says, holding her right arm out, then swinging it across her body, "to another."

Both women are laughing. Claire is no longer trying to be ladylike about it. Renée is laughing harder than I've ever seen her, harder than at any movie, harder than at any joke.

I try not to be angry. I tell myself that this is just Renée's way of trying to make a new friend. I remember how Renée had been after the gas man saw her naked, how she'd been before she started taking her classes.

All I say is, "Well, I guess the joke's on me."

When she stops laughing, Renée squeezes my shoulder. "We're just teasing you, Hamilton. Don't get upset."

And I say, "I'm not."

"I think it's cute," Claire says. "My boyfriend's like that, too. Not with toast, but with clothes. Everything has to be arranged in order of color. The red shirts have to be together, then the blue ones, then the white ones. I swear, men are such children."

"Remind me to tell you about his chicken shirt," Renée says.

And Claire says, "His *chicken* shirt?"

Renée sets a plate down in front of Claire, then returns to the counter to pick up her plate and mine.

"So, Claire," I say, "are you in Renée's archeology class?"

Claire holds a hand up while she chews. "No," she answers after swallowing. "Film."

I KNEW it. It was in the skin, the pale white skin.

I look at Claire more closely—her flat chin, her small, sharp nose—and have the strange feeling that I can tell what her father looks like. I lift my sandwich to my mouth and take a large bite. Renée and Claire are watching me chew, leaning forward like they're watching a science experiment. Then they fall back laughing.

When they stop laughing, I turn to Claire and say, "Film, huh?"

And she says, "Yes." She and Renée look at each other and begin laughing again. "A chicken shirt?" Claire says. And I say, "Yes."

I take another bite of my sandwich. Claire and Renée speak with their eyes. They look at me. They look at my sandwich. They look at each other.

I say, "So, what are you studying in your film class?"

And Claire says, "This and that. Mostly that."

"No, really," I say. "What are you doing?"

And Claire says, "It's really not very interesting. Why don't we talk about something else?"

And I say, "No, it sounds very interesting. What are you studying?"

Claire inhales deeply. "Listen, Hamilton, I don't want to offend you, but you don't really seem to be the artistic type."

To which Renée says, "You're right about that." I notice

that she hasn't touched her sandwich yet.

"I am so artistic," I say. "I'm as artistic as the next guy."

And Renée says, "If the next guy's a construction worker." Renée smiles, and Claire laughs.

And I say, "I am so artistic." Then before I know it, I say, "Do you know anything about poetry, Claire?"

And she says, "A little."

And I say, "Well, I happen to love a good poem."

Renée raises one of her eyebrows the way you would if you smelled a gas leak.

I'm hoping Claire will ask me who my favorite poet is, and sure enough she does. "Who are your favorite poets then?" she says.

And I say, "I don't know, there are so many."

And she says, "Who comes to mind first?"

And I smile a little and say, "Keats, Yeats, Browning, Frost."

Claire tips her head and says, "Hmm."

Except when I look at Renée, she's shaking her head side to side.

It's only then I remember that I'd once told her our high school cheer:

Keats, Yeats, Browning, Frost,
The Cadbury Poets have never lost.

I give her a look to ask her not to embarrass me, not to tell her friend how I know those names.

Renée doesn't say anything. She just keeps shaking her head, and I go back to the bedroom and finish my sandwich there.

I liked it better when she was singing stupid songs about dogs without ears. I liked that MUCH better.

CHAPTER 11: BETTER THAN RUTH

I've been through this before.

Maybe not THIS exactly, but close enough.

I've been through this feeling like I don't even belong in my own home. It's a terrible feeling. It's a terrible feeling that you wouldn't wish on your worst enemy.

After we married, Shellie and I stayed in Cadbury. We rented a little house, and we painted it on the weekends and tended to the garden. I have memories of the two years we spent there that are still as sweet as the frosting on a cupcake. A Christmas Day spent in bed, playing board games. New Year's Day doing the same. Shellie in overalls, with streaks of paint on her face. Shellie in a bathing suit on my grandfather's boat, her face and bare limbs turning brown. Shooting basketballs together on the courts behind the high school. *Keats, Yeats, Browning, Frost.*

One day, Shellie came home from work and said she couldn't live there anymore. She said she couldn't live in Cadbury knowing that the person who had helped kill her brother, the one who had burned his palm, could be anyone we saw on the street, anyone we saw in church.

"Everyone I see, I ask myself, 'Is it him?' 'Or him?'" she said. "Everyone, all day long."

I understood, so we moved to Atlanta. We didn't even

have jobs. We just packed everything into a car and drove. We stayed with Carl and Judy for a few days, until we found an apartment just off Peachtree Street, over by the A&P grocery store. And Shellie started to hate me soon after we moved in. You could tell. And you couldn't blame her. She deserved to hate me, even though she could never put her finger on why.

The particular day I'm thinking of, the sun didn't seem to give off much heat even though it was June and it was nearly three o'clock and the birds were making noises outside the window, the sort of noises birds usually make when it's warm and the air is thick and sweet. The birds had built a nest in one of the tall, thick oaks outside our apartment building, but the nest was too high to see. It was hidden by branches and leaves and the thick, black power lines that ran from building to building. All there was was the sound of the birds to remind you that they were there on a summer day, to remind you that it even was the summer and that somewhere people were dressed in bathing suits or drinking cool drinks in tall glasses.

Beside the window and the trees and beneath the nest, I was holding the Saturday newspaper open at the card table I used for a desk. I wasn't dressed in a bathing suit, and I wasn't drinking a cool drink in a tall glass. I was reading an article about something that had happened in Russia, about a woman who had lost her job baking bread and now, to buy bread, she had to wait in a line that was long and curved like a river. I was reading about an unhappy man who leaped in front of a train and lost his foot at the ankle, only to have the doctors reattach it through some new medical procedure that left his foot cool and tingly, like it had merely fallen asleep and had not been lying alone on the tracks like a lost mitten; the man sued the railroad and the surgeons. I was reading, and I didn't notice when Shellie entered the room.

"What are you doing?" Shellie said.

And I said, "What?"

And she said, "I asked what you're doing," only she said it like she'd caught me doing something wrong.

I patted the newspaper.

Shellie huffed. "You could answer a question with an answer, you know."

And I said, "I'm reading, Sweet Potato?"

And she said, "I know you're reading. That's all you ever do now is come in here and read. Newspapers, magazines, books. Read, read, read, read, *read*."

And, very politely, I said, "That's what I'm doing."

And she said, "But why? That's what I want to know. I want to know why."

And I said, "You should know why."

And she said, "I don't."

And I said, "You're the one who wants me to be more ambitious. You're the one who thinks I need to get better jobs and make more money like Carl."

And she said, "So, what does reading have to do with it?"

And I said, "I'm building my knowledge," which was true. Or at least I was trying to build my knowledge. It wasn't working as well as I'd hoped. I'd read an article in a magazine about some new medical discovery or some political issue or something else of that nature, and I'd make myself memorize it because it might come in handy in a job interview. Two days later, I couldn't remember the name of the article. Two days after THAT, I couldn't remember the name of the magazine.

Carl could remember everything. I don't know how he did it.

Shellie clapped her hands and said, "Building your knowledge? Building your knowledge?" Then she let out a noise that, in my memory, sounded like, "Ha!"

And I said, "That's what I'm doing. I'm building my knowledge. I read so I can learn about things, and then I can use those things in my life, when I talk to people, when I have conversations with people on the street or at work. That way I can sound like I know something, and people will say, 'You know, that Hamilton Ashe's pretty smart. He has a good future ahead of him.' That's how you get ahead. So that's what I'm doing. I'm building my knowledge."

Shellie was smart: she knew it wasn't working.

She said, "My husband thinks that they're going to make him the president of General Motors because he reads a couple of newspapers. I've got the only husband in the world who spends all of his time building his knowledge, and for what? Deep down, there's nothing you really want to do. It's not like you want to be a scientist or a doctor or a lawyer. Besides, there are movies and plays and beaches. We could be walking out in the sun. But, no, my husband wants to stay inside and build his knowledge." She kept saying "my husband" as if she were talking to someone else in the room, but it was just us. Why would she do that? Why would she tell me I had to get better jobs, then tell me we should be outside walking in the sun? How could you do both? How?

I said, "If that's the way you feel, maybe you should think about getting another husband," which I meant as a JOKE. Who knew she'd take me seriously.

And Shellie said, "Don't think I haven't thought about it."

And I said, "I'll bet you have."

I listened for Shellie to leave the room, but she stood behind me, making noises in her throat.

Finally, I said, "This is a good one," and I gave the paper a shake.

And Shellie said, "What's a good one?"

"This one here, the one I just read. See, a boy caught a fish and found a watch in its stomach when he slit it open, and the watch was still ticking."

"Hum," Shellie said, and she leaned over to read the article. "That is a good one, isn't it?"

And I said, "That would be a good advertisement for that watch company. You know, the one that has the commercials where they drop a boulder on a watch, but the watch still works. Or they'll shoot it with a bullet and the watch keeps working. You know what I mean? What's the name of that watch company?"

And she said, "I don't know," even though I KNEW she knew. Everyone knows the name of that watch company. It's Timex.

So I said, "Shellie, I know you know the name of it. You know, the watch company. The one with those advertisements. What's the name of that company? You know it. What's the name?"

She said, "You're kidding, right?"

I laughed and said, "I *know* the name of the company. It's Timex. 'It takes a licking and keeps on ticking' is their slogan. I knew that, but I was just trying to make conversation with you."

"I don't want to make conversation."

"If you don't want to make conversation, would you

mind just letting me read?"

Shellie didn't answer. She sighed and sat on the edge of the card table, not putting her full weight on it, but keeping her feet on the floor. She tapped at the tabletop with her fingernails. They were long and painted blue to match nothing she was wearing. She picked up a letter opener and ran her finger over the plastic handle. She set it down, then picked up a baseball in a clear plastic case. The baseball was the yellow-brown color of tobacco spit, except for a streak of black ink along one side. It was a scribbled signature that looked like someone wrote it on a moving train or car. The letters jerked left and right, up and down, where they shouldn't have, and the letters that should have had loops had pointed ends instead. Shellie removed the plastic cover and pulled the ball out, rolling it between her palms, and I jumped up from my chair.

"Don't touch that!" I said. "Don't take that out of the case! That's Ty Cobb, for godsakes."

"I know whose signature it is," Shellie said, clutching the baseball to her chest in both hands to keep me from snatching it away from her. "I've heard about it a thousand times. A hundred thousand times. A hundred, million, billion, zillion, kabillion times. 'This is the baseball that Ty Cobb signed for my grandfather,'" she said. "'My grandfather met him in a parking lot outside a restaurant, and Ty Cobb signed the ball. Ty Freaking Cobb,'" only she didn't say "Freaking." "'Do you know who Ty Cobb *was*? He's in the Hall of Fame, for godsakes. He played for the Tigers, and he was one of the greatest of all time, maybe even the greatest. Everybody's heard of Babe Ruth, but Cobb was better. He was better than Ruth, better than Willie Mays, better than

Lou Gehrig, better than Kubla Khan, better than Tiny Tim, better than the Venus de Milo. Blah blah blah Ty Cobb blah blah blah *blah*.'"

"Listen," I said, "I don't care if you want to make fun of me. I really don't. That's your prerogative. I married you for better or worse, and maybe the worse part means that I'm required by law to listen to you make fun of me once in a while. Fine. That's fine. But please put the ball back in the case so you don't smudge it. You can play with it all you want then. You can dangle it over a fire if you want, I just don't want you to smudge it."

And Shellie said, "I'm not going to smudge it. You're treating me like a five-year-old. I know how to handle things so they don't smudge."

And I said, "Please, Sweet Potato."

And she said, "No."

So I said, "Please," again.

And she said, "Oh, okay," and put the ball back in its case and set it back on the card table. "There, are you happy now? I've put it back. I've put it back precisely where it was before without a single smudge on it." She slid off the table and moved slowly around the room, her hands clasped behind her back, her elbows pointing out in a way that was girlish and pretty. In the next apartment, someone began practicing fingering exercises on the piano—pink-pink-pink-pink-*pink*, pink-pink-pink-pink-*pink*. Shellie yawned and rested her head against the wall and put her hands on top of her head.

"That's very soothing," she said, and she closed her eyes. I picked up the newspaper from the floor, but I had trouble concentrating. I read the same lines over and over.

"Ham," Shellie said at last. "Ham, I can't go on like this.

I mean it. I can't go on like this."

And I said, "You can't go on like what?" I patted my knee and held my arms out for her to sit on my lap, but she shook her head no.

"Like *this*," she said, and she held her arms out to her sides. She wiped at her eyes, which were dry. Her nose was pink. "Like this. This is no way for a woman my age to live, Ham."

"I work hard," I said. I was working for a printing company at the time. She was working as a secretary in a dentist's office. We were barely making enough money to pay for rent and food. "I work very hard," I said again.

And she said, "I know you do." She sniffed, and when she did, the tears started. "I know you do, darling, I'm not saying you don't work hard, but this is all we have to show for it. This. We have a tiny little apartment with old furniture. I'm embarrassed to have my family over. I'm embarrassed to invite friends. And I hate myself for being embarrassed. Does that make sense? I'm becoming a terrible, bitter, spiteful woman, and I have to stop that."

And I said, "We'll move into a better apartment. My luck will change, and we'll move into a better apartment, a bigger one."

And she said, "You've been saying that for months. Years."

And I said, "It's the economy, sweetheart. It's the economy. I don't control the economy. I wish I did, but I don't. You should read about the economy. It's terrible. It looks like it's getting better, all these bigwigs say it's getting better, only it's not because the economy has a mind of its own. The economy doesn't understand anything about logic or scientific facts or emotions. It's the economy that's doing this. But once the economy improves, things will get better and we'll be able to afford a better apartment. Maybe even a house. And not one of those tiny houses that looks like it was built for chickens or dogs or dolls, but a real house. I promise."

And Shellie said, "And clothes, too. It's not just the apartment, Ham, but it's clothes, too. I haven't bought a new blouse in a year. I feel like I haven't bought a new dress since the Civil War, since the Spanish Inquisition."

And I said, "You're exaggerating. You bought a new dress during World War I. Remember? It was red. Remember?"

Shellie wiped her nose with the heel of her hand, then sniffed. She licked her lips. She had beautiful lips. "Don't make me laugh, Ham. I haven't bought clothes in years. Look what I'm wearing. Look. Look. I'm not saying I should be dressed like the Queen or some movie star, but look. Look."

She was wearing a flowered blouse I'd seen her wear for many years and a black skirt that came to her knee, with white stockings covering her legs. She had a brilliant red-orange handkerchief tied around her neck. The handkerchief was almost the same color as her hair. Her hair hung over her forehead like a canopy.

"You look lovely," I said, and I meant it. "You look as lovely now as you did that first summer." I could picture her sitting on top of one of the washing machines at the appliance store. I could picture her demonstrating the new mixers or the new vacuum cleaners, smiling, smiling, smiling like a parade was going by.

And she said, "But the clothes, Ham. I need new clothes. I can't go out anywhere like this."

And I said, "I don't know what I can do. I can only work so much. You know that I work day and night. You know that, don't you? Don't you?"

And she said, "Yes. Of course. Of course."

And I said, "I don't have a solution, Sweet Potato. I don't have an answer. I'm sorry. I'm sorry." I was ashamed, and I rested my head in my hands, which only made me feel more embarrassed because I knew what I looked like sitting there like that. The hunched shoulders, the hung head. I'd promised to make her happy, to give her everything she wanted, and I was breaking the promise every day.

That's when Shellie said, "You could sell that." Something about her voice made her words sound rehearsed, as if she'd been practicing those words over and over. "You could sell *that*," I could hear her say. "You could *sell* that." "You *could* sell that." When I lifted my head, I saw that she was smiling a little. A blue fingernail was pointing to the baseball in the plastic case. She wanted me to sell my grandfather's baseball.

"What?" I said.

And she said, "You could sell your baseball."

I shook my head and said, "It's autographed by Ty Cobb, Sweet Potato. My grandfather gave that to me. You know that. It's autographed by Ty Cobb."

And she said, "I know, I know. But I talked to a man in a store, and he said he'd give us a thousand dollars for it. Can you imagine that? A thousand dollars!"

And I said, "A man in a store?"

And she said, "Yes."

And I said, "What, did you take it to a store to see how much they'd give you for it?"

And she said, "No, Ham, no, it's not like that at all. The ball's never left the apartment. No. You see, I was in a store, and there was a man talking to his son about baseball, this cute little boy, and he was telling him how good a ballplayer Babe Ruth was. I was in a talkative mood, so I said, 'Did you ever hear about a ballplayer by the name of Ty Cobb?' And before I knew it, I'd told him about your baseball, and the man said he'd give me a thousand dollars for it if it's authentic."

And I said, "Of course it's authentic."

And she said, "A thousand dollars, Ham. Do you know how many dresses I could buy? Do you know how much food we could buy?"

I thought for a moment, then shook my head again. "I can't do that. It's Ty Cobb."

Shellie tightened her jaw and raised her voice, not much, but enough. "Who do you love more, Ham, Ty Cobb or me? Who did you marry, Ty Cobb or me? Who takes care of you? Who? Who, Ham, who?"

She liked to repeat questions several times. It's a habit I picked up from her, I'm afraid, although it makes me smile a bit every time I catch myself doing it.

And I said, "Shellie, it's not that bad. Things will get better. Things will improve, and we'll get out of here. It's just a matter of time, of patience."

And she said, "Patience is for people who can afford to be patient. Patience is a luxury, Ham, like caviar and champagne and fur coats and a million other things we don't have. Me, I can't be patient much longer. I'm not a young girl anymore. I'm not. We should have things. I go places and I see things and I think, 'Shouldn't we have this? Shouldn't we have that?' And the answer's yes. Yes, we should have things. We deserve things. I should be able to go out with my head held high. You could sell the stupid baseball and it would fix everything, at least for a while."

And I said, "Shellie, please."

Then she said, "Don't 'Shellie, please' me. If you don't do this, I'll leave and I won't come back."

I could tell she meant it.

And I said, "I can't sell it. It has meaning to me. My grandfather gave it to me. My grandfather. I don't have much to remember him by."

Shellie wrinkled her nose, sneering a little. "That's sad if that's all you have to remember him by. That's very, very sad. A stupid baseball. A stupid, rotten baseball. It even looks rotten. It looks like an apple when you bite into it then leave it out in the air. It gets all brown and rotten. Look at it, Ham. It's just a brown ugly thing. Go ahead, look at it. I dare you to look at it."

She was right: it was a brown, ugly thing.

"Now," she said, "if you're telling me this is the only thing you have to remind you of your grandfather, then I feel sorry for you. That's the most pathetic thing I've ever heard. A grown man whose only memory of his grandfather is a stinking rotten old baseball."

And I said, "I have other things. I have other memories," which was true. I remember him taking me fishing. I remember him telling me about the shark he caught. I remember him saying, "Blessed are the little fishies."

And Shellie said, "Then you don't need the stupid baseball, do you? We can sell it and get the things we really need."

I looked at Shellie, with her hair falling across her forehead and her round sad eyes. I slumped in my chair.

"Is that what you want?" I said to her.

And she said, "Yes, Ham, that's what I want. That's precisely what I want at this instant in time."

And I said, "Fine. Fine. Sell the baseball. Take it. Take it and sell it. I don't want to hear another word about it. I don't want to see the money. Just take it."

Shellie tipped her head to one side. "Are you sure? I don't want to do it if you're not sure."

And I said, "I'm sure."

And she said, "Really?"

And I said, "Yes."

Shellie looped her arms around my neck and pressed her lips against my jaw.

"I love you," she said. "I'm sorry about the things I said before, the things I said about you. You know I didn't mean them, that I just said them out of frustration. You know I love you, don't you?"

And I said, "I know."

She lifted the baseball from the card table, and she said, "This is the right thing to do. A thousand dollars, Ham. A thousand dollars. And it's not just for me. It's for you, too. You need things. You know what you could use? You could use some gabardine slacks. You always looked good in gabardine slacks, and we could buy you some new ones, with a new leather belt and maybe some shoes. Huh, Ham? Huh?"

And I said, "We can talk about it later. Try to negotiate a better deal if you can. Try to get an extra hundred dollars. Can you do that?"

And she said, "I think so."

And I said, "Well, try. Try."

And she said, "I will."

And I said, "Here's what you do: tell the guy all about

Cobb, then tell him you want twelve hundred dollars. Maybe you should tell him you want more than that, but settle for eleven hundred dollars. Negotiate. That's the key. Negotiate. Make him think you'll walk away from the deal if he doesn't give you eleven hundred. I know about these things."

And she said, "I know you do, Ham."

And I said, "You have to make him think that you don't really care about whether you sell it, that you'll just go home if he doesn't give you eleven hundred."

And she said, "I will, Ham."

And I said, "Don't let him swindle you."

And she said, "I won't."

I watched her stuff the ball into her shoulder bag. I hadn't even noticed that she had the shoulder bag with her. She smiled and scratched at her nose with her blue fingernails.

"Can you start dinner while I'm gone?" she said.

I nodded, and she walked over to me and kissed me on the top of my head.

"Ham's a pig," she whispered, then she turned and left.

"Tell him he was better than Ruth," I called out as I heard the front door open. "Tell him he was better than Mays. Willie Mays," I shouted. I listened for her to say something, and when she didn't I got up and went to the open window and waited for my wife to walk past the trees. There were boys and girls playing in the street, and cars speeding past too quickly, making noises that sounded like they needed more oil. Then I saw my wife, only for a moment through the branches, but long enough to recognize her as a beautiful woman, what with her tiny waist and those legs, with that long red hair flapping. A beautiful woman who deserved things. I knew she would leave me soon, that she'd file for divorce and meet someone who could take better care of her. When she had passed from sight, I sat down at the card table. I returned to building my knowledge.

But building knowledge is for people like my brother Carl, not me. Knowledge is for people like Shellie and Renée and Guitar Walter and Claire and all the others.

For people like me, it's a luxury. Like caviar and champagne. It's a luxury you don't fully understand. It's a luxury that's wasted on you.

CHAPTER 12: MY BLACK THREAD

Broom Hilda stole my spool of black thread.

When I left work to go home, I had a large spool of black thread sitting next to my machine. Right NEXT to it. It's a spool of cotton-wrapped polyester thread that you can use on all natural fibers and synthetics. When I show up for work in the morning, though, it's gone. And it's not as if someone broke into the shop in the middle of the night and stole it. It's not as if someone would break in, leave the cash register alone, leave the sewing machines alone, leave the clothes alone, and only take one spool of black cotton-wrapped polyester thread.

Who would do something like that?'

Who?

No one.

So who stole the thread?

Who?

Broom Hilda.

Who else could it be?

Who else on earth could it be?

No one.

This time I don't say anything to Palmeyer. The last time I did, the last time Broom Hilda stole my thread, she made me look like a fool.

"Are you accusing me of being a thief?" she said.

And I said, "I'm accusing you of stealing my thread."

And she said, "That's accusing me of being a thief."

So I said, "If the shoe fits."

And she said, "If the shoe fits, what?"

And I said, "That's the whole expression: If the shoe fits."

And she said, "The expression is, 'If the shoe fits, wear it.' Is that what you're saying? Are you saying if the shoe fits, I should wear it?"

"Yes."

"So, you're accusing me of being a thief. You're lucky I don't sue you for defamation. You'd better have a good lawyer."

"For your information, I have an excellent lawyer. My brother Carl is a lawyer."

"Well, you ought to talk with him about what happens to people who accuse other people of being thieves."

"And you ought to talk to the police to see what happens to people who steal."

"You're going to look funny when I sue you for every penny you have."

"And you're going to look funny in handcuffs. Or should I say funnier?"

Just then, Palmeyer walked in, and Broom Hilda told him I'd accused her of being a thief.

Without even letting me say anything, Palmeyer said, "You ought to be ashamed of yourself, Salami. Debbie is old enough to be your mother. You ought to show her respect." Then he gave HER the rest of the day off.

So this time when Broom Hilda steals my black thread, I keep my mouth shut. I keep my mouth shut and use the blue.

Every once in a while, I see her look over at me, the corners of her mouth turned up. I can tell what she's thinking: *I've got your black thread. I've got it.*

Big deal. You can keep the black thread. I won't be here much longer. I'll find a new job, then I'll leave here.

★

At lunchtime, I drive downtown to Carl's office. I call him first so he knows what I'm coming for. Only when I get there, Cecily looks surprised to see me.

"Ham," she says, "I didn't know you'd be stopping by today, or else I'd have worn something pretty."

She looks pretty as it is, and I tell her that. She's wearing a raisin-colored blouse with a short black skirt that shows off her legs. She's wearing pearl earrings and a matching necklace.

Cecily leads me into Carl's office.

"Look what I found in the hall," she says.

And Carl says, "Why'd you drag it in here?"

He's wearing gray pants with a white shirt. He has suspenders, which make him look tall and fit. He's standing in front of the newspaper articles. For the first time, I notice the horse is almost the exact same color as Carl's hair. He's going bald on top. That's one thing I have over Carl: I still have all my hair.

When Cecily leaves, I say, "Carl, listen, I really hate to do this again."

And he says, "It's okay. How much do you need?"

"How about a hundred?"

He writes a check and hands it to me. It's written in his perfect handwriting.

I say, "You know I'll pay you back."

And he says, "It's not a problem if you don't. Why don't

you sit down," which I do.

We talk for a little while about Judy and the boys. The boys are playing pee-wee football. We talk a little about our parents, who are thinking of moving to Florida. Then I tell Carl about Renée. I tell him about how she hasn't been the same after the gas man saw her naked, and how she doesn't play the guitar anymore, and how she started taking night classes, and how she has new friends who come over all the time, and how they act like monks whenever I come into the kitchen, and about *Keats, Yeats, Browning, Frost.* Then I tell him about work. I tell him about Broom Hilda and Palmeyer, and how they always say, "Do you remember," and how they play big band music all day, and how there isn't as much overtime as there used to be.

That's when I say, "Listen, can I ask you a legal question?"

"Is it about common-law marriage?"

"No."

"Good."

"Are you familiar with an area of law called defamation?"

"Sure am."

"Can someone sue you if you say they stole something?"

"Can you *prove* they stole it?"

"Can I *prove* it? No, I can't prove it."

"Then, yes, they can sue you for defamation. If you accuse someone of being a criminal, but you can't prove they committed a crime, you could be sued for defamation."

I say, "Darn it," only I don't say "darn."

"Is someone suing you?"

"Not yet."

"Is it that Walter boy with the guitar?"

"Guitar Walter?"

"Yes."

"No."

"Is it that Broom Hilda lady?"

"Yes."

"Why don't you just leave her alone? You act like you're jealous of her."

I'm about to say, "No, I'm not," only I think about it for a second. Instead, I say, "I hope I'm not."

Then Carl says, "You know, I'll bet if you made an effort to be nice to her, she'd be nice back."

And I say, "Maybe."

It's the kind of advice he probably gives to his boys, and it makes sense if you think about it. So, on the way back to the shop, I stop at the Krispy Kreme doughnut store. There's a flashing red sign on the front window that says, HOT DONUTS. I get a box to take back for Broom Hilda and Palmeyer. And wouldn't you know it, but Broom Hilda LOVES Krispy Kreme doughnuts. They're her favorites. She eats three of them with a cup of black coffee. When she doesn't think I'm watching, she eats a fourth. I see her licking her fingertips.

Then, a little while later, she stops at my machine and hands me the spool of black thread.

"I borrowed your thread this morning for a job," she says. "Sorry I didn't get a chance to ask."

And I say, "It's okay." Then I say, "Do you remember how you and Palmeyer were talking about Mario Lanza the other day?"

And she says, "Yes."

And I say, "Well, I was at an Italian restaurant the other night, and the maître d' told me that Mario Lanza had once eaten there."

Her eyes get so big you'd have thought I told her she had just won a brand-new car. For the next fifteen minutes she tells me all about Mario Lanza.

"I can lend you some of his records if you'd like," she says.

And I say, "That'd be great."

For a minute I think that maybe I won't look for a new job after all.

★

After work, I stop at Fat Matt's Rib Shack for dinner. I eat by myself, have a few beers and a few cigarettes, then I go home to wait for Renée so I can tell her about how I bought the Krispy Kreme doughnuts and how Broom Hilda is being friendly to me now. I watch television in the living room while I'm waiting, even though there's nothing on that I'm interested in. The first show's a comedy about a woman with two children. So's the next. I sit on the couch and mend one of Renée's blouses. I fix the hem on one of her skirts. The phone rings, and I think that maybe it's Renée calling to say she'll be late, which happens more and more lately. I set Renée's skirt down on the arm of the couch and answer the phone.

"Hello," I say.

It's not Renée, though. It's a man. He says, "Hello. Is this Hamilton Ashe?"

I think it might be a salesman. I say, "Yes. Who's this?"

And that's when he says, "You're not going to believe this, but this is Hamilton Ashe. I mean to say, that's my name, too."

I don't know what to say, so I say, "Is this some kind of joke or something?"

And he says, "No. I swear to God, my name's Hamilton Ashe. I live in Baltimore, Maryland, and I heard that there was someone in Atlanta with the same name as mine."

I'm not sure whether he's pulling my leg, so I say again, "Is this some kind of joke?"

And he says, "No. It really is my name."

So I say, "How did you find out that I had the same name?"

And he says, "I was up in New York City on business, and I had dinner with some people, and there was a woman there by the name of Shellie Haller. She gave me your number."

That's when I know he's telling the truth.

I say, "That was my wife. Shellie Haller was my wife. She used to be Shellie O'Connell, then we got married and she was Shellie Ashe, then we got divorced, then she got married again and became Shellie Haller."

And he says, "I know. You should have seen the look on her face when they introduced us. They said, 'This is Hamilton Ashe,' and she turned white like she drank some spoiled milk. I thought she was going to have a heart attack."

I laugh picturing that, picturing Shellie meeting some complete stranger whose name is Ham Ashe. I laugh picturing Shellie turning white. I laugh louder than I had at any of the television shows I'd been watching.

"This is incredible," I say. "How does she look? Does she still look the same?"

And he says, "I don't know what she looked like before, so I don't know if she looks the same. But she's a very attractive woman."

And I say, "I know. Does she look happy?"

And he says, "Yes," which makes me a little happy and a little sad at the same time.

"This is incredible," I say, again. "Another person with my name." It probably happens all the time with people named John Smith or Bob Johnson. But not with Hamilton Ashe. I've never heard of anyone having the same first name, let alone the same FIRST and last names. I say, "I can't believe someone has the same name as mine."

And he says, "Me neither."

And I say, "It's an unusual name."

And he says, "Not as unusual as it was five minutes ago, is it?"

And I say, "I guess not." Then I say, "Listen, when were you born?"

And he says, "June 6, why?"

And I say, "I just thought it would be funny if we had the same birthday, too."

And he says, "Do we?"

And I say, "No. I'm November 28."

For a couple seconds, neither one of us says anything. Finally, I say, "How'd you get your name? My mother named me after a man she once knew."

And he says, "I was named after a watch."

And I say, "A watch?"

And he says, "Yes. It's the name of a watch company. Hamilton Watches."

I look at my watch. "Good thing my mother didn't do that or I might be named Casio Water Resistant Ashe."

The other Hamilton Ashe laughs at my joke, which is nice of him.

Then I say, "Listen, are we related?"

And he says, "I wouldn't be surprised if we are. What's your father's first name?"

And I say, "Samuel Ashe."

And he says, "No, that doesn't ring a bell."

And I say, "What's your father's name?"

And he says, "Alex."

And I say, "I don't know any Alex Ashes."

We spend ten minutes or so trying to figure out whether we're related. We go through parents and aunts and uncles and cousins and grandparents, and we can't come up with anyone in common.

Then he asks me, "Did people ever make fun of your name?"

And I say, "Of course."

And he says, "Me, too. They used to call me Bologna or Salami—"

And I say, "That's what my boss calls me. Salami."

And he says, "Let me ask you this. Did you *ever* think it was funny?"

And I say, "Maybe the first time I heard it when I was four or five."

And he says, "Same here. Everyone always thinks they're the first one to realize that ham is a type of meat."

That's when I tell him the story of how Shellie was elected class president by putting up posters that said, HAM IS A PIG.

He laughs a little and says, "I know. She told me about it at dinner."

And I say, "She did?"

And he says, "Yes. After she made me show her my driver's license to prove that I'm really Hamilton Ashe."

There is a pause, and I say, "We don't talk anymore."

And he says, "I'm sorry to hear that."

And I say, "It's okay." Then I say, "So, are you married?"

And he says, "Yes. My wife's name is Angie. We have two daughters, Katie and Claire."

And I say, "Those are nice names."

And he says, "Thanks. How about you? Did you get married again?"

And I say, "No. No wife, no kids. I'm living with a girl, though. Her name's Renée. She's taking classes tonight."

And he says, "Oh. What's she studying to be?"

And I say, "Smart." Then I say, "Really, I don't know what she's studying to be."

Again, a few seconds pass without either one of us saying anything.

Then he says, "I wonder if we look alike."

We both describe ourselves. We don't look alike at all.

Then he says, "What do you do for a living?"

And I say, "I'm a tailor. How about you?"

And he says, "I'm a school teacher. I used to be a lawyer."

And I say, "That's funny, That's what my brother does. I mean, he's a lawyer."

And he says, "Really?"

And I say, "Really. His name's Carl Ashe."

And he says, "Wouldn't it be a coincidence if I had a brother named Carl?"

And I say, "Do you?"

And he says, "No. I was just thinking what a coincidence it would be."

He tells me a little about when he was a lawyer. It sounds like he worked long hours, just like Carl. The way he tells it, it sounds dull and tedious and not all that different from my job. Then he tells me about how he's teaching at a high school now, and he tells me how much he likes it.

I tell him a little about working with Palmeyer. I try to make it sound interesting, but there's only so much you can say about being a tailor. I tell him a little about Palmeyer. I tell him a little about Broom Hilda, only I call her Debbie when I do. I tell him about what happened with the black thread and the Krispy Kreme doughnuts, and how Debbie is friendly to me now.

"Good," he says, "I'm glad. It's important to like the people you work with."

And I say, "I agree."

He tells me about his wife. She sounds like a very pleasant woman.

I tell him a little about Renée. I leave out a lot. I don't mention anything about the song about the dog missing its ear.

He tells me a little about Baltimore. I've never been there, and it sounds like a beautiful place, the way he describes it.

I tell him a little about Atlanta. I try to focus on all the beautiful trees and the monuments. I make a point of not telling him about what it's like here in August, when you can't even go outside because the air is so thick.

We talk about baseball and movies and music.

Before I notice, we've been on the phone for more than an hour. Finally, he says, "This has been interesting, Ham. I didn't mean to keep you on the phone so long."

And I say, "It's okay. Renée's not here."

And he says, "Look, if you're ever up in Baltimore, you'll have to give me a call. We'll take you out to dinner." Then he gives me his telephone number. I write it down on the back of one of Renée's *Redbook* magazines. It's the one with Oprah Winfrey on the cover.

I say, "If you're ever down here in Atlanta, you'll have to call me, too."

And he says, "I will."

And I say, "Good."

And he says, "Well, good night, Ham."

And I say, "Good night, Ham."

Then we both hang up.

★

Now I have two things to tell Renée about: Broom Hilda and the other Hamilton Ashe. I can hardly sit down, I'm so excited. I can't pay attention to anything on television. I finish mending the hem of Renée's skirt, then just pace around the apartment waiting for Renée to come home so I can tell her about my day.

Only Renée doesn't come home.

CHAPTER 13: A THOUSAND BREATHLESS SUMMERS

When your girlfriend doesn't come home at night, you're supposed to think, *I hope she's all right. I hope she wasn't in an accident.* Or you're supposed to think, *Maybe I should call the police. Maybe I should call the hospitals.*

Or you're supposed to think, *I wonder if she's left me*, especially if that's what your wife did.

Only I don't think that at all.

Instead, I think, *Guitar Walter.*

Guitar Walter.

Guitar Walter.

GUITAR WALTER.

Guitar Walter with his guitar.

Guitar Walter with his oily hair.

Guitar Walter with his college books, sitting in the kitchen, drinking coffee I paid for.

Guitar Walter sitting on my couch and smelling my girlfriend's perfume like a dog sniffing around for a treat.

Guitar Walter with his hands all over my girlfriend.

At two o'clock in the morning, all I can think about is Renée and Guitar Walter kissing.

What I think about at three o'clock is worse, bare arms and legs everywhere.

What I think about at four is horrible.

★

I shower. I shave. I make a pot of coffee. I get dressed. Renée still isn't home when I leave for work. She hasn't called. I don't know any of her new friends' telephone numbers. I don't even know their last names, so I can't look up their telephone numbers or call directory assistance. You can't dial 411 and say, "I'd like the telephone number for Guitar Walter." You can't say, "I'd like the number for a girl named Claire Something-or-other with red hair and pale skin." You can't.

I stop on the way to work to get some more Krispy Kreme doughnuts, and when I get to the shop I tell Debbie and Palmeyer about how Renée didn't come home last night. Debbie makes an "O" with her mouth, then covers it with her palm.

"That's terrible," she says. "Did you call the hospitals?"

I tell her, "No," and she says, "We'd better."

For the next half hour, we take turns calling the hospitals. I look up the numbers in the phone book, then Debbie calls them.

"Is there a girl there named Renée Yates?" Debbie says, and after a little while she looks at me and shakes her head side-to-side, no.

"Ask if there's a Renée Ashe," I say.

And Debbie does, and then she shakes her head, no, again.

We call all of the hospitals that are listed in the phone book. There are more hospitals than you can imagine. There must be more sick people in Atlanta than anywhere in the world. Or else they're very small hospitals.

No Renée Yates at any of them.

No Renée Ashe.

Then we call all of the police stations in the area. Hands. Feet. Legs. Breasts. I try to put them together in my mind to complete two naked bodies, but I can't.

Same thing.

Then I start picturing her with Guitar Walter again.

I try to call her at home, but there's no answer. I just keep getting our answering machine saying, "Hello, this is Renée Ashe. My husband and I are out at the present moment. Please leave a message."

I work on a sports jacket for five minutes, fixing the buttons on the sleeves, then I call home again. Still no answer, just Renée's voice.

I work a little more, then call home again.

Then I work a little more.

Then I call home again.

It's not until ten-thirty that Renée answers the phone, only now I don't know what to say to her.

"Renée," I say, "is that you?"

And she says, "Yes."

And I say, "Renée, I was worried sick. We've been calling the hospitals and the police stations."

And she says, "Who?"

And I say, "Me and Debbie."

And she says, "Who?"

And I whisper, "Broom Hilda."

And she says, "Why have you and Broom Hilda been calling the hospitals and the police stations?"

And I say, "I thought maybe something happened to you when you didn't come home last night."

And she says, "I'm fine. I ended up staying the night at Claire's."

Film Claire. Claire from the kitchen.

And I say, "I wish you would have called to tell me. I didn't sleep at all last night, I was so worried."

And Renée says, "I tried to call you a thousand times, but you were on the phone all night," which I hadn't even thought of. I was on the phone with the other Hamilton Ashe. Then Renée says, "Finally, we just fell asleep."

And I say, "That makes sense." And she says, "Then I tried to call you at work all morning, but the number has been busy."

And I say, "We've been trying to find you. I was just so worried."

And she says, "What did you think happened to me?"

When I don't say anything right away, she gets angry and says, "You're a pig, do you know that?"

And I say, "Why?"

And she says, "You thought I was fooling around with Walter, didn't you?"

And I say, "Well, to be honest—"

Before I can finish, she says, "For your information, I didn't even see Walter last night. I was out with Claire. Just me and Claire."

And I say, "Okay."

Because it's a Friday, Renée doesn't have classes, so I say, "Well, I'll be home at about six. What do you say we catch a movie tonight?"

And she says, "I can't. There's a party tonight." Then, very quickly she says, "You don't have to go if you don't want to."

And I say, "Where is it?"

And she says, "It's over in Virginia Highlands," which is the name of the artsy part of town. It's filled with shops and art galleries and little stores that sell nothing but expensive coffees. "But you don't have to go," she says again.

She keeps telling me that I don't have to go, over and over again. If I had a dollar for every time she says it, I'd have ten or twelve dollars.

It's pretty clear that she doesn't want me anywhere near her friends' party, or why else would she keep telling me I don't need to go?

Why?

Which is exactly why I'm going to go.

★

"This isn't a suit-and-tie affair," Renée says while I'm getting dressed. You can tell she's still angry with me for thinking she'd been with Guitar Walter last night. "It's more of a pants-and-shirt type."

She stands in front of the bedroom mirror, changing her clothes, her arms twisted behind her like a full nelson as she tries to hook her bra. Dressed in just my shorts, I walk to her side and fasten the tiny metal hook for her, turning it in my fingers, and she pats my forearm once, then twice, and thanks me.

"You know," she says, "you really don't have to come tonight. If you'd be uncomfortable, I'll go by myself."

And I say, "No, no, I'm going to go. Where is it again?"

And she says, "At Walter's."

And I say, "Which one is Walter?"

And she says, "You know which one is Walter." She puts her hand on the small of my back and gives me a shove. "Now, go shower already."

I pull a pair of dark slacks and an Oxford shirt from the closet and hold them up for Renée's approval—she nods her head in the mirror—then lay them on the bed. I pick a pair of boxer shorts from my underwear drawer and carry them into the bathroom, then I shower, and when I return to the bedroom in my shorts and wet feet, Renée is still in front of the mirror, brushing on eye shadow now. She's wearing a loose black sweater and a dark skirt with the pattern of blooming flowers. She doesn't look a thing like the Archaeologies or the Films.

I put my hands on Renée's waist, fanning my fingers, then rest my chin on her shoulder. I can't think of anything romantic to say, so we both just stand there, looking at ourselves in the mirror. Renée holds the brush to her eye shadow next to her face. It's the same position as if she were holding an umbrella over both of us.

I consider saying, "You look beautiful, Sweet Potato," or "I love you, Sweet Potato," but I don't. I almost say, "Sweet Potato, do you want me to do your eye shadow," but I don't say that either.

After a moment, Renée says, "Ham?"

And I say, "Yes?"

And she says, "Ham, we've got to get going. It's past nine already."

"Maybe we could be a little late," I say, trying to be seductive, and I bring my hands to her breasts and press my lips to her neck, but Renée pulls free.

"No, Ham," she says sternly.

I release her, and she waits for a moment before starting to apply the eye shadow again, holding the little brush as if she were only holding the umbrella over herself now.

I dress, then sit on the bed and pull my socks and shoes on. On the drive, I tell Renée about Broom Hilda and the

Krispy Kreme doughnuts. I tell her about the other Hamilton Ashe, but I don't mention how he met Shellie. She doesn't need to hear about Shellie.

Renée smiles when I talk, but she doesn't say anything. Instead, she sits quietly for most of the drive, holding her hands on her lap, occasionally running her fingers over her cheeks to blend her rouge. I can tell that she's thinking about all the new words she's been learning. *Effervescent. Translucent. Dollyshot. Ubiquitous. Pharaoh.* You can see her lips move if you pay attention. Tiny, tiny movements, but they're doing it. Renée knows that she doesn't sound comfortable with her new words, I'm sure of that. Once, when she was showering, I pressed my ear against the bathroom door, and through the roar of the water I heard, "Hy*per*bole. *Hy*perbole. Hyper*bole. Hy*perbole."

She knows.

I almost drive past Guitar Walter's apartment because Renée isn't paying attention. I have to nudge Renée to ask, "Is this the street?"

She says, "Oh, oh, yes," and I park the car around the corner.

Walking to the apartment building, I keep my hands in my pants pockets. I extend my elbow in case Renée wants to clutch it, but she doesn't. Her lips are making those tiny movements, fluttering.

The party is on the third floor of a sorry-looking apartment building. There's no elevator, and the air in the stairwell STINKS. There are bags of rotting garbage left to one side and forgotten. Five or six other people climb the stairs with us. All of them are wearing black clothes. They're all Films, I can tell. They all say hello to Renée. Me, they don't say anything to. They don't even ask if I'm Renée's boyfriend, and I wonder whether she's even told them about me.

As soon as we enter the apartment, a man hugs Renée to him. He kisses her on the cheek. If I've met him before, I don't remember. I try to picture him sitting at our kitchen table, but I can't. Still, there's a chance that he's been over to the house and I simply hadn't paid any attention to him.

The man takes Renée's coat and drapes it over his arm. I look around the room, but I don't recognize anyone. There's loud music playing, but no one is dancing. They just stand in small circles, talking and drinking from plastic cups.

Renée takes my coat and hands it to the man, and we follow him to a small table with an assortment of wine bottles on it. There may be thirty bottles in all.

"Please help yourself," he says. "I'll put these in the bedroom."

Renée fingers several bottles, reading the labels, then selects one and pours red wine into two plastic cups. She hands me a cup.

"Where's Walter?" I ask.

Renée searches the room. Her hand is on her hip, her hip cocked slightly. I have never seen her stand like that before. It's provocative and sexy. Then she stands on tiptoe, and, when she does, I notice she's removed her shoes. They're dangling from her fingertips, twisting like hooked trout.

When Renée spots Walter, she waves her arm high and smiles broadly as if she's greeting him at the airport.

A tall, thin man walks up to us. He grabs Renée's wrist, making a bracelet of his thumb and index finger, then kisses her cheek. His mouth, which is pretty for a man, breaks into a grin.

"Syd," she says, "this is Ham, my boyfriend."

See, she said "boyfriend," not "husband."

See, she's NOT my wife.

The man leads Renée toward Walter, leaving me alone. There's a small group standing in the doorway to Walter's kitchen. There are four men and two women in a semicircle, all listening to a chubby man with a goatee. They're tipped forward toward him, as if there were a strong wind at their backs. I've never seen any of them before, but I join the group anyway, standing just outside the semicircle, looking between the shoulders of two of the men. They stop talking when I arrive. They all look at me.

"Hey," one of the men says, "aren't you Renée's boyfriend?" He's a thin, round-shouldered man with hair cropped so closely to his scalp that it looks like a felt cap.

"Yes, I am," I say, even though I don't recognize the man. "Have we met before?"

And he says, "Yes, we did. We met at your house. In your kitchen." The man taps his temple with two fingers. "Now, don't tell me. I remember your name."

And I say, "It's —"

"— No, don't tell me. I remember. It's some kind of meat, isn't it?" The man turns to the rest of the group. "His name is some kind of meat," he announces.

"You're named after meat?" one of the women asks.

And I say, "No," and shake my head. I start to say that I was named after my mother's first love, then stop myself.

"I know," the man says, pointing a finger. "You're Sausage."

There's a burst of laughter, but I don't say anything.

And the man says, "Am I right? Is it Sausage?"

I smile weakly.

"Pepperoni?" one of the women asks.

"Bologna? Is that your name, Bologna Ashe?"

"Liverwurst?"

"Who would name their child Liverwurst?"

"Don't mock me—you guessed Pepperoni. As if Pepperoni's a more reasonable answer than Liverwurst."

"Ground Beef?"

"Is it Chuck Steak?"

"Tongue? Could it be Tongue?"

It's like being in my own kitchen, except that there are fifty people now, not just one or two. I can't just go off somewhere by myself like I can in our bedroom or our living room. I can't just sit on the steps outside and smoke a cigarette, or drive down to the convenience store. You can ignore one or two of them, but you can't ignore fifty. Fifty overwhelms you.

Finally, I interrupt them. "Very cute," I say. "My name's Hamilton."

"Ham!" the man shouts, then shakes a fist in the air, laughing. "Didn't I tell you he was named after meat? Want to know something else about him? He only eats sandwiches on toast! And it has to be *warm* toast!"

Renée!

When the group stops laughing at me—and it isn't soon that they do—they turn their backs to me and return their attention to the man with the goatee, who seems disturbed at having been ignored for two minutes. The man is dressed in all black. A black turtleneck sweater, black pants, black shoes. He stares at me meanly.

"Sorry for the interruption, Jules," one of the women

says. "Now, you were saying that you don't consider your work to be avant-garde?"

"It depends upon your definition of avant-garde," he says. "If you mean odd or self-indulgent, then no, it's not avant-garde. But if you mean advanced or experimental or unconventional or in some other way more contemplative than the norm, then, yes, it's avant-garde. As avant as garde can get."

Everyone nods. I place my wine glass on the counter and ignore it as if it were someone else's.

One of the men in front of me, the same one who'd teased me about my name, asks Jules a question. "What do the markings on your films mean?"

And Jules says, "Are you referring to the slashes and the triangles that appear in each of my frames?"

And the man says, "Yes."

"In the corners?"

"Yes."

And Jules says, "Well, what do *you* think they mean?"

The man in front of me cups his chin, rubbing it like smart people do when they're deep in thought. Finally, he says, "I see it as an indication of the fleeting nature of film. As if to say, 'This is a film. This is not reality, but just a facsimile, and it will end shortly.'"

Jules smiles. "Yes, yes," he says. "Bravo. You're very perceptive."

There's a pause, and for some reason I decide to say something. "You know," I say, "I don't feel very intelligent around here. I don't know a thing about films. I mean, I still call them movies."

I wait for laughter, but there is none. One of the women

contorts her face.

There's laughter across the room, and I look over to see a circle of twenty people or so. At the center are Renée and Walter. His hand is on her waist, and her wine is almost gone.

★

Throughout the night, the apartment rings with laughter, the deep laughs that come from your stomach. A burst here, then there, then one in the corner, like a string of firecrackers. *Pop-pop-pop-pop.*

I circle the room, trying to become invisible like a ghost in winter, moving among the people. I can't find a group I want to join. I find myself back with the same group I'd been with earlier. They've grown in number, still listening to Jules and his black clothes and his goatee. I'm beginning to get a headache.

Jules points to a wooden chair at the kitchen table.

"See there," he says. "You look at that and what do you see? You see the chair and the floor. The chair and the floor, two distinct objects. The chair and the floor."

"But with film," he says, "with film we can work miracles. We can break down the laws of science. If we focus on it for ten minutes, it becomes chair-floor. Chair-floor. Chair-floor. One object." He says it swiftly, as if it were a single word: *chair-floor.*

No one says anything, and I wonder whether they're all as confused as I am. When I look at their faces, though, I can tell that they aren't confused at all; they're just being quiet.

Jules touches his eyebrow with his finger.

"Chair," he continues, moving his hand slowly from his forehead down to his waist, "floor. One object."

There's an empty wine bottle on the counter behind me.

Bottle-head, I think. *Bottle-head*. One object. The bottle and Jules' head. The thought makes me snort out loud. Again, I move away from the kitchen and circle the room. I eavesdrop on conversations, acting as if I'm not listening, acting as if I'm looking at the posters on the walls, the view of the city, the books on the crowded bookshelf.

"It's the difference between color and black-and-white," a man says.

A thin, plain woman says, "I never wanted the apple sauce, I always wanted the apple butter," and it sounds like she's about to cry.

A short woman with a cap says, "Your words seem so true that the truth seems like a lie in comparison."

What does that mean?

What could that possibly MEAN?

"We had a love-hate relationship," another woman says. It's Claire. Claire, from the kitchen. "We both loved him and hated me. But that was a long time ago. Mark's perfect for me."

A man with heavy glasses says, "It's the darkness of the theater that makes film so exquisite, because only in the darkness can we truly see ourselves."

A woman says, "He knows my every thought. It's like he's been talking to my therapist."

A woman is talking about Fellini.

A man is telling a story about a pair of shoes he bought.

A man says, "I used to believe that there was a beauty and purpose to everything in life. But how do you explain carnival workers?"

Two women are talking in a doorway.

"The next thing I knew," one says, "he married Lisa, the She-Dog from Hell."

"Oh," the other says, "so she kept her maiden name?"

And the first woman says, "Well, it was already on her checks."

A man is talking to a woman. "She wants to know what everything feels like. If I eat a sandwich, she wants to know what it feels like. If I go for a jog, she wants to know what it feels like. If I go to the bathroom, well, let's just say it's getting a bit restrictive."

A man says, "Have you ever noticed that all the great cartoon characters have three-syllable names? Mickey Mouse. Donald Duck. Porky Pig. Fred Flintstone. Bugs Bunny. Elmer Fudd. Daffy Duck."

"What about Magilla Gorilla?"

"Oh, please, Magilla Gorilla wasn't a star. He can't even get a job anymore."

I walk to the center of the room.

"How was my day? Sweetheart, my day was like a thousand breathless summers."

I don't recognize the voice. Then I see it's Renée talking to Walter.

"That's wonderful," Walter says. "That's superb."

"I feel as if, finally, everything is starting to mean something."

I touch Renée on the waist to get her attention, but when she turns around, for a second it's as if she doesn't recognize me, as if we'd never met, as if the past four years were just a dream. There's a look on her face as if she were already starting to forget me.

"Renée," I say. I don't know what I'm about to tell her, but I want to leave. "I'm hungry. I'm going to head home. Here are the keys to the car—" I fish the keys out of my pants pocket—"and I'll just get a cab."

"Ham," she says, "I'm not going to drive this late at night, especially if I'm drinking. You take the car. I'll get a ride from someone."

And I say, "Are you sure?"

And Renée says, "Yes."

Walter shakes my hand.

"I'm sorry we didn't get a chance to talk," he says. "I would've enjoyed getting your perspective on things."

"Maybe some other time," I say. "Thanks for inviting me to the party. I really should be headed home, though."

"That's fine, Ham. Whatever you want to do is fine."

And that's when I say, "Your words seem so true that the truth seems like a lie in comparison."

Renée shoots me a disapproving look, then shakes her head. She says, "I'll get a ride, Ham. Good night."

And I say, "Good night."

I get my coat from a pile in the bedroom. I brush the lint off it, and walk toward the front door. Walter's hand is on Renée's waist again, and neither one of them looks at me.

A young man wearing a New York Yankees baseball cap stands on a chair, and the apartment quiets down as everyone gathers around him. The man removes his cap and places it over his heart and says, "Today today today...I consider myself myself myself...the luckiest man man man...on the face of the earth earth earth."

I get out of the apartment as everyone applauds. I move down the stairwell and out to the street.

★

Do I really believe that Renée's having an affair with that boy Guitar Walter? No. But for a moment, a hair of time, the thought enters my mind again and I feel it changing me, the way a drop of alcohol changes a drink.

When I get home, I remove my coat, folding it over a chair in the living room.

I want to talk to someone about Renée and Guitar Walter, only there's no one to talk to. It's too late to call Carl. And, when I think about it, I realize that the only people I could talk to are Palmeyer and Debbie. But I'll have to wait until Monday to talk with them. I think about calling the other Ham Ashe, but it's too late at night to call a stranger, even if he does have the same name as you.

I walk to the kitchen. There are dirty dishes on the countertop. I wash the dishes and put them in the rack next to the sink.

I think about what I'll say to Renée when she comes home. I can't help thinking about how things have changed. There was a then, and there's a now, and there's no confusing the two. First, it was the guitar. Then, it was the gas man. Now, it's her classes. Soon, we're going to start hating each other. We'll hate each other, but will we ever be brutal like some people are? I think about grabbing her by the arms and shaking her and saying, "Renée, look what's going to happen to us." I want to hold her until she sobs, but Renée never sobs anymore. She studies. She talks. She has breathless summers.

I'm tired but not sleepy, and my mouth tastes like old wine. I decide to fix a sandwich, even though I'm not really hungry. I pull the toaster out of the cabinet next to the sink, drop two pieces of white bread in, and unwrap a few slices of American cheese. I eat the sandwich quickly, while the toast is still warm, but don't put the toaster back in the cabinet when I'm done. I just sit and look at it. I remember how I once pretended to do a magic trick for Renée.

"Look," I said. "It's bread. Now I put it in here"—I dropped two slices in the toaster, and when the toast popped I said, "What happened to the bread? It disappeared."

I take the loaf of bread out of the refrigerator again, and, two at a time, I toast every slice. It takes fifteen minutes, and when I'm done, I put all of the slices back in the bag, then return the bag to the refrigerator.

★

It's two-fifteen, and only God knows where Renée is. I'm not going to call the police and the hospitals. I've already done THAT once today. I undress and toss my clothes in the bathroom hamper, then climb into bed and just lie there. I picture Shellie sitting on the washing machines at the appliance store. I picture her laughing and brushing her hair out of her eyes. Then I picture Shellie telling me about her brother, about how he wanted to be an astronaut and a baseball player, and how the only thing I could do to stop her from crying was to tell her I loved her over and over again.

I hear Renée when she unlocks the front door, but I don't move. I don't even open my eyes.

I hear the bedroom door swing open, hear her unbuckle her belt and unzip her skirt, hear her pull off her skirt and her sweater. She opens and closes drawers in the dark, slips into a nightgown and then gets into bed.

Sometime during the night, my hand finds its way to Renée's hip. She doesn't wake, and I keep my hand there.

Her back is to me, and I try to remember what her face looks like, but can't. Then, suddenly, I remember. I remember what she looked like on that trip to Sea World, when she held the fish over the tank, and I fall asleep, keeping my hand still on her hip.

In the morning, I hear Renée calling to me from the kitchen.

"Ham," she calls. "Ham, what happened to the bread?"

And I call back, "What? What?"

And she says, "The *bread*. What happened to the *bread*?"

CHAPTER 14: SOMEONE FELL AND WE ALL LAUGHED

Renée's in the kitchen chopping vegetables like she's playing the drums: chop-chop-chop-*chop*, chop-chop-chop-*chop*. I'm in the bedroom, but the sound of the chopping carries throughout the apartment. I walk to the kitchen and pour a glass of soda as Renée chops. Chop-*chop*. The toaster is still in the same spot where I'd left it. Renée doesn't look up from her work, her fingers moving, chop-*chop*, and I return to the bedroom.

A short time later, the doorbell rings. Before I can say anything, Renée calls out, "I'll get it," as if she'd been waiting for someone. She hadn't said anything about company. I hear her say, "Hello," then I hear footsteps moving toward the kitchen. I can't tell if they're Films or Archeologies with her. Probably Films. Probably some of them from the party last night.

Probably Guitar Walter.

Guitar Walter, who had his hand on Renée's waist like it belonged there.

I take my wallet off the bureau and slip it into my pocket. I'm going to pick up a newspaper at the pharmacy and then watch a football game on television. Before I leave the bedroom, though, I hear a crash in the kitchen, and then a scream.

It's Renée.

I race to the kitchen to find Renée sitting on the floor beside the toaster. There's no mistaking her pain: it washes up in her face like high tide. I pick up the toaster and put it on the counter beside the cutting board.

"She knocked it off the counter when she was reaching to get coffee from the cabinet," Guitar Walter says. He sounds excited. "It hit her right on the foot. Right there, on the front."

Guitar Walter's hands flutter. Claire is standing behind him with her hand over her mouth.

I remain calm. I bend down and rub my fingertips over Renée's ankle. A bone along her foot juts out like a broken umbrella rib, and Renée winces and pulls back.

"It's broken, Sweet Potato," I say.

And she says, "Are you sure?"

And I say, "It's too ugly not to be broken."

Renée licks her lower lip, then says, "God, Ham, it really hurts."

And I say, "You'll be okay. I'm right here." Then, to Guitar Walter, I say, "Give me a hand, will you?"

Guitar Walter helps me lift Renée from the floor. She leans against me, keeping her injured foot an inch or so above the floor. It's already turning purple-blue, like a piece of bruised fruit, and it's begun to swell. I pull a chair away from the kitchen table and help lower her into it.

"Now, Guitar Walter," I say, "go out and open the doors to the car, will you?"

He gives me a puzzled look, and I realize that I just called him "Guitar Walter" instead of just "Walter."

So sue me.

I pull my keys from my pants pocket and hand them to

Guitar Walter. Guitar Walter gallops out of the kitchen and nearly trips in the living room. We hear a *clump-clump* as he bumps against the recliner, and Renée and I smile at each other.

"You should move that chair," she says. "Someone's going to break a leg on that someday."

And I say, "People don't break their legs on chairs, Sweet Potato. They break them on kitchen appliances."

She grins at me.

And I say, "I read that in a medical journal. Forty percent of all broken legs are caused by toasters. I think twelve percent are caused by blenders. Food processors are responsible for ten percent."

And she says, "What about refrigerators?"

And I say, "That depends. Now, your regular refrigerator is responsible for six, maybe seven percent of all broken legs. If you're talking about one of those models with the ice machines on the door, well, those are killers. Twenty, maybe twenty-five percent of all broken legs are caused by those things. They're monsters. They really should be outlawed."

I realize that Claire hasn't said a word. She's standing against the wall, her hand over her mouth.

"It's okay, Claire," I say. "It's just an accident."

Walter returns. He's out of breath. He says, "Where are you? Shouldn't we hurry up?"

And I say, "She's not having a baby, Walter. Now, go get Renée's blue coat from the hall closet. There's no reason to panic. Let's all stay calm."

Guitar Walter brings the coat into the kitchen, and I help Renée stand again and slip her coat on.

Renée's eyes are moist. "Are you *sure* it's broken?"

And I say, "I didn't go to medical school for three years for nothing."

And she says, "Ham, you didn't go to medical school."

And I say, "Medical school, high school—what's the difference?"

I wipe a teardrop from Renée's nose, then lift her in my arms like a fireman. Her arms loop around my neck, and I carry her through the apartment and out to the car.

Guitar Walter holds the car door open. "Can I help?" he says.

"It's okay," I say, "she's my girlfriend," then slide her into the back seat and drive to the hospital.

★

Renée's foot is broken, all right, just as I said. The doctor in the emergency room is a young black man with a receding hairline and an athletic build. He puts a cast on it and tells her to stay in bed for a few days. He gives her a pair of crutches and a prescription for painkillers, which I have filled at the pharmacy on the way home. If I'd remembered, I would've picked up a newspaper while I was there.

I park the car in the parking lot, then carry Renée into the apartment, weaving through the living room and to the bedroom, and set her down on the bed. I'm careful not to bump her cast against the doorjambs or the walls. Claire keeps Renée company while Guitar Walter and I go to the kitchen to make some tea. On closer inspection, Guitar Walter isn't handsome at all. His nose is bony. His cheeks, too. He has the gangly, startled look of a teenager unsure what to do with his arms and legs. He folds his arms across his chest, then unfolds them, then folds them again. I'm making him very nervous, which is fine with me.

"So, Walter," I say, "do you just go to school, or do you work, too?"

And he says, "I work."

And I say, "Do you mind if I ask what you do for a living?"

"Where I work we sell electrical supplies. Not electrical supplies like lamps and light bulbs, but supplies like wiring and conduit. Most of our clients are large construction companies right here in Atlanta."

And I say, "That sounds very interesting," to be polite.

He says, "It is. It really is. You know, when I first saw the advertisement for the job in the paper, I remember what I thought the company would be like: boring with a capital B. But it isn't like that at all. In fact, it's just the opposite. Someday I'm going to sit down and write a movie script about it, about all the funny things that happen at work. The hard part for me is that sometimes something comical will happen at work, and I won't write it down right away, and then I'll forget all about it. Sometimes, when I get home, I'll tell my mom about the funny things that happened that day, and she won't even laugh. She doesn't have much of a sense of humor, being from the South."

"You live with your mother?"

He nods his head. "I'm thinking about renting a place for myself. I did that once before, but then I moved back so my mother didn't have to eat alone, which will give you a sinking feeling."

"I didn't notice her at your party last night."

"Oh, she wasn't there. She was out of town. Hell, she'd *never* let me have a party." Guitar Walter tugs at the collar of his shirt with his middle and index fingers. "Want to hear something funny that happened the other day at work?" he says. Before I can answer, he says, "Bob Gaffrey, Nancy Syms, and I were engaged in a conversation when Cliff Whalen passed by. When he was a good ways away, Bob Gaffrey said, 'Cliff Whalen's so old that when he was in school they didn't teach history.' We all laughed and laughed when he said that, and Nancy Syms turned red. 'Stop it,' she said, 'just stop it. I'm going to pee in my pants, I'm laughing so hard.' Funny things like that happen all the time at work. They just happen right out of the blue."

I nod and look away, but Guitar Walter continues: "You know, one of the first people I met at work is named Wilson Downey, who has the cubicle next to mine. Wilson Downey is black, and he does crazy things that will make you laugh. For instance, sometimes I'll be on the telephone talking to a customer, and he'll stick his head over the top of my cubicle and stick his tongue out or make a face at me so I'll burst out laughing on the phone. And if you try not to laugh, you'll just laugh louder. Also, sometimes Wilson Downey will pretend he's sticking his finger up his nostril when he really isn't. I'd like to have Bill Cosby play Wilson Downey in the movie. Bill Cosby was in some funny TV shows. He does some very hysterical things."

I'm beginning to feel ridiculous for having been jealous of this boy.

Guitar Walter keeps talking. "Theresa Valvano has some very entertaining sayings tacked up on her bulletin board. One says, 'The Floggings Will Continue Until Morale Improves,' which is very ironic. Another says, 'A Waist Is A Terrible Thing to Mind.' Last year on my birthday, Theresa brought me a cupcake with a candle in it, and everybody stood around my cubicle and sang the song 'Happy Birthday to You.' Theresa Valvano looks like Shirley MacLaine, only with black hair and not red. After they finished singing, I said to Theresa Valvano, 'Theresa, I can't believe you remembered my birthday.' To which she replied, 'I remember everything. My mind's like a steel trap. Sometimes it even sets off the metal detectors at the airport.' Everyone laughed and laughed because she's so witty. Don't you think?"

And I say, "Yes, she sounds very witty."

Guitar Walter bounces on his toes. He grins, showing two uneven rows of teeth.

Then he says, "Bob Gaffrey once put a sign on the bathroom door that said, 'Ed Standell Memorial Library' because Ed Standell will oftentimes read the newspaper while he's using the facilities. Bob also has some very hilarious nicknames for everyone at work. He calls Henry Mueller 'the Astrodome' because Henry Mueller has a bald head that looks like a picture of the Astrodome in Houston, Texas. He calls Sarah Feelney "Sarah Feel Me," which is a sexy play on words. He calls Susan Nile 'Porky Pig' because she has a pushed-up kind of nose. He calls Ed Standell 'Mr. Ed' after the horse on the TV show called *Mr. Ed*, which was about a horse that had the power of speech. He calls Melissa Horn 'Melissa Horny,' which is another sexy play on words."

What was taking the water so long to boil?

WHAT?

Then he says, "I remember one time it was winter, and the parking lot outside became like a sheet of ice. It looked like an ice skating rink. Sarah Feelney was looking out the window, and she yelled out, 'Hey, everyone, come look at this!' So we all went over to the window, and when we looked outside we saw cars sliding all over the parking lot, which was very funny to view. The people who were walking on the ice kept slipping and sliding around, then someone fell, and we all laughed. Not five minutes later, someone *else* fell."

Guitar Walter smiles broadly, and I make myself smile, too.

Then he says, "Not only am I writing a movie about work, but I'm still writing songs. I hope to have an album out soon."

And I say, "Really?"

And he says, "Yes." Then he says, "Would you like to hear one of my best songs?"

Before I can say anything, he starts singing a song to me right in the middle of the kitchen. He closes his eyes tight when he sings. It's a song about a boy who eats an entire apple, including the seeds, and an apple tree grows in his stomach.

AN APPLE TREE!

It's WORSE than Renée's song about the dog who ran away and came back with his ear missing.

When he sings—

Johnny,
Johnny Apple Tree,
Apples for you,
Apples for me

it's all I can do not to laugh out loud.

"That's very good," I say when he's through.

And he says, "Do you want to hear another? It's about a girl who's an ugly ducking, then ends up being a beautiful swan. It's called 'Beautiful Swan.'"

Then he closes his eyes and winces like someone stepped on his toes.

Then he sings:

Oh, you used to be ugly,
And you used to be round,
And you had pimples on your face,
And you weighed 200 pounds,
But now you're so beautiful,
Like a beautiful swan,
But now you're so beautiful,
And your pimples are gone

I can't believe he wrote a song that uses the word "pimples." TWICE.

Just then the teapot whistles. I practically run with the tray into the bedroom. Claire is sitting on the edge of Renée's bed.

"Tea," I say, "get it while it's hot."

For the rest of the afternoon, we sit on the bed and watch old movies on the television, which I carry into the bedroom from the living room. Me, Renée, Guitar Walter, and Claire.

★

When Renée falls asleep, I walk Guitar Walter and Claire to the door, then return to the bedroom. Renée is still dressed in her blouse and skirt, so I take the chicken shirt out of a drawer, then pull her by her arms into a sitting position.

"What are you doing?" she says. She's half-awake.

I say, "I'm helping you get changed, that's what I'm doing."

Renée lifts herself up with her arms, and I undo her skirt and slide it off, careful as I pull it over her cast. I notice that Guitar Walter and Claire have already signed her cast. Over Guitar Walter's signature it says, "This autograph will be worth millions when 'Beautiful Swan' is a #1 hit!"

Renée pulls her blouse off herself, and I bunch up my chicken shirt so she can slip her arms through, then pull it down to cover her body. Then Renée lies down and closes her eyes, resting her head on her hands.

"Listen," I say, "you know what they tell you about falling off a horse, how you have to get right back on?"

And she says, "Mm hmm."

And I say, "Well, I don't want you to be afraid. As soon as you're able, I want you to march right in there and make some toast."

Renée smiles and says, "Okay," and then she's gone.

CHAPTER 15: MY DEAD WIFE

As far as I know, Renée stays in bed for the next four days, lying there with her cast and watching television and reading her magazines. Maybe she moves around the house when I'm at work, maybe not. Who knows. Still, I bring her her breakfast and dinner on trays. I even come home from work at lunchtime to bring her a sandwich and some of the leftover Krispy Kreme doughnuts. The pills the doctor gave her make Renée hungry, and, despite her diet, she eats, and eating seems to make her feel stronger.

Claire and Guitar Walter and some of the others come by each night to bring her the assignments for her night classes and to share their notes, and, gradually, our bedroom becomes our kitchen. Coffee, cake, cookies, sandwiches, you name it, and me in another room by myself. Without a television to watch.

By Thursday, Renée is feeling strong enough to move about. She's able to do some of the cooking and some of the cleaning, but it tires her out, and she's asleep early that night. Eight o'clock, maybe earlier.

Claire shows up by herself, and when I tell her that Renée's asleep, she stays to help me with the dishes and cleaning the living room, which is nice of her. When we're through, we sit in the kitchen and eat some brownies.

"Can I ask you a question?" she says to me.

And I say, "Sure."

And she says, "Is it normal for a man to wear colored underwear?"

And I say, "What do you mean, is it normal?"

And she says, "My boyfriend Mark goes to the gym a lot, and he doesn't like to wear an athletic supporter, so instead he just wears some tight bikini briefs. But they're all colored. Red, blue, purple. Is that normal?"

I shrug, and I say, "I have no idea if it's normal. I have no idea at all what kind of underwear other men wear. They could all be wearing lacy underpants and garters for all I know."

"I thought Renée said you used to play basketball. You must've seen hundreds of men in their underwear."

"It's true I played basketball, but I haven't seen many men in their underwear."

"Even walking around the locker room? Men just seem so comfortable walking around undressed. Like the showers. In ladies' locker rooms, we all have individual shower stalls. But guys all stand around under one big showerhead. They're more comfortable being naked."

I raise a finger like I'm about to make some big announcement, and I say, "Aha, that's where you're wrong. We're not comfortable at all. That's why we have rules. You can walk around naked, but you have to keep your eyes to yourself. You look straight ahead. You look at your locker. At the urinal, you stare straight ahead at the wall like there's something interesting there. You...cannot...look...at... another...man."

"But what if you're talking to someone in the locker room?"

"Then you look him straight in the eyes." I make a chopping motion with one hand, slicing the air. "You make eye contact the entire time. You can't let your eyes drop even an inch. The last thing you want is for someone to think you were looking at him. A man's goal is to get through life seeing only one man naked—himself."

"That's crazy."

"It might be crazy, but it's a rule."

"You're exaggerating, Ham." She takes a bite of her brownie.

"Not at all. Not even the littlest bit. You can't look. You could be in a locker room, and—poof!—a guy's crotch could catch on fire. There could be flames everywhere, and no one would say a word. No one."

"No one?"

"What, and admit you were looking? No, we'd let our best friend's crotch turn into a bonfire before we'd admit we were looking."

"You're exaggerating, Ham."

"Stop saying I'm exaggerating."

"Fine, then just give me your opinion. Do you think colored underwear is normal?"

"It *could* be normal. Then again, maybe not."

"Let me try this another way. Would you wear colored underwear?"

"Not in a million years."

"Why not?"

"Well, let's just say Renée and I have a son someday, and that our son sees me parading around in purple bikini underwear. He'll assume that's normal and—bing, bang, boom—before you know it, he's dressing like Marilyn

Monroe. It could happen. It happened to my cousin Robbie."

I didn't realize how much noise Claire and I were making, talking and laughing, until Renée walks in and says, "Will you ladies puh-leeze be quiet so I can sleep."

★

Renée clomps around the apartment in her cast. It's funny watching her trying to learn how to use her crutches. She makes faces and strange noises. But, before you know it, she's off to her night classes and I'm home alone again. Home or at Fat Matt's Rib Shack, listening to music and eating ribs or chicken. At least I can put the television back in the living room where it belongs.

One night, I fall asleep on the sofa with the news on, and when I wake up Renée's still not home, so I go to bed. I wake up a few hours later to hear her cast clomping in the hall. I sit up in the bed.

"How was class tonight, Sweet Potato?" I say.

I expect her to say "Fine," like she always does. Instead she says, "Don't you dare call me that."

And I say, "What?"

And she says, "Don't you dare call me that." Her voice is dark and grinding.

I have no idea what she's mad about, so I say, "What on earth are you talking about?"

Things have been going so well lately. I felt like things were getting back to normal, even if it was a different kind of normal.

Renée starts to take her sweater off. She hops on one foot. "I'm not in the mood to talk about it now," she says. I've never seen her this angry before. Never.

And I say, "If you're mad at me about something, I'd like

to know what it is."

And she says, "Fine. What do you call me?"

And I say, "What?"

And she says, "What do you call me?"

And I say, "I call you Renée."

And she says, "That's not what I mean. I mean, what nickname do you call me? You just called me it five seconds ago. What do you call me?"

And I say, "Sweet Potato."

And she says, "See!" like she's caught me robbing a bank.

"See, what?"

"You call me Sweet Potato, you admit it."

"Of course I admit it. I always call you that."

"Then let me ask you a little question then."

I say, "Go right ahead."

She hops closer to me, so we're face to face, and she says, "Remember your wife Shellie?"

And I say, "Yes."

And she says, "So you do remember her?"

And I say, "I don't have amnesia. Of course I remember her. And she's my ex-wife, not my wife."

Renée says, "Don't try to change the subject."

And I say, "I don't even know what the subject *is*."

And she says, "I'll bet you had a nickname for her, too, didn't you?"

And I say, "Yes."

And she says, "What was it?" But before I can answer, she says, "It was Sweet Potato, wasn't it?"

I think about lying, because lying would be easy, but I don't.

I say, "Yes."

And she says, "You're a jerk," only she doesn't say "jerk." She calls me a name that rhymes with "glasshole."

"Why is that?"

And she says, "Because it's the *same* name."

And I say, "What's the big deal? It's just a nickname."

"What's the big deal? What's the big deal? It's a huge deal, an enormous deal. How do I know that when you say Sweet Potato you're even thinking of me? For all I know, every time you've ever called me Sweet Potato, you were thinking of her."

And I say, "I wasn't," which is true. I hardly ever think of Shellie unless someone mentions her name. Or unless someone with my exact same name just happens to call from Baltimore to say he bumped into her.

And she says, "How do I know that?"

And I say, "Because I'm telling you that. In my mind, it's like she's dead. It's like she's not even on this planet anymore."

"Is that so?"

"Yes. I'm thinking of you whenever I call you Sweet Potato."

"That's not good enough. For all I know, the whole time you've been with me you've been thinking of her. Every single time you were thinking of her."

"I wasn't."

"Regardless, from now on, you're forbidden from calling me Sweet Potato. Do you understand?"

"Yes."

She says, "Do you UNDERSTAND?" like she's talking to a child who's misbehaved.

Then I figure it out. I sit up in bed. I point a finger at her.

"Who put you up to this?" I say.

And she says, "What do you mean?"

And I say, "Who put you up to this? Claire? Guitar Walter? One of them had to put this idea in your head. Which one was it?"

And she says, "For your information, I do have a mind of my own."

I know she's lying. One of them put her up to this. Just when I was starting to like them, just when I was starting to think they might be decent human beings after all, one of them put this idea into her head. This stupid, stupid, STUPID idea.

"I want to know which one of them did this," I say. "I want names."

She says, "It was my idea."

And I say, "Are you telling me you didn't even discuss this with any of them?"

And she says, "You're changing the subject again. The point is that you're forbidden from calling me Sweet Potato ever again. Do you understand?"

And I say, "Sweet Potato, Sweet Potato, Sweet Potato," for no good reason other than to prove to her that I still have a say about some things.

Before I know it, we're having an argument and I'm spending the night in a hotel. A hotel I can't afford.

★

It's seven o'clock in the morning when the woman at the front desk rings my room to wake me, though she may have tried earlier. I was brushing my teeth in the bathroom, and it's possible the phone rang and I didn't hear it. It's only when I turn off the faucet that I hear the phone ringing, and

I spit the toothpaste into the sink and answer the phone.

"Hello?" I say.

The woman at the front desk says, "Good morning, it's seven ay-yem. This is your wake-up call."

It's the same woman I spoke with when I arrived at the hotel last night. She has yellow hair, the color of shredded wheat, and her eyebrows are shaved and drawn back in with black pencil, making her look surprised, like a photograph of a child opening a Christmas package.

I thank her politely, then hang up. I finish tying my shoes, then sit on the bed and pick up the phone. First I call Palmeyer.

"Hello," he says.

I say, "Hello, Palmeyer, it's Ham."

And he says, "Who?"

And I say, "Ham."

And he says, "Who?"

And I say, "Hamilton Ashe."

And he says, "WHO?"

Finally, I say, "It's Salami."

And he says, "What do you want, Salami?"

And I say, "I'm not feeling well."

And he says, "Who is?"

And I say, "Really, Palmeyer, I'm sick. I'm going to have to stay home today."

And he says, "I'm not going to pay you for today."

And I say, "I didn't think you would."

And he says, "You better come in tomorrow. Me and Debbie can't do all the work."

I almost say, "*I'm* the one who does all the work," but I don't. Instead, I just hang up, then I dial home, and I wait for

Renée to answer. Two rings, three rings, four, five, six. There's no answer. I don't know what I would have said if she had answered anyway. I get the answering machine. She's changed the message. "Hi, this is Renée Yates. My roommate and I aren't home now. Please leave a message."

My roommate?

My ROOMMATE?

I take the elevator down to the lobby. I'm hungry. I head to the coffee shop, stopping on the way to buy a newspaper from the rack. The coffee shop is practically empty, and I take a seat in one of the booths at the back of the shop and open the paper to the sports page.

"Coffee?"

It's one of the waitresses. There are only two: mine, and an older woman eating chocolate chip cookies and listening to the radio. My waitress is young, probably just out of high school, with black hair, shoulder length, thin lips, and gray eyes the color of mice.

"Please," I say, and she turns my cup over and fills it while I read. I pour in two packets of sugar.

The girl hands me a plastic menu and says, "In town for business?"

I nod and say, "Sort of. Really, I guess you could say I'm always in town for business. My apartment is only a couple miles away from here."

She says, "Stop by for a quick bite on the way to work, then?"

I look up from my paper and she's smiling. I can tell that she isn't trying to pry, that she just wants to talk. The other waitress is still off in the corner eating. Because of the difference in the waitresses' ages, they probably have little to talk about. Just like me and Palmeyer.

The tag on my waitress' blouse reads SUSAN, so I say, "Yes, Susan. Just a quick bite."

I order two poached eggs and buttered toast, and, when she's written that down and starts back toward the kitchen, I call to her to bring some juice, too. Several minutes later, when she brings me my eggs, they're fried instead of poached, but I don't send them back. Actually, I prefer fried eggs better, it's just that I always forget to order them in restaurants and, at home, Renée always burns the bottoms. Shellie did, too.

The toast is still warm, and I butter a slice.

"More?" Susan asks. She's holding the coffee pot, poised to pour another cup.

I swallow and say, "Yes, thanks."

When I finish my meal, I turn to the front page, looking over the headlines. There's a story about a murder in a parking garage. There's a picture of the mayor looking unhappy. I look up from the paper to see Susan leaning against the counter, reading a paperback book with her mouth slightly open. When I catch her attention, I gesture for more coffee, holding my fist out and rolling it.

Susan returns with another pot and fills my cup.

She says, "You know, that's the universal signal for 'pour me another cup of coffee.'"

I say, "What is?"

And she says, "What you just did," and she copies the gesture I had made, making a fist and rolling it. "I'll bet if you did that in a restaurant in Indonesia, they'd know to bring you more coffee."

I smile. "You might be right. I've never been to Indonesia."

"And this"—she scribbles on her left palm with an imaginary pen—"is the universal signal for 'bring me my check.'"

I say, "You're probably right about that, too."

"Trust me, I am," she says. "You know, you don't seem to be in much of a hurry to get to work today. If I didn't know better, I'd think you were playing hooky."

There's something strange about her eyes, other than their color, and I try to figure out what it is. Maybe they aren't straight. Maybe the left one is a little off. Not a lot. Maybe just a hair.

"Actually," I say, "I won't be going in at all today. I'm taking the day off."

And she says, "Not feeling well?"

And I say, "No, not really. Things haven't been going very well lately. You know, sometimes it's good to just take a day off now and again to sort things out."

And she says, "You're right about that. A mental health day, that's what I call it. Sometimes I'll call in sick, and when I come in the next day I feel like a whole new woman. Maybe the same thing will happen for you. Not that you'll feel like a new *woman*, but, well, you know what I mean."

She doesn't leave, though, she doesn't even move an inch from her spot in front of me, so I decide to tell her everything, or nearly so. I begin with, "Renée is NOT my wife."

It takes almost two hours, with Susan rushing off now and then to wait on other customers who arrive, and I work my way through four more cups of coffee and an apple danish that Susan had recommended. "It's simply otherworldly," she said, "like it was sent from another galaxy," and, in fact, it is very good.

Before I know it, it's lunchtime, and I still haven't

reached the part where Renée told me I'm not allowed to call her Sweet Potato anymore. The coffee shop has grown busy. There are only Susan and the older woman to cover the whole shop, so Susan can only stay at my table for a minute or so at a time. My story isn't going anywhere, and Susan keeps giving me apologetic glances or mouthing, "I'm sorry," looking up from her pad while she takes orders.

I'm stuck at the part where Renée broke her foot on the toaster, and every time Susan comes back, I have to start that all over again. After the fifth try, I swallow the last of my coffee and tuck my newspaper under my arm.

"Oh, don't go," she says. "I want to hear more."

I take my wallet out and remove a ten-dollar bill to pay my bill. "Look," I say, "I'm staying up in Room 404. Why don't you give me a ring when the place quiets down a bit and I'll come down and tell you the rest."

She says, "Great, Room 404," and she writes the numbers on the back of her hand, then walks toward the kitchen.

"Oh, hey," she says, "what's your name?"

And I say, "Ham."

And she says, "*Ham*?"

And I say, "Yes."

And she says, "Ham, like the food?"

I nod.

And she says, "Ham, like 'green eggs and ham'?"

I nod again. "It's short for Hamilton. I was named after my mother's first boyfriend."

★

I sit on the edge of the bed, looking out the window at the giant red-and-blue K-mart sign down the block, wondering whether I should call Renée to let her know that I'm all right. She may be very worried. But I decide to let her worry, and I just end up watching television. There's a pretty blonde woman named Martha Something-or-other talking about stocks and bonds. Her hair's the color of butter.

After a while, someone knocks on my door. I open it, and it's Susan, carrying a tray with two turkey sandwiches, cut into halves, and two large glasses of grape drink. The turkey is on TOAST.

How did she know?

Then I remember I'd told her about the time Renée and Claire had teased me in the kitchen about how I liked toast.

"I'm on my break now," she says. "I only have half an hour. Think that's enough time to finish up your story?"

I nod and step back from the door so Susan can get past me.

"Thanks for the food," I say.

And she says, "Don't thank me, I charged it to your room. I gave myself a big tip, too. A huge tip. You'd be surprised at how generous you are."

I laugh. I can't afford any of this. Already I'm trying to think of how I'll ask Carl to lend me money to pay for everything.

Susan sets the tray down on the bed and sits down beside it. I pick up one of the plates and a glass and carry them to the desk, then sit in the desk chair. I take a bite of the sandwich. The toast is still warm. I close my eyes while I chew.

After I swallow the first bite, I say, "Now, let's see. I was telling you about when Renée broke her foot, wasn't I?"

"Yup."

"About how I took her to the hospital?"

"Yup."

"And how her friends stayed over all day?"

"Yup."

I pick up where I'd left off, telling her about everything that happened. Susan takes little bites of her sandwich and little sips from her glass while I talk. As I do, I look at her gray eyes, trying to figure out what's wrong with them.

Then I reach the part about Renée wanting me to stop calling her Sweet Potato.

"Now, here's why I'm here at the hotel," I say. "So, you have the whole scenario now, right?"

And she says, "Right."

And I say, "About how there's something always happening, and it's not even related to anything else?"

And she says, "Right?"

And I say, "Like how she wanted to be a singer, right?"

"Right."

And I say, "And how I got her the guitar?"

"Right."

"And how the gas man saw her naked?"

"Right."

"And how she started taking classes?"

"Right."

"And how since she started taking her classes Renée's been doing things that she would never have dreamed up herself?"

"Right."

"And how Renée has been acting strange?"

"Right."

"Well, get this. Last night, Renée came home from her classes, and I was lying there in bed sleeping and dreaming and thinking that everything's okay again. Only when I called her Sweet Potato, she said, 'Don't you dare call me that.' Well, I didn't have the slightest idea what she was talking about, and she said she didn't want me to call her Sweet Potato anymore. She said that if I call her Sweet Potato, how can she know that I'm not thinking of my ex-wife because I used to call her that, too. So I said that's the stupidest thing I've ever heard and how she's out of her mind if she doesn't think I love her. I told her that, in my mind, Shellie doesn't even exist anymore. Then she starts screaming about how I'm *forbidden* from calling her Sweet Potato ever again. Forbidden. Who *forbids* people from doing things? Who has that kind of power? But that's what she says, that I'm forbidden from calling her Sweet Potato ever again."

I look over at Susan.

"So tell me," I say, "am I the crazy one?"

And she says, "Yup," and I'm so surprised that for a moment I can't think of anything to say.

Finally, I say, "You're kidding, aren't you?"

And she says, "No, I think you're crazy. If your wife doesn't want you to call her the same thing you used to call your dead wife, then you shouldn't. Case closed." She holds both hands in front of her like she's carrying a bag of groceries.

And I say, "What? My wife and my dead wife?" I try to explain, "Renée's not my wife, she's my girlfriend. And Shellie's not dead, she's my ex-wife. She's alive and well, as far as I know."

And Susan says, "Well, that's just splitting hairs, isn't it?"

And I say, "What," because I can't think of anything else to say.

And she says, "If your wife—or your girlfriend, or whatever she is—if she doesn't want you to call her Sweet Potato, then you don't call her Sweet Potato. It's as simple as that."

Again, I can't think of anything to say right away. "But I always call her Sweet Potato," I say.

Susan gets up off the bed and starts rummaging through her purse.

"It wouldn't be that big of a deal," she says as she looks through the purse, pulling tissues and makeup out. "It wouldn't be any great sacrifice if that's what's going to make her happy."

And then I say, "But."

And she says, "Listen, let me tell you something about your wife," only she keeps talking before I can tell her that Renée is NOT my wife. "You should just do what she asks. I know sometimes Greg thinks that the things that would make me happy are stupid. Greg, he's my boyfriend, if you can call him that. He doesn't understand women at all, just like you. He doesn't think it's a big deal to walk around with his hand on my rear end, but I don't think that's very lady-like. It makes a girl look cheap, and I told him that, and he just laughed. So he kept on doing it, and I kept on telling him to cut it out. Finally, I just said, 'Listen here, buster, if you ever do that again, I'm never going to talk to you again.' So, what does he do? He puts his hand on my rear end like he's going to show me who's the boss. So I said, 'You think you're the boss? I'll tell you who's the boss. Tony Danza's the boss, that's who,' and I just slapped him across the face"—she swipes at the air—"and then I walked home, more then two miles. The next day he came over to my house with a big thing of flowers for me."

I put a piece of my turkey sandwich in my mouth. The toast has grown cold. Susan catches her breath.

"Tony Danza?" I say.

And she says, "He was on a TV show called *Who's the Boss?*"

And I say, "Oh."

And she says, "That's the problem with men." She points at my chest. She doesn't poke me, but she comes close enough. "All of you think you're such big shots. 'Do this for me. Do that for me.' 'Me, me, me, me, me.' You think it makes you a big shot if you can get away with being rotten to your girlfriends or your wives or whoever. You think that if you do what they don't want you to do, it proves that you're more important. Well, it wouldn't be all that difficult to do a simple little thing just to make your wife happy. In fact, it'd probably be pretty easy. I'll bet she does a million little things like that to make you happy. A million. And you can't even do one because you're such a big shot."

Susan's face becomes red, and she starts talking faster and faster. It's hard to understand what she's saying. They're just ugly sounds coming out of her mouth.

"Mumbo jumbo mumbo jumbo jerks mumbo jumbo," she's saying. "Mumbo jumbo unnecessary mumbo jumbo mumbo foolish jumbo."

She keeps talking, pacing, flapping her arms, her mouth getting bigger and bigger, bigger and bigger, her teeth getting larger and larger, her mouth getting bigger and bigger, moving closer and closer until her white face is directly before me and I feel as if she's going to swallow me.

Before I know what I'm doing, I grab the girl by her bony elbows and pull her to me, kissing her. She has moist lips. She pulls free, her eyes large now.

"What are you doing?"

I step back, and I put a hand over my mouth and whisper, "Oh, my God."

And she says, "What was that for?"

And I say, "I'm sorry," and I take a step toward her. "I'm so sorry. It's just everything that's happened. I just needed to kiss someone. I just needed to hold someone for a second. I didn't mean it really."

My eyes are wet, and I wipe away the wetness with the back of my hand. The girl puts the pillow aside and walks to me. She stands in front of me. She's quiet. Her eyes are dry, and her mouth is closed, a thin line of purple on her lips.

"Okay," she says, "just don't touch anything," and she lets me hug her to me, my hands on her back. I rub her back and stroke her hair. I say I'm sorry, over and over, and I call her Sweet Potato when I do, though I don't know whether I mean Shellie or Renée.

CHAPTER 16: SHE HASN'T PAID A DIME

So I stop calling Renée "Sweet Potato."

Susan was right: it isn't that hard after all.

Sometimes I catch myself just before I say it. I'll say, "Sweet," then catch myself and say "heart." Once, I say, "Sweet Pea." I only say "Sweet Potato" once, and Renée just gives me a cross look, but doesn't make a big issue of it. After a while, I don't even think of saying it anymore. It just gets lost somewhere in my mind, with old phone numbers I don't call anymore and the names of people I haven't seen in years and years and may never see again.

Weeks pass without so much as an argument.

Maybe that's why I don't see it coming.

Maybe that's why it's such a surprise.

If we'd been arguing, I might have anticipated it. I might have said, "Oh, boy, here it comes."

But we haven't been arguing. We've hardly seen each other enough to argue.

The lease on our apartment ends in a few weeks, and we have to decide whether to renew it or move to another apartment. On the one hand, I'd like to stay because I think it's a nice apartment. The living room's large enough, the bedroom has a nice view of the Atlanta skyline. On the other hand, I can't keep borrowing money from Carl. Eventually,

I'll owe him so much money that I'll never pay him back unless I win the lottery. Which won't happen because I never buy lottery tickets. I can't ask Palmeyer for a raise. He can barely afford to pay for both me and Debbie as it is. I don't know how to tell Renée we have to move, so I keep putting it off.

Finally, one night after she returns from her classes, I say to her, "Renée, I think we need to talk."

And she says, "About what?"

And I say, "About the future."

And she says, "Spaceships and robots?" She laughs as she gets undressed. She's wearing navy blue underwear that she bought at the mall. It's the kind that looks like a "T" from behind.

And I say, "No, I mean the immediate future. The lease on the apartment is coming up."

And she says, "I know. I saw the envelope they slipped into the apartment." The envelope contained the new lease. They want an extra twenty-five dollars a month on top of what they're already charging us. That's an extra twenty-five dollars we don't have.

"Well," I say, "I don't think we can afford to stay here anymore."

And Renée says, "I agree."

And I say, "I think we should start looking for another place. Maybe off Collier Road," which is a nice area with older apartment buildings. They're not as expensive, and there are some nice parks nearby.

And then Renée says, "There's something I think we should talk about, too."

She seems to be breathing too slowly, as if she has a secret she's guarding. She sits on the bed.

And I say, "What's that?" and I get ready for the same old talk about how we're married or how we should get married. Or how we should get divorced. We haven't had one of THOSE talks in months.

Only Renée doesn't say that at all. Instead, she says, "Maybe we should talk about getting separate places."

And I say, "Really?" It sounds like it's going to be a trick, only I don't know what the trick is. If I know what the trick is, maybe I can figure out how to avoid it, working backwards from the end of the trick until I get to this moment so I'll know exactly what to say. Then I look at her and I can tell it is NOT a trick. She's serious.

Renée says, "Really. What do you think?"

And I say, "Why do you think we should do that?"

And she says, "Because I don't think we're really dating anymore."

And I say, "What does that mean?"

And she says, "Things have changed," which I can't really dispute.

Still, I say, "It's only been a couple months that you've been taking your classes. How much can things change in a couple months?"

And she says, "A lot."

Before I can stop myself I hear myself say, "Is this about Guitar Walter?" I know it has NOTHING to do with Guitar Walter.

Guitar Walter with his Johnny Apple Tree song.

And the one about the girl with the pimples.

This has nothing to do with Guitar Walter.

Renée says, "This has nothing whatsoever to do with Walter."

And I say, "Then what does it have to do with?"

And she says, "Everything."

And I say, "Everything's a lot. That means that there's nothing that this ISN'T about."

Renée squints and says, "I don't get it."

And I say, "Does this have anything to do with the oven?"

And she says, "No."

So I say, "See, then it isn't everything. There are some things this has nothing to do with."

She sighs a little and says, "You're right, Ham. This has nothing to do with the oven. You've just made a very valid point. It has nothing to do with the goshdarn oven."

And I say, "Does it have anything to do with the doorknobs? Or the ceiling? Or the mailbox?"

And she says, "We don't have a mailbox," which is true. We just have a mail slot in the front door. That's how they gave us our new lease.

I say, "My point is the same. There are a lot of things this has nothing to do with." I have NO idea what my point is. I'm not even sure I HAVE a point. The more I talk, the more I'm embarrassing myself. I need to shut up. But I can't. I keep talking. I don't know what I'm saying. The words are just spilling out of me like I'm a punctured oil can. At one point I say something about the *Hindenburg* and Mario Lanza and Harry S. Truman and penny candy and the Lindbergh baby. I say, "Remember the time we got a flat tire? Remember the time we went dancing and your shoe broke?"

Finally, Renée puts a hand up in front of her face like a crossing guard stopping traffic. Then she says, "Just the same, I think we should get separate places."

And I breathe deeply and say, "Okay."

And she says, "Okay."

I say, "Okay." again.

And she says, "Actually, Claire and I have been talking about maybe sharing an apartment."

Claire.

CLAIRE.

I knew it.

Sort of.

She's the one who puts Renée up to everything.

I say, "Oh, really? You and Claire?"

And she says, "Yes."

And I say, "Have you started looking yet?"

Then, out of nowhere she says, "Actually, we're thinking of just keeping this place."

They're thinking of keeping OUR apartment?

And I say, "OUR apartment?"

And she says, "Yes."

And I say, "So *I* have to move out?"

And she says, "Yes. Remember, it was my apartment before you moved in," which is true. I used to live in an apartment by myself in Midtown before I met Renée.

And I say, "I know it was your apartment first, but I'm the one who's been paying rent," which is also true. Renée hasn't paid a DIME in rent since she lost her job at the hospital. Not a DIME. Now she wants me to move out.

And she says, "It's the way it's supposed to work, Ham. The guy is the one who leaves."

And I say, "Who told you that? One of the Films? One of the Archaeologies?"

Renée smiles and says, "It's just the way it's done in civilized society, Ham. It's the way people act when they choose to live in a civilization. The man is the one who moves out."

And I say, "Show me where that's written? Is it in the Constitution of the United States of America? I don't think it's in the Constitution of the United States of America. We studied the Constitution of the United States of America, and this issue wasn't addressed at all in the Constitution of the United States of America."

And she says, "A) Please stop saying 'the Constitution of the United States of America.' B) No, it's not an issue that's addressed in the Constitution of the United States of America. And C) regardless of whether it's written down, that's the way things are done by self-respecting men and women in our country. The man is the one who moves out."

And I say, "But you're the one whose suitcase is already packed." I point in the general direction of the bedroom closet as if she forgot where it was.

And she says, "No, it's not. I unpacked it a couple months ago."

And I say, "It's still there in the closet, on the floor. It's in there next to the guitar and the tape recorder and the microphone."

THE SUITCASE.

AND THE GUITAR.

AND THE TAPE RECORDER.

AND THE MICROPHONE.

AND THE COWBOY OUTFIT. THE SKIRT. THE BOOTS. THE COWBOY HAT.

I HATE that closet.

And Renée says, "But the suitcase is empty."

And I say, "What?"

And she says, "The suitcase. It's empty. There's nothing in it."

It's been UNPACKED this whole time. She just wanted me to think it was packed. Now, I get angry. I say, "So you've been pretending it was packed for a couple months?"

And she says, "I never said it was still packed."

And I say, "But you wanted me to think it was packed, didn't you? You wanted me to think you were going to leave at the drop of a hat, didn't you?"

And she says, "I won't dignify that question with a response."

Then I say, "How are you going to afford this place?"

And she says, "I got a job at the card store in the shopping center. You know, the one with the picture of the puppies in the window. I start in a couple days."

And I say, "So NOW you decide to get a job?"

And she says, "Well, I NEED a job if I'm going to live here, don't I?"

I just keep shaking my head. This isn't the conversation I'd been planning on having. After a couple moments, I say, "This was pretty rotten of you, Renée. This whole thing. Now not only do you want to break up, but you're throwing me out of the apartment. That stinks, Renée. That really stinks."

And she says, "I'm not throwing you out. I'm asking." She says it in a soft voice while she's sitting there in her blue underwear.

And I say, "Fine. I don't really care." And then I call her "Sweet Potato," not once, but twice.

But I DO care. Why should I have to leave when I'm the one who pays the rent? Why? It just doesn't make any sense.

I stay mad for a couple hours.

It's only when I'm driving to the convenience store for cigarettes that I remember that I wanted to leave the apartment in the first place because we can't afford it.

But I'm still angry.

Why am I the one who has to leave?

Why?

★

I go in to work early to work on a zipper on a pair of suit pants for a man named Prozzi. The teeth are rusted and broken. They look like the mouth of a man who hasn't brushed in years.

Before I started working for Palmeyer, I thought a zipper was just a zipper. But it's not. There are all types of zippers. There are polyester zippers that you can use for skirts and pants and dresses of all different fabrics. There are metal zippers, which are stronger than the polyester ones; you can use them for sportswear. There are brass jean zippers, which you use on jeans. There are metal separating zippers, which you can use on jackets. There are plastic separating zippers, which you can use on outdoor wear.

Not only are there all different types of zippers, but there are all different ways to sew them. You can lap them so the fabric conceals the zippers, which is what you have to do if the zipper is not the same color as the fabric. You can center the zipper, which is what you do on women's skirts. You can also do what's called a fly-front zipper, which is what you do on most pants.

It's a lot more complicated than you would think. The same is true of buttonholes. I must know a dozen different ways to make a buttonhole. Overedge buttonholes. One-step buttonholes. Universal attachment buttonholes. Built-in buttonholes. There are more.

When I finish with Prozzi's pants—they need a new metal zipper—I move on to a shirt for a man named Bauer. That's what I'm working on when Debbie arrives. We say hello, then she pours herself a cup of coffee and takes one of the Krispy Kreme doughnuts I brought in. I put the shirt aside, and I tell Debbie all about what happened with Renée. I tell her about how I was living in my own apartment before I met Renée, and how I moved in with her, and about how I paid all the rent after she lost her job at the hospital, and how she wants me to move out.

"Debbie," I say, "why am I the one who has to leave?"

She has two pins tucked between her lips. "What difference does it make?" she says.

And I say, "It's a matter of pride."

And she says, "Well, you need to swallow your pride."

And I say, "If I swallowed my pride, there'd be nothing left of me."

And she says, "That's sad. That's so very, very sad."

And I say, "Thanks."

And she says, "No, that's not the word I was looking for. The word I was looking for was 'pathetic.'"

And I say, "Oh, that makes me feel better," which it doesn't.

And she says, "I don't mean to make you feel bad, but have a little dignity. Act like a man. Move on and be a gentleman about it."

Then Palmeyer says, "Salami, I have an idea that will take your mind off all of this."

And I say, "What's that?"

And he says, "How about doing some WORK," which I do. I fix the tail of a dress shirt for a man named Van Dyke.

It's a fairly simple job. You just turn the edge under about one-fourth of an inch, then stitch near the edge of the fold. Then you hem using a slipstitch or a blindstitch. It takes my mind off things, but only for a couple of minutes. When I'm done with that, I repair the pleats on a pair of dress pants for a man by the name of McGee. That takes my mind off things for a few minutes, too.

After work, I stop by a few apartment complexes to see if I can find one I like. They're all too expensive or, if they're not too expensive, they're in bad neighborhoods.

It takes almost two weeks to find a new place. Two weeks of sleeping on the couch and pretending I don't see Renée when I bump into her in the bathroom or the kitchen or the stairwell, as the case may be.

My new apartment is furnished, which is good because that means I won't have to buy new furniture right away. But I have to give them a security deposit, which I explain to Carl when I drop by his office. This time he doesn't smile, and he doesn't call me "buddy."

He says, "How much do you need?"

I say, "A hundred dollars."

Carl writes the check and hands it to me, and I put it in my pocket without looking at it.

"Listen," he says, "I really need to get back to work."

And I say, "Okay. I understand." Then I say, "You're not angry with me, are you?"

And he says, "Ham, I've got a lot of work to do, okay? I'll talk to you later."

And I say, "But just tell me, are you angry with me for asking to borrow money again?"

And he says, "Ham, just go home."

Then he picks up some papers on his desk and starts reading them.

Now I've lost my girlfriend, I've been thrown out of my apartment, and my brother's upset with me about something.

All in all, it's a bad couple of weeks.

I have a few beers.

I smoke a few cigarettes.

I go home and go to sleep on the couch.

CHAPTER 17: DO YOU LOVE ME YET?

The apartment building where I'm moving is an old one. There's an elevator cage made of iron, flecked with rust. There's a dumbwaiter boarded up. There's an old swimming pool out back with leaves floating on top of the water like milk clouds in a cup of coffee. The apartment itself isn't large, but it's roomy enough, crowded with someone's old attic furniture. The paint is chipping in spots, and below there are two other coats of paint that you can find with your thumbnail. It's clearly been through a lot of tenants, and I have the strange sense that each one left something in it. I can smell a woman cooking dinner. I can hear a child learning the piano. I can see lovers arguing, someone filling the tub, a party, the television, a baby crying, a dog yelping at the door, someone slipping on wet tile.

Two women are sitting on the stoop in front of the building as I carry the first carload of boxes into the apartment. They're heavy women with their hair up in nets, and they speak as if they have stuffy noses. The women lean to the side to let me pass as I carry the boxes from the car, and I rest the boxes on my hip as I press the elevator button.

I return to get another box from the car, and it's then that I spot Guitar Walter lurking on the other side of the street. His shoulders are drawn together to form a U. He looks away, then looks back at me. There's an awkward moment where we both decide whether we should acknowledge each other. Finally, Guitar Walter puts his head down and walks toward the car, and he pulls a box from the trunk and follows me into the building. It's a kind gesture, I realize, only it makes me feel mean and small. He doesn't mention Renée at all.

"I'm thinking of getting a place of my own, too," he says.

I say, "Good. I think you'd enjoy it."

"Yes, that's what my mother says, too."

"She's probably right about that."

"Yes, she's a smart woman. She was on *Wheel of Fortune* once."

We make two more trips from the car to the apartment and back again, and when the last of this load of boxes is in the apartment, I shake Guitar Walter's hand and thank him, then walk to the car.

"You know," he says, "there's nothing going on with me and Renée."

And I say, "I know."

And he says, "I thought it was important to tell you."

And I say, "Thanks."

And he says, "I just figured that since you were moving out —"

And I interrupt him and say, "Thanks."

Renée isn't helping me move at all. When I return to finish packing the last of the boxes, Renée's just sitting in the living room watching television like it's any other Saturday morning. Only it's not any other Saturday morning. The man she was living is moving out. The man she said was her HUSBAND is moving out. And she's sitting on the sofa, eating a banana and watching cartoons.

I keep carrying the boxes through the living room and out to the car, and if Renée even looks up once I don't see it. Eventually, she shuts off the television. I'm packing up one of the last boxes in the bedroom, and now she's in the living room listening to the radio. I'm packing up my socks and underwear, and she's listening to some girl singing about love.

This is my song,
— the girl sings —
It's still very new.
This is my song,
I wrote it for you.

The first verse I wrote
When I was feeling all wrong.
It's a little too silly,
It's a little too long.
The second verse I wrote
At a French restaurant.
I was thinking of you
While I ate a croissant.

And this is the chorus,
The part where you hum,
La di di di di da,
La di di di di dum.
This is the chorus,
The part you can't forget,
So sing it with me,
Do you love me yet?

It's a pretty song. I don't listen to the radio much anymore other than the big band music at work, so I haven't heard the song. I keep packing.

> *This is the next verse,*
> *Which I wrote in the car.*
> *I wonder who you're with now*
> *I wonder where you are.*
> *Does she have pretty hair?*
> *Is it blonde, is it long?*
> *Does she say that she loves you?*
> *Did she write you a song?*

There's a pause for a second, then the girl repeats the last two lines of the song. Only when the song's finished, the radio station doesn't play another song. I keep packing, and a minute or so passes. Still the radio station isn't playing another song. Then the radio station starts playing the SAME song again.

> *This is my song*
> — the girl sings again —
> *And it goes like this:*
> *Verse, verse, chorus,*
> *Verse, chorus.*

It's only then that I realize that it's NOT the radio.
It's RENÉE.
My Renée.

I come to the doorway and watch her, her head leaning forward while she strums her guitar, her eyes closed, the ends of her hair touching the top of the guitar. I watch her, and I feel terrible. I feel like I'm drowning. My chest hurts. I feel like I'm sinking in the middle of the ocean, a thousand miles from the shore. I feel myself go down three times, but I only come up twice.

Finally, I walk out to the living room with a box. I say, "That was a nice song."

Without even looking up from her guitar she says, "Thanks."

And I say, "Really, I mean it."

And she says, "Thanks," again.

And I say, "I didn't know you were still writing songs."

And she says, "I never stopped."

And I say, "Oh."

As I'm carrying one of the last boxes out to the car, I pass Renée in the hallway. Her upper lip disappears when she sees me. She clutches her arms in front of her chest as if she were cold. She's not cold. It's July, and the air conditioner isn't even on.

"Is that everything?" she says, and she nods toward the box I'm holding.

And I say, "Just about. I still have to get my stuff out of the bathroom."

And she says, "Well, okay then. I'm just going to go out and run some errands with Claire." She jingles her car keys.

And I say, "Okay then."

Then we both say, "Bye."

She stops clutching her arms, and I think she's going to hug me good-bye, only she doesn't. Instead, she just walks toward the front door. She's almost there when she turns around and says, "By the way, Ham, I know we weren't married."

And I say, "Really?"

And she says, "Mm-hmm. I was just wishing out loud."

★

I unpack a few of the boxes, then I take the elevator downstairs and go out to the street. I'll finish unpacking later. I'm hungry, but there's no food in the apartment yet, so I walk around looking for a restaurant. I stop at the first one I see, a Japanese restaurant with a neon sign above the door. Even though I don't like Japanese food, I go in. A pretty, black-haired woman greets me at the door. She isn't Japanese, but you have to look closely to tell that. She's wearing a short red kimono and too much makeup, which makes her look like a doll.

"You alone?" she asks.

And I say, "Yes."

And she says, "Well, that can be rough, being single in Atlanta. Actually," she smiles, "that sounds like the name of a horror movie, doesn't it? *Single in Atlanta*. Rated R. Parental discretion advised." She smiles again. "I can joke about it because I'm single, too."

And I say, "Oh."

She leads me to a small table in the back of the restaurant. Moments later, she returns and hands me a menu and fills my water glass. When I glance around the room, I see a couple at a table near the bar that looks familiar. Who are they? Who? They look like they could be the Archaeologies. I'm not sure if it's them or not. I try to picture them sitting in our kitchen, but I'm not sure. I don't remember if they're married or not. The man seems to be enjoying himself, laughing, scooping a piece of sushi into his mouth, chewing, laughing, chewing, laughing, laughing, laughing. The woman seems a little bored.

They probably aren't Archaeologies at all, but why take a chance? I don't need to deal with Guitar Walter AND the

Archaeologies in the same day.

Before they can spot me, I slide out of my chair and leave the restaurant, then walk the sidewalks aimlessly. It gets dark, then darker, and I get tired. I feel a blister growing on my heel. My hunger pains come and go, but I don't enter any other restaurants.

Walking on, I hear the faint sound of music. As I move along, the singing grows louder, and I can recognize it as a woman's voice. In the background, I heard the sound of a roller-rink organ. I keep walking, and when I hear the singing at its strongest, pouring out of one of the houses on the other side of the street, I look up to see a tall, skinny black woman in one of the windows. She's dancing to a song on the radio. The woman smiles in embarrassment when she sees me, but she keeps dancing anyway.

The song ends, and a commercial comes on the radio. I wave to her, and she smiles. Then I walk home. When I reach the building, I'm happy to see that the lights of some of the other apartments are on. I watch television, I read, I rearrange the furniture to cover the stains and holes in the carpeting, then I unpack some more of the boxes. I hang my shirts in the closet. I put some books on the bookshelves. In one of the boxes, I find an envelope addressed to Renée Ashe. It's already been opened. I take the letter out and read it:

> *Dear Mrs. Ashe:*
> *Thank you for sending us your cassette tape. We*
> *had an opportunity to listen to it. Unfortunately, we*
> *did not believe it was of the quality we demand of our*
> *artists at Cowpoke Records. Because you did not*
> *enclose a self-addressed stamped envelope, we will not*
> *be able to return the tape to you.*

We wish you luck.
Sincerely,
Colin Campbell
Vice President, Artist Development

I throw the letter in the trash, then get changed. I put on my chicken shirt and some shorts and go to bed, sleeping on stiff, new sheets, fresh out of the package.

Sometime in the night, I'm awakened from a dream by the sound of voices. They seem to be in the same room, as if someone snuck in to share a secret with me, and my heart beats rapidly. Burglars? Then I realize that they're the voices of people in the apartment below, their voices seeping through the floor and curling around my bed.

"Oh, baby," I hear a man say.

And a woman says, "You are so good, baby. Give it to me. Oh, cook me," only she doesn't say "cook."

And he says, "Oh."

And she says, "Cook me. Cook me. Cook me with your porcupine."

And he says, "Oh, your fishbowl is so tight."

They don't say "porcupine" or "fishbowl."

And she says, "Oh."

And he says, "Oh."

And she says, "Oh, God, this should be illegal."

Then he says, "Oh."

Then she says, "Oh."

And it goes on and on.

"Oh."

"Oh."

"Oh."

"Oh."

"Oh."

"Oh."

I try to block out the noise, first with other thoughts, then with my pillow, but I can't. They're making too much noise.

"Oh, cook me," I hear. "Cook me like you've never cooked anyone before. Cook me like you were cooking for royalty."

The strange thing is that they actually DO say "royalty."

What could that possibly MEAN?

"Oh."

"Oh."

"Oh."

Finally, I pull the telephone off the nightstand and call Renée.

"Sweet Potato," I say. "Sweet Potato, it's me."

"Ham, leave me alone," Renée says.

And I say, "Renée, please."

And she says, "Ham, did you forget that we're not dating anymore?"

And I say, "If I could just kiss you."

And she hangs up.

The ruckus in the downstairs apartment continues.

"Cook me, cook me, cook me."

"I am."

"Then cook me harder, for goshsakes."

With nothing else to do, I lie on my back and close my eyes and think of Renée and moan at the ceiling.

Moan, moan, MOAN.

I'm feeling sorry for myself, but I know I shouldn't.

It's like the boy who kills his parents, then, when he goes

to trial, pleads for mercy because he's an orphan: it's my own fault I'm alone.

I know that.

I KNOW.

CHAPTER 18: WHAT GOD HAS TORN APART

"Have I got the girl for you," Debbie says one morning. It's fall now, and the mornings are dark and brisk and unpleasant. It always looks like it's about to rain. It reminds me of the car wash where I used to work.

I say, "Good morning, Debbie. How are you?"

"Fine. I've got just the girl for you. I wanted to talk to you about my daughter, Angela."

"Your daughter? I didn't know you had a daughter. I thought you just had a son," which is true. She's told me about her son Donald a thousand times. About how he graduated from college and is working for a computer company, and about how he got married to his college girlfriend, and about how they can't have babies because her ovaries are crossed. But she's never mentioned her daughter. Ever.

She says, "No, I have a daughter, Angela. I'm sure I've mentioned her before. She's a beautiful girl. You know, when I was a girl—of course, this was a long, long time ago—when I was a girl, I was beautiful. I had a beautiful smile. It was the kind of smile that would knock you out of your tree. That's what the boys used to say about it, that I'd smile and they'd just stop *dead* in their tracks. You know, you might find this hard to believe, but I even dated the president of our class in high school. Twice we went out. Once to the movies, and once to a dance. He was the most handsome boy I'd ever seen, but God knows what he looks like today. Few things in life stay the same, don't you agree?"

I say, "I don't know about that. Some things get better, some things get worse. I'm sure some things stay the same."

"Well, anyhow, I was never as pretty as Angela. She's a million times prettier than I ever was, and I was pretty. To make a long story short, Angela was dating this boy named Jack Caliban for the past two years, and they just broke up, and she's not seeing anyone at all. A sweet girl like that. So, I was thinking to myself, 'Wouldn't it be nice if she started seeing a nice young man around here.' Then, all of a sudden, it hit me that I should fix you up with her. I mean, I know you and your wife are separated. And I was just thinking that you're such a nice, young man."

"Well, thank you for thinking of me, but we're trying to work things out," which is a lie. I haven't talked to Renée at all. "I'm flattered, though."

And she says, "Well, if things don't work out between you and—" She pauses.

And I say, "Renée."

And she says, "That's right. If things don't work out between you and Renée, I've got the girl for you."

And I say, "Well, we'll see."

She touches my arm lightly, then squeezes my fingers. "She's a terrific girl. You two would be perfect together. You're both so nice. That's what everyone always says about Angela, that she's so nice. We raised her right. And you, well, you seem like such a nice young man, even if you do tease me. So, that's why it all makes sense. That's why it's so *logical*. Nice people should see each other, don't you think? I never liked that Jack much. He was such a know-it-all. I mean, he was very intelligent, but he always had to show you he was intelligent. Not like you. You come across like a nice person."

She releases my fingers.

I say, "Thank you. That's sweet of you to say that."

Debbie isn't listening to me. "Maybe I'll just have Angela stop by some time to say hello. What I'll do is I'll tell her that I need her to pick me up at work. Then you two can meet *naturally* that way, and if anything comes of it, well, so be it."

"So be it," I say, "but I've really got to get back to work. I've got a lot of work to do, and miles to go before I sleep. Or something like that." Then we both go back to work. The radio's playing an Artie Shaw song.

It's very nice of Debbie to try to fix me up with her daughter. It just would be too strange to be dating a girl while you're working with her mother.

But I have to admit that I think about it a few times over the next couple weeks. Angela with the pretty smile. Usually, it's late at night when I'm sitting in my new apartment by myself watching television or reading the newspaper or doing something of that nature. Sometimes it's when the couple downstairs is making a racket, making noises that seep into my bedroom like water leaking.

"Oh, cook me, you madman."

"Oh."

"Oh."

"Cook me, cook me."

"Oh, baby."

"Cook me like you're cooking for royalty."

There it is again: "Cook me like you're cooking for royalty." What could that possibly mean?

It's all I can do not to go down a flight of stairs and pound on the door and say, "What does that mean? What could that possibly MEAN?"

But I don't.

Then I'll think of Angela or the girl at the grocery store or the woman who brought her dress in to have us fix the buttons or the girl I saw jogging on the sidewalk on my way to work.

★

It's only a few weeks later that I receive a telephone call at work, and I have no trouble recognizing the voice. It makes me smile, which I haven't done much of in a while.

"We haven't talked in a long time," she says.

And I say, "That's true. How have you been?"

And she says, "I've missed you."

And I say, "Me, too," which is true.

And she says, "Will you meet me for lunch?"

And I say, "Yes."

And she says, "When are you free?"

And I say, "Any day but December twenty-fifth. I have plans that day."

And she says, "Really?" and laughs a little.

And I say, "Yes. It's someone's birthday," and she laughs a little more.

And she says, "Well, I'd really rather see you sooner than that anyway. How about tomorrow?"

And I say, "Tomorrow's fine."

Then we make plans. I can hardly concentrate on my work the rest of the day, and I can hardly sleep at night. When I wake up, I put on my favorite shirt and favorite pants. The pants feel funny.

They've split open in the seat.

★

I still can't concentrate at work. I sew a hem all wrong and have to take it apart and restitch it. I almost catch my index finger in the bobbin.

I watch the clock.

I watch the clock.

I watch the clock, then leave for lunch far too early. I arrive ten minutes before we're supposed to meet. I'm more than a bit nervous. I take a seat at a table across from the front door, and I order a soda while I wait. The waitress is a young woman, light-haired and thin-hipped with red eyes like a sheep, and I flirt with her for a moment when she returns with my soda.

"The food here must be horrible," I say.

And she says, "Why?"

And I say, "Well, look how thin you are. You're as thin as a rail."

She blushes.

I drink some soda and check my wristwatch. The front door opens, and a pair of businessmen enter. Several minutes later, two women in navy blue business suits enter and walk through the restaurant, finally sitting at a table in the back, near the restrooms. Then, the front door opens again, and, gradually, part by part, a woman appears. Hands, arms, breasts, face, hair.

I rise from my seat. I watch Bobbie Jean as she approaches. She's even prettier than I remembered. Bobbie Jean is wearing high heels, which I've never seen her do before. Her heels click on the tiles like ice cubes rattling in a glass. Suddenly, she stumbles. She puts a hand on a table to balance herself, then pulls off her shoes, letting them dangle from her fingertips.

"Damn heels," she says when she arrives at the table, and she drops the shoes to the floor. "Am I late? I'm always late."

And I say, "No. It's no problem."

Bobbie Jean drapes her coat over an empty chair and takes the seat across from me. She's wearing a red scarf around her neck and large, silver earrings that look like half moons.

"So," I say. "It's good to see you."

And she says, "It's been a while, hasn't it?"

And I say, "Yes. Aren't you working today?"

And she says, "I took the day off. I figure they can do without me for a day. I'm working over at Phipps Plaza."

And I say, "I know. You told me."

And she says, "That's right, that's right. Anyway, I did some shopping this morning, stuff like that. I picked up my vacuum cleaner from the repair shop, then I went to the Department of Motor Vehicles."

And I say, "Bobbie Jean, I don't mean to sound like a know-it-all, but I don't think you have to register your vacuum cleaner with the Department of Motor Vehicle Safety."

She puts her hand on mine. "They're unrelated events, Ham."

The waitress returns to the table with our menus. As we read through them, Bobbie Jean looks over hers and says, "You know, we really shouldn't be here."

I lower my menu to look at her, and I say, "Why, is the food bad? Have you heard bad things about the food?"

And she says, "You know what I mean—we shouldn't be here *together*." She whispers "together" as if it were a dirty word. "I was thinking that on the drive over. People might get the wrong idea."

And I say, "Are we doing something wrong?"

And she says, "No. At least I don't think so. But I know I feel guilty, and normally I only feel guilty if I'm doing something wrong."

And I say, "What are we doing wrong?"

And she says, "Does your girlfriend know we're here?"

And I say, "She's not my girlfriend anymore."

Bobbie Jean smiles a little at the corners of her mouth. "Is that right?"

And I say, "Yes, we broke up a few months ago."

And she says, "Well, you know what they say at weddings—what God has torn apart, let no man put together. Or something like that."

And I say, "I guess so."

And Bobbie Jean smiles and says, "So that's why we're at a romantic restaurant?"

I look around the restaurant and I say, "Bobbie Jean, this place has a salad bar, for godssakes. A place can't have a salad bar *and* be romantic at the same time. Everyone knows that. In fact, I think it's even written in the *Bible*."

And she says, "In the *Bible*?"

And I say, "Well, I know it's written somewhere. Maybe I saw it on the wall in the men's room. In any case, it's true. They're mutually exclusive. If you looked at all the romantic places in the world, you'd find that none have salad bars. Paris—no salad bars. They're outlawed. Anyone caught with a salad bar is tarred and feathered. The same thing in Rome."

And she says, "Are you sure?"

And I say, "Well, they're not tarred and feathered in

Rome. There, I think they're flogged with bamboo rods."

"I don't know," Bobbie Jean says, and she returns her eyes to the menu.

And I say, "Let me ask you this—have you ever seen Fred Astaire waltz Ginger Rogers over by the salad bar? No. Have you ever seen young lovers look at each other longingly as they picked up little tomatoes with those metal tongs? No."

"You know," she says, leaning in toward me, "I hate those sneeze guards that they have at salad bars. You know, those plastic sheets they put above them. It just makes people more comfortable about sneezing around other people's food." She waits a second, then leans forward and says, "You're sure you don't find this romantic, me and you having lunch together?"

And I say, "There's a salad bar, for godssakes."

And she says, "Well, let me ask you this, then."

And I say, "Shoot."

And she says, "Did you tell Palmeyer you were meeting me for lunch? I think he's still mad at me for quitting."

And I say, "No, but I never tell him who I'm having lunch with. Never. Whether it's man or woman, fish or fowl, I never tell him. I could have lunch with the Queen of England and I wouldn't tell him."

And she says, "That wasn't my question. My question was, did you tell Palmeyer you were having lunch with *me*?"

And I say, "No."

And she says, "He's still mad at me, isn't he?"

And I say, "Technically, he's a little mad." Technically, he's VERY mad, although he's gotten better since Debbie started.

And she says, "Well, maybe if he'd paid me a little more."

And I say, "Maybe."

And she says, "Won't Palmeyer be mad if he finds out you had lunch with me? Isn't it a little dangerous?"

And I say, "It can't be dangerous if it has a salad bar."

And Bobbie Jean says, "I thought it couldn't be *romantic* if it has a salad bar."

And I say, "It can't be dangerous, either."

And she says, "And I suppose that's in the Bible, too."

And I say, "Well, maybe if you read it, you'd know," which makes her laugh a little.

Bobbie Jean takes a bite of her roll. The flakes stick to her lip. I take the napkin from my lap and reach across the table to sweep them away.

"Thanks," she says.

I excuse myself and go to the rest room. When I return, I stand behind Bobbie Jean. She twists her head to look up at me.

"Excuse me," I say, "would you like to dance?"

Bobbie Jean looks puzzled. "There's no music."

And I say, "We don't need music." I extend a hand to her. Bobbie Jean lifts the napkin from her lap and sets it down on the table, then slips her long fingers into my palm. I squeeze them a little, then help her to her feet. I place my other hand on her waist, keeping our bodies separated like couples at a church dance, then I push her backward in small circles through the tables to the song that's playing in my head. Bobbie Jean seems to hear the same song. She smells of soap and water and of some simple perfume.

"You know," she says, "I'll bet the two of us are going to be good friends. I can just sense it."

And I say, "Maybe."

And she says, "Even though we have nothing in common."

"That's not true," I say. "We have plenty in common."

And she says, "Like what?"

And I say, "We both sew all day."

And she says, "I know, but what *else* do we have in common?"

And I say, "Yugoslavia."

And she says, "I've never been to Yugoslavia."

And I say, "Me neither. See, that's something we have in common." I pause before saying, "Have you ever been to Italy?"

And she says, "No."

And I say, "See what I mean? Just look how much we have in common. How about Spain?"

And she says, "No."

And I say, "France?"

And she says, "Actually, yes."

And I say, "You've been to France?"

And she says, "Mm-hmm. Right after I graduated from high school."

And I say, "You won't believe this, but I also graduated from high school!"

And she says, "See, there's something else we have in common."

Then I say, "Where else have you been?"

And she whispers, "Why don't you just shut up and dance."

I continue to spin Bobbie Jean around the restaurant. She twirls the way you twirl a flower stem between your fingers. The voices of the other customers surround us, but what they were saying I can't say. They make the noises you imagine are made by people in a blurred photograph. We dance past the cashier's stand, past the restroom and the metal kitchen doors. When we reach the salad bar, I pluck out two small tomatoes, placing one in her mouth, then one in my own. We rock back and forth as we chew, and when Bobbie Jean swallows, I dip her.

"No, the salad bar isn't romantic," Bobbie Jean says, and I say, "See, I told you so."

I lead Bobbie Jean back to our table. The other customers applaud. Bobbie Jean curtsies and says, "Thank you. Thank you all very much. I adore you all," then blows kisses.

"Do you want some dessert?" I ask her at the end of the meal.

And she says, "Of course I want dessert. Wasn't that the reason we went through the formality of eating that other food, to get to the dessert?"

★

That evening, I watch a little television and read the newspaper. I have a hard time falling asleep listening to the couple downstairs cooking and grilling and marinating.

"Oh."

"Oh."

I finally fall asleep thinking about work, about how I have three suits I have to finish by lunchtime. But when I awake the next morning, I'm not thinking about work at all. I'm thinking, *Bobbie Jean, Bobbie Jean, Bobbie Jean.*

CHAPTER 19: MON PRESIDENT, MON AMOUR

Bobbie Jean calls me at work the next day while I'm marking the fabric for a suit for a man by the name of Duguay. I'm marking the cuffs with chalk when the phone rings. I have to leave Duguay standing in front of the mirrors while I go to answer the phone.

"I called to thank you for lunch," Bobbie Jean says.

And I say, "You already thanked me."

And she says, "Actually, I called for another reason."

And I say, "What was that?"

"You know," she says softly, "I had a dream about you last night."

And I say, "Is that so? What was I doing?"

And she says, "Eating chicken."

And I say, "Eating chicken?"

And she says, "Mm-hmm. You were sitting at a table eating chicken."

And I say, "Is that all?"

"No. I think there were mashed potatoes, too."

I smile.

Then she says, "Do you have any plans tonight?"

"Nothing important," which means that I don't have any plans at all. I was just going to go home and watch television, maybe have a beer.

Then she says, "What do you say we go for a drive tonight?"

"Okay."

I can see Palmeyer watching me.

STOP EAVESDROPPING, I write on a ticket.

And he writes, THEN STOP TALKING SO LOUD.

I look at Duguay standing in front of the mirrors. He shifts his weight from one foot to the other. He pushes his jacket sleeve up so I can see him look at his watch.

"Where should we go?" I say.

And she says, "Anywhere we want."

And I say, "Anywhere?"

And she says, "Anywhere," and laughs.

She says good-bye, and I return to marking up Duguay's suit. I think about her the rest of the day.

★

I drive to Bobbie Jean's apartment after work. She's wearing a red sundress. She bounces on her toes when she runs to the car.

"How was your day?" I say.

She says, "Fine. I sewed things. How was yours?"

And I say, "Fine. I sewed things."

"So, where are we going?"

"I thought you wanted to go anywhere."

"Anywhere sounds good. I think it's that way." She points to the right, and I drive that way.

We drive off in this direction, then that. As we do, she tells me a story about a boy she once knew who plays professional football now. We drive past apartment buildings and office buildings. We drive past the building where Carl works. We drive past a high school, past the airport, past an industrial area. Warehouses. Factories. Small metal huts. Not far beyond, the landscape changes, and we reach the plush coun-tryside. The roads narrow. The sky grows black, and the sign for a motel appears over a hill, rising in the air like a balloon.

"There," Bobbie Jean says, interrupting her story.

I say, "What?"

She points out the window and says, "That motel. I think we should stop there."

When I look at her, she doesn't wink exactly, but she does something with her eyes that has the same effect. This is not the way I'd planned things, but then I really hadn't planned them at all. I imagine her in her underwear. I imagine her naked.

"Do you not want to go there?" she says.

And I say, "No, by all means, let's go."

The motel is set among a series of hills as round as plump knees. It's painted the dirty cream color you think of when you think of schools and prisons and government buildings. I park the car beneath the motel sign, which says "Arcola Motor Lodge" in red cursive letters.

"Are you sure you want to do this?" I say.

And she says, "It's either this or go to a movie."

And I say, "There's nothing out that I want to see."

And she says, "Me neither."

We get out of the car and walk toward the office. A light rain falls upon us as we walk. There's no one there, so I call out, "Hello? Hello?"

I can hear the sound of a television in the back room.

"Hello?" I call out loudly. "Is there anyone working here?"

A boy emerges from the room, walking backward, his eyes still on the television. He drags his feet as if it would require too much exertion to lift them. He only turns when he bumps into the counter. He's a round-faced boy, no more than twenty, with long, curly hair, almost as long and almost as curly as Bobbie Jean's.

"Hi," he says. He places a soda can on the counter and digs his hands into his pockets. "Can I help you?"

And I say, "We want a room."

And he says, "For how long?"

And Bobbie Jean says, "Three hours ought to be enough, don't you think, honey?"

And I can feel myself blushing a little.

And the boy says, "That's fine. You've got to pay up first." He pulls a clipboard from beneath the counter.

"Okay," he says, "can I get your name?"

Before I can say anything, Bobbie Jean says, "His name is Eisenhower. Mr. Dwight D. Eisenhower."

Bobbie Jean watches the boy as he completes the form. "It begins with an E," she says, "E-I-S-E-N-H-O-W-E-R."

And the boy says, "Like the junior high school?"

And she says, "Exactly."

This time, she does wink when she looks at me.

The boy says, "That'll be twenty dollars."

I pay him, and he places a key on the counter and returns to the television.

As we walk to the room, I say, "Dwight D. Eisenhower?"

"It was the first thing to come to mind."

"Why didn't you give him our real names?"

"So we could be the first persons in history to give their real names to a motel clerk? I don't think so. Besides, it's more exciting this way."

"So I'm Dwight D. Eisenhower?"

Bobbie Jean arches her eyebrows and says, "Unless you'd

rather I be him."

And I say, "No, that's fine. But if I'm Eisenhower, who does that make you?"

And she says, "Who would you like me to be?"

And I say, "I think his wife's name was Mamie." I remember Palmeyer asking Debbie, "Do you remember Mamie Eisenhower?" And I remember her answer: "Yes, yes. Do you remember Creamsicles?"

Bobbie Jean says, "I don't want to be a Mamie. What a horrible name. What if instead of being your wife, I'm your secretary."

And I say, "Fine."

And she says, "What's my name?"

I say, "How about Jane," because it's the first name that comes into my head.

She frowns a bit. "I don't like Jane. It's too plain."

I say, "You can make up whatever you like."

"How about Blanche? I always wanted to be called Blanche."

"Fine, Blanche," I say, "we're here," and I unlock the door to the room, then stick my head in first as if testing the water. We step inside, me first, and we inspect the room. It's a drab room. There's a double bed, covered with a thin, shiny bedspread. There's a small, chipped bureau, and an old television set with rabbit ear antennas. The smell of stale beer fills the air, mingling with the odor of a thousand cigarettes, and I feel the beginning of an upset stomach.

"It's not exactly the Hilton, is it?" Bobbie Jean says with a shrug.

And I say, "You can say that again."

And she says, "It's not exactly the Hilton," and she

bumps me with her hip, then drops her purse to the floor. "It's okay, though. On the positive side, at least we don't have to worry about getting dirt on the squalor."

I say, "That's true."

And she says, "Anyway, affairs are supposed to be seamy. If they were neat and clean and orderly, only debutantes would have them."

I force a smile and I say, "Affair?"

And she says, "Well, President Eisenhower, I can only assume that your wife doesn't know that you've brought me here. And seeing as there's no typewriter in this room, I don't imagine you've brought me here to take dictation."

I walk to the window and force it open to let some fresh air in. A breeze blows at the curtains. The rain begins to fall in long, silver streaks. Across the street, I can see a giant billboard advertising cigarettes, a man on horseback wearing a bright yellow slicker. Next to that, one for malt liquor.

I leave the window open, then tug at the curtains. They won't close completely—a piece of fabric is caught on the rod above—and I can't jerk it free. A small crack remains. I return to Bobbie Jean, who's balanced on the edge of the bureau. We're several feet apart, listening to the whip and snap of the curtains.

Bobbie Jean bites her lower lip.

How do we start this, I wonder, but no sooner have I completed the thought than Bobbie Jean has her arms around my waist and gives me a shy and passionate kiss.

She pulls away for a second, then says, "I'm going to make you feel *so* good, Mr. President. So good." And then she kisses me again, her mouth unexpectedly large, her tongue slipping into my mouth, over my tongue, then running over my teeth. Her mouth tastes of coffee.

She unbuttons my shirt, slides it off my shoulders, tosses it on the bed, loosens my belt, unfastens the button of my pants, slides my zipper down, slides her hand into my boxer shorts, runs her hand up and down, smiles at me, says, "It's good to see the men are at attention," drops to her knees, licks me, says, "You taste great," smiles at me again, takes me in her mouth, puts her hands on my rear end, pulls me toward her again and again, runs her teeth over me, pulls me toward her again and again until I start to feel a little light-headed, then stands up, squeezes me in her fingers, lowers my pants and shorts to my ankles, pulls them off, pushes me onto the bed, forcing me onto my back, onto the greasy bed-spread that smells of drugstore perfume, releases me, pulls her sundress over her head, unfastens her bra, caresses one small breast, then the other, says, "Don't they look nice," pulls off her underpants, runs her fingers between her legs, closes her eyes, joins me on the bed, runs her fingertips over my thighs, my stomach, my chest, moves on top of me, then says, "I want to cook you hard"—though she doesn't say "cook"—lowers herself onto me, rolls her hips, bounces on my lap, moving loosely as if she were missing some essential bones, says, "Oh, yes, that feels good, Mr. President," bounces again and again, reaches down to move my hands to her breasts, says, "Oh, that feels good," bounces more quickly, says, "Oh, Mr. President. Oh, Ike," bounces, bounces, bounces, moans, bounces, bounces, bounces again and again until drops of sweat ski down her neck and over her breasts and drop onto my stomach, says, "Do it, do it, don't stop, keep cooking," bounces, moves my hands to her buttocks, says, "That feels so good, Mr. President," bounces, bounces,

bounces as the curtains rustle, *sheesh-sheesh-sheesh*, bounces, says, "Oh, Mr. President, you feel so good inside me," bounces more and more violently, bounces, says, "Marinate me," bounces, bounces, says, "Season me," bounces, twists, says, "Bake me. Sautée me with onions. Barbeque me, fry me like an egg, boil me, broil me, grill me," laughs, said, "Mon President, mon amour, don't stop, don't stop," begins to shake, then exhales loudly, her breathing deep, exhales again, says, "That was great," begins bouncing again, more slowly now, says, "Now it's your turn, Mr. President," rolls her hips, bounces slowly, squeezes me, making it clear that she has the power to control my excitement, and, when I'm through, she closes her eyes and continues to sit across my hips. Finally, she falls to the bed beside me and throws her arms over her head, exposing the sugar-white flesh of her armpits. She exhales sharply.

"I think I just saw the face of God," she says.

I smile and say, "You sure it wasn't Santa Claus? They look a lot alike, you know."

She reaches over and scratches my chest with her finger-nails.

Though I'd barely moved, I'm exhausted. I'm surprised, confused, exhilarated. My perspiration is so heavy that it stings my eyes. I listen to the rain on the cheap shingled roof.

"You were so quiet," Bobbie Jean says. Her breathing is still heavy, and she folds her arms beneath her breasts. "I swear you didn't make a noise the whole time."

And I say, "I usually don't."

And she says, "Seems like that would take the fun out of things. I like the noise. I like to talk, you know, provide color commentary when I'm cooking."

And I say, "Well, your language certainly is colorful."

She sits up suddenly and says, "Do you have a problem with that?"

And I say, "No, no. I'm just not used to it."

Bobbie Jean lowers her head to my chest.

"Yeah, well," she says, "Tom was always complaining about my language, saying that I have a foul mouth, that it's not ladylike. If I want someone to grill me, I'll tell them so. If I want to be marinated, I'll say that, too. I'm a take-charge type of person. Does it bother you?"

"No," I say. "It's exciting."

And she says, "Well, I don't like to be quiet. I love sex, don't you? I figure everyone has an obsession, so what better obsession than sex? It feels great."

And I say, "And it whitens your teeth and freshens your breath."

"That, too," she laughs. "What's that expression—man can't live on sex alone? Well, I'm not so sure about that."

Bobbie Jean spreads her fingers on my hip. Her fingers creep toward my groin as slowly as a spider. I close my eyes.

"Now it's your turn to do some work," she says.

And I say, "Okay."

And she says, "Don't forget to call me Blanche."

And I say, "Okay."

And she says, "Okay, who?"

And I say, "Okay, Blanche."

I kiss her and run my hand over her breasts, then along the flat of her stomach, down her hip, and along her solid thighs. She curves like a trout, and I run my hand along the inside of her thigh, then between her legs. I begin to climb between her legs, but she stops me by placing a hand forcefully against my chest.

"Not that way," she says, and she turns over onto her elbows and knees, her hair falling over one shoulder. She looks over the other shoulder. "This way."

I kneel behind her and run my hand over her rear end. I call her Blanche over and over again, which doesn't make me feel as silly as I'd thought it would. On the floor beside the bed, my socks lie like dead black snakes. And beside them are Bobbie Jean's underpants, with a hole on the hip the size of a nickel.

Then something strange happens.

Or something stranger.

When we're done in bed, I start to get dressed. I put on my underwear and my socks. Bobbie Jean sits on the edge of the bed watching me get dressed. Not five minutes after she was using language that would embarrass a dock worker—not five minutes—she suddenly gets up from the bed and says, "I need to go potty," then heads to the bathroom.

She says it in a voice meant to sound like a little girl: "I need to go potty."

CHAPTER 20:

THE PRESIDENT OF THE ROBERT De NIRO FAN CLUB

It happens every time we see each other after that. At some point, she'll say, "I need to go potty."

That, or "I need to tinkle."

Or, "I have to go tee-tee."

She'll say it at the movies or in a bar or in one of our apartments. She'll even say it in a restaurant. We'll be eating dinner, and she'll slide out of her chair and say, "I'll be right back. I need to tinkle."

Who talks like that?

Who says "I need to go potty"?

Who says "I need to tinkle"?

Who says, "I have to go tee-tee"?

Who?

Who?

Everything about her is so strange.

EVERYTHING.

★

There are all different types of hand stitching. Running stitches. Backstitches. Prickstitches. Slipstitches. Catchstitches. Blindstitches. I know how to do them all. I didn't know any of them before I met Palmeyer, but now I do.

I'm stitching a woman's skirt. I'm using a catchstitch.

The way you do it is you work from left to right with the needle pointing to the left. You take a small horizontal stitch in the hem edge. You take another small horizontal stitch in the fabric about one-fourth of an inch from the first stitch, and you cross stitches. Then you alternate stitches in a zigzag pattern. You work the blind catchstitch the same way you work the blindstitch, folding the hem away from you.

Bobbie Jean calls me, and I have to put a piece of tape over the last stitch so it won't come apart while I'm on the phone. Catchstitches don't come apart very often, but you can't be too careful..

"Yes?" I say when I pick up the phone.

"Is this President Eisenhower?" Bobbie Jean says.

And I say, "Bobbie Jean?"

And she says, "Call me Blanche." Then she says, "Are you going to be able to get away tonight?"

And I say, "Maybe later," even though I have enough work to keep me busy until midnight.

Palmeyer taped a list on the wall of people who are waiting for their clothes:

Garrison
Lillie
Barch
Novak
Carkhuff
Mayne
Van Dyke
Gordon
Lloyd
Rhodes
Vaeth

Paltell

Johnson

Sliwinski

The list goes on and on. The ones who have called to complain are circled in red.

"Well, I hope you can get away," Bobbie Jean says, lowering her voice to a whisper. "I've been thinking about you all day. Have you been thinking about me?"

"Mm-hmm." It was true, I had been: *Bobbie Jean, Bobbie Jean, Bobbie Jean.*

And she says, "Yes?"

And I say, "Yes."

And she says, "A lot or a little?"

And I say, "A lot."

And she says, "What have you been thinking?"

"Bobbie Jean," I say, feeling the color rise in my face, "I'm not going to tell you over the telephone."

And she says, "I'll tell you what I'm thinking then. I'm imagining that you're here...and we're kissing...and you're running your tongue over my lips...and you're sticking your tongue in my mouth...and you're kissing my lips and my cheek and my neck...and I'm kissing you on your cheek...and I'm running my tongue in and out of your ear...in and out, in and out...and I'm talking to you in French...and I'm saying, 'Oh, mon president, mon amour'...and I'm running my hands over your back and over your rear end...and you're caressing my breasts...oui, mon amour, oui...and you take off my dress...and you take off my bra...and you run your hands over my breasts...and I take your shirt off...and you kiss my breasts...you kiss them on the sides...and on the tops...and on the bottoms…oui, oui, oui…and then you take one of my doo-das in your mouth…and you nibble on it…and you bite it…and you lick it…and then you take the other doo-da in your mouth…and you bite on it and…. Ham?"

And I say, "Yes?"

And she says, "I'm imagining you biting my doo-da…oh, mon amour…and then you take my underpants off…and then you kiss my shoulders…and my stomach… and my hips…and my thighs…and your hands are squeezing my breasts…and you run your hands along my legs…and along my rear end…and you squeeze my cheeks…and you stick your finger into my sassafrass and move it in and out, in and out…and then you slide up…and you kiss me on the lips…and I spread my legs wide…and I take you in my hands and I guide you inside me…and you move in and out…in and out…in and out…in and out…in and out…faster and faster…faster and faster…harder and harder…faster and faster…and I keep saying, 'Cook me, mon amour, cook me'…and you're going in and out…in and out…in and out…Ham?"

Is this the way normal people act?

Is this the way people talk to each other when they're dating?

Is it?

Again, she says, "Ham?"

I hear myself say, "What?"

And she says, "Ham, do you think we can get together today?"

And I say, "Yes."

And she says, "When?"

And I say, "I don't know."

And she says, "Tell Palmeyer you have an errand to run, then meet me at my apartment."

And I hear myself say, "Okay. Can you get away from work?"

And she says, "I'm not *at* work. I called up and told them that I was sick. I told them it was a 'woman thing,' and they didn't ask any questions."

Within half an hour, I'm following Bobbie Jean into her apartment.

"Are you sure it's okay?" I say. "Are you sure your room-mate won't walk in?"

She has a roommate named Kate.

Bobbie Jean says, "Positive."

I approach her from behind, running my hands over her breasts, then her hips, before snaking a hand between her legs.

"In the bedroom," she says. "Not here. In the bedroom."

She takes my hand, then leads me down the narrow hallway toward the bedroom. The hall smells of air fresh-ener. At the end of the hallway, the bathroom door is ajar, and I twist my hand free from hers, gesture toward the bath-room with a flick of my head, and enter. I close the door behind me and look at the catastrophe that surrounds the basin. An open lipstick tube. Two kinds of deodorant. Per-fume. An uncapped bottle of aspirin. Eye shadow. Three light blue plastic razors. Cotton swabs. A mound of cotton balls. Mouthwash. A bottle of baby oil, a small oil slick around its base. Toothpaste. Three toothbrushes. Bottle caps. An ashtray with half a dozen bronze cigarette butts. An empty panty hose package.

I use the toilet, then turn on the faucet. I root through the mess, looking for a bar of soap. I pick up a green compact case and pop it open: Bobbie Jean's birth control pills. I knock over a bottle of perfume, then set it straight, wiping the spilled perfume into the sink with my palm. Finally, I find a bar of soap beneath the plastic bag of cotton balls. I wash my hands, wiping them on a soiled towel hanging over the shower stall, then walk to the bedroom.

Bobbie Jean has already drawn the drapes, and she's kicking off her shoes when I enter. Again, I hug her from behind.

"I hope you don't mind," I say, wedging my chin in the crook of her neck and locking my fingers together at her waist, "but I had some of those mints you left out in the bathroom."

And she says, "What?"

And I say, "Those mints in the bathroom."

Bobbie Jean lets her head fall back. "What mints?"

And I say, "Those mints in that little green case."

Bobbie Jean breaks free and whirls to face me. "Ham, those aren't mints. Please tell me you didn't eat any of those."

And I say, "I had six or seven. You know, they must've been stale or something, because they didn't have any flavor to them at all."

And she says, "Please tell me you're joking. Those are birth control pills! Do you know what they'd do to a man!" Her eyes are huge, and when she sees that I am joking, she clenches her teeth. "You're going to drive me crazy," she says, then kisses me quickly on the lips.

I say, "By the way, your bathroom."

"What about it?"

"Who cleans it?"

"Oh, clean shmean."

I move to the nightstand. There are magazines there and drinking glasses, but the magazines are dog-eared and old, and the glasses are empty. I turn the radio on. A big band tune jumps out, and I give Bobbie Jean a smile, then turn the dial, moving from station to station until I hear a song I recognize. I snap my fingers and swing my hips.

"You can't leave that station on," Bobbie Jean says.

And I say, "Why?"

And she says, "Because whenever I hear singing, I always want to sing along."

And I say, "Sing all you want."

Bobbie Jean is wearing a baggy sweater. Her breasts are lost in it. I feel for her waist in the folds of the sweater, then kiss her gingerly. I pull the sweater over her head, turning it inside out, then finger the lace of her bra. There's a rip on one of the cups. She begins to sing along to the song on the radio, her voice thin and sour.

I slide the straps of her bra off her freckled shoulders, then unsnap it and let it drop to the floor.

Bobbie Jean sings. She undoes my tie, tugs it through the tunnel of my collar, then lets it fall on top of her sweater.

I run my hands over Bobbie Jean's breasts, spreading my fingers over them.

She sings in my ear. She unbuttons my shirt, then forces my hands off her breasts. I pull my shirt off myself, then my belt and pants. I dip my head to run my mouth over her breasts. They smell of soap.

Bobbie Jean sings.

My hand finds her thigh, working its way up.

Bobbie Jean stops singing for a moment, forgetting the words, then begins again, a faint mustache of perspiration forming on her lip.

I push her onto the bed. The sheets are as cool as lemonade. I unzip her jeans, and she raises her rear end off the bed as I tug her pants down her legs. She lifts her feet, letting them dangle near my chest, and I yank her pants off. Her underpants don't match her bra. They're old and gray. I pull her underpants off and push her legs apart with my knees.

Bobbie Jean sings louder.

She guides me inside her, then puts her hands on my back, and I swing into her. Bobbie Jean stops singing, and the song on the radio changes and is lost in the sounds we're making.

Just, "Oh."

"Oh."

"Oh, God."

"Don't stop."

"Oh."

"Oh, mon president, mon amour."

"Oh."

"Oh."

"Oh, Sweet Potato."

"Call me Blanche."

"Oh, Blanche."

I'd called Bobbie Jean Sweet Potato.

"Oh, mon president."

"Oh, Blanche."

"Oh."

"Oh."

This goes on and on and on. When we're done, I'm exhausted. There's sweat everywhere. My hair, my eyes, my chest, my face.

Bobbie Jean kisses me on the cheek.

Then she goes to tinkle.

We're not always President Eisenhower and his secretary.

Sometime we're the King and Queen of England.

Sometimes I'm an Indian chief and Bobbie Jean's an Indian princess.

Sometimes I'm Babe Ruth and she's Marilyn Monroe.

Sometimes she's Madonna and I'm her makeup artist.

Sometimes I'm a college professor and she's a student who failed her final exam.

Sometimes SHE's a college professor and I'm a student who failed HIS final exam.

Sometimes I'm Robert De Niro and she's the president of the Robert De Niro Fan Club.

Sometimes she's a lonely housewife and I'm the boy who cuts the lawn.

There are others.

But we are never ourselves. NEVER. We're never Ham and Bobbie Jean. It's gotten to the point where I miss hearing my name. I've almost forgotten what it sounds like. I wouldn't even mind hearing it mispronounced.

CHAPTER 21: KISSING SAM

I have dinner at Carl's. I don't bring Bobbie Jean with me. What if she said she had to tinkle? What if she called me President Eisenhower by mistake? What then?

It's a very nice dinner. Chicken and rice, with chocolate mousse for dessert. While we eat, I talk with the boys about baseball and movies and other things I imagine boys their age like to talk about.

"Tell your Uncle Ham about the election," Carl says to Jon, the oldest boy. You can tell Carl's proud of their boys.

Jon gets excited and says, "I got elected vice president of our class."

I say, "That's terrific. Congratulations."

And he says, "The best part is that if Doug Brandy dies, I become president."

I laugh.

Carl and Judy laugh, too, even though you can tell they've already heard their son say this before.

"Tell them about when you ran for president," Carl says to me. "Go ahead, Ham, tell them."

I tell the boys about how I ran for class president, and how I lost to Shellie, and how Shellie's campaign was "HAM IS A PIG!" They don't understand. I have to explain that ham is made from pigs. Even then they don't find it funny.

When we're finished, the boys bring their schoolbooks down to the table to do their homework. I help Judy clear the table. On one of the trips, Judy pulls me aside in the kitchen.

"Can I talk to you for a moment?" she says.

And I say, "Yes."

And she says, "It's about the money."

"The money?"

"It's about the money Carl's been lending you."

"Oh."

"I don't want you to take this the wrong way, Ham, because you're family, but we've got kids we need to take care of. You know, we need to put aside money for college."

And I say, "Of course."

And she says, "You know Carl would never say no to you if you asked for money. So I'm asking you, as a favor, if maybe you could use a little more discretion."

And I say, "Okay."

Judy winces, and she says, "I'm sorry, Ham, I guess that didn't come out right."

"No, it's okay. I just had a rough time with my finances. I promise I'll pay it all back."

"No, no, that's not what I'm saying. I'm not asking you to pay it back. I'm just asking if you could be a little more careful in the future."

"Of course."

She takes my hand and says, "Forget I said anything, Ham. It didn't come out right, so please forget I said anything. Let's go back," which we do.

We walk together into the dining room. Carl and the boys are talking and laughing, sitting at a beautiful cherry table with expensive dishes and silverware and glasses. Judy stands behind him and throws her arms around his neck like a scarf. She kisses the top of his head.

At moments like that, it's easy to be reminded how much better things have turned out for him than for you. It's easy to be reminded of what he has and what you don't: everything.

"Well, you blew your chance," Debbie says when I arrive at work. Palmeyer is on vacation with his wife. They're in Acapulco for a week, so it's only me and Debbie in the shop.

I say, "What chance did I blow?"

Debbie says, "With Angela."

I must give her a puzzled look because she adds, "My daughter."

I say, "Oh."

And she says, "Yes, she met a nice boy named Vincent. Vincent Conigliaro. He works for an insurance company."

"Oh."

And she says, "Are you dating anyone now?"

"No one serious."

I don't want to tell her about Bobbie Jean. I'm afraid if I start, I'll tell her about Bobbie Jean's underwear and about "tinkle" and "potty." I'm afraid I'll tell her about Eisenhower and Madonna and the Ice Capades and the Green Bay Packers.

We go back to work. The radio's playing. Since Palmeyer's gone, I have it set on the classic rock station.

Debbie says, "Ham, do you remember the Beatles?"

And I say, "Yes."

And she says, "I like that song they did." She says "that song" as if the Beatles only had ONE song. But it's sweet the way she says it. It makes me think she was a very good mother.

I say, "Which song?"

And she says, "You know, that one. That one they did about love."

I almost say, "Debbie, EVERY Beatles song was about love," which is true, more or less, but I don't. Instead, I say, "Yes, I remember."

And Debbie says, "Well, it's true what they said."

And I say, "What was that?"

And she says, "Love is a very splendid thing."

And I nod.

The line is, "Love is a many-splendored thing."

And it wasn't the Beatles. I don't know WHO it was, but I know it wasn't the Beatles.

And she says, "It's true. Love is a very splendid thing. I remember when I was engaged to this boy I was dating named Pete. This was many, many years ago, of course. We'd been dating for a year or so, and he had a good job, and in those days that was the person you married. I was working as a secretary in those days, and there was this man at work named Sam. He was a normal-looking man, but he had the most wonderful personality. He could always make me laugh. One day, we went for a drink after work, a whole group of us, nothing indecent, and it got dark so he offered to walk me to the bus stop. Before you knew it, we were kissing, I'm ashamed to say. It wasn't planned, it just happened before either one of us could say anything. There I am, practically engaged, kissing another man, kissing Sam. I put a stop to it, even though I wanted to keep kissing him, and Sam went home. After that, Sam and I would see each other at work, and we'd just look at each other sadly. This went on for weeks, we'd just look at each other, and I realized

I was falling in love with him. He was so different from Pete. I thought about him day and night. Finally, we spoke again, and he was a perfect gentleman. He said, "I just want to apologize, but I would like to see you. I understand that you're dating someone else, and I don't want anyone's feelings to be hurt, but if someone's feelings have to be hurt, I'd rather they be his.'"

And I say, "So you married Sam?"

And she says, "No. I broke things off with Pete, and then I started dating Sam, only things didn't work out. I ended up marrying my husband a few years later. He was more like Sam than Pete. It's funny, but I got a call from Sam many years later. He said he wanted to know how everything had turned out, and I told him everything was fantastic. A terrific husband, a terrific daughter, a terrific son. And he said, 'Then you owe me,' which is true. If he hadn't come along, I would've married Pete, and I would've been miserable."

I think about it for a second before I say, "Debbie, what does this have to do with me?"

She puts her hand on top of mine and says, "Hamilton, dear, I never said it had anything to do with you. I was just telling you a story."

★

Bobbie Jean keeps leaving her underwear at my apartment. One day it's her bra. The next day it's her underpants. Some days it's both. I can't believe she just forgot them. I can't believe that she'll be driving home and all of a sudden she'll think, "Hey, I'm not wearing my bra." Or underpants. Or both, as the case may be.

At first, I keep her underwear for her, then slip it into her purse when she's in another room. But I don't do that with the old ones or the ones with the holes in them like they were attacked by moths. Those I try to fix with a needle and thread. If I can't fix them, I throw them out.

Sometimes, Bobbie Jean will start looking through my drawers and she'll say, "Do you have my underpants?"

And I'll say, "Which ones?"

And she'll say, "The pink ones."

The pink ones were the worst. They looked like they had bulletholes in the back. They look like Mafia hitmen shot her in the rear end with a machine gun, that's how bad they were. Who keeps underwear like that? Who?

And I'll say, "Didn't you take the pink ones home?"

And she'll say, "No, I'm pretty sure I left them here."

And I'll say, "Well, I don't know where they are," which technically is true. I DON'T know where they are. They could be in the town dump. They could be in a garbage truck. They could be in an incinerator somewhere, melting.

"They were my favorites," she'll say.

It's all I can do not to laugh.

Her favorite underwear has holes in the back big enough to stick your finger through. And she's a SEAMSTRESS. It would take her all of two minutes to fix the holes if she wanted to, but she doesn't do it. Instead, she's running all over town in underpants with holes in them.

Except when she's running around in no underpants at all because she left them at my apartment.

She calls me at work one day to ask about them.

"Ham," she says, "have you seen my black-and-white underpants?"

And I say, "No," even though I just saw them the other day as I was stuffing them in the trash can.

And she says, "I know I had them at your place."

And I say, "I don't remember them."

And she says, "Yes, you do," which is true. She was wearing them when she was the President of the Robert De Niro Fan Club.

And I say, "Oh, well. Maybe you'll have to buy a new pair."

And she says, "I guess so. It's such a shame," like someone died.

And I say, "Yes, a shame."

"You know, I had a daydream about you today," she says. "I dreamed you and I were on a plane together and —"

And I say, "Bobbie Jean, please don't do this."

"Ham, it's okay. It's a perfectly normal dream. I dreamed we were on this plane together, and it was dark, and everyone was sleeping. You and I started kissing each other…running our tongues inside each other's mouth…and you started squeezing my breasts…and pinching my nipples through my blouse…and I unzipped your pants and pulled out your sandwich and started running my hand up and down, up and down…and then a stewardess came over and told us we couldn't do that out in the open…so we went to the lavatory, and it was a huge lavatory…and you closed the toilet seat and sat down on it…and I laid down across your lap, face down…and you lifted up my skirt and ran your hand over my sassafrass, going round and round in circles…round and round…round and round…and then you pulled down my underpants and ran your hands over my sassafrass again…round and round…round and round…and then you spread my legs and ran your hand over my eggplant…up and down…up and down…and I kept saying,

'That feels good, that feels good'…and then you ran your hand over my sassafrass again…round and round…round and round…round and round…and then you put your hand on my eggplant again and moved it up and down…up and down…up and down…and then you moved your hand to my sassafrass again, and you spanked me lightly…and then you spanked me again…and I said, 'Spank me, Ham, spank me'…and you spanked me again…I can practically feel it now…and then you helped me to my feet and helped me up on the counter and lifted my skirt…and I spread my legs and said, 'Lick me, Ham, lick my eggplant'…and you started licking me…moving your tongue up and down…up and down…up and down…and then you stuck your tongue inside me and moved it in and out…in and out…in and out…and I kept saying, 'Lick me, Ham, lick my eggplant'…and then you helped me off the counter and turned me around so my sassafrass was toward you, and you lifted up my skirt and ran your hand between my legs…and then you slid up inside me and moved in and out slowly…in and out…in and out…in and out…faster and faster…faster and faster…and I kept saying, 'Cook me, Ham, cook me'…and you kept moving in and out…faster and faster…harder and harder…faster and faster…and I kept saying, 'Cook me, cook me hard'…. Can you feel that, Ham? Wouldn't that be great, Ham?"

"Okay," I say. "Let's get together."

"Great," Bobbie Jean says. "I'll meet you at your apartment at six o'clock."

"Six o'clock," I repeat. And, sure enough, at six o'clock I'm back at my apartment.

Bobbie Jean is waiting on the steps in front of the building.

The first thing she says is, "If you even *try* to spank me, so help me God I'll break your arm off."

★

We spend the entire evening in bed.

We listen to the couple downstairs.

"Oh, baby."

"You're the best cook I've ever had."

"Oh."

"Oh."

"Oh."

"You're a master chef."

"Oh."

"Grill me."

"I am."

"Cook me like you're cooking for royalty."

When the news comes on at eleven o'clock, Bobbie Jean walks to the bathroom.

"Potty time," she says.

I make myself smile.

Bobbie Jean's still going potty when the phone rings, and I use the remote control to turn the volume down on the television set before I pick up the phone. I answer it after the third or fourth ring and say "Hello?" only there's no answer. Again, I say, "Hello?" and I'm just about to hang up when I hear someone say "Hello."

I say, "Hello. Who is this?"

And a young man says, "Hello." His voice is on the verge of cracking. "I'm sorry to be calling you so late, but there's a problem."

Bobbie Jean sticks her head out of the bathroom. "Is it for me?" she asks, and I shrug in response. Bobbie Jean walks back into the bedroom.

"There's a problem?" I say to the man on the phone.

And he says, "Yes. It's just that, well, I don't even know where to start."

And I say, "Calm down, calm down. Just tell me what the problem is."

And he says, "I'm sorry. I didn't mean to do that. It's just that, well, do you know where the Tara Theater is?"

And I say, "Yes, of course." I know exactly where the Tara is: it's right near where Renée and I used to live. It's where we saw *Sleepless in Seattle*.

The man says, "Well, you see, that's where I'm calling from right now. The Tara Movie Theater. You see, I work here, and the last show just let out. So, I went into the theater to clean things up, you know, popcorn boxes and soda cups, and, well, I didn't even notice her at first."

And I hear myself say, "Oh, God." I can't control it, it just comes out of me like a breath, and I put my hand right over my heart. "Who is it? What happened?"

Bobbie Jean covers her mouth for a moment, then removes her fingers to say, "What's the matter?"

I hold up a hand to quiet her.

The man says, "You see, she was just lying there on the floor, and I couldn't wake her up, and I thought she was dead, but she wasn't."

And I say, "Thank God."

And he says, "Yes, you're right about that. Like I said, I thought she was dead, but she wasn't because when I shook her, she sort of let this sound out of her mouth."

And I say, "Thank God. Thank God." My heart begins to calm down some. I catch my breath and say, "You still haven't told me who it is."

Bobbie Jean sits on the bed beside me, and I twist the phone slightly so we can both listen.

The man says, "Well, that's just it. I wish I knew who she was, but I don't. You see, I didn't know what to do when I found her because I'm the only one left here. Everyone else is gone, and I was just supposed to clean up and then shut off the lights and lock up, but then I found her lying on the floor. Maybe I should've called the police or something, but for some reason I decided to check her purse to see if I could find out who she is. You know, maybe there would be something in her purse that would explain why she was lying there on the floor. Like one of those medical cards, or something like that. But there wasn't one of those, and there wasn't even a driver's license in there. All there was was a piece of paper with your telephone number on it."

And I say, "My telephone number?"

Bobbie Jean puts a hand on my forearm lightly.

The man says, "Yes. That's why I called you, because I had your telephone number."

And I say, "Oh my God. Who is it? Who is it?" I'm trying so hard to figure out who it could be that I can't think of anyone at all. "Is it Carol Mosca?" I finally say. Carol Mosca was a girl I knew in grade school.

The man says, "I don't know. I'm sorry, but I don't know." He sounds apologetic, and he seems to be just as scared as I am.

I try to put my thoughts in order. "What does she look like?" I ask.

And he says, "I don't know, I'm not very good at describing people. She's white. She's got long blonde hair. I don't know how tall she is because she's lying down all crooked."

And I say, "How old is she?"

And he says, "I don't know. Twenty-five, thirty maybe."

And I say, "My God, I can't think of who it could be." But then it comes to me: Renée? Maybe she dyed her hair. Maybe it's Renée.

Bobbie Jean puts her hand over the mouthpiece.

"Hang up the phone," she says. "Ham, hang up the phone."

And I say, "What? I can't hang up the phone. There's trouble."

And Bobbie Jean says, "Hang up the phone. It's just kids. They're making a prank phone call. They did the same thing to my friend Amy last week. They're probably drunk and don't have anything better to do. Just hang up the phone."

And I say, "Bobbie Jean, it's a Thursday night. Kids have school tomorrow. It couldn't possibly be kids," but she just says, "Trust me. Hang up the phone."

I say, "Good-bye," into the mouthpiece before hanging up and getting into bed. I can't fall asleep, though; is it Renée? I try counting backwards from one hundred to make myself sleepy. I get to seventy-seven, seventy-six, seventy-five, and then I think about Renée lying on the floor in the movie theater and I forget where I am.

The phone rings again almost an hour later, and even though I'm wide awake I'm still startled. I have to put my hand over my heart again.

"Hello?" I say. "Hello? Hello? Is that you?"

"It's me," the man says. "Where *are* you?"

And I say, "What?" I keep my voice down so I won't wake

Bobbie Jean up, and I cup my hand over the mouthpiece.

The man says, "It's me, from the movies. When you hung up I thought you were coming to get your friend, but then you didn't show, and I started worrying that maybe something happened to you. I started thinking that maybe you were in an accident or something and that maybe I should call the police."

"No," I say, "I'm still here."

And he says, "I don't understand. That doesn't make any sense. Your friend is here, and, well, I just don't understand."

And I say, "She's not my friend. I mean, at least I don't think she is. I don't have any idea who you're talking about."

And he says, "But she had your phone number written down on a piece of paper in her purse. I have the piece of paper right here. I'm looking at it right now."

"Hang up the phone, Ham," Bobbie Jean says. Her voice surprises me, just like the telephone ringing had. "It's just kids. It's probably some boys from the high school who got your number somehow, that's all."

I hang up the phone, but, still I can't sleep at all. I can't close my eyes for more than ten seconds at a time. I just sit upright and fold my arms across my chest, waiting for the phone to ring again, but it doesn't. Several times I think it's about to, I think I hear the faint beginning of a ring, the *brr* of the *brrriiinnggg*, but I'm wrong. Once I even pick up the receiver to see if the phone is still working and hear the dial tone, so I know it isn't the phone.

Finally, I turn and hang my legs over the side of the bed, push my feet into my slippers, and sneak down the hall, my shoulders hunched up, moving as quietly as possible. I take my coat from the closet and pull it on over my shorts. I walk out to the street, and when I start the engine, I close my eyes for a moment and inhale deeply before shifting the car into reverse, then drive slowly, moving in small bursts. When I turn the corner of our street, I allow the car to move for longer stretches before forcing it to a stop.

The streets are mostly empty, and I begin to drive more normally until I reach Piedmont Road. There are a couple of cars on the street, but that only makes me feel more uncomfortable than I already felt: what kind of people would be up and around at this hour of the night? I lock the door on the driver's side by pushing the button down with my elbow. The other side is already locked. I can feel myself sweating in my coat.

I steer the car past the restaurants and the shops. I drive through two red lights because I can't stand waiting, being as close as I am. I imagine Renée on the floor of the movie theater. If she passed out from drinking, I'll take her to the doughnut shop to get some hot black coffee to get the blood circulating in her veins again. If it's something more serious, I'll put her in the back of the car and race to the hospital.

From a distance I can see the movie theater. The marquee lights are turned off, but you can still make out the names of the movies. One movie is *Meet Me in Brazil*, the other is *Every Whisper is A Beat of My Heart*.

I pull the car into the No Parking zone in front of the movie theater and switch off the headlights, then I lean over and look out the passenger's side window and see that the lights in the theater have been turned off. The only light inside is a yellow neon sign that says: "Buttered Popcorn!"

I look up and down the street to make sure it's safe to get out of the car, then check in the rearview mirror. There's no one there, so I step out of the car, locking the door first and clutching my coat closed as if it were winter and chilly out. I walk to the main door and knock against the glass, then look up and down the street again. When no one answers, I knock again, harder this time, then put my hands to the glass and peer in. I prepare myself for someone to appear suddenly on the other side of the glass, or for a hand to touch my shoulder, but neither happens. I can only see the candy counter inside and, off to the side, the restrooms. Next, I walk to the ticket window and look in. Still, nothing.

I walk back to the main door, look in again, then take several steps back.

"Hello?" I call out. I try not to be too loud. "Hello, is anyone there?"

I wait a couple seconds before I say, "I'm here about the girl. Hello? I'm here about the girl," then step backward until I'm standing beside the car. I look up and down the street, at the Original Pancake House across the parking lot, a Thai restaurant, a gas station, then at the theater. The movie poster next to the ticket window is of a man and woman embracing, their eyes closed like nutshells.

"Hello?" I call. "Hello? I'm Ham Ashe. You called me about the girl. Hello? Renée? Hello?"

I climb back into the car and lock the door. I start up the engine and listen to the radio, stretching my neck out every few minutes to see if I can spot anyone in the movie theater. I keep looking in the rearview mirror and the side mirrors, too.

When I finally convince myself that it was just a prank phone call, like Bobbie Jean had said, I shift the car out of park and head back home. When I get home, I pick up the phone and I dial Renée's number. It rings seven or eight times before she answers.

"Hello," she says. It's the voice she uses when she talks in her sleep.

I can't think of anything to say.

"Hello," she says again. "Hello. Hello."

I hang up the phone.

Renée's fine.

I'm embarrassed by how foolish I'd been, driving all the way to the movie theater because of some kids playing a prank.

But what if it HAD been Renée?

What then?

CHAPTER 22:
KEATS, YEATS, BROWNING, FROST AGAIN

I have to break up with Bobbie Jean.

I HAVE to.

I'm not President Eisenhower, and I'm not Robert De Niro, and I'm not a college student who failed his test.

I'm Hamilton Ashe.

I'm Hamilton Ashe, and I'm a normal man. I don't leave work early to go to bed with a girl. I don't say dirty things in bed. I don't date girls who say dirty things in bed. I'm just Hamilton Ashe, that's all I am.

I have to break up with her. I just don't know what I'm going to say.

After work, I drive to Bobbie Jean's apartment to pick her up for dinner. I walk up to her apartment. She's wearing a blue-and-orange sweater with black-and-red pants. She has a blue kerchief in her hair. She looks like something glimpsed through a kaleidoscope. She kisses me on the cheek, then puts a hand on my chest.

"I have a surprise for you," she says. She holds up a finger. "Just have a seat and I'll be right out." She gestures toward the couch in the living room. There's a blue blanket with little yellow suns draped across the back.

I say, "Okay."

And she says, "Read a magazine or something."

She runs back to the bedroom.

I sit on the couch and wait for her to come out. I look at the magazines on her coffee table. They're all fashion magazines. *Glamour. Vogue. Cosmopolitan.* They all have pictures on the cover of girls who look like scarecrows.

I start leafing though one of them. There aren't any articles about sewing. There's an article about how eating two artichokes a day will help you lose weight. Who wants to eat two artichokes a day? There's another article about eye shadow. It's six pages long. That's much too long an article about eye shadow. It's a few minutes before I hear the door open, and when Bobbie Jean comes out she's wearing a cheerleader uniform. A yellow sweater with a blue-and-white skirt, little white socks, saddle shoes. There's a white megaphone sewn onto the sweater with the word "Raiders" stitched on it in script.

"Surprise," she says.

And I say, "Surprise what?"

And she says, "I figured every man's fantasy is to be with a cheerleader."

And I say, "Oh."

And she says, "So, tonight I'm the head cheerleader, and you're the captain of the football team, and my parents are out of town for the weekend."

And I say, "Oh."

And she says, "Come on, play along."

She stands in front of the television, and she starts to do a cheer. She shakes her pompons. She kicks her legs. She does a cheer that goes like this:

Ham, Ham,

He's our man,
If he can't do it,
No one can.
Yeah, HAM!

Then she starts another cheer. It sounds familiar at first:

The other team is dumb,
The other team is smelly,
But we're clean and smart,
Like Percy Bysshe Shelley.

Then she starts clapping rapidly and stomping her feet like there's an army of ants beneath her. She shouts:

Keats, Yeats, Browning, Frost,
The Cadbury Poets have never lost.

I'm confused.

"That was our school cheer," I say.

And she says, "I know."

And I say, "How did you know the words?"

And she says, "I called your brother."

I've never even introduced her to Carl. Carl doesn't even know she EXISTS.

"You called my brother?" I say.

"Yes."

"My brother?"

"Yes." She smiles proudly.

"Carl?"

"Yes."

"Why on earth would you call Carl?"

"To get the words to your high school cheer."

"I wish you hadn't done that," I say. "He's very busy."

She tries to pull me from the couch, but I don't move.

"Come on," she says, "you're not playing along. You're supposed to be the captain of the football team. You're supposed to rip my uniform off, then carry me to my parents' bedroom."

And I say, "I don't want to play, Bobbie Jean."

And she says, "I'm not Bobbie Jean. My name is Sammie Jo, and I'm the head cheerleader, and I'm a complete slut. Just last night I slept with your best friend Skip, the halfback."

And I say, "Bobbie Jean."

And she says, "Sammie Jo."

And I say, "Bobbie Jean."

And she says, "Come on. Isn't this every man's fantasy, to be with a cheerleader?"

And I say, "For your information, I married a cheerleader."

And she says, "Oh, I didn't know that." Then she says, "We could do something else. I could be the editor of the yearbook, and you could be the president of the photography club."

I just stand there motionless for a moment. I think of Shellie, and I think of high school, and I think of how her brother died. I think of working with her at the appliance store, and I think of how we got married, and I think of how I tried to become intelligent so we could have a happy life together, but I failed. Then I think of Renée, and how we met, and how we moved in together, and everything that happened after she lost her job at the hospital.

It's the saddest moment of my life. I'm remembering everything. I'm missing EVERYTHING.

I say, "Listen, Bobbie Jean, you're a very nice girl, but I don't think we should see each other anymore."

I expect her to be disappointed or angry, but she isn't. All she says is, "Okay." She puts the pompons on top of the *Cosmopolitan* magazine.

And I say, "So I'm going to leave now."

And she say, "Okay."

I walk to the door.

And she says, "Ham, are you all right?"

"I'm fine. I've just been having a bad day."

"Something at work?"

I say, "Yes," which isn't true at all. Work is the only place I like to be anymore.

"Do you want to talk about it?

"Not really."

"Okay," she says. "Give me a call if you ever feel like fooling around."

I get back in the car and stop at Fat Matt's Rib Shack for some chicken. I have a few beers and smoke a few cigarettes before heading home. When I get there, I wait for the elevator. A couple waits with me, a thin young woman with an older man. She looks like she hasn't eaten since last week. He's heavy with a thin mustache that sits above a silly mouth. He has a big billboard of a forehead and wormy blue veins on the backs of his hands. They're the silliest looking couple I've seen in hours. They're the silliest looking couple I've seen since me and Bobbie Jean.

I step aside to let them on the elevator before me when it arrives. They smile to thank me. The doors close, and none of us says anything as the elevator rises, rocking a little. They step off on the floor below mine.

"Have a good evening," the woman says to me.

I say, "Thanks."

As the doors close, I hear the man say, "It's a night fit for royalty," in the same voice that seeps through my floor most nights. "Yes, a night fit for royalty."

CHAPTER 23: TELL ME SOMETHING I DON'T KNOW

There's an expression that I heard a long time ago, I don't know where.

It goes like this: Life would be funny if it weren't so sad. Or, Life would be sad if it weren't so funny.

I don't remember which.

But I believe it's true.

After work one Friday, I say good night to Palmeyer and Debbie, then drive to Buckhead, which is an area of town filled with bars and restaurants. I'm tired, but I want to have a few beers, maybe see if I meet someone nice.

I have one beer here, then one beer there. I talk to a few girls. Nothing serious, nothing personal. Just "How are you?" and "What do you do?" and topics of that nature. They're nice girls, but I find myself looking over their shoulders.

I end up on the deck outside a bar called CJ's Landing, where they play live music and sometimes have contests where you can win trips to exotic places. It's crowded, all the young girls in their short skirts and sleeveless blouses, all the young men with their hair combed back and wet like they've just stepped out of the shower. And me in my work clothes, smoking a cigarette.

I push my way through the crowd to the bar.

"Hey!" I yell to the bartender. "Hey!"

Either he doesn't hear me or he ignores me.

"Hey, over here!" I say, but the bartender walks right by me.

That time I KNOW he heard me.

Then I hear a girl behind me say, "Let me give it a try for you." She puts a hand on my waist. I turn, and there's a pretty, brown-haired girl standing there. She has very white teeth like you'd see in a toothpaste commercial or on the cover of a magazine. She's wearing sunglasses even though the sky's starting to get dark. You can see the reddish-orange of the sun setting behind the buildings, like on a postcard.

"Yoo hoo," she says, and she waves at the bartender. "Oh, yoo hoo."

I laugh a little and say, "Yoo hoo? Did you actually say yoo hoo?"

She smiles a little and says, "If it works, it works."

"Does it work?"

"See for yourself."

Sure enough, when I turn around the bartender is standing in front of us.

"I'll have a Budweiser," the girl says. "And he'll have…."

I say, "A Budweiser sounds good," even though I don't really like Budweiser that much. I just say it because it's the first thing that comes out of my mouth.

She says, "Two Budweisers," and holds up two fingers. I check: she's not wearing an engagement ring.

I reach for my wallet, but the girl puts her hand on my wrist. "I'll get this round," she says.

And I say, "Okay, but I'll get the next."

And she says, "Then I'm ordering something really expensive next round."

And I say, "Like what?"

And she shrugs her shoulders and says, "A Mercedes."

And I say, "I thought we were limiting this to drinks."

And she says, "You should have read the contract before you signed it."

The bartender hands us each a bottle of beer, and the girl pays him, then takes a sip.

"What's your name?" she says.

And I say, "Ham. It's short for Hamilton."

I wait for her to make a comment about my name, but she doesn't. Instead, she says, "I'm Anna," and sticks her hand out for me to shake, which I do.

"Pleased to meet you," I say.

And she says, "You won't be after I make you buy me that Mercedes." Then she says, "Quick, let's move," and points toward a table where a couple is just standing up to leave. "Come on," she says, "don't dilly-dally."

I follow Anna as she races through the crowd, and she slips into one of the seats and places her bottle on the table to mark her territory just before another girl reaches the table.

"Sorry," Anna says to her, "but the race goes to the swiftest." Then to me she says, "I ran track in high school. There was no way that girl was going to beat me here."

"But what if someone got in your way?"

"No problem. I ran hurdles."

I sit across from her. She takes off her sunglasses. She has pretty green eyes, the color of grapes.

"So, what do you do?" she says.

Just then the band starts playing behind me, so I have to speak up a bit, but not too much.

"I'm a tailor," I say.

And she says, "What?" and cups a hand around her ear like you'd expect an elderly woman to do.

And I say, "I'm a tailor," a little louder.

And she says, "That sounds like fun." There's a chance she thought I said "sailor."

I say, "It's not bad. How about you. What do you do?"

And she says, "Would you believe it if I told you I'm a top fashion model?"

And I say, "Yes."

And she opens her eyes wide and says, "Really? Well, that's very nice of you to say, Ham."

And I say, "So, are you a model?"

And she says, "I WISH. Work two hours a month and make a million dollars. That's a sweet life. No," she says, "I'm a lawyer."

And I say, "Really? So's my brother."

And she says, "What's his name?"

And I say, "Carl."

And she says, "What's his LAST name, silly?"

And I say, "Ashe."

And her eyes get wide again, and she says, "You're Carl Ashe's brother?"

And I say, "Yes."

And she says, "THE Carl Ashe?"

And I say, "Yes."

And she says, "You're the brother of THE Carl Ashe?"

And I say, "Yes. Do you know him?"

And she says, "Everyone knows him. I've met him a couple times. He's got a great reputation. He's supposed to be one of the best lawyers in town."

And I say, "I didn't know that."

And she says, "It's true. He speaks at a lot of conferences. I heard him give a talk at a conference in Savannah last year." Then she squints a little and says, "I guess you look sort of like him."

And I say, "People say that sometimes." It's the nose.

She makes some movements with her hands like she's tugging at a piece of clay. "I guess if we stretched you out a little bit, and pushed your chin in a little, you'd look just like him."

And I say, "Maybe."

And she says, "Of course, we'd have to make you look pretentious and self-satisfied."

I don't say anything.

And she says, "And we'd have to pull out some of your hair up top."

And I say, "I'd rather we not do that."

And she says, "Aren't you the party pooper, Ham." She takes a sip of her beer, then sets the bottle on the table again. That's when she leans closer and says, "So, what really happened? Give me the dirt. I promise I won't tell anyone."

The band has gotten louder, so I have to speak up again. "What do you mean?" I say.

And she says, "I bought you a beer, so now you have to tell me the truth. Did his wife really leave him because he got his secretary pregnant?"

And I say, "WHAT?"

WHAT?

Anna repeats her question a little louder this time because she thinks I didn't hear her over the noise of the band. But I heard the question just fine. It just took me by surprise.

Judy left Carl?

Carl got Cecily pregnant?

WHAT?

"His wife left him?" I say.

Anna tips her head to one side and says, "You said your brother's Carl Ashe, right?"

And I say, "Right."

And she says, "Carl Ashe, the lawyer?"

And I say, "Yes."

And she says, "I thought his wife left him a month ago."

I don't say anything, then Anna closes her eyes and says, "Uh-oh." She shakes her head side to side.

And I say, "Are you sure about this?"

And she says, "Ham, I'm sorry. I just assumed."

I stand up and say, "I've got to go call my brother," though I don't know what I'm going to say when I reach him.

Carl was cheating on Judy?

With Cecily?

It doesn't make sense.

Anna says, "I'm sorry."

And I say, "It's not your fault. I'll be right back."

I turn around to look for a telephone, looking past the bar, past all the customers, past the band, past their singer, who's holding the microphone in one hand and twirling her cowboy hat with the other.

And who's the girl who's singing?

Renée.

MY Renée.

Life would be funny if it weren't so sad.

Or the other way around.

★

I stand in place for a moment. I couldn't move if I wanted to.

It's the first time I've seen Renée since I moved out of the apartment. It's been months and months and months and months.

Renée looks beautiful. She's lost some weight, and she's smiling. She seems to be composed of sunlight and open air, dancing a little on stage, swinging her hips. There are three men in the band, none of whom look familiar. For a moment, I think one of them is Guitar Walter, but I'm wrong. It's just another thin guy with oily hair.

Renée's wearing a long black skirt and a beige top with thin straps. She's singing a song about the rain. Her eyes are closed.

> *Georgia rain,*
> — she sings —
> *Let it fall upon my face,*
> *Georgia rain,*
> *Wash away my fear and my disgrace,*
> *Georgia rain.*

It's a pretty song. Then Renée opens her eyes, and she sings a little more, but after a few more words she sees me standing there, and her mouth hangs open for a moment, the way it does when someone tells you a surprise, like your brother's wife left him because he got his secretary pregnant. Renée forgets to sing a couple words. Instead, she says, "Um um um."

It's that moment, that instant when we see each other and her mouth falls open, that I realize that she's going to be my wife after all.

"I'll be right back," I mouth to her.

She finds the words and starts singing again, but taps her ear to let me know she can't hear me.

So I mouth, "I'll be right back" again, more slowly this time, and I hold up one finger, though I don't know why. She nods like she understands.

I push my way through the crowd toward the restrooms, figuring that might be where the phone is. I'm right, only there's a girl on the phone, twisting her hair into curlicues. I stand next to her, waiting, waiting. I can see Renée dancing in the distance.

"You said that the last time," the girl says into the receiver.

After a few seconds, she says, "In your dreams you will."

I can hear Renée singing in the background:

For all the things that haunt me
That I just can't explain,
For all the things that tear through me
Faster than a train,
For all the things that keep me up at night
I have just one refrain:
Clean me, Georgia rain.

"I don't want to go to hell," the girl says into the receiver. "Want to know why? Because I'm afraid if I do, they'll make YOU my roommate for time eternal."

There's a pause, and then the girl laughs and says, "I did so think of that myself."

Then she says, "Okay, ten-thirty. Don't be late." Then she hangs up.

I put a quarter in the phone and dial Carl's home. I hope

he answers. I hope the girl's wrong. I hope she's thinking about someone else's brother, about some other lawyer whose name sounds similar to Carl's. Maybe she's confusing Carl with Cecily's boyfriend. Maybe Cecily's boyfriend was married, and maybe HE was cheating on HIS wife.

Only Carl doesn't answer. Judy answers.

"Hi, Judy, it's Ham," I say, trying to sound pleasant.

Judy says, "Ham?"

And I say, "Yes."

And she says, "I can hardly hear you. What's all the noise?"

"I'm at a bar," I say. "How are you?" Renée is standing still now, holding the microphone to her lips. Her shoulders are hunched.

Judy says, "I'm fine. Are you drunk, Ham?"

"No, no, I've only had one beer. Not even the whole thing. How are the kids?"

"They're fine."

"Good, good. I'm glad to hear that." Then, casually, I say, "Listen, Judy, can you put Carl on the phone for a minute?"

There's a pause that grows longer and longer and longer until I know that everything the girl just told me is true, absolutely true. Finally, Judy says, "You're looking for Carl here?"

"Yes."

"Here?"

"Yes."

"Jesus, Ham," she says, "don't tell me he didn't tell you."

"Tell me what?"

"This is incredible. I shouldn't have to tell you this. That's his responsibility."

"Tell me what?"

"Carl doesn't live with us anymore. It's been a couple weeks."

"What happened?"

"It's not my place to tell you. He's your brother."

"What did he do, Judy?"

"He'll tell you."

"Where can I reach him?"

"Why don't you call his secretary," she says.

"Cecily?"

"The one and only."

I can hear Renée singing in the background. She's singing the song about the whisper and the wild horse.

I say, "Judy, are you going to be okay?"

"God knows," she says, "God knows." Then she says, "Ham, I want to apologize to you if I've ever been rude to you or didn't seem as welcoming as I could have been."

And I say, "Judy, you've been great."

"No, Ham, I'm sorry. We should have had you over more, and I should have been kinder to you. Want to know the worst part?"

"I guess."

"For about a year he'd been telling me that *you* were having an affair with Cecily. And like an idiot, I believed him, and I said and thought some horrible things about you. Like it would make sense for you to do something like that, for you to cheat on that sweet girl you were dating, but it was actually my own husband who was doing it. I'm so sorry, Ham. I'm so sorry for the things I said and thought."

And I say, "It's okay, Judy. It really is. I'm going to come by the next day or so to see you and the boys, okay?

"That would be nice."

I say goodbye, then hang up. I head back toward the bar. I have to decide whether to try to find Carl or stay to talk with Renée. I have to decide which is the right thing to do.

I stay to talk with Renée.

★

It's two-thirty in the morning, and Renée and I are sitting at one of the tables on the deck at CJ's Landing. They've herded everyone else out, so it's just me and Renée and the employees, who are sweeping up and wiping off the tables with dirty rags. I'm running my fingers over the back of her hand while we talk.

I tell her about Carl and Judy, and about Carl and Cecily. I tell her everything I know.

"What am I supposed to say to him?" I ask.

And she says, "I have no idea. Whatever pops in your head. Just make sure it's something you can take back later, if you have to. He is your brother, after all."

And I say, "That sounds like good advice."

And she says, "That's what I was shooting for."

We don't talk for a few minutes. We just look at each other. I look into her eyes, not where they're blue, but near the center where they're turning black. I keep running my fingers over the back of her hand, and she closes her eyes.

"That feels nice," she says.

And I say, "Good."

And she says, "Did you know we were playing here tonight?"

"No."

"It's just a coincidence that you showed up?"

"A complete coincidence."

"Either way, it's nice. If you came to see me, it's nice. If it was just luck, luck's nice, too."

"I'm glad you think so."

"I do," she says. Then she says, "Why did you hang up?"

"What?"

"A couple months ago you called me late at night, only you hung up."

"No, I didn't."

She says, "Hay-yum."

I remember the night the boy called and said he'd found a girl in the movie theater. I tell Renée about it, about how I'd been worried about her.

"How did you know it was me who called?" I say.

She shrugs and says, "I don't know, I just could tell."

We sit a few more minutes.

"I thought you had to go talk to Carl," she says.

"I think it can wait until morning."

"Are you sure?"

"I'm sure."

"Okay."

That's when I say, "Listen, Renée, what do you say we grab lunch sometime?"

She smiles and says, "I would love to."

And I say, "How about tomorrow, after I find Carl?"

And she says, "Tomorrow would be perfect."

Then I lean across the table to kiss her on the cheek, a quick little kiss that catches a little of her lips. I'd almost forgotten how soft her skin was.

★

I don't know Cecily's last name, I just know her as Cecily, so I can't look up her number in the phone book. I'm sure Judy would know her name, but I don't want to call her. Why make her feel worse?

I could try calling one of his friends, only I don't know any of his friends. I don't even know if he has any friends.

Even though it's Saturday morning, maybe he's at his office. I call there, but there's no answer.

I drive around town aimlessly for a while, thinking I might see him or his car, but I don't. I drive by his house three or four times, but only Judy's car is in the driveway. Once, I see Judy working in the garden, and I drive by fast so she won't see me.

After a while, I drive downtown to see if Carl's gone to the office after all. The building is open, but the front door to the law firm is closed and locked. I knock, but no one answers.

"Carl," I yell. "Carl Ashe. Come out if you're in there."

Still, there's no answer.

Just as I'm getting ready to leave, a man comes down the hallway carrying a briefcase. It's a man I met once at dinner at Carl's house, only I can't remember his name. Weymer or Wyler or something like that. He's an older man, our father's age, with silver hair and a deep suntan.

He gives me a puzzled look when he sees me. He doesn't remember my name either, which makes me feel better.

"Can I help you?" he says.

And I say, "Yes, I'm Carl Ashe's brother, Ham. I think we met before."

And he says, "Yes, yes. I'm Dave Wyman, Carl's partner." He sticks his hand out, and I shake it. He has a stronger grip than you'd expect.

"Is there something I can help you with?" Wyman says.

I say, "I thought Carl might be here." I don't want to say anything about Cecily. There's no sense causing any trouble if he hasn't already heard..

And he says, "Well, come on in and we'll give it a look."

He unlocks the door, and the two of us walk down the hallway toward Carl's office. There's a smell in the hallway like the interior of an antique desk drawer. When we get to Carl's office, the lights are off.

"Darn it," I say.

And Wyman says, "Sorry."

Only when I turn around, I see a gold nameplate on top of Cecily's computer. It says: CECILY OLSEN.

"It's okay," I say to Wyman. "Thanks for your help. Would you mind if I made a quick phone call?"

"No, by all means go ahead. Why don't you use Carl's office."

Wyman leaves, and I thank him again. I turn on the lights, and I walk into Carl's office. I walk over to his desk and sit in his red leather chair. I sit across from where I usually sit when I'm asking Carl to lend me money. His desk is a mess. There are papers scattered all over the place like there had been a storm.

I dial information, and while I wait for the operator to give me Cecily's number I try to find a clean sheet of paper to write the number on. I can't find any. I open up Carl's top desk drawer and find a small notepad there. I write Cecily's number on the top sheet and tear it off. When I put the notepad back, I see my name written on another sheet of paper. It says:

MONEY LENT TO HAM

$500- rent

$175- miscellaneous

$100- clothing

$100- rent

$100- rent

$75 - miscellaneous

$250- rent

$125- car expenses

$1000- insurance

$250- rent

$100- miscellaneous

$100- gifts

$50 - unknown

$100- miscellaneous

$500- rent

$500- car expenses

$500- miscellaneous

The list goes on and on in Carl's perfect handwriting.

There's only one problem: the numbers are all WRONG.

I only borrowed $1,100 from Carl. I know it. I kept track in my head. The total is $1,100. I don't know where the other numbers came from.

Where?

And it's not as if he knows someone else named Ham.

I dial Cecily's number. I expect her to answer, but she doesn't. Carl answers on the third ring.

"Hello," he says.

And I say, "Carl?"

And he says, "Yes."

And I say, "Carl, it's me."

He breathes heavily into the phone. "How did you know to call me here?" he says.

And I say, "I found out last night."

And he says, "What do you know?"

And I say, "I know I don't owe you a million dollars."

And he says, "What?"

"I know I don't owe you a million dollars."

"What the heck are you talking about?"

"I'm sitting in your office. I came here to see if I could find you, and when I went to get a piece of paper I found a list that says I owe you a million dollars."

And Carl says, "Oh, that. The list in my desk drawer? That list isn't right. You know that."

And I say, "What is it then?"

And he says, "A couple months ago Judy wanted to know where all the money in our checking account went. I couldn't tell her where it really went, so I told her I was lending it to you."

And I say, "Darn it, Carl, she must hate me."

And he says, "Not at all. When I told her I'd lent it to you, she was a little upset, but she got over it. When she found out where it really went, that's when she went through the roof."

"Where did it really go?"

And that's when he says, "Different things. Gifts, restaurants, hotels. You know. The usual."

And I say, "So it's true?"

And he says, "Yes."

And I say, "Are you in love with her?"

And he says, "Who? Judy or Cecily?"

And I say, "Cecily."

And he says, "I don't know."

And I say, "Are you still in love with Judy?"

And he says, "I don't know."

Neither one of us says anything for a while. I pull open Carl's bottom desk drawer and prop my feet up on it as I lean back in his desk chair.

Finally I say, "You told Judy that I was the one having the affair with Cecily?"

And he says, "Yes."

"Why?"

"It just seemed like a good idea at the time."

"Well, it wasn't."

"I know."

"Were you ever going to tell me about this?"

"Eventually."

"Have you told Mom and Dad?"

"It's on my list of things to do." He huffs into the phone.

I say, "This is a pretty rotten thing you're doing to Judy and the kids."

And he says, "Of course it is."

And I say, "I can't believe you're doing this."

And he says, "Ham, please do me a favor. Please don't lecture me. I've gotten lectures from everyone. My partners, Judy, Judy's friends. I don't think I could bear a lecture from my brother at this particular moment."

"Can I lecture you later?"

"Sure. We'll have dinner sometime next week, and we can talk all about it."

"Okay."

"So, how are you doing?"

"Me? I'm great."

"Really?"

"Yes, really. You'll never guess who I'm having lunch with today."

"Shellie?

"No. Don't be an idiot."

"Renée?"

"Yes."

"That's great, Ham. Really great. She's a good girl."

"Tell me something I don't know."

"I'm happy for you."

"If things work out, would you be interested in being my best man?"

"Again?"

"Yes."

"Okay."

Then we both hang up. I lean forward in Carl's chair and push his bottom drawer closed with my foot, and as I do something catches my eye for an instant, like the glimpse of a car in your side-view mirror as it's passing you. At the bottom of the drawer, beneath a stack of documents, I see a little sliver of plastic. I almost didn't see it at all. I push the papers aside, and I see a small, clear plastic cube. Inside, the Ty Cobb baseball.

I'm confused.

Is it a different baseball?

No, it's the same one. I recognize it. I haven't seen it in years, but it's the same one, the one my grandfather gave me.

But how could Carl have the Ty Cobb baseball?

How?

Shellie sold it to a man for a lot of money. For too much money. It was enough money for us to pay the rent for a couple months. There was enough money left over for Shellie to buy a new dress.

I pick up the phone to call Carl back, to ask him how he got the ball, but I figure everything out while the phone is ringing.

When Carl answers, I say, "By the way, I meant to thank you for all the times you lent me money."

And he says, "No problem."

And I say, "No, I don't just mean recently. I mean the times you lent me and Shellie money, too."

And he says, "Think nothing of it."

We say good-bye again. I push the papers back so they cover the plastic cube, then close the bottom desk drawer.

CHAPTER 24: OUR LITTLE ANGEL

Renée likes the movies. I don't like them as much as she does, but I used to go with her anyway. The problem with the movies is that they're all the same. I don't mean they're identical, but they're close enough that they may as well be. Nine times out of ten, you can guess the ending before the movie even starts. For instance, if it's a movie with Sandra Bullock and Hugh Grant in it, you know they're going to end up together in the end. You KNOW it. They may argue a little, or they may pretend they don't like each other, but you know that they'll be kissing at the end of the movie, kissing with their eyes closed while music plays.

Or, if it's a detective movie, or a police movie, you know they'll catch the criminal in the end. You KNOW it. You may not know exactly how they'll do it, but you can probably figure it out pretty quickly if you pay attention. If the criminal plays the piano in the beginning of the movie, then it will be the piano that leads the detectives to him. If he eats Fig Newton cookies, it'll be the cookies. It always is. And if it's one of those movies where you have to figure out WHICH person did it, it is never the obvious one. It's always the one you're not supposed to suspect, the one who appears to be helpful. The one who appears to be nobody.

I can guess every time. Every time I would lean over to

Renée and say, "It's the guy with the curly black hair. Right there! THAT one! The one pretending to be helpful!"

The dramas are more difficult. You can't always predict exactly what's going to happen in them, but you can predict one thing: someone has a deep, dark secret. Maybe he doesn't want to go to the beach with his wife, and finally he'll start crying and tell her that his father drowned in a terrible boating accident. Maybe he doesn't like to fly on planes, and he'll finally say that his father was in the Air Force and got shot down in Vietnam. Maybe he doesn't like to eat hamburgers. Maybe it's because he once had a pet cow. Maybe he doesn't like candy because he got caught shoplifting a chocolate bar.

It's always something like that, which is fine with me. Everyone has a secret like that. Everyone has a secret. But that's why I don't like the movies so much. There's always a scene where someone starts crying and tells someone else about his deep, dark secret. It always happens. But in the real world, you keep the secret to yourself. The darker it is, the more you'll try to keep it to yourself, the more you'll try to keep it from the people you love the most, because they might stop loving you if they knew. You might think about it, but you never tell anyone. Isn't that why they call it a secret in the first place? Isn't it?

But you always know how the movie's going to end. You always know who's going to fall in love. You always know who's going to get caught. You always know who has a secret.

"There's never any surprise," I used to say to Renée.

And she'd say, "So what?"

And I'd say, "There needs to be a surprise."

And sometimes that would be the end of the conversation.

And sometimes she would put her hand on my lap and start to unzip my pants and whisper, "Surprise!"

★

We're going to a little Mexican restaurant called Jalisco's for lunch. Renée picked it out, which is fine with me. I like Mexican food. I like refried beans. I like fajitas, although someone told me they're not really Mexican food.

I take a shower, and then I shave. While I'm putting the shaving cream on my face, I picture the future. I see it clearly, like it's a memory of something that's already happened.

I picture myself sitting in the audience at Eddie's Attic. Renée is on the stage, singing.

At the table next to me, two men are talking.

"Can you please be quiet," I say, "so I can hear the young lady sing?"

And one of the men says to me, "Who is she to you?"

And I say, "She's my wife."

But she isn't my wife.

Yet.

And I picture our rehearsal dinner the night before our wedding. I picture us at a little restaurant on the river called Canoe. It's Renée's favorite because the waiter there once told her she looked young enough to be my daughter. He gave her a free drink.

I picture Renée wearing a loose sundress and a cowboy hat. My parents are there, sitting at the same table as Renée's parents. Carl is there, and so is Judy. They're back together and happy. Their boys are there, too, dressed in little tuxedos. Renée's sisters are there with their boyfriends. Palmeyer and his wife. Debbie and her husband. Guitar Walter. Claire. The Films. The Archaeologies. They're all there.

We're all drinking wine and eating fish. Someone's brought a box of cigars, and the air is blue with smoke. After dinner, people begin to stand up one by one to say nice things about me and Renée. Some of them are funny, some of them are sad, some of them make no sense at all.

Palmeyer says he's going to give me a raise now that I have a family to feed, which is nice of him to say, only I don't know if he means it or if it's a joke. I think he means it because he calls me "Ham," which I've never heard him say before.

Carl says something about when we used to share a bedroom when we were children.

Shellie is there. She says she's sorry she left me.

My mother cries like she's never seen one of her sons get married before, which doesn't make any sense because she's already been to one wedding each for me and Carl.

Renée's father says it's the happiest day in his life, except for the day the Braves won the World Series.

Then Guitar Walter stands up. He's holding a guitar. I think he's going to start playing one of his songs, but he doesn't. Instead, he says, "Ladies and gentlemen, I'd like to make a special request. Renée?" He holds the guitar high in the air.

Renée blushes and shakes her head, no.

"Come on, Renée," Guitar Walter says.

Everyone starts clapping.

"Should I?" Renée says to me.

And I say, "Of course. Get up there." I almost say "Sweet Potato," but I don't. I lean over and kiss her on the cheek.

Renée stands up and walks over to Guitar Walter. Everyone claps even louder. Some people whistle.

Renée takes the guitar from Guitar Walter and sits down.

"Ladies and gentlemen," Guitar Walter says, "for the last time anywhere, we're proud to present Ms. Renée Yates."

Everyone applauds again, and Renée starts plucking the strings. She stops playing and closes her eyes and sniffs.

"Ham got me this guitar," she says, and everyone looks at me and claps like I've done something special, which I didn't. You buy a guitar for your girlfriend if she wants a guitar. You buy her whatever will make her happy.

"So," Renée says, "this song is for Ham."

She purses her lips and blows me a kiss, then starts strumming the guitar again.

After the first few notes, I know what song she's playing.

I know.

I KNOW.

But I don't care, that's how happy I am.

And then I see our wedding day. I picture Renée walking down the aisle, dressed in white, looking like an angel. My angel. I imagine that she's floating down the isle, floating toward me.

The priest asks me if I take her to be my bride, and I smile and say, "Yes."

Then he asks her if she takes me to be her husband, and she smiles and says, "Hay-yum is not a pig."

And I see a honeymoon on some island somewhere, and a baby, and diapers, and a swing set, and school recitals, and a daughter who is smarter than her father but loves him just the same. I see all this and more.

I look in the mirror as I get ready to shave, and through the shaving cream I realize that I'm smiling. I'm smiling like a parade is going past.

I drive to the old apartment to pick Renée up for lunch. I beep the horn, and she descends the stairs, her blonde hair flapping. She's smiling, smiling, smiling.

She waves at me, and I think, *My wife is waving at me.*

She reaches the bottom of the stairwell.

I notice a man descending the stairs behind her. He's tall, taller than me, and very handsome. He must be a new neighbor. He calls out to Renée.

He calls out to my wife.

And my wife stops and turns.

And he says something.

And she says something back.

And he says something else.

And she laughs.

And he takes her hand. He takes my angel's hand.

And she leans toward him like she's being tipped by the wind.

And she kisses him, her chest touching his.

And he smiles.

And they walk to my car, hand in hand.

And my wife waves at me with her free hand.

And she opens the door and says, "Ham, this is Bob. Bob, this is Ham. Old boyfriend, meet new boyfriend, and vice versa."

My wife has a boyfriend.

SURPRISE!

CHAPTER 25:
WHAT WILL BIGMOUTH SAY ABOUT
THE BANANA PUDDING?

It's a Tuesday. It's Cab Calloway's birthday, so the radio station is playing "All Cab, All Day." Only between the commercials and the announcements that they're playing "All Cab, All Day," they only play four or five songs an hour. And they keep repeating the SAME songs. I've already heard "Minnie the Moocher" four times today. I don't need to hear it again.

Palmeyer, Debbie and I are talking about the time Debbie got lost in Stone Mountain, which is pretty difficult to do considering the path is straight up and straight down, when Minnifield comes in. He's the guy who had us alter a suit for him on short notice by pretending he was going to a wedding. I'm sure he doesn't remember that, but I do, and I'll bet Palmeyer does, too.

"Hey, boys," Minnifield says. He has a suit jacket folded over his arm.

And Palmeyer says, "Hello there, Mr. Minnifield. Haven't seen you around here in a while."

And Minnifield says, "No. I haven't been here in a while."

Minnifield nods toward me, and I nod back, then I return to my machine.

"Last time you were here," Palmeyer says, "I think we were altering a suit for you for your nephew's wedding."

And Minnifield says, "What?"

And Palmeyer says, "Weren't we altering a suit for you for your nephew's wedding?"

And Minnifield touches his temple and says, "You know, I believe you're right. It was for my nephew's wedding."

The liar. He told us it was for his NIECE's wedding.

And Palmeyer says, "What was the bride's name again? It was Anna, wasn't it?"

And Minnifield says, "Yes, that's right, that's right. You have a good memory."

Liar, liar, LIAR. He never told us the bride's name. Besides, the bride supposedly was his niece.

"Anyway," Minnifield says, "I've got a bit of a problem I hope you can fix." He places the suit jacket flat on the counter and points to a black circle on the right sleeve. He didn't have to point, you could see it from where I was sitting.

"I got a little careless," he says, "when I was smoking."

Palmeyer lifts up the sleeve and brings it close to his face.

"Minnie the Moocher" comes on the radio. AGAIN.

Palmeyer turns the sleeve inside-out, then folds it back again, staring at the black circle like a surgeon examining an X-ray.

"It's a tough job," Palmeyer says, "but my boy Salami here can fix it."

Me?

Why me?

As if I'm not busy enough as it is. As if I don't already have a stack of clothes to alter.

He hands the jacket to me. I run my thumb over the black circle. There is a tough, thick crust surrounding it. It'll be difficult to repair, even worse than a tear. At least with a tear, you can reweave the fabric. This, I could try a patch, but the patch might show if the material is not identical. More likely, I'll have to remove the sleeve entirely and try to shift the material so the burn will be hidden behind a seam. It'd be easier to build a new jacket from scratch.

Cigarette burns are the worst.

I hate the cigarette burns.

And every time we get a jacket or a pair of pants with a cigarette burn, every single time, I end up thinking about what happened in Cadbury, Georgia. About what Victor Smalls did. About body parts only a doctor could imagine. About that boy's hand with the cigarette burn in him. About how Victor Smalls did not smoke. About how people speculated that he might have had an accomplice. An accomplice who smoked. I know that sounds ridiculous, like a flashback from a movie where someone keeps remembering the time he almost drowned, but it's true. It happens every single time. Usually, I'll see the cigarette burn and I'll say to myself, *It's just a piece of clothing. Don't let yourself think about that other stuff.* But then I'm trying so hard not to think about the other stuff that I end up thinking about it even more.

I hate working on the cigarette burns.

I HATE it.

★

Palmeyer tells Minnifield that it'll be a week before we can get his jacket back.

"Any chance I can get it earlier?" he says.

And Palmeyer says, "What, another wedding?"

Minnifield thinks for a second, but finally says, "No, no, a week will be fine," then leaves.

When he's gone, I say, "That guy's such a liar, Palmeyer."

And he says, "I know, I know. But he pays for the work we do."

And Debbie says, "What did he lie about?"

And I say, "He told us a big fat lie about needing a suit for a wedding, so we had to rush to get it done even though we were backed up."

And she says, "His nephew's wedding?"

And before I can say anything, Palmeyer says, "Last time, he said it was his niece's wedding."

And I say, "The guy is a big fat liar."

And Palmeyer says, "Regardless," and tries to hand me the coat, only I don't take it.

I say, "Come on, Palmeyer, can't you do it?"

And he says, "I'm too backed up."

And I say, "Well, I'm backed up too, look, look." I point toward a rack full of clothes, then to two piles of clothes.

And he says, "I want you to do it. You'll do a better job on it than I would."

I ignore his compliment, even though it may be the first one he's ever given me, and I say, "Listen to me. I don't want to do it. I don't want to fix that big fat liar's goshdarn jacket. Goshdarn this place. Goshdarn this whole friggin' place."

No one says anything. Debbie and Palmeyer both stare at me.

Finally, Debbie says to Palmeyer, "Do you mind if Ham and I talk outside for a minute?"

Palmeyer doesn't say anything. He doesn't move at all.

Debbie and I walk outside, and we stand on the sidewalk.

"What's the matter, honey? she says. She's never called me honey before.

And I say, "Nothing."

And she says, "You can tell me."

And I say, "Nothing. Really. I'm sorry I swore."

And she says, "It's okay to swear. I'm a big girl. I've heard it all before. Frankly, I think people should swear more often. It's a good way to release some of your emotions."

And I say, "Really?"

And she says, "Fuck, yes."

And I laugh a little.

And she says, "What's the matter?"

I almost tell her everything. I almost tell her everything about Shellie. I almost tell her everything about Renée. Instead, I say, "I hate working on the goddam cigarette burns. I hate the GODDAM, MOTHERFUCKING, COCK-SUCKING, SON-OF-A-BITCH CIGARETTE BURNS."

She puts her arm around my shoulder and says, "It's okay, honey. I'll work on the cigarette burn. I'll take care of it."

And, into her shoulder, I say, "Goddam motherfucking cigarette burns."

And she says, "Yes, yes, I know. They are motherfuckers, aren't they?"

And I say, "Yes."

And she says, "Goddam, bitch, ass-licking mother-fuckers."

And I say, "Yes, yes."

★

What do I think about sometimes? What do I think about when I'm working on cigarette burns? I think about how thin the walls of our home were when we lived in Cadbury.

They were so thin that I could hear something my mother was saying on the phone, and she was downstairs in the kitchen, and I was up in my bedroom, and my door was closed and locked.

"Oh," she was saying. "Oh, my. Yes. I understand that. I agree that tests are very important."

You could hear everything that went on in that house. Everything, even if you weren't trying. Talking. The television. The dishwasher. Mrs. Cantor, when she came to visit my mother. Clementine. That was our dog. Everything, every little noise, floated around in that house.

Sometimes, in our bedroom—we shared one, Carl and me—one of us would sneeze, and someone would say, "Bless you," from the den or the kitchen or, once, from the garage even. From the *garage,* that's how thin the walls were.

"No, we haven't been to a doctor yet," she said. "It hasn't seemed to be that severe. Nagging is the word I'd use to describe it. A nagging condition." She's talking to someone at the high school, probably the principal's secretary. I can tell.

"He's upstairs in bed right now. Sleeping like a baby. I really couldn't say when he'll be feeling up to it."

They wanted to know why I hadn't been in school all week is what they wanted to know. My mother was trying to explain. She isn't really sure why herself. She keeps asking me, "Is it your head? Your stomach? Is it your chest?" "It's everything," I kept telling her. It's everything all put together.

"Yes, yes," she said to the secretary. "That would be good. That would be very good."

It sounded like they were talking about sending my homework home. I didn't want to listen. Homework was the last thing on my mind. I'd think of the ballet before I'd think of homework.

I turned the clock radio on and then sandwiched my head between my pillows until my mother's voice sounded like a car engine revving. It stuttered and started, like it's winter outside.

So, why hadn't I been to school all week? Bigmouth, that's why. Thomas was his given name, but everyone called him Bigmouth. That was because he was one of those guys who always had to raise his hand in class and give the teacher the right answer. Always, it was, "Who knows the answer to this problem? Yes, Thomas?" Or "Who would like to go to the blackboard for this one? Thank you, Thomas." It was not so much that it made the rest of us look dumb, it was just, why did he DO it? Why did he have to be such a bigmouth? He wouldn't have been half bad otherwise. Even the girls called him Bigmouth, though.

My mother was off the phone. No more of the car engine, and I took the pillows off my head and lay there, listening to myself breathe, in and out, and to the radio. I couldn't make myself breathe in time to the songs. In and out, in and out, in three-four time. I played the trombone in fifth-grade band, so I knew a thing or two about music and keeping time. I quit so I could play soccer.

"Ham, are you okay?"

It was my mother. She tapped her fingernails against my door, and I couldn't decide whether to pretend I was asleep. I didn't feel much like talking to anyone.

"Ham, sweetie?"

And I said, "What?"because I couldn't have been asleep, or else how did the bedroom door get locked?

And she said, "I asked if you're okay."

And I said, "I guess so." There was no inflection in my voice. Nothing. It was just dull and flat, but not sickly, and that was the way I should have sounded. If I sounded sick, then I would have had to see the doctor.

And she said, "That was Mrs. Agee on the phone, from up at the high school. She's going to send some work back with Robbie Sincore this afternoon. She says you've already missed a quiz in U.S. history. She says it was on the Battle of Bull Run or some other such thing."

And I said, "Bull Run was right. It was in the Civil War." We had started on the Civil War three weeks ago.

And she said, "She says you can make up the quiz when you get back. You can make it up after school one afternoon."

And I said, "Okay."

And she said, "Or you can do it during your free period. I told her you've got soccer practice, so she said you could take it during your free period instead. Whichever you like. And there's a quiz in Mr. Lair's class tomorrow."

And I said, "He has one every Friday."

And she said, "Oh, my. Every Friday, is that right? My, well, just as long as you know."

I listened to my mother move down the hall and into her bedroom. I heard her turn the television on to some game show. I knew it was a game show. I could hear the host, and I could hear the audience going wild, screaming, and I swear that I could just about hear all the lights, they were so loud. She was making the bed, probably, and watching a game show at the same time. You don't need to concentrate much when you're making the bed.

Next, I listened to the man on the radio, the DJ. He told

a joke about a lady who eats too much. She eats so much that she can't get into her car, and someone else tells her to hang the license plate around her neck. That was not the end of the joke, but it may as well have been. It was a dumb joke.

I listened to myself breathe. In and out, in and out.

I wanted to apologize, but what would people think if I apologized to Bigmouth? They'd think I was crazy is what they'd think. That, or they'd think I was kidding around.

I listened. This was what the world sounded like when I was in school. A commercial. The vacuum. The telephone ringing. The DJ. A song I don't like. In and out, in and out. The washing machine. Clementine in the backyard, pulling against her chain. My mother talking on the phone to one of her friends, something about a picnic. A lady won a dining room set. A song. In and out, in and out. A bathroom faucet. "Just like Mama used to make."

It was me speaking, only it sounded like someone else. It *felt* like someone else. Usually, I didn't hear what I said because I was too busy saying it to listen, but this I heard like it was someone else, someone with a deeper voice standing beside my bed or beneath it or somewhere else close by. Carl's bureau, maybe. I was remembering, is what I was doing. It was because of the song on the radio. It was a slow song, slow with a lot of pianos, and the signer was singing about he lost his girlfriend. It was music to remember by. That was what my mother calls music like that. Sometimes she would stop doing whatever she was doing and half-close her eyes, like a cat, listening. "Oh, Ham," she would say to me, "I just remembered something sad." That's what I was doing: remembering.

When I heard my mother turn the shower on, I climbed

out of my bed and flicked the lights on and stood in front of the mirror in my gym shorts, nothing else. No shirt. I needed to do sit-ups is what I needed to do. My stomach was getting fat. I flexed my muscles like the men in the Mr. Universe contest and held my breath. Why was I doing this? To make myself laugh, only I didn't. I just looked silly standing there is all.

When I was done with that, I let my breath out and went back to the nightstand. I turned the radio up louder, then went back to the mirror and danced in front of it. I tried to dance like the dancers on *American Bandstand*, kicking my legs up, swirling my head around and around, rubbing my hands all over my chest, the whole time making a face like I just drank a whole glass of grapefruit juice. It didn't work. I was still not laughing, and I shut the radio off, pulled on a T-shirt, the one that said CADBURY HIGH SCHOOL on the front, turned off the lights, and headed downstairs.

The kitchen was clean and all the chairs were pushed in at the table. My mother had already put away everything that she and my father and Carl had for breakfast, which meant that I had to cook for myself. I would have to clean up afterwards too.

I usually did not eat breakfast, but what else was I going to do? That was what I was doing all week—eating—and most of the time I wasn't even hungry. It was just something to do to pass the time. Tuesday, I ate an entire chocolate cake, one of those in the boxes that you bought at the supermarket. Not in one sitting. Spread out over the whole day. But it's the same number of calories regardless of whether you ate it in one sitting or spread it out.

I cracked a couple of eggs into a coffee mug and mixed them up with a spoon. I was not very good at cracking eggs, and little white pieces of shell fell in, but I left them. I just stirred them in until I couldn't see them anymore.

After I beat the eggs, I melted some margarine in a pan and poured the eggs in, then scrambled them like my mother did, adding a little sugar and a little pepper, making plenty of noise. I forgot to put some bread in the toaster, so I ate the eggs by themselves, which was probably good for me calories-wise. I drank a glass of soda, too. It made my stomach tingle, and I thought of someone at school who said you can clean pennies with soda. I don't remember who.

It's not until I put everything in the sink and started working on the frying pan with an SOS pad that I looked at the clock, and I was surprised to see that it was already eleven. At school, it was almost lunchtime. We ate early. Fourth period. Biology got out in fifteen minutes, and then it was lunch, then gym, which was no treat right after lunch.

Eleven also meant that my father was going to call soon, in half an hour maybe. I knew it. It was the same time he had called every day that week, just before he left the office to eat, and I knew he was going to ask me the same questions he had asked every day that week. He was going to ask me how I was feeling. He was going to ask me If I needed anything. He was going to ask me if I wanted to tell him what was the matter. Tuesday, I almost told him about Bigmouth. I almost said, "There's this guy in my class with the name of Thomas," but I had a piece of cake instead. I almost told him, though, and I almost told Carl once, too, but he wouldn't understand. He was too young.

I took all of the clean dishes and silverware and glasses out of the dishwasher and put them away in the cabinets and drawers, then I put my things in. I walked into the den and turned on the television, then lay down on the carpet in front of it. There was a soap opera on, the one I had been watching all week. I didn't usually watch soap operas, I was usually in school, but this was a good one. It was the one with Bob and Cheryl in it. Bob was a lawyer, and I had not figured out exactly what Cheryl did. They were trying to find the baby that Cheryl put up for adoption when she was eighteen or nineteen.

"He's there. Somewhere in the world, he's out there," Cheryl said. She was looking out an enormous window into the woods behind their house. We had a window just like that that looked out onto the street.

And Bob said, "I know, I know," and he put his arms around her shoulder. "And somehow we'll find him."

And Cheryl said, "But who knows where he could be. He could be in New York or Ohio or London."

And Bob said, "Or even right here in Springport."

The music gets louder. Dum-da-da-dum-dum-dum, only they can't hear it. The boy's right there in Springport. I knew it. I could feel it. It was probably the boy who raked their leaves. He was on the show yesterday, raking.

"But where do we start, Bob?" Cheryl said.

And he said, "We start at the hospital, that's where. We have to find the hospital records and talk to the doctors."

The phone rang. Our phone.

"Hi," my mother said. "Fine, fine. Nothing new, just the usual, cleaning."

"But the hospital's not there anymore."

"What?"

"It's not there anymore."

"Mm-hmm. He's still in his bedroom. He says he's all

right."

"It closed ten years ago."

"But someone must still have the records. Do you remember the doctor's name?"

Cheryl looked puzzled, and her eyes got as big as a spaniel's. That's what Clementine was, a spaniel.

"Oh, God, Bob, I can't think of it!"

"Stay calm, stay calm. There's no hurry. It'll come to you."

"Well, why don't you talk to him? He doesn't say much to me."

I heard my mother walk down the hall to my room. She knocked on my door, opened it, closed it, then headed back down the hallway and stopped at the top of the staircase.

"Ham? Ham, are you downstairs?" she said.

And I said, "Yeah."

And she said, "Ham, your father's on the phone. He wants to talk to you."

And I said, "Okay, I'll pick it up down here."

I walked into the kitchen and took the phone from the wall.

"I've got it, Mom," I called up to her, and I waited for her to hang up before speaking, as if I had a secret to keep from her. I did, about Bigmouth, but even if I had told my father about it, she would hear it through the floor.

"How's my big boy feeling?" my father said.

And I said, "Okay. A little tired, but okay. I guess."

I looked into the den. Cheryl was looking out the window.

And my father said, "Okay? Are you still sick? Are you feeling feverish?"

And I said, "A little feverish, I guess." I remembered what my mother said. "It's a nagging condition," I told him.

And I said, "Well, is there anything you need?"

"No, not really. Maybe the new *Playboy*," I said, trying to be funny, only he didn't get it. He didn't laugh, and I didn't either. Some days you can't make yourself laugh no matter how hard you try.

And he said, "Do you want to talk about it?"

And I said, "About what?"

And he said, "Ham, I know you're not sick. Or if you are sick, you're not very sick. I know something's the matter. You can tell me. I'm your father. We're pals."

And I said, "I know. Nothing's the matter, though."

And he said, "Are you having problems with your classes? Is it your grades? Are you worrying too much about the grades?"

And I said, "No."

And he said, "Soccer then? Are you having trouble with the coach? I'd be happy to go talk to him if you're having trouble, Ham."

And I said, "No, Dad. Really, nothing's the matter."

And he said, "Really?"

And I said, "Really."

My eyes hurt. I wanted to tell someone about Bigmouth and about how Bigmouth's mother packed him sandwiches and a thermos full of homemade banana pudding for lunch. I wanted to tell someone about how Wiper sat on Bigmouth's stomach in the locker room while Everett and I held his arms down, how Wiper thumped his thumbnail against Bigmouth's chest—the Chinese Torture Test—until he said, "Scott Wiper is the greatest guy in the world," and how everything went crazy all of a sudden, how Henshaw pulled a banana out of his lunch bag, how he crushed it in his hands and said, "Just like Mama used to make," how Bigmouth clenched his teeth and twisted his head back and forth so Everett and Henshaw couldn't pry his mouth open at first, how he said, "Don't," while Henshaw smeared the banana on his cheeks and lips, how I couldn't stop because what would Everett and Wiper and Henshaw think of me, how everyone laughed, how Wiper said, "Damn right, Scott Wiper's the greatest guy in the world" before he asked me for one of my cigarettes and lit it and burned a dozen holes in Bigmouth's pants, then pressed the cigarette into Bigmouth's palm until Bigmouth was screaming, how Wiper finally got off him, how Bigmouth got undressed at his locker, his face all red and moist, how I sat on a rock out in the middle of the woods all through gym and geometry and English and soccer practice, thinking, "What will Bigmouth say about the banana pudding," and how I didn't walk home until dark, how I can't go to school, how I'm eating and eating.

I couldn't tell my father any of this. If I told anyone, it would've been him, but I couldn't tell him. When he was a boy, when he was my age, he was the kind of guy who studied all the time and wrote poems and things like that. He was like Bigmouth, he wasn't like me at all. Once, when I was little, he told me about the time he went to a dance at school and some guy came up to shake hands, only the guy punched him in the gut instead. My father was the kind of guy who had people sit on his chest and give him the Chinese Torture Test, not the kind who *gave* it.

"Are you sure you're okay?" my father said.

And I said, "Sure." I couldn't say anything else. If I even

mentioned Bigmouth, if I started to tell him anything, I'd end up telling him everything. He'd hate me. I listened to myself breathe. In, in, in, in, in, in.

And he said, "We'll talk when I get home then. I'll bring you a present to cheer you up. A surprise."

And I said, "Okay."

I hung up the phone and went back to the television. Bob was holding Cheryl. His arms were wrapped around her waist. I shut my eyes.

"I never should have done it," she said.

And Bob said, "Never should have done what?"

And she said, "I never should have given the baby up. I should have kept him. He's a part of me, my own flesh and blood."

And Bob said, "But you were so young then, and alone. You couldn't have given him the home he deserved."

And Cheryl said, "I'm his mother." She was crying. Her head bounced against his chest. "His *mother*. A child only has one mother."

Again, there was music, then a commercial. I walked back into the kitchen and pulled a carton of ice cream out of the freezer. Chocolate. I made a sundae with whipped cream and Bosco and cherries and nuts. The works, the way I liked them. I sat at the kitchen table, eating, listening to my mother's footsteps in the bedroom, hoping that Bob and Cheryl find the boy soon, before I have to go back to school. Check out in the yard, I wanted to tell them. It's the kid who's raking the yard. Right outside your window.

★

Two days later, Bigmouth went to the store to buy a new pair of pants to replace the ones that had been ruined.

Two days after that, they found his body in the bay. Actually, parts of his body.

And on his right hand, they found a fresh cigarette burn, like a little crater on the moon.

A few years after that, I married his twin sister.

CHAPTER 26: YOU ARE HAMILTON ASHE

You be me for a minute or a day.

You see how it feels.

Go ahead. Try it.

You are Hamilton Ashe.

You are thirty-six years old.

You are divorced.

Your girlfriend left you.

You are the kind of person who hates TV shows or movies where it's revealed that a character has some horrible secret in his past, yet you have a secret in YOUR past, a horrible, terrible secret.

You set off a series of events that resulted in a boy being murdered, a boy who wanted to be an astronaut and a professional football player and a private detective.

You are an accomplice in that boy's murder. Maybe not legally speaking, but in every other way.

You meet the boy's sister, and you think that somehow you're going to make her happy again, that you can take away all the sadness you created.

You marry her.

You marry the one person in the world you can never tell your secret to. NEVER. Because if you tell her, she'll hate you.

You tell her she's wrong every time she says, "Ham, something's bothering you. I can tell. Please tell me what's bothering you."

You tell her you have nothing to say when she says, "Ham, we never talk. You never tell me what you're thinking." Because what you're thinking about is the very thing you can never tell her about.

You make her unhappy, and you rearrange your memories of her just a little bit so you can pretend she was cruel or demanding or unappreciative. You tell people a story about how she made you sell an autographed baseball your grandfather once gave you, and every time you tell it you tell it a little worse, to make yourself feel a little better. Only when you have a few beers, or when you're sleepy, you remember the truth, you remember that she was beautiful and kind and sweet, and that she made you laugh. You remember that she loved you. Which only makes you feel worse.

You know you need to tell someone about what you did, just so you can say it out loud, just so someone—ANYONE—can tell you, "It's all right, Ham. You weren't an accomplice. You didn't kill anyone." Only you won't see a psychiatrist because you know you're not crazy. So you see women instead. One after another, and they stroke your hair and rub your chest in bed and tell you everything will be okay, but they don't know WHAT it is that needs to be okay.

You meet a woman in a bar one night. She's pretty and funny and reminds you of your ex-wife just a little. She works in the gift shop at a hospital, and you can tell she's falling in love with you. Soon, you move into her apartment with her, and it's only once you're there that you realize why it is that you like her, why it is that she reminds you of your ex-wife: she's sad, too. You don't know why, but you can tell, and you want to make her happy. But how can you make her happy if you don't know why she's sad? How?

You have two secrets that you can't tell her. You can't tell her that you were an accomplice, and you can't tell her how you couldn't tell your ex-wife that you were an accomplice.

You lose her, too, and you do the same thing you did when your wife left: you rearrange your memories. You tell stories about her and her friends talking in the kitchen, or about the way she behaved at a party, and each time you do you change the details just a little to make her appear worse, to make yourself feel a little better.

You go to work.

You smoke your cigarettes.

You have a few beers.

You go to bed with women who don't know you, and you leave them before they do. You leave them before they start asking too many questions.

You eat.

You sleep.

You shower.

You shave.

You rearrange your memories. You rearrange and rearrange and rearrange.

You try not to hate yourself too much.

But you always end up hating yourself more than anyone else possibly could.

CHAPTER 27: MARCO. POLO.

Palmeyer's gone.

Debbie's gone.

It's just me and my machine and the big band music to fill the room and make you think that you're not alone when you really are. It's eight o'clock, and I have no plans for the night other than to make a sandwich and watch television. I'll watch a baseball game, then the news, then go to sleep.

I know all the big band songs by heart now. I can recognize them after a few notes. When Palmeyer and Debbie are here, we see who can guess the song first. "Tuxedo Junction" and "The Nearness of You" and "Don't Get Around Much Anymore" and "Dinah" and "The Lady's in Love with You." When Palmeyer and Debbie aren't here, I just listen. I listen for the horns. I listen for the cymbals. I listen for the moment when one song ends, just before the next one begins. That moment of absolute, stone-cold silence that could be followed by anything, anything at all.

I'm fixing the collar of a woman's sweater. It got caught on a hanger, and there are loose threads everywhere like the weedy grass before a haunted house. This one I have to fix by hand: it's too delicate for the machine.

There's a knock on the glass of the front door. It startles me because it's so late. Everyone knows we close at five.

There's a sign that says that, too. I look up. It's a couple about my age with a small boy. The boy looks about seven or eight. They wave to me, and I point at my watch to let them know that we're closed. "We're closed," I mouth. "Closed." We've been closed for three hours.

But they knock again, and this time they wave me toward the door. Even the boy's waving, making a motion like he's trying to catch fireflies in his palm.

I get up from my chair and unlock the door, then open it a crack.

"I'm sorry," I say, "but we're closed for the night."

And the woman says, "Please, it's an emergency. It's a tailoring emergency."

And I say, "An emergency?"

And she says, "Yes. We're leaving first thing tomorrow morning to go to Washington for a reunion, and my husband waited until tonight to try on his tuxedo."

The man holds up a black garment bag and smiles. It's an uneasy smile, like he's embarrassed.

"Exhibit A," he says.

And I say, "What's the problem?"

The man starts to answer, but before he can say anything, the woman pokes his stomach and says, "Exhibit B. Too many hamburgers and pizzas and desserts."

It's late enough already, and I have the sweater to work on. But I open the door anyway and say, "Come on in. I've got nothing better to do."

And the woman says, "Thank you. Thank you so much," and she pats my forearm as she walks past.

"Thank you," the man says. "You have no idea how much this means to us."

Even the boy says, "Thank you." I doubt he knows why he's thanking me.

The man steps into the dressing room to try his tuxedo on. The woman and the boy sit down next to me in front of my machine.

"It's *his* reunion," the woman says. "You'd figure he'd try on the tuxedo earlier."

When the dressing room door opens, it's worse than I'd imagined. Nothing fits. NOTHING. The man might as well have been trying on his son's clothes. The jacket sleeves are too short, showing about three inches of his shirt sleeves. The jacket's too tight to button. The pants won't close at all. One of the cuffs has come loose.

The boy sees his father and laughs, then stops suddenly when his mother gives him a scolding look.

The man holds his arms flat to his sides.

"Well?" he says. "Is it a lost cause?"

I walk a circle around him. It's a big circle. I walk around him again.

"Well?" he says.

And I say, "We've got some work to do."

I get my ruler and pins and chalk, and I start working.

I start with the jacket, letting all the material out of the back.

"A Simple Wish" is playing on the radio.

There's not enough material at the bottom of the sleeves to lengthen them, but I find a little extra material tucked up in the shoulder, which lets me pull the sleeves down. I shift the buttons.

"Party at Bob's House" is playing.

I take the pants apart and get as much material as I can

out of the seat and thighs.

"Popcorn Time."

I repair the cuff.

"Queen of Mine."

I replace the zipper and the pants button.

I press the jacket.

I press the pants.

It takes almost three hours, and the family sits with me the whole time, not saying much, but saying enough to let me know how important the tuxedo is to them. I show the boy how to operate the machine while I'm working.

"This is the take-up lever," I say.

And, "This is the bobbin winder tension."

"This is the bobbin winder spindle."

"This is the reverse stitch push button."

"These are the thread guides."

"This is the slide plate."

I show him the seam gauge and the tracing wheel.

I show him the bent-handle shears and the seam ripper and the pinking shears and the pressing mitt and the seam roll. I let him play with the magnetic pin catcher and the pin cushions.

Eventually, the boy falls asleep under Palmeyer's table with basting tape stuck to his shirt and his pants.

The woman snaps her fingers to the music on the radio.

The man just sits in Debbie's chair the whole time, watching me work.

When I'm done, I give the tuxedo to the man and say, "Let's give it a try."

He carries the pieces back into the dressing room. His wife crosses her fingers in front of her face.

"It couldn't hurt," she says.

I cross my fingers in front of my face, too, and she smiles. She has a pretty mouth and bright blue eyes.

The dressing room door creaks open, and the man steps out. The tuxedo fits perfectly now, or close to perfectly: the sleeves might be just a little too short, but there's nothing more I can do with them.

"Oh, my gosh," the woman says. She puts her hands over her mouth the way someone would if she opened a box on Christmas and found a diamond necklace or a string of pearls or something of that nature. She looks at her husband. She looks at me.

"Is it okay?" the man says.

And I say, "As long as you stay away from hamburgers and pizzas and desserts for the next 24 hours. Go ahead and look." I gesture toward the mirrors.

The man steps up to the mirrors and looks at his reflection, first up, then down. He turns sideways, then looks up and down again.

He looks at me in the mirror and mouths, "Thanks."

I mouth, "No problem."

His wife walks to the mirrors.

"Let me look at you," she says, and she takes him by the hand. She pulls him away from the mirrors and into the middle of the room.

"You look fantastic," she says to him. "Absolutely fantastic."

He tugs her toward him and puts his hand on the small of her back, and they dance several steps to the song on the radio.

The song is called "Wonderful, Wonderful You."

When they're done dancing, he walks back to the dressing room to get changed. The woman helps me clean up the mess around my work area. They pay me for fixing the tuxedo, and I put the money in the cash register. Then the woman hands me an envelope.

"This is for you," she says. "Thanks."

I watch them walk to their car. I watch the man carry his son to the car and place him sleeping on the back seat. I watch him hang the tuxedo on the hook in the back of the car, then hold the passenger door open for his wife. I watch him get in the car. I watch the headlights pop on. I think they wave to me, but I can't tell through the headlights. Then they drive off.

I open the envelope. There's fifty dollars inside. I take a pen and write CARL on the envelope, then stuff it in my jacket pocket and head home.

★

I work, and I work, and I work, and I find some pleasure in working. The rhythm of the machine, the ticking of the bobbin, the comfort of the cloth, even the prick of the needle on my fingertip. People bring their clothes in with tears or rips or holes, a pair of pants or a jacket for instance, and they beg you to fix them, they need you to fix them because they love those pants or that jacket, because those were the pants or the jacket they were wearing when they first met So-and-so, or when their daughter graduated from middle school, or something else of that nature. And sometimes you can fix it. You move some material from another part of the jacket, or you put a few invisible threads under a cuff, and it makes them happier than you could ever imagine.

Sometimes I stay at work late, finishing up a suit jacket

or a dress as the case may be, trying to keep from getting too far behind. Sometimes it's nine o'clock before I go home. Sometimes it's later.

Sometimes I have lunch with Debbie and Palmeyer, and we talk about World War II or Red Buttons, the comedian, and we'll remember things we thought we'd forgotten.

Sometimes I go to Carl's apartment and sit on the couch with him and watch television. Sometimes, on weekends when he visits with the boys, we take them to a Braves base-ball game. Sometimes we take them back to Cadbury and show them how to bait a hook. We teach them how to peel shrimp. We teach them how to scrub their stinking little hands with lemon so they won't attract cats and flies.

Sometimes I stay at home and read a magazine or a newspaper.

Sometimes I stay at home and drink a beer or smoke a cigarette.

Sometimes I go sit out by the cracked little swimming pool at the apartment building and listen to the children playing, trying to find each other with their eyes closed, trying to find each other just from the briefest sounds of their voices.

One child will say, "Marco."

And the other will say, "Polo."

Then, "Marco."

Then, "Polo."

"Marco."

"Polo."

And so on, and so on, until the first child finds the second. Then, the next day at work, I'll say to Debbie and Palmeyer, "Do you remember that game you used to play in the pool called Marco Polo?"

Sometimes I go to sleep early, or I rent a video from the video store down the street.

Sometimes I go to Fat Matt's Rib Shack and eat a plate of ribs and drink a beer and smoke and listen to the band.

Sometimes I go to the laundromat and wash my clothes because the machines at my apartment building aren't very good. One of them ended up ripping my chicken shirt so badly that I couldn't fix it. It was nothing to get upset about. It was just a shirt.

Sometimes I go to the grocery store.

Sometimes I go on a date..

Mary Beth, who's short and has to tip her head back like she's in a dentist's chair whenever we kiss.

Nancy, who won't eat meat.

Lauren, who will.

Carrie, who likes to smoke and dance.

Jackie, who likes to drink and dance.

Susan, who talks about her dead mother.

Ann, who has freckles everywhere and giggles at all my jokes.

Kathryn, who gets migraine headaches.

Teresa, who sleeps in a Mickey Mouse T-shirt.

Serena, who likes to watch football on television.

Maria, who has two children.

Tracy, who wears short skirts.

Vickie, who wears long, flowery skirts.

Molly, who listens to books on tape.

Laurie, who likes to climb mountains.

Cindy, who smells of perfume.

Monica, who smells of potato chips.

Sherrie, who smells of bananas.

Wendy, who smells of lemons.

There are others whose names I don't remember. They're all nice women, but if you don't love them, it's easy to forget almost everything about them. They just become names. Then they disappear altogether. Like I'm sure I've disappeared in their minds. I become Ham Something, then I become No One.

Sometimes I go to the movies, walking into the theater just as they're dimming the lights so no one will know that it's me and that I'm alone.

Sometimes I drive to Eddie's Attic on Wednesday nights and pretend I arrived by chance.

I know what I'll say if I see Renée there.

"Oh, I just stopped by because I became such a big music fan listening to you play," I'll say.

That, or "I happened to be driving past and thought I'd stop by for a beer and a smoke."

Whichever feels right.

I sit in a booth at the back where I can see both the entrance and the stage. Sometimes the door will swing open and the streetlights will flicker through, and I'll see a woman standing in the doorway wearing a cowboy hat and boots, and for a second I'll think it's Renée. Only it never is. All women look alike when they're wearing cowboy hats and boots, especially from a distance, especially in the dark. Still, my heart jumps a little each time it happens. My heart jumps when I scan the sea of cowboy hats in front of me.

Is that her?

Is that her?

Is THAT her?

Or her?

Or her?

Or her?

Sometimes I stay until closing time, drinking and smoking until everyone has finished playing their guitars and singing their songs. Songs about husbands and wives and boyfriends and girlfriends who broke their hearts. Songs about cars and trucks and trees that smell like June. And people who died. And people who didn't. And people they loved but who didn't love them back. And people they kissed, and people they didn't. Songs about the ocean. Songs about birds and long walks at night when the moon looks like a melon ripe for picking.

Listening to those songs, it's hard not to think of yourself and your own life. It's hard not to think of your own songs in your mind, songs you'd sing if you knew how. Maybe a song about a girl you loved and who loved you back. About how she loved you so much that it frightened you. It frightened you because you knew in your heart that she couldn't always feel that way; you knew that the way you knew the sky was blue and your mother loved you. How you knew that you'd just end up making her sad and sorry. And you'd sing about how she left you, and how you'd wished she'd said something cruel when she left, only she didn't. And you'd sing about how you drove all over town hoping to see her, how you saw images of her here and there like the ghosts that remain after the pop of a flashbulb, how you would drive past her apartment at night just so you could see the glow of the light in her bedroom and knew that if she looked out the window at that precise moment you'd be looking at the same sky. And in the song, she'd come back to you unexpectedly, and she'd look a little different, and she'd sound a little different, but she'd still be the same, more or less. Not perfect, but she would be yours, and you would love her for not being perfect.

That would be your song.

And if you wrote a song like that, what would you call it? What?

Maybe you would call it "Winona Forever."

Maybe you would call it "Winona Forever," and you'd cry just a little bit every time you sang it.

THE END